A
LIFELONG
DREAM

Emmy's Story, Part 14

By
Kenneth Lee McGee

This is for Mom.

Elsie Tockstein McGee
She passed away in July
at the age of ninety-two.

A special thanks to Sue Midlock for creating the cover.

I would like to thank Denise and Stephanie for their support and for sharing their knowledge and opinions. I will forever be indebted to the people of WriteOn Joliet.

I want to thank the people from my church who continue to inspire me.

I want to thank my wife Sheila for spending countless hours pouring over my manuscripts.

Chapter One

"Don't worry, Robby. We are making the right choice," Regina whispered and then smiled.

Robinson Collins held his wife Regina's hand as they sat facing Pastor Tyler Hammond in his office at Crest Ridge United Nazarene.

"I think you're right." Robby glanced over his shoulder looked through the window into the hallway and saw Pastor Darren Eaton talking to Pastor Herb Ausland.

Regina's eyes wandered over the photos of Tyler, his wife Liz and their three kids in the floor-to-ceiling bookcases to her right. She shifted her gaze to to the other side of the room and whispered to Robby, "Pastor Tyler sure has lots of books. I wonder who built these bookcases."

"No idea," he answered.

Tyler replaced the phone in its cradle. "Sorry for the interruption. That was one of our seasoned members. She wanted to let me know she wouldn't be here this morning but that she was all right."

"Mrs. Thompkins?" Regina asked.

Tyler sighed, nodded and said, "She hasn't been the same since she broke her hip."

"Some people might say that's a good thing." Regina smiled slyly but then waved a hand, shook her head and let her dreadlocks bounce around her oval face. "The change in her attitude. Not her falling."

"I understood what you meant, and I overheard Emmy say that to Liz last Sunday," Tyler said and then watched as Robby flexed his large forearms and made fists with his enormous hands. "Have you guys made a decision on the board's offer?"

Robby and Regina looked at each other.

"We have, Pastor Tyler, and as much as we appreciate the offer, we don't feel we have the time necessary to put a hundred percent into the position. The worship leader is too important a responsibility."

"I know how many hours Liz put in on her job as a teacher

7

here at the church's school before she had the baby. You are both teachers at Roosevelt High. That can't be easy."

Regina rolled her expressive brown eyes. "You do realize she has a name. You don't have to call her the baby any more."

Robby rubbed a hand over his shining bald head and laughed. "You better tell him, Regina."

Tyler shifted his attention from Robby to Regina and chuckled. "What's going on?"

Regina grinned and patted her stomach. "There's something else that will taking up a lot of our time..."

"We're expecting our first in October," Robby blurted out. "That's why we won't have the time."

"Congratulations! I'm happy for both of you." Tyler stood up and extended a hand.

Robby stood up reached across the cluttered desk and vigorously shook Tyler's hand. "Thanks. I hope you can find a permanent worship leader soon."

"Is it all right to tell Liz, or are you guys keeping this a secret?"

"We are heading to the music suite now. We planned to tell everyone."

"I'm sure Liz and Emmy will be excited to hear the news."

"Where are Robby and Regina? We need to get going." Emmy Colasanti-Colwell glanced toward the double door leading into the music suite while holding almost three-month-old Phoebe Grace Hammond in her arms. "Are you smiling at me, Phoebe?" Emmy rocked her gently as she cooed at Emmy.

"They were meeting with Tyler," Liz said.

"About the worship pastor job? I hope they take it. They've been doing a great job since Chase and Yvonne left. I'm doing a show in Toledo in June, I think," Emmy said and then bit her lip. "I'll have to make sure they have tickets."

"I'm not positive, but I assume that's why they're meeting."

Regina entered the music suite followed by Robby.

"About time you guys got here!" Emmy walked up to them. "We do need to rehearse even though we know these songs."

Robby looked down into Emmy's sparkling blue eyes,

smiled and said, "You can't keep her."

"I know, but I want to hold her for a while. Did you guys decide?"

Robby nodded. "If I could have your attention for a moment. Regina and I have some news."

The worship team gathered and stood in front of Robby and Regina.

"Should I tell them, Regina?"

Regina nudged his side. "Go ahead. You know you want to."

"First of all," Robby said. He paused to look at each member of the worship team and then added, "We have decided not to take the position."

Several people moaned.

"Let me explain. It's not because we haven't enjoyed it, but it's a matter of time management." Robby looked around the room and ended up looking at Emmy again. "We don't feel we will have enough time to devote to the team."

"There are others who work full-time, Robby. Surely, we can help you guys out." Emmy bounced on her toes as she rocked Phoebe Grace.

Regina shook her head and then flipped her dreadlocks out of her face. "What he is trying to say is that we are expecting a baby in October, and that's why we won't have the time."

Emmy didn't speak for a few seconds, but then she understood. "Are you serious? Are you really pregnant?"

Robby put his muscular arms around Regina's waist and pulled her close. He kissed her cheek and smiled. "Baby's due in October."

Regina smiled at her husband but then broke away. "I already said that. Now that we have that out of the way, we need to go over the songs for this morning."

Kenny Colwell answered the landline in the kitchen later that night. "Hi, Sofia. What's up?"

"Is it too late for Niles and I to come over to talk to you and Emmy?"

"No, Emmy is getting Kevin Michael settled and the girls

are taking a bath. Come on over."

"We'll be there in fifteen or twenty minutes," Sofia replied.

"The garage door is unlocked."

Twenty minutes later Niles pulled up to the security building at the entrance to the gated community of Bristol Ridge. The guard stepped out and waved.

"Good evening, Sofia. Hello, Niles. Are they expecting you?"

"Yes," Niles answered.

The guard reached inside and pressed the button to raise the gate. "Have a good night."

Niles drove through the gate and quickly reached Kenny and Emmy's driveway on the left. "Do they ever close these gates?" Niles drove through the wrought iron gates and admired the brick entrance.

"Kenny probably opened them from the house," Sofia spotted two deer in the woods to her right.

Niles drove up the winding asphalt drive, came around the final curve and parked in front of the six-bay garage at the side of the large, two-story brick and stone house. They walked inside, through the garage and mudroom and paused in the kitchen.

"That was quick," Kenny wiped the granite island and tossed the towel in the direction of the counter close to the sink. "Em's still upstairs. I'll go get her."

"We'll wait in the family room. We don't want to disturb the kids. It's their bedtime."

Kenny took the wide stairs two at a time. He found Emmy in the twins' bedroom and waited in the doorway.

"Mommy, can we read before we have to turn out the lights?" Eight-year-old Isabella Marie held up two books.

"Two books but then it's time for bed."

"Three books!" Heather Rose, the older twin, tried to negotiate for more time.

"I said two," Emmy replied and then walked over to Kenny. "Did I hear someone come in?"

Kenny nodded. "Sofia and Niles."

Emmy turned back to the girls. "I will be back up later to

10

check. I expect you to be asleep."

Kenny checked Kevin Michael's room. "You are supposed to be in bed."

"I want to play with my new firetruck," Kevin Michael replied without looking at his father.

"Ten minutes and then lights out. I will tuck you in later," Kenny said.

"I'm almost six. I don't need to be tucked in like a baby," Kevin Michael insisted.

"Ten minutes, and then I'm turning out all the lights. I have my phone with me." Emmy held up her new smart phone and stared at the screen. She followed Kenny down the stairs. "I love how I can control everything from here."

"Technology is a beautiful thing," he said. "When it works."

Emmy scooted past Kenny and dashed into the family room. "Hey, guys. How are you?" Emmy plopped into her recliner and set her phone on the end table next to her. She smiled at Sofia and Niles on the leather couch. *So cute. You guys are holding hands.*

Kenny picked up a toy police car and then sat in his recliner.

Niles turned his attention from the stone fireplace to Kenny and Emmy. "We're sorry for coming over so late."

"It's only eight o'clock, Niles. We don't go to bed this early," Emmy said with a grin.

Sofia noticed the stack of Junie B. Jones books on the coffee table and then looked at Emmy. "Em, I'm giving you my notice. The kids are getting older, and you don't really need me anymore."

Emmy sat up straight. "But you don't have to leave. We can find something for you to do. I need help with the bills and groceries and stuff. The girls and Kevin love you. You don't have to leave."

"I do because," Sofia said and then looked at Niles, "we are going to have a baby."

Emmy launched herself from the recliner. "You are!?

11

When? How long have you known?" She sat next to Sofia and hugged her.

"If you let me breath, I'll tell you."

"Sorry, you are the second person to tell me they are expecting today. Regina Collins is having a baby, too. Now tell me, please."

"My due date is September 23. It's too early to know the sex, so don't even ask."

Kenny nodded at Niles. "Congratulations about the baby and the promotion at work."

"Thanks," Niles replied.

"I'll be here for another month. That should give you time to find a replacement," Sofia said.

"The girls will be so sad to hear you're leaving. Do you guys want something to drink? I could make some coffee, or we have water and pop."

"We're good, Emmy. We should go before the kids know we're here."

Emmy walked them to the garage service door. "Night, guys. I'm so happy for you."

She walked back inside and saw Kenny sitting on one of the barstools at the kitchen island. "Want something to drink?"

"I grabbed some water."

Emmy opened the fridge and picked up a bottle of water, but then set it back and took a can of Dr Pepper instead. She sat on the barstool next to Kenny. "I can't say I'm surprised Sofia's leaving, but I didn't know she was already expecting."

"You said they were trying," Kenny replied and then picked up a banana from the fruit bowl in the center of the island. "This one could be used for banana drop cookies."

"Like I have time for that." She checked the other bananas in the bowl. "I need to make the kids eat more fruit." She turned to Kenny. "Do we even need to look for another nanny? The kids are getting older. We're going to be home most of the year. What do you think?"

"This might be the perfect time to cut expenses and go solo."

12

"I agree. We've been very fortunate to have Mary and Sofia as nannies. If we hire another one, we might not be so lucky."

"Who's going to tell the girls?" Kenny asked.

Emmy held out her hands. "Rock, paper, scissors."

"No way. You always cheat. You can tell the girls. I'll tell Kevin."

"Wimp! Kevin Michael won't care."

Later that night as Kenny slipped into bed beside Emmy, he heard a soft cry. "Em, are you upset?"

"No."

He put an arm over her. "Then why are you crying?"

Emmy turned over to face him. "Do you think we made a mistake when I got my tubes tied?"

Kenny shook his head. "No, Em. Dr. Walsh said it was the right thing to do."

"I miss having a baby in the house."

"You could always borrow Conor, or one of the babies from church," he suggested.

"Not the same. Liz has a baby. Regina and Sofia are going to have babies. Mary might have a baby sometime. I want one, too."

Kenny held her close and kissed her ear. "I know you do, but we need to remember God gave us three babies already. You never thought you could have a baby, but we have three great kids."

Emmy bit her lip. "Am I being ungrateful? Am I a spoiled brat?"

"Tony would say you're a spoiled brat, but I don't agree."

"I'm sorry for acting like this. Do you think we could pretend we're trying to have another baby?"

Even in the dark Kenny could see Emmy's blue eyes sparkling. "We can pretend, m'lady."

She giggled and then said, "You are such a dork, but I love you anyway."

Chapter Two

Roy Posey, the senior construction supervisor, stood outside the sanctuary of the Crest Ridge United Nazarene and looked at the building going up next door. "We've been lucky with the weather. Now it won't matter because everything is indoors."

Garrick Winston, the project manager, looked up at Roy, "If you ask Tony, he will say it's because of all the prayers of the people who attend church here."

"I suppose that didn't hurt," Roy said and then pointed to a minivan pulling into the parking lot. "They're here. Do we have the hardhats?"

Garrick hooked a thumb over his shoulder. "Over there."

Tony Bertucci pulled the minivan to the front entrance and stopped. John Randolph jumped out and opened the side door for his father-in-law. "Do you need your cane?"

Seventy-four-year-old Daniel Keasling waved his hand. "I'm good. The new hip is much less painful than the old one." He exited the van and saw Roy and Garrick. "There's Mutt and Jeff."

Carl Tomanek, the architect who designed the building, exited the van on the driver's side.

Tony walked around the van and laughed. "Uncle Daniel, no one knows who Mutt and Jeff are anymore."

John hit the button to close the van doors and patted the Bertucci and Keasling Construction logo on the side. "Is Roy seven feet tall?"

"An inch or two short, and Garrick is five and a half at the most," Tony answered.

Daniel Keasling walked up to Roy and Garrick and shook their hands. "I've been hearing good reports about our progress."

Garrick checked his iPad. "As of this morning we are three days and eight hours ahead of schedule. That should increase now that weather won't be a factor."

Roy put a hand to his mouth and coughed. "Geek."

Tony and John smiled. Carl Tomanek shielded his eyes against the sun and looked up.

"I have to admit it, Garrick. We were never as organized in

14

the old days," Mr. Keasling said.

Daniel Keasling and Peter Bertucci, Tony's late father, founded Bertucci and Keasling Construction over fifty years previously. Since then it had become one of the largest construction companies in the state and entire Midwest. Few other local companies employed as many of South Hampshire's people as did B 'n' K, as the locals called it. The new sanctuary at the church was their highest priority project at the moment.

"I can't imagine doing a project like this without modern technology," Garrick said. "Are you ready to take a look inside?"

"Lead the way," Mr. Keasling said as he pointed.

Roy gathered up the hardhats and passed them around. Tony noticed each one had a name on it.

"Right this way, boss." Roy held the door open.

Mr. Keasling smoothed out his gray hair and then put on his hardhat. "Roy, are you ever going to let Gladys retire?"

"She claims the company would fall apart if she retires."

Mr. Keasling laughed. "She's probably right. Even Kristen relies on Gladys for answers. Speaking of my daughter, when is she going to bring my grandkids over to see me?" Mr. Keasling asked as he looked up at John.

"I'll remind her you and Grandma need to see the kids."

Mr. Keasling laughed as he replied, "You know Karla will smack you if she hears you call her Grandma. She might be fifty-six in real years, but she stopped counting a long time ago."

Tyler Hammond walked out of the older building with his hardhat already on. "Mrs. Millner told me you were here. She knows everything that goes on around the church."

"Tell Harriet hello for me," Mr. Keasling said. *What would we ever do without these ladies.*

Roy ducked inside and straightened out his gray ponytail. "It's a little loud in here, but we could have the crews take a break."

"I may be old, but I can still hear," Mr. Keasling said.

"What?" Tony asked.

John shook his head at his college roommate and former teammate on the Chicago Bears.

15

"Couldn't resist." Tony shrugged.

"Emmy's right. You are a goofball."

Garrick led the way through the interior of the large building. He pointed to the roof. "The steel is finished."

"How high is that?" Mr. Keasling craned his neck.

"The center part is fifty feet above the floor," Roy explained. "I need a ladder to reach it."

"I need to talk to Carl for a moment," Garrick said. He and Mr. Tomanek walked away to discuss some changes.

Roy finished leading the bosses around the work site.

"It appears we are in good shape," Mr. Keasling said to Tony and John as he exited the building. "Please, keep me informed if there are any issues."

"We will, but Roy and Garrick can handle anything that comes up."

Carl joined them a couple of minutes later, and they headed back to the company headquarters.

"Anything serious?" Mr. Keasling asked Carl.

"Just a couple of minor issues. Garrick will handle them."

"It's going to be a very functional building when it's finished," Tony said.

"True," Carl agreed. "They don't build churches the same nowadays. Functionality is more important than form. Makes my job easier."

The next morning Pastor Tyler and Darren Eaton waited in Tyler's office for the arrival of a couple Chase Hillman had recommended as strong candidates for the worship leader position. Tyler scanned the letter once again and read the highlights.

"How does Chase know them?" Darren asked.

"According to Chase's letter they met when Riordan and Sadie were at Point Loma Nazarene University out in San Diego about ten years ago." Tyler read more of the letter. "They are both from Pasadena."

"I wonder if they've been to the Rose Bowl?" Darren asked as he read the liner notes to one of the Schulenberg's CDs.

"Why would that matter?" Tyler asked.

16

"It wouldn't. I think it's a cool stadium."

"Have you ever listened to either of their CDs?"

"I've got the first one, but I haven't heard this newer one. Should we play it?" Darren popped the CD out of the jewel case.

"Would it be weird if they get here and we're listening to their CD?"

"Yeah, maybe. Do they have any kids? How long have they been married?"

Tyler handed Darren the letter. "You can read it. They got married while at Point Loma, and have a son named Jude."

Darren skimmed through the letter while Tyler listened to phone messages.

"Chase thinks they would be a good fit. He and Yvonne really like them," Darren said as he read further. "It says here they actually resigned from their church two months ago because they felt God telling them to leave before they started a short tour. Riordan told Chase he definitely felt the Holy Spirit telling them to leave like God told Abraham to leave his country in Genesis 12:1. Do you think our congregation would accept a couple from California?"

"Why wouldn't they?" Tyler shrugged. "Dr. Behren came from California."

"He wasn't a native Californian. Wasn't he originally from Iowa? That's a big difference. Native Californians are a different species."

"They look rather normal on the CD." Tyler laughed as he stared at the photo.

"I heard that." Harriet Millner frowned as she stood in the doorway and tapped the frame with a pencil. "I thought you might want to know the Schulenbergs are here. They are waiting in my office. Should I bring them in here?"

Tyler jumped up. "No, Darren and I will go to them."

Harriet glanced at Tyler's desk. "If they get hired, they will eventually realize you have a messy desk."

"I'll organize the mess one of these days," Tyler replied.

Harriet raised her eyebrows. "Uh-huh, where have I heard that before." She replaced the pencil in her gray hair above her ear.

17

Tyler and Darren followed Mrs. Millner back to her office.

"Hello, I'm Tyler and this is Darren Eaton, my associate."

Riordan and Sadie turned around. "It's a pleasure to meet you, Pastor Tyler." Riordan offered a hand. "You, too, Pastor Darren."

"We're not that formal around here," Tyler chuckled.

Darren shook hands with Riordan. *You guys look even better in person. You could be the poster people for surfers. I always thought blondes had fair skin. You guys have great tans and it's March.*

"I'm Sadie," she said. "But you probably knew that. I talked to Liz on the phone yesterday. We are all about the same age."

"Darren is the old man on the staff," Tyler teased his friend.

Mrs. Millner frowned again. *Are you forgetting about Pastor Herb?*

"Would you like to take a tour of the place, or would you rather talk in my office first?" Tyler asked.

"We'd love a tour," Sadie said. "Chase and Yvonne told us about the volunteers you have on the worship team. We'd like to meet some of them later if that would be possible."

"Robby and Regina did contact the musicians who are scheduled for tomorrow. They will be here in about an hour to rehearse with you."

"When will the new sanctuary be finished?" Riordan asked as he glanced at the photos of the former pastors and their spouses on the hallway wall.

"We are shooting for early November," Darren answered.

"If we go this way, I can show you the music suite. Chase had his office there." Tyler led the way to the right. He explained what some of the other rooms were used for as they walked past. "This used to be the teen center but it was remodeled when they expanded the music suite. Of course when the new building is finished, the music suite will be moved." Tyler opened one of the double doors leading into the music suite. "There are two offices on this side." He led the way into the main room. "The choir used to rehearse in here back in the day."

"It's pretty large," Riordan said. "Looks like enough room for the entire worship team to gather for meetings and stuff."

Tyler pointed to a door. "There is a video production room through there."

"Will we rehearse in here or the sanctuary?" Sadie asked.

"The team usually uses the sanctuary for rehearsals, but it is possible to rehearse in here."

"We like to rehearse where we'll be performing. I like to get a feel of the room," Riordan explained.

Sadie continued, "The acoustics are always different, and we like to make sure the technicians are familiar with the room."

"We have some very capable volunteers," Tyler remarked.

"Oh, you don't have people on the staff for production?" Riordan sat at the baby grand piano and played some chords. "It's in tune."

"Several of our volunteers work at Steward Music. You might call them pros," Darren said. "Perhaps you've heard of Fridays At Five. Some of our techs work for the band."

"Would you like to see the sanctuary now?" Tyler asked as he stared at Darren.

"Yes, please." Sadie smiled.

Tyler cut across the hallway to one of the rear entrances to the platform in the sanctuary. He flipped on a light, they walked up the stairs and came out at the side of the platform.

"Very nice." Sadie touched the black wall.

Riordan looked out at the sanctuary and then up at the ceiling. "Is the church planning to move these lights to the new building?"

Tyler shook his head. "No, everything will be new. DelSasso Sound is doing all the audio and video designing. I hate to say how much we're spending, but we have some very generous people in the church."

Tyler didn't reveal the new building would not have a mortgage.

"Would you guys like to grab some lunch? We have an hour before the worship team shows up."

"Sure, Pastor Tyler. Anywhere is all right with us, but I am

19

partial to Mexican food," Sadie said.

"I know a place you might like," Tyler said. "I'll drive."

When they returned from lunch, most of the worship team was in the music suite. Tyler introduced Riordan and Sadie to the team.

"It's a pleasure to meet you," Riordan said as he looked around the room. "Chase Hillman has told me how much he appreciated working with such a talented group."

After talking to the musicians and taking a quick look at the songs previously chosen for the next day, everyone moved to the sanctuary.

"Would it be possible to make a couple of changes?" Riordan asked Tyler. "Nothing major, but could the keyboards be moved out of the center? I assume that's where Chase positioned himself."

"I'm sure we can move them for you." Tyler turned to Cam Frees, who played one of the two sets of electronic keyboards on the platform. "Can we move them?"

"Certainly. It's easy."

"And I'd like to add a song," Riordan said.

Ten minutes later, with the keyboards re-positioned, Riordan began playing the introduction to the song on his expensive Martin D-28 acoustic guitar. "Is everyone familiar with this song?" he asked the musicians.

"We've played it a few times," Cam answered.

Ross Knapp played the lead line on his new Gibson Les Paul, looked at his wife Heidi and shrugged.

Sadie sang the first verse and Riordan joined her on the chorus.

"Let's stop for a minute," Sadie said after the second verse. She looked at Heidi and Regina. "What parts do you normally sing on this song?"

"I sang lead on it the only time I ever sang it at church," Regina said.

"I haven't sung it before. Our group doesn't usually sing songs that Emmy writes," Heidi confessed.

"We sang this one several times back home. Our church

20

really liked the message," Sadie said without hearing Heidi's answer.

"Let's move on to the other songs," Riordan suggested.

Thirty minutes later Riordan and Sadie called a halt to the rehearsal.

Riordan turned to look at the musicians. "Does anyone have any questions about any of the songs? Are we clear on the arrangements?"

Everyone understood the simple arrangements.

"Thank you all for coming in today," Sadie said. "Normally we would have played to tracks on such short notice, but Chase assured us you could pick up these songs quickly."

Ross Knapp whispered to Jackson Brewster, who played the bass guitar for this team, "Don't they realize how simple these songs are?"

Jackson shrugged and said, "I guess not. I don't think they even realize Emmy goes to church here."

Ross set his guitar in its stand. "Yeah, I got that feeling, too. Why are they doing one of Emmy's songs anyway? Our crowd is used to hearing Emmy sing them. Nothing better than the original, I always say."

"Wouldn't you think Chase would have told them about Emmy?" Jackson asked. "That's a sweet looking guitar. When did you get it?"

"Heidi bought it for my birthday." He laughed and then added, "She gave me the money. I picked out the guitar."

Regina and Heidi walked up to Riordan and Sadie and waited until they had finished talking to Pastor Tyler.

Sadie smiled at the ladies. "You have beautiful voices. You blend together very well."

"Thank you," Regina responded. "Are you planning to sing these songs for both services? We usually include some hymns for the early service. It's a more blended service than the second one."

"Oh, I didn't realize that. We haven't sung hymns at our home church for years," Sadie said.

"Heidi and I could sing the hymns if you'd like," Regina volunteered.

Riordan joined the conversation. "Actually, Sadie and I are only going to join you during the second service. We thought the team knew that."

"That's not a problem." Regina waved a hand. "We rehearsed on Thursday for both services. We can handle it."

Kenny and Emmy sat in the same row as Kristen, Tony and Sloane for the second service the next morning.

"Kristen, have you heard about the couple leading worship this morning?" Emmy asked.

"No idea what you're talking about, Em. What couple? Where are Regina and Robby? Are they moving?"

"Liz told me Regina is pregnant, so they turned down the offer to be the official worship pastors. Chase recommended this other couple, and they happened to be available today. Liz said it's like an audition for the board members, but Chase knows them and really thinks they would be a good fit."

Tony leaned forward and faced Emmy. "Are you going to keep jawing for the whole service?"

Emmy made a face at him. "I was just talking to Kristen about something."

Sloane poked her husband in the side. "Don't pester Emmy."

Pastor Tyler walked onto the platform, greeted the crowd and began the service with a prayer. Then he introduced Riordan and Sadie. "Please, make them feel welcome."

The congregation clapped politely.

"Hey, brat, have you heard of them?" Tony asked Emmy.

"Shush!" Kristen warned.

Emmy shook her head. "Not until Liz mentioned them."

Riordan and Sadie took turns singing lead on the four songs. They sang the song Emmy had written last.

"They sound pretty good," Kristen said to Emmy as the worship band left the platform. "Is the church going to hire them full-time?"

"Maybe," Emmy answered. "They really do sound good together, but it felt forced. Too slick. Not very spontaneous."

"You guys always rehearse," Kristen whispered.

"We rehearse the songs, but not the actions. I bet she uses the same motions every time she sings those songs."

Kenny put an arm around Emmy. "You don't know that, Em. Maybe that's their way of worshiping."

"Yeah, whatever." Emmy sat back in her seat. *Maybe it's a California thing.*

Kenny said, "She didn't sound as good as you on your song."

"She didn't sing the chorus right at the end. I always go up the final time."

After the video announcements and the offering, Riordan and Sadie returned to the platform without the other musicians.

"We want to thank you for having us here today," Riordan said. "We would like to do a song from our first CD for you." Riordan looked up at the sound tech and the track began to play.

Emmy leaned closer to Kristen and whispered, "Are they going to tell us they have merchandise for sale in the foyer?"

"I didn't see any," Kristen replied.

"I was kidding," Emmy sat back and listened.

The congregation clapped and several people even rose to their feet after they finished. Emmy noticed some of the older people standing.

"Thank you so much," Sadie said after the people stopped applauding. "If I may take a couple of minutes..."

Emmy poked Kristen's arm. "Here comes the sales pitch."

"...I'd like to tell you how I came to accept Christ into my life," Sadie closed her eyes as she spoke.

Kristen turned to Emmy and frowned.

"Fine! I'll give them a chance."

Tyler looked around the large conference table at the church board members the next evening. "Now that we have the old business out of the way, we need to discuss the worship leader position. Did all of you have a chance to talk to Riordan and Sadie after the service yesterday?"

"I didn't talk to them, but I listened as they talked to

people," Jim Rosek spoke up. "I was impressed by their attitude. I can't comment on their musical ability because I can't sing a lick and couldn't play an instrument to save my life."

All of the other board members talked in positive terms about Riordan and Sadie.

Roger Goldman waited until the others voiced their opinions. "I happen to know Riordan's parents, and I have known Riordan all of his life from afar. Chase and Yvonne highly recommend them, and I agree. I actually attended their church last fall when I was in California. I thought they would be a good fit for us even back then."

The board spent fifteen more minutes discussing the couple.

"Do we have an idea of what we could offer as a salary?" Dylan Michaelis asked. "Would we pay them as much as we paid Chase?"

Roger, who headed the finance action team, answered the question. "We don't need to start them off where Chase ended up, but we can afford to offer a generous package. We have one big advantage," Roger paused to smile. "The housing costs here are less than a third of what they probably paid in Pasadena."

The board members laughed. After more discussion, a motion was passed to offer the position to the Schulenbergs.

Tyler chuckled, "I will call them later tonight because they assured me they wouldn't be able to sleep until they heard from us."

Twenty minutes later, Tyler closed the meeting with prayer. He called Riordan as soon as he got back to his office and presented the board's offer.

"We have been praying almost nonstop for the last two days," Riordan said. "We were prepared to take the position, if offered, no matter what the salary was. We definitely feel this is where God wants us to be."

"So, can I tell everyone you accept the offer?" Tyler chuckled again.

"Yes!" Riordan exclaimed. "And we can start this week if you'd like."

"Where will you stay? The church doesn't have a vacant property at the moment."

"We will stay with the Goldmans until we can find a place to rent. They are family friends from way back."

"Hi, Liz, can you tell me anything about the board meeting?" Emmy asked after getting the kids to school on Tuesday morning.

Liz grinned over the phone. "If you are asking about the Schulenbergs, I can tell you."

"So tell me!" Emmy's voice rose in pitch.

"The board unanimously agreed to hire them, and they are starting immediately."

"I was afraid of that," Emmy said with a sigh.

"Didn't you like them?"

"I did like how they sounded, but maybe not so much how they led the service."

"Sadie told me later that she was more nervous then ever before. She said she thought no one would hire them because of how awful they were."

"She really said that?"

"Yes. Would I lie to you?"

"No, of course not. I feel guilty now because of what I thought."

"You will have a chance to meet them on Thursday if not before. I'm sure you will like them. Sadie is so down-to-earth and Riordan has a wicked sense of humor."

"Are they going to turn the worship team into another Hillsong? We already have enough singers, and with the addition of the two of them..."

"I don't think they will make any drastic changes," Liz said. "Oh, you'll love this. Tyler was talking to them this morning and your name came up."

"Why?"

"Tyler mentioned the song they sang of yours."

"She didn't sing the verse right at the end," Emmy said. "She didn't go up a half-step."

25

"I caught that, but Tyler said they aren't aware that you live here and don't know you're a part of the worship team. Can you believe it!?"

"Why would they know?" Emmy asked quietly.

"Em! You are kind of a celebrity in the Christian music field. Most people know stuff about you."

"I am not a celebrity! I don't even think of Kenny like that."

"That's because you guys have lived here all your life and locals don't treat you like that. If you showed up at my home church, people would want your autograph."

"I've been to Hillside Nazarene and no one treated me any different than anyone else," Emmy insisted.

"Oh, do the teens in our church ask for your picture every week?"

Emmy bit her lip. "No, but... nevermind. Did Tyler tell them I live here?"

"I don't think so. I know he gave Riordan a list of the worship team members, but you're listed as Emily Colwell."

"Chase did that to tease me. Hasn't it been changed?"

"Guess not, so if they look at the printout, they still won't realize who you are. I want to see their faces on Thursday when you come to practice."

"They might not recognize me," Emmy said.

"You do realize your face is on the cover of your CDs, right. I'm sure Sadie has one or two of them."

"I hope they don't think I'm a diva."

Liz laughed. "More likely, they will think you're one of the singers from the teen worship band."

"Very funny, Liz! Can you see me sticking out my tongue?"

"I got to run. I'll talk to you later."

Tyler and Darren met with Riordan and Sadie for lunch the next day.

"Have you had a chance to look for a place to live?" Tyler asked. "I could talk to the Van Diens and see if there are any open apartments in the complex where they live. It's close."

26

Darren added, "The church owns three houses, but none of them are empty."

Riordan waved a hand and smiled. "No need. Mr. Goldman set up an appointment with Heidi Knapp yesterday. She located a house to rent rather close to the church. We checked it out and couldn't believe the price. We signed a lease right there. We even have the option to purchase it later if we so choose."

"Wow! Things are certainly falling into place for you guys."

"We definitely feel God has opened the doors for us to be here," Sadie said.

"Have you thought about the music for this Sunday?" Tyler asked. "Did you have a chance to read the email with my sermon topics for the next two months?"

"We did, and we have chosen some songs. Regina emailed us a list of the songs the team has done in the past plus their contact information and short bios."

"Really?" Tyler glanced at Darren.

"I can't wait to meet them."

"Were there photos of the team members?" Tyler asked and then took a sip of water.

Sadie looked at Riordan and then back at Tyler and Darren. "There were photos of everyone."

"What Sadie is trying to tactfully say is that all the team members are young people except for one of the singers."

Darren held one of his fries close to his mouth. "Which one? Ross and Heidi Knapp are the oldest members of the team, and they're in their forties. That's not old."

"This singer looked like she might be in her seventies," Sadie said.

Darren looked at Tyler. Tyler grinned.

"The info listed her name as Olivia something. I can't remember, and it said she had been a part of the team for over forty years. Chase wrote in the comments that she has trouble hearing, but still insists of being a part of the team."

Darren's face dropped.

"I don't want to create an issue," Riordan said.

27

"Olivia tries very hard to find the right part to sing," Tyler said. "We can talk about her later."

Darren gave Tyler a confused look.

"One other thing I might mention," Riordan changed the subject. "We owe our record company one more CD. We thought we might be able to do a live recording using the worship team. Has anyone ever mentioned something like that before?"

Tyler tapped a finger to his chin. "The team did a live recording years ago. I'd have to talk to some of the tech guys to see if that would still be possible."

"We really shouldn't take up anymore of your time, Pastor Tyler," Sadie said. "We need to work on the songs for Sunday, and we have to make arrangements for our furniture and belongings to be delivered to SoHam. Did I say that correctly. One of the team members told me that's what locals call the city."

"That is correct."

"We put our stuff in storage until we knew where we would live," Riordan explained.

"We will see you tomorrow night if not sooner," Tyler said.

Riordan and Sadie left, and Darren began to laugh.

"What is so funny?" Tyler grinned.

"You know why I'm laughing. Chase never changed Emmy's fake info in the system. They don't even realize she goes to church here, and you didn't exactly tell the whole truth."

"I did not lie. I said that Olivia tries very hard to find her part. I meant Olivia Whittenburg."

"Mrs. Whittenburg passed away two years ago."

"Did I forget to mention that?" Tyler asked with a straight face.

"I want to be there Thursday night."

"Are you going to audition for the team? I know you can sing better than me."

"This should be priceless." Darren laughed again.

Chapter Three

"Are you nervous about tonight?" Riordan asked Sadie on the way to the church Thursday evening after dinner with the Goldmans.

"A little bit, but I shouldn't be. Jude will be fine."

"Not what I meant," Riordan said while watching a blue Honda Civic roar past him.

Sadie shook her head. "That driver deserves a speeding ticket."

"What will we do if this Olivia is there?"

"We will deal with her when the time comes. Pastor Tyler emailed me and said almost all of the worship team will be there."

"Great," Riordan sighed. "That means Olivia will probably be there, too. What will we do with a seventy-year-old deaf singer?"

Emmy parked her Civic Si in the back and entered the music suite. She saw Liz Hammond talking with Regina and Heidi and ran over and grabbed Liz's arm.

"Are they here yet?" Emmy asked.

"Is who here?" Liz asked with a straight face.

"You know who I mean, and are you going to start singing again? What if Phoebe needs to be fed in the middle of the service?"

"I have a plan for that," Liz grinned. "And they aren't here yet."

Emmy bit her lip and shifted her weight back and forth on her feet.

"Why are you nervous, Em?"

"What if they don't like me or my songs?"

"You are silly. They sang one of your songs last Sunday." Liz twisted her long blonde hair into a braid.

Heidi and Regina looked at each other and walked away.

"Apparently Liz isn't in on the surprise." Regina laughed and her dreadlocks shook.

"How can the Schulenbergs not know Emmy goes to church here?" Heidi asked. "They have a list of team members."

29

Regina explained Chase's practical joke.

"Oh, I get it. I'm glad I didn't mention Emmy the other day."

Riordan and Sadie walked into the room a few minutes later accompanied by Tyler and Darren.

"Can I have everyone's attention, please," Tyler shouted to be heard above the noise. He introduced the Schulenbergs to everyone and turned the meeting over to them.

Riordan held Sadie's hand as he prayed and then looked around the room. "I want to thank all of you for coming out. This was a last-minute request, and I know not all of you are scheduled for this Sunday. I would also like to thank you for the warm welcome Sadie and I have received."

"Jude, too," Sadie said.

"And our son Jude, as well," Riordan added. "I'd like to say we plan to stick with the teams Robby and Regina have organized. The only change is Sadie and I will be a part of every group other than the teens. Pastor Jake will remain in charge of that team." He chuckled, "I've never had a week off every month. We're looking forward to that."

Sadie scoped out the people in the room. *Hmmm, I don't see anyone who looks over fifty. Maybe Olivia decided not to make an appearance.*

"I have looked over the schedule of songs for the next month, and I know most of them. I have to say if will be great to know what songs we will be singing that far in advance."

"We will make one small change," Sadie announced. "For the next few weeks Riordan and I will be singing for the offering. After the offering. During... You know what I mean. That is something we did back home in Pasadena, and we'd like to continue that here."

Riordan talked about his goals for the team. He mentioned the recording he would like to plan and a few other things.

"Sadie and I have met several of you, and we have seen most of your faces either at the church or online. We apologize in advance if we have trouble remembering everyone's name. Please bear with us, and we will try to get to know each of you as soon as possible. Right now I'd like to let each of you introduce yourself and remind us what you do within the team. To make it easier, I'll start. I'm Riordan and I sing and play acoustic guitar. Let's start in front and go down each row."

One by one the team members introduced themselves. Emmy sat between Liz and Bobby O'Connor and fidgeted in her seat. Liz introduced herself loud and clear and then waited for Emmy.

"Your turn, Em," Liz poked Emmy's arm.

"Hi, I'm Emmy and I sing whatever part is needed," she said softly.

Riordan and Sadie didn't react to Emmy other than to point to the next person in line.

Bobby O'Connor introduced himself as the best drummer in his seat and got a laugh from everyone. Soon everyone had introduced themselves.

"We have some cookies, crackers and cheese and a couple of veggie trays to munch on. Riordan and I would like to rehearse with the musicians on the schedule for this Sunday for just a few minutes. Then we can all come back here and mingle. We would like to meet with the different teams. That will help us get to know you better."

Bobby stood behind Emmy, put his hands on her shoulders and whispered, "Why didn't you speak up when you introduced yourself? I doubt if they even heard you."

Emmy turned to face Bobby and bit her lip. "I don't know. I feel kinda shy around them. They are celebrities out in California."

"You're a goof, Em." Bobby touched Emmy's nose just as Riordan and Sadie looked in their direction.

"Who is that young lady with Bobby the drummer?" Sadie asked. "She looks familiar in a way. Is she one of the singers with the teen group. Tyler mentioned some of them are in college."

Riordan shrugged. "Not sure. I couldn't hear her name. She might be Bobby's girlfriend. We should practice for Sunday."

Riordan only needed fifteen minutes for the rehearsal. Some of the team members appreciated his no-nonsense, organized method while others thought he might be a bit bossy. The team

31

returned to the music suite. Riordan and Sadie mingled with the different groups.

"Are you through stuffing your face, Em?" Bobby asked.

"Sorry, but I didn't have time for dinner. Kevin Michael needed a bath."

"Here come the new bosses. Better be on your best behavior," Bobby said.

Emmy elbowed him in the side.

"Hello, I guess you are the last group other than the teens," Riordan said and then looked at Emmy. *I'm guessing you're one of the college students.*

Emmy moved closer to Bobby and he put an arm around her waist.

"We met some of the teen musicians and Pastor Jake last night. Would it be all right if we took seats over there and talked for a moment?" Riordan pointed a circle of seats in the corner and led the way.

Emmy sat between Bobby and Adam Vicini. Liz had excused herself to feed Phoebe Grace.

"I apologize for this, but could we introduce ourselves again. We could start with Bobby and go from there." Riordan noticed the colorful tattoos on Bobby's arms.

"I'm Bobby O'Connor, and I've been playing with the worship team here since I was a teenager. I've worked with various local bands, too." He grinned at Emmy.

Riordan took that as meaning he and Emmy were together.

"I'm Mason Williams, and we met when my father talked to you." Mason's father was Pastor Don Williams, who taught a Sunday School class when he wasn't doing pulpit supply for other churches.

Boyd Goldman spoke next. "I'm Boyd Goldman. No relation to Roger Goldman. I play guitar. Electric most of the time. I was formerly a member of The Only Hope Band."

Riordan interrupted him. "I remember that band. Sadie and I saw you guys in concert once. Sorry, please continue."

"We recorded a couple of CDs, but then some of us got married or moved to other bands, so we broke up the group for the time being. We have talked about reuniting to record another CD, but that's in the future."

"I'm Micah Hurst and in addition to playing acoustic guitar for the worship team, I am a member of a local band, who are getting ready to go on tour real soon." He grinned at Emmy, but neither Riordan nor Sadie noticed.

"You look mighty familiar," Riordan said to Adam. "Should I know you?"

"I was also a member of The Only Hope," Adam said.

Bobby laughed. "Aren't you now a member of some other group? What is their name?"

Boyd waved his hand at Adam. "I remember. Aren't they called Friday Afternoon, or something like that?"

Riordan and Sadie immediately caught on. "You're the new keyboard player for Fridays At Five. I knew we recognized you. We caught you guys in Los Angeles. Fantastic show. Chase mentioned that Kenny Colwell grew up in SoHam and was once a part of the team here. That must have been so amazing. He's a great songwriter. I'm pretty sure we have all their CDs."

Adam looked at Emmy, who was trying to hide behind him and Bobby, and said, "He does still attend church here whenever he can. FYI, we are starting our Dangerous Circumstances Tour tomorrow night at the United Center. I might be able to get you a couple of passes if you're interested."

"That would be awesome," Sadie said. "We would need a babysitter, but I think the Goldmans would watch Jude."

"I'll see what I can do." Adam grinned and nudged Emmy. "What is your name? I forgot."

"Yes, we didn't hear you before. You don't need to be shy," Riordan said and the whole circle of guys began to laugh.

Riordan and Sadie looked at each other and then at Bobby. "Are we missing something? Is this your girlfriend? Is she part of the teen team?"

The guys laughed even harder some wiping their eyes.

Adam patted Emmy's knee, and the guys settled down a bit. "May I have the honor of introducing..."

Emmy poked Adam in the ribs.

"Well, I consider it a privilege if not an honor, Em," Adam said. He turned his attention back to the Schulenbergs. "I can understand why you don't recognize her. She is more petite in person than she appears in photos."

Riordan tilted his head as he stared at Emmy. Sadie stared for a moment and then put a hand to her mouth. "Oh, my God!"

Adam continued, "May I introduce my friend Emily Olivia Colwell, perhaps better known as Emmy Colasanti. That's her professional name."

Emmy bit her lip and waved weakly at Riordan and Sadie.

"Chase sometimes called her Olivia when he wanted to get under her skin," Bobby explained.

"I don't know what to say," Sadie said after a brief silence. "We sang your song on Sunday. Now I feel like a fool."

Riordan added, "We didn't know you were part of the team."

"Do you know who Emmy's married to?" Boyd asked.

Riordan and Sadie looked at Bobby.

"Not me!" Bobby hollered. "No way I would ever be interested in her."

Emmy kicked Bobby's leg. "You're a creep, Bobby, and I hate you with all my heart."

Adam grabbed Emmy's arm to keep her from hitting Bobby again. "Emmy sometimes lets her Italian blood get the better of her. She's actually married to Kenny."

"Kenny? Kenny who?" Riordan asked.

"Kenny Colwell!" Everyone shouted.

Sadie turned ghostly pale. Riordan froze with his mouth open.

On the other side of the room Tyler chuckled and said to Darren, "I guess they know now. Should we make sure they're okay?"

"We probably should."

Sadie finally regained the ability to talk and looked at Emmy. "Are they kidding?"

Emmy shook her head. "We've been best friends since I was seven..."

34

"That was ten years ago," Bobby teased.

Emmy was about to slug him when Adam stopped her.

"We met when I was seven. I'm thirty-three now, and we've been married for almost eleven years."

"I think I'm going to be sick," Sadie said.

"We are so sorry we didn't recognize you," Riordan apologized. "I thought you looked familiar, but I couldn't remember why. You do look different in person than the pictures on your CDs."

"They use trick photography on the CDs to make her look like an adult," Bobby teased.

"I would have never guessed you were older than us," Sadie said.

"She's one of the older members of the team," Tyler explained.

Emmy glared at him.

"I meant in terms of seniority, Emmy. Not in actual age."

Emmy looked around. "Shoot! I am older than most everyone. I guess I've been a part of the worship team longer than anyone else."

"But you were a child when you started, Em," Bobby said and everyone laughed.

"Didn't Chase ever mention me?" Emmy asked.

"He mentioned an Olivia Colwell and an Olivia Porter, but we never made the connection," Riordan explained.

Emmy blushed as she thought about Rory Porter.

Adam came to her rescue. "Emmy uses Olivia Porter to check into hotels on the road. It affords her a bit of privacy."

"In the files Chase referred to a seventy-year-old lady named Olivia Colwell. He said she couldn't sing and was partially deaf."

Boyd looked at Bobby and Adam. "That sounds about right."

Tyler chuckled, shook his head and said, "You guys are going to pay for all the times you've teased Emmy."

"We know, but it's so much fun," Bobby said and then patted her knee.

After most of the team had left, Tyler and Darren remained to talk to Riordan and Sadie.

"I probably owe you guys an apology because I knew about Chase's joke in Emmy's file," Tyler said.

Riordan laughed. "I admit I had some concern about Olivia. I'm glad to know she's a fictional character."

"She's not entirely fictional. Chase told me about a lady who was part of the team when he first arrived. She couldn't sing a lick on key, but sang very enthusiastically."

"How did he resolve the issue?" Sadie asked.

"If I remember correctly, the husband convinced his wife to give up singing with the team."

"Can I ask you something serious, Pastor Tyler?"

"Sure, Riordan. What is it?"

"You have so many talented people in the church already. Why do you need us?"

Tyler chuckled. "We are blessed with an abundance of talent, but... How can I explain this? People like Kenny and Emmy and a few of the other people are professionals. The Bender cousins used to be in a band. Most of Emmy's former band are part of the team. They earn their living with their talents, so they aren't always here. Emmy is the perfect example. She would be a great worship leader. I've heard stories about her being so in tune with the Holy Spirit that she makes changes at the last moment to the set list because she senses a need."

"She seemed so shy. I never would have imagined she would be who she is. Does that make any sense?"

"Totally, Sadie," Tyler said. "Have you ever seen her in concert?"

Riordan looked at Sadie.

"Not that I recall," she answered.

"You would remember," Tyler said then chuckled.

"Why is that?"

"Wait until you see her sing with the worship team. She is like a butterfly changing from a caterpillar. That's a weird example. Please, don't tell her I said so, okay?"

"We won't, but I think I know what you mean."

36

"She is more reserved in church than when she first started. That's according to people who knew her then. But she can let go on tour. I've seen her perform, and she is pretty amazing. She learned a lot from Kenny about how to connect with her audience."

"That's something we need to work on. Maybe Emmy would be willing to give us a few pointers."

"If you ask her in the right way."

"Oh, is she kinda... uh..."

Tyler waved a hand. "You misunderstood me. Emmy isn't like a diva in the least. I meant you would need to convince her she has something to teach you. She doesn't realize how talented she is. You should hear her girls sing. They are going to be something when they grow up."

"We are looking forward to being part of the team at Crest Ridge," Riordan shook Tyler's hand.

"Mom, are we going to watch Daddy play his guitar tonight?" Heather asked and then took another bite of her grilled cheese sandwich.

"Yes, we are," Emmy flipped another grilled cheese sandwich over on the grill section of her stove. "I could make you something else if you want."

Father James smiled at his half-sister. "It's not easy to get a really good grilled cheese sandwich anymore."

Emmy rolled her eyes as she slid the sandwich onto a plate. "Give me a break." She slid the plate across the island to Father James.

Isabella brought her clean plate back into the kitchen from the breakfast nook. "I'm all done. Can I play outside?"

"Make sure you wear your boots and keep your mittens on. It's still cold outside."

Isabella dashed into the mudroom to get ready.

"I want to play, too," Kevin Michael hollered.

Emmy glanced in his direction. "Did you finish your sandwich?"

He shoved the last third of his cut-in-two sandwich into his mouth. "All done."

"You can play, but you have to stay in the backyard where I can see you," Emmy insisted.

"Can we go into the woods if we stay where we can see the house?"

"All right, but not too far, and make sure Kevin Michael stays with you. Will you help him get his boots on, please?"

"Are you going outside, Heather?" Father James asked.

Heather brought her plate back into the kitchen. "Nope! I'm going upstairs and listen to Daddy's CDs. I want to sing along when he plays his guitar." Heather sprinted out of the room and ran up the stairs to the room she shared with Isabella.

Isabella helped her brother with his coat, and they went out through the garage. She turned and waved at Emmy who was looking out the window above the kitchen sink.

"Have you been working on that book of yours?" Father James asked and then took a sip of water.

"Not much. I've been writing some short stories about growing up in Raynor Park. I like doing them more."

"Do you go back there often? And I don't mean just going to Darby's."

Emmy thought about the locally-owned, one-of-a-kind hot dog stand where she worked as a teenager. "Trips to Darby's are getting fewer and farther between. It's not like when I lived at home. I passed it everyday coming back from Roosevelt High."

"Do you think it will ever close?"

"Do you mean because it's losing money?"

Father James nodded while he chewed his sandwich.

"Danny is still making money. He bought new picnic tables last year. He repaved the parking lot. People who used to live in SoHam still come back to Darby's. Danny should be all right for as long as he wants to keep working."

"How old is he? Do you know?"

Emmy put a finger to her chin. "I think he's ten years older than me."

"Which car are you driving tonight?"

"Kenny said I should take the Odyssey, but I haven't decided," Emmy answered.

"We can't take the Si."

"Ya think."

"What time did Kenny leave?"

Emmy glanced outside in time to see Isabella throw a snowball at her brother. "He got picked up around ten. The guys were doing a couple of interviews and a meet-and-greet thing."

"What time do we need to leave?"

"Why? Do you want to take a nap first?" she teased.

"I wouldn't mind a nap. I will be sixty next year."

Emmy grabbed a Coke from the fridge. "You're getting so old. You're old enough to be my father instead of my brother."

"Not my fault. Are you going to answer my question?"

"Do you want to see the opening act?"

"Who is it? Did you already tell me?" He picked up an apple from the fruit bowl in the center of the island and took a bite.

"BearFace."

"What? Are you referring to my beard?"

Emmy laughed, "No, that's Pastor Jeremiah's band. They're opening tonight and tomorrow."

"Would I like their music?"

"I doubt it. They don't do any Frank Sinatra songs. Is that apple any good?"

"Not bad. Why?"

"It's been sitting there for a month," she said.

"Will the kids want to watch Pastor Jeremiah's band?"

"Yes."

Father James sighed and stroked his beard. "Then why did you even ask?"

Emmy shrugged. "Just being polite. We need to leave around five thirty."

"Is that new worship leader going?"

"Adam got passes for them, so as far as I know they're going."

"Backstage passes?" Father James took a closer look at the apple. "This hasn't been there for a month."

"I meant yesterday, and they have parking and backstage passes. The works."

"Christians shouldn't lie. Do you think we will run into them?"

"Probably at some point. Why?"

"You didn't sound too positive about them the other day."

Emmy looked out the window and watched as Isabella and Kevin worked together to build a snowman. "I got to know them better last night. They're okay."

Emmy drove her BMW X3 to the United Center later that evening. She parked in the VIP lot, entered the building and saw Andy Walker, Fridays At Five's longtime manager, talking to Ty Dalicandro, the new tour manager for the band. The kids spotted Andy and raced toward him.

"Uncle Andy!" the girls yelled.

He turned, saw the kids and opened his arms. "How are my princesses tonight?" He picked up both girls.

"We're going to watch Pastor Jeremiah tonight," Heather explained.

"What about your father?"

"We'll watch him, too, but we like to watch Pastor Jeremiah more."

"Let's not tell that to your father, okay?" Andy set the girls down. "What have you got there?" he asked Kevin.

"I brought a firetruck to play with in case the music is too loud."

"That's a good idea." Andy smiled at Emmy and Father James. "Howdy, cousin, or should I say cousins?"

"I've disowned you, so you're not my cousin anymore. You were barely related to begin with." Emmy looked up at Andy and frowned.

Andy shook hands with Father James. "What did I do?"

Father James shrugged. "She said something about never calling her."

"I have been rather busy making sure this tour makes money."

"What a load of... manure. You don't do anything anymore. You make your employees do all the work. You just show up at concerts and boss people around to prove how important you are."

40

"Wow! Do I detect some hostility?"

"Yes. Have you seen the new worship leader and his wife?" Emmy glanced around the crowded backstage area.

"I was there last Sunday. Why?"

"I meant tonight. They're supposed to be here."

"I haven't seen them, but then again, I might not recognize them. They could be standing right behind you for all I know."

Emmy spun around fast enough to move her curly dark hair into her eyes.

"Hello, Emmy. We thought that was you," Riordan said as he smiled. "Are these your kids?"

"Yes, and this is Father James. My half-brother."

Father James shook hands with Riordan and Sadie.

"I would love to hang out and chitchat, but I have a job to do," Andy said and then walked away.

Emmy looked up at Riordan. "Did you have any trouble at the gate, or with parking?"

"Not a bit." He touched the laminated all-access pass hanging down the front of his jacket.

"Who are you?" Kevin Michael asked. "Do you know my daddy?"

Riordan offered a hand. "My name is Riordan and this is my wife Sadie. We are the new worship leaders at church.

"Oh, you're Mommy's new boss. Are you really going to ruin the worship team?"

Emmy turned as red as possible. "Kevin Michael! I never said that. Go play with your sisters and Father James."

"I'll keep an eye on them," Father James said. He waved to the two security people assigned to the kids tonight and they walked around trying to find the catering area.

"I might have said something about turning the team into Hillsong with too many singers," Emmy admitted.

"We don't want that to happen, but we don't want anyone to lose their spot on the team," Sadie explained.

"Will we have a chance to meet your husband?" Riordan asked to change the subject.

"Yeah, I'll find Jana Cordell. That's his assistant. She's from

41

the church. She will know where he is and when he'll have time to hang out."

"Adam said Pastor Jeremiah's band is here tonight."

"BearFace is opening the show. Have you met Jeremiah and Mia? The kids adore them."

"We did meet Pastor Tolla and his wife at a staff meeting."

"When they first arrived, the girls thought he looked like Jesus because of his beard. The other two guys in his band have these heavy beards, too. That's where they got the name, I guess."

"Hey, Emmy, when did you get here?" Stephanie Grachan waved as she approached.

"We just got here a few minutes ago. Oh, this is Riordan and Sadie Schulenberg. They are the new worship pastors at church. This is Stephanie Grachan. She's in charge of press relations for the band. She's got four boys who all play soccer."

"Nice to meet you," Sadie said.

"Have you seen Jana," Emmy asked.

"Saw her five minutes ago. No telling where she might be now. You know how hectic the first night of a tour can be. I gotta run. Say hi to the kids for me." Stephanie disappeared into the crowd.

"Is it always like this?" Sadie asked. "We've never been backstage at a big rock show before. We do concerts, but nothing like this."

"This isn't too bad. Some venues are smaller and you can barely move backstage. If you want to stay with me, I'll see if I can find Kenny."

"What about the kids?" Riordan looked around but couldn't see the kids or Father James.

"Father James is with them," Emmy said. "Oh, and they have a security detail that never lets them out of their sight. Their passes have chips in them, too."

"All the time?"

"No, just in places like this when the band's on tour."

"Do you have a security team with you when you go on tour?" Sadie asked.

"Nowadays I do. I never did in the old days, but things are

42

different now," Emmy said. *Todd Delaney's crazy brother caused that.*

Sadie glanced at Riordan. "I hope we never have to resort to that."

Though she tried, Emmy couldn't introduce Kenny to the Schulenbergs because he was kept busy until showtime. The Schulenbergs watched the show from their seats in the audience. Heather and Isabella watched BearFace from the side of the stage where it was not as loud. Then they joined Father James and Kevin Michael in a secure area backstage.

Halfway though the Fridays At Five concert, Kenny brought Emmy out on stage.

"Will you sing one of your songs for me?" Kenny asked while using his microphone.

"Do you guys know how to play any of my songs? I have a professional band that I use," she teased.

Kenny stared at the audience and waited for their reaction. The crowd exploded with laughter.

"Just one song, but I want it to be a fast one. Not those sappy ballads you guys play."

The crowed roared again.

Riordan hollered into Sadie's ear, "Do you think they always do this?"

Sadie shook her head. "No, Emmy told me she was going to pull a fast one on him tonight. I think his reactions are real."

Emmy grabbed Kenny's wireless mic and sang one of her uptempo songs. She danced and raced all over the wide stage to the delight of the crowd. She received a standing ovation as she left the stage.

"Wow! She's really good," Sadie shouted to Riordan.

"I never would have believed it after last night."

Chapter Four

Emmy added lunches to each of the kids backpacks. "We need to get going. Isa, will you make sure Kevin Michael's hands are clean."

"They're clean, Mom. See!" Kevin held his hands up to be inspected.

"They look clean to me, Mommy." Isabella tried to look at his hands, but he pushed her away.

Kenny sat the kitchen island sipping his second cup of coffee. "Kevin Michael! Knock it off."

Emmy grabbed her purse and keys and looked at Kenny. "Will you remember to pick them up after school?"

"I will remember. I won't be working in the studio all day. I have to run over to DelSasso Sound. Sean said he found a guitar I might like."

"Don't you have enough guitars already?" Emmy asked. "You can only play one at a time."

"I like collecting vintage guitars and amps."

"Just remember to pick up the kids. I don't want to get a call from Kristen saying you forgot."

"That only happened once," Kenny admitted. "Kristen brought them home."

"I'll see you tonight. I'm going to stop and see my mother before I head over to the warehouse. I hope she's doing better today. Last week she complained about Daddy like he was still alive."

"I hope she remembers your name, Em."

"Does Grandma remember who we are?" Heather asked.

"Sometimes she does, but she has trouble remembering names. Scoot! We need to get to school." Emmy shooed the kids out to the garage.

Kenny finished his coffee, grabbed a banana and headed downstairs to his state-of-the-art recording studio. He would work on demos of songs for the new Fridays At Five project for most of the day.

Emmy dropped the kids off at the Crest Ridge United

Nazarene School and then headed to Sunrise Garden to visit her mother in the memory care facility. She left after thirty minutes because Patricia Colasanti insisted Emmy needed to get to school. Emmy called her older sister Diane as she drove away.

"How did your visit go?" Diane Robertson asked.

"Not too bad. I think she was pretty calm until she insisted I get to school," Emmy answered while darting around slower traffic. "Did Brady leave already?"

"Yeah, he left about an hour ago."

"Where was he going this week?" Emmy asked.

"Madrid and Lisbon. I wish I could have gone with him. I'd love to visit those cities," Diane said as she nursed five-month-old Conor.

"You should make Brady take you and the younger kids along. Kenny and I can watch Carson and Caden if you don't want them to miss any school."

"I could, but traveling with two little ones is not my idea of a vacation. I don't think Brady realized how much he would be away from home when he and Bennett started this company."

"He should make Bennett do his share," Emmy suggested.

"You know his brother can't be away from the Academy during the school year. He's the headmaster."

"Just sayin'," Emmy punched the gas pedal as the light turned green.

"Where are you going now?" Diane asked as she tried to get Conor to burp without spitting up.

"Band rehearsal. We're starting today."

"Why? I didn't think your tour started until May."

"It doesn't, but Christian will be gone the whole month of April. He's doing a gig with another band from LA. They needed a lead guitar player for a short tour and he needed the money."

"Are you still using that old brick warehouse in the Gordon Hill neighborhood? That area used to be so rundown."

"We're still using the same place, and the area has really changed over the last few years. Young couples have moved into the area and started fixing up the properties. I read an article in the *Herald* about Gordon Hill being one of most desirable

45

neighborhoods in SoHam now. The warehouse right across the street is now condos. The band could sell their warehouse and make a ton of money. I'd live in the area if I was a kid with no kids."

"Yeah, but you're a goof, Em. Shoot! I gotta go. Conor spit up all over my top. Call me sometime."

Emmy ended the call. *I thought living just down the street from each other would allow us to get together more often. Guess I was wrong. We're too busy with our own lives.*

Thursday evening before the worship team met to rehearse, Pastor Tyler met with Robby Collins and Riordan Schulenberg in Riordan's office.

"As much as I dislike having to do this, I believe it is necessary," Tyler said.

Robby leaned against the wall and nodded. "This is the second time. He was lucky to get off the last time. He had Jenara in the car with him this time. Apparently, she had been drinking, too."

"Who is Jenara?" Riordan asked.

"His girlfriend," Robby said. "His live-in girlfriend. They should get married."

Riordan sat on the front edge of his desk. "I've never had to deal with a situation like this, so I will defer to your judgment. But I think he needs to resign from the team."

"Are we all in agreement?" Tyler looked at the other two men.

"Yes," Robby nodded.

"I concur," Riordan said.

"I'll see if Skip is here and bring him into the office." Tyler walked out into the music suite and saw Skip Mason standing alone by the stack of chairs against the back wall. Tyler motioned and Skip walked over with his head down.

"Let's use Riordan's office, Skip," Tyler said and then closed the outer door to the two offices. He followed Skip into the inner office and closed that door as well.

"I'm sorry about what happened." Skip stared at the floor.

46

"We're sorry, too," Tyler said. "Would you like to sit down?"

Skip glanced at the chairs. "No, I'm good."

Robby put his massive arm around Skip's thin shoulders. "We've talked about this before."

Skip met Robby's eyes for only a split-second before looking down at the floor again. "I know. I was clean for almost a month."

Robby looked at Tyler.

Tyler took a deep breath. "Skip, the global Nazarene Church recognizes the consumption of alcohol as one of the things we should avoid. You do understand this, right?"

"Yeah, I know. I have a problem following that rule."

"Please don't think I'm unaware that other members of the team have a drink occasionally," Robby said. "But you have an abuse problem. You've been charged with a DUI. That's serious, Skip."

"Yeah, I'm going to lose my license."

"You could face jail time, Skip," Tyler added.

Skip shifted his weight back and forth while staring at the floor. The other three men looked at each other. No one spoke for a time.

"Skip, we are going to ask you to resign from the worship team effective immediately. I think it might be appropriate for you to write an apology to the team," Tyler said softly.

"I really let everyone down, huh?"

"You let yourself down, Skip." Robby placed his hand on Skip's back.

"I guess I should leave, huh?" Skip looked around the office. "I've never been in here before. There's not a back door by any chance."

"Sorry, Skip," Riordan said.

"Would you let us pray for you before you leave?" Pastor Tyler asked.

Skip nodded.

Tyler, Robby and Riordan circled around Skip and put a hand on him. Tyler prayed first and then Robby and Riordan

47

prayed for Skip.

"What will you do now, Skip?" Tyler asked. "Will you lose your job?"

"I'm not sure. The school board kinda frowns on teachers getting arrested for drunk driving."

"Please, let us know if there's anything we can do to help. We are here for you, Skip."

"I appreciate that, Pastor Tyler." Skip looked him in the eye. "I will beat this addiction one way or another."

"Everyone makes mistakes in life," Robby said. "The people who learn from their mistakes... well, I'm sure you know the rest."

"Can I leave now?" Skip asked.

"You are free to go, and you are free to come back to church on Sunday," Riordan said.

Skip left the office and the music suite without stopping to say goodbye to anyone.

"Now we have to explain to the team what happened," Riordan said.

"I'm pretty sure they already know," Tyler replied as he walked out of the office. "Bad news travels faster than the speed of light."

"Do we have a replacement for Skip?" Riordan asked.

Robby nodded and pointed to a young man standing beside the drum kit. "We do. His name is Danny Alcantar, and he's been playing drums for the teen band for about three years. He's not as experienced as Skip, but he's not bad."

"Does he always wear a Golden State Warriors cap?" Riordan asked.

"No, sometimes he wears a Cubs' hat," Robby joked. "He wears it in church. It used to bother me, but..." Robby shrugged then added, "Now I don't think about it. I guess if it was important enough, God would let him know to take it off."

"Did you have a good day at the office, Daddy?" Grace Randolph ran up to her father and wrapped her arms around his legs. "I helped Mommy make dinner. We're having spaghetti."

John picked up his not-quite-six-year-old daughter and smothered her with kisses. "I can't wait to taste your spaghetti, but first I need to talk to your mother. Where is she?"

Grace shrugged, "I don't know. We had a party at school today because Kevin Michael turned six. How long do I have to wait until I'm six?"

"Just over a month," he answered. "Where are you, Kristen?"

"In the family room," Kristen hollered. "Did you hear from North Park?"

John set Grace down and walked into the family room. He sat next to Kristen on the couch and kissed her. "I got the offer. The money's not bad."

"Is it half of what you make now?"

John shook his head. "More like a third."

"I could go back to work full-time," Kristen offered.

"No, we would need to get a nanny for the kids. I don't mind you working at the office while the kids are in school, but I'd rather you didn't work more hours than that."

"Have you decided? How soon do you have to let North Park know your decision?"

"They gave me until Friday to decide. I want to talk to my brothers before I make a decision." John put an arm around Kristen and pulled her closer. "Are you going to get your hair trimmed the next time Gracie gets hers cut?"

Kristen bunched her long, blonde hair behind her neck. "I could be like Emmy and keep it short."

"Your hair isn't as curly as hers." John ran a hand through Kristen's silky hair.

"Quit changing the subject. When are you going to talk to Kirk and Keith?"

"After dinner. I hear we are having spaghetti and Gracie helped you cook."

John's two older brothers both coached at the college level back in Ohio. Keith served as the head coach at John Carroll University located in a suburb of Cleveland. Kirk, the oldest brother, coached linebackers at Bowling Green State University.

49

After dinner, John called Kirk and told him about his offer and the important details.

"Can you live on that salary?" Kirk asked.

"We'd have to make some adjustments in our lifestyle," John admitted.

The brothers talked for several minutes about the pros and cons.

"My advice would be to stay with Bertucci and Keasling. It's a lot more secure than a head coaching position. You could always coach part-time down the road if you still had the bug."

John talked to Keith who offered the same advice.

"What did they say?" Kristen asked when John slipped into bed later that night.

"They said to stay with Bertucci and Keasling."

"What are you going to do?"

"I'm going to take a couple days and think about it. I might even pray about it, too."

"I know you love football, John. Don't worry about the money. We will be all right."

The next afternoon Diane invited her in-laws and Emmy over to the house to celebrate Lily's second birthday.

"Why did you decide not to throw a big party, Diane?" Emmy asked.

"Because Lily and Conor are the only two little kids from the neighborhood not in school. I didn't want to have the party at night."

"I guess it doesn't matter," Emmy said and then laughed. "They are having fun with Grandma and Grandpa."

Diane sighed. "Bill and Mona spoil them too much."

"It's because they don't have any other little grandkids anymore," Emmy said. "They might have great-grandkids soon."

Diane thought about Bennett Robertson's children, snorted and said, "No way! Spencer and Abigail aren't interested in having kids."

"Are they both still at Stanford?" Emmy asked while watching Conor laugh at his grandfather making faces at him.

"Spencer is working on his PHD, and Abigail is either in her second or third year," Diane explained.

"Too bad Brady isn't home."

"Tell me about it." Diane picked up Conor and checked his diaper. "You wanna change his diaper? You always say you want another baby."

Emmy pinched her nose. "I'll pass. I can smell it from here."

John returned home after work on Wednesday, put his arms around Kristen's waist, lifted her hair out of the way and kissed her neck. "I made up my mind."

She turned to face him. "What did you decide?"

"I declined the offer. I'm staying with Bertucci and Keasling." He looked at the oven. "What are you making?"

"Lasagna. Are you hungry?" John opened the oven door to take in the aroma. "Did you make this from scratch, or should I ask?"

Grace walked into the kitchen carrying one of her dolls in time to hear John's question and shook her head. "Mama put it together after school and I watched. Uncle Tony didn't want Mama to let Mommy bring it home."

"Thanks for spilling the beans, Gracie," Kristen said.

John laughed and then said, "Everyone uses Mama Bertucci's recipe for lasagna. Even Emmy and she's a good cook."

Kristen placed her hands on her hips and frowned at John. "I did put the salad together without help."

"And I'm sure it will be delicious," John teased.

Chapter Five

"Is there anything else you need us to do?" Emmy asked Liz Hammond after filling the last balloon with helium.

"I think we're good to go," Liz said as she looked around the all-purpose room at church. "Thank you so much for your help, Em."

"My pleasure. What time will Dany and Darian be here?"

"I told them to be here by two. Most of the guests should have arrived by then." Liz counted the places set up. "If we need more chairs, Darian can help."

"Kenny wasn't at my bridal shower," Emmy said.

"Neither was Tyler, but Dany insisted he be here for a little bit."

Dany and Darian arrived shortly after two. He held her hand as they walked into the room.

"What?" Dany asked as Darian came to a stop.

"I'm the only guy here," he said scanning the room.

"Of course. Who else did you expect to be here?"

"Eli, Tyler, someone, anyone. I feel weird with all these women staring at me."

Dany squeezed his hand. "You don't have to stay for the whole thing. I just wanted everyone to see you. Some of my friends and relatives haven't met you."

Cora Michaelis walked up to Dany and Darian with her daughters Mary and Dahlia. "You look so pretty, Dany. Is my son giving you a hard time about being here?"

"Ma!" Darian protested. "Guys don't go to wedding showers."

Dahlia grinned at her older brother. "They do now."

Darian asked Mary, "Was Jonah at your shower?"

"Yes, and he stayed for the whole thing. Without complaining," Mary said.

Darian took a deep breath and then smiled at Dany. "I will stay as long as you wish."

Two hours later Darian kissed Dany, waved to the guests and left.

Dahlia walked out with him. "That wasn't too terrible, was it?"

"I survived, but what are we going to do with some of those gifts? Who needs that many sets of sheets, or that many gravy bowls?"

"You can always exchange them for something more useful," Dahlia said.

Darian grinned. "Like a new Xbox."

Dahlia smacked his arm. "You won't be using your Xbox after you get married."

"Sofia, will you sit by me for lunch?" Heather pulled Sofia into the breakfast nook.

"But I want to sit by Sofia," Isabella whined.

Emmy pointed to the three chairs along one side of the table. "You can sit on either side of Sofia, but you have to stop pestering her and let her eat. You've been bothering her all day long."

"I don't mind," Sofia replied as she took her seat.

Heather stared at Sofia's stomach. "Are you going to get real big like Miss Liz?"

"Heather! That's not nice," Emmy said as she set the taco salad on the table.

"But she was big until Phoebe was born," Isabella shrugged.

Kevin Michael raced into the breakfast nook, set a firetruck on the table and climbed into his seat. "When is Daddy coming home?"

"He will be home later this afternoon. Their plane was delayed because of a blizzard in Utah, and we do not need firetrucks on the table while we eat."

Isabella turned to Sofia. "Utah is a state out west. We saw it on the map. Do you like taco salad?"

Sofia smiled. "I do, and I requested it for lunch today."

"Who wants to say the prayer?" Emmy sat down and looked at the girls.

Heather and Isabella both said a short prayer.

"I don't want tomatoes in my taco salad," Kevin Michael stared into the large Tupperware bowl searching for any sign of tomatoes.

"I didn't put any in the big bowl," Emmy assured him. "I have grape tomatoes if anyone wants to add them."

"It looks delicious, Mommy," Isabella said as she reached for the slotted spoon to fill her bowl. "Here, Sofia. You can go first."

"Thank you, Isa," Sofia said and then took the spoon.

Later, Emmy set the Tupperware bowl in the sink. "I can't believe we ate the whole bowl without Kenny or Tony here."

Sofia brought the dirty bowls and silverware into the kitchen. "I had three helpings, Em. It tasted even better than usual. Did you change your recipe?"

"I bought a different spice packet, a cheaper brand, and I cut down on the beans a little. Nothing drastic."

"Were we supposed to save some for Kenny?" Sofia asked.

Emmy shrugged. "He can find something to eat."

"What time do you need to leave, Emmy?"

Emmy checked the clock on the microwave. "Two thirty or so. That's why we went to the early service today. The crew is already in Green Bay. The guys and I are cutting it close, but we should make it on time. Nelson checked the weather, and there shouldn't be any delay." Emmy referred to Nelson Grapella her band's manager. "Oh, the girls have going away presents for you."

"Should we take care of that now? I don't want you to be late."

Emmy wiped her hands on a towel. "We can sit in the family room." Emmy used the intercom to tell the kids to come downstairs.

"We'll be there in a minute, Mom. We are finishing something," Isabella answered.

Emmy cleared a spot and she and Sofia sat on the leather couch.

"What do you plan to do until the baby comes?"

Sofia turned to face Emmy. "I'm going to be working part-time at the church. Pastor Tyler needed help in the office."

"He's going to have to hire more people. The church can't continue to rely on volunteers forever."

Heather, Isabella and Kevin Michael raced into the room.

Heather held a gift bag. "We have something for the baby, Sofia."

"And we made cards for you," Isabella handed the homemade cards to Sofia.

"Thank you so much." Sofia read the cards.

"We helped Kevin with his card, but he wrote his name," Isabella said.

"These are so much better than store-bought cards. Thank you."

"You should look in the bag," Heather handed it to Sofia.

Sofia removed the fancy paper, lifted two onesies out and held them up.

"Mommy helped us pick out the clothes. She said the baby could wear them even if it's a boy," Heather explained.

"They look so pretty. Thank you."

Heather looked at Isabella as Kevin Michael stared at Sofia.

After a moment Isabella moved close to Sofia. "We are getting bigger, so we don't need a nanny, but we will miss you."

Sofia reached out to hug all three kids. "I will miss you, but we will still see each other at school and church." She released the girls but Kevin clung tightly to her.

Emmy noticed the tears streaming down Kevin Michael's cheeks but didn't say anything which might embarrass him.

"I've been calling you all day," Emmy shouted. "Where have you been, and why didn't you answer my calls?"

"Sorry, but I was kinda busy," Father James answered.

"Doing what?" Emmy walked into the kitchen from the pantry. *I need more cereal for the kids.*

"I had two funeral masses today. That took most of my time. For some reason the families thought I should be there."

"Sorry, I didn't know," Emmy apologized.

"It's all right. They were both really old. What's on your mind, child?"

"Nothing too important," Emmy said and then bit her lip.

"Yeah, right. Come on. Spill it. You wouldn't have called five times if something wasn't bothering you." He waited several seconds before she answered.

"I don't think the new worship leaders like me."

Father James shook his head as he waited for Emmy to explain. She didn't.

"Why don't they like you?" he finally asked.

"I don't know! They just don't. They won't let me sing like before. They sing lead on every song, and all I do is sing harmony."

"But isn't their job to be the leaders?"

Emmy didn't answer.

"Are you there?"

"I'm still here."

"Is there more to it than that?"

"Well, they are real particular about the music. Riordan got after one of the musicians because he played a D instead of a B. Chase would have never done that in front of everyone."

"Was it an obvious mistake? Did it ruin the song?"

"No! I doubt if anyone even noticed. And another thing." Emmy sat on a barstool at the island. "They are choreographing the singers. Sadie wants the singers to stand in certain spots and raise our hands at the same time."

"Like the Supremes?"

"Who?"

"Never mind."

"I have never done things like that. I dance around and stuff because that's how I feel at the moment. It feels so fake otherwise."

"When does your tour start?" Father James asked.

Emmy looked at the calendar on the fridge. "Sometime in May."

"Do you think you will keep singing with the worship team until then?"

"Well, yeah, I'm not going to quit. I'm only scheduled once a month as it is, so no one would even notice if I did."

"Are you scheduled tomorrow?"

56

"Nope! I can sleep late if I want. I might just decide to stay home. Kenny will be back in time to take the kids to church."

"I have an idea," he said.

"What?"

"Come to mass at St. John's. It's St. Peter Regalado day."

"Who's that. Never heard of him."

Father James gave Emmy some background info.

"I could show up if you want me to," Emmy agreed.

"Come to the eleven o'clock mass, and then we can do lunch. My treat."

Emmy laughed. "That means we're going to Darby's because Danny lets you eat for free."

"But you like Darby's."

"Fine! We can eat there," Emmy said and then put the phone on speaker-mode and leaned on her elbows. "Can I take communion, or is that against the rules?"

"It's against the rules. You should know that."

"So if I got in line with everyone, would you refuse me? Would you make a scene about it?"

He thought for a moment. "I wouldn't refuse you because I know you, but if the Bishop found out, he would get on my case."

"So what? You don't like the guy. Why do you even care?"

"He is my boss, and even a rebellious priest like me needs to follow some rules."

"Don't tell me you're getting serious in your old age," Emmy said and then chuckled.

"I'm not that old, and I do take my calling seriously when it comes to certain aspects. The parishioners expect it."

"I don't want to get you into trouble with the boss."

"I wouldn't do anything God would not approve of, and you better not either, young lady."

"I try not to, but I am human."

He shook a finger even though she couldn't see him. "That's no excuse. You told me what Pastor Tyler said in one of his messages."

"I'm never telling you anything again," Emmy made a face at the phone. "Do I have to dress up, or can I wear jeans and a sweatshirt? I can find a clean one."

"I'll let the Holy Spirit guide your decision, my child."

"I'm hanging up. I'll try to make it at eleven."

The next morning Emmy sat near the back for the eleven o'clock mass. She responded along with the other parishioners. *I remember more than I thought. That's strange. I haven't been to a regular mass for twenty years.*

Later, she got in line with the other worshipers to take communion. *Should I take communion? I am a believer.* She paused as the person in front of her took the wafer. She heard Father James say, "The body of Christ," and the lady stepped aside.

Father James frowned as he looked at Emmy.

She looked up at him and slowly crossed her arms.

"Bless you, my child," Father James said.

Emmy returned to her seat.

She stood in the foyer later after everyone had left. She bit her lip as she saw Father James approaching. "Are you pissed at me?" she asked when he got close.

He had changed into jeans and a dress shirt. He put on his black leather jacket. "I have been going back and forth in my mind over whether I should be mad or not."

"Did you decide?" she asked while looking up at him with an innocent expression in her eyes. "I didn't take the host."

He shook his head and then chuckled. "It's no use. I can't stay upset with you, and stop looking at me like that."

She put her hand through his arm. "Like what?"

"You get this look in your eyes that makes me think of you as an innocent, guileless child."

"Maybe I am," she said as her eyes sparkled.

"And I might be the pope one day."

"Isn't that being blasphemous?"

"Fine! I'll go to confession next week. Are you driving?"

"It's too cold to walk."

He opened the door for her and followed her out to the parking lot. "Where's the BMW?"

58

She clicked her remote to unlock the Civic Si. "I wanted to drive this today."

He lowered himself into the passenger seat. "I didn't think you drove this in the winter."

"I usually don't, but the streets are relatively clear. Of snow, I mean. There's still tons of salt on the roads. I'll have to run this through the car wash later." She started the car, revved the engine and let out the clutch.

Father James shook his head as the tires squealed. "Are you trying to ruin the engine? You need to let it warm up before you do that."

"It's still kinda warm, and I don't do it all the time." She passed a SoHam squad car doing ten miles-an-hour over the limit.

"One of these days," Father James said.

"I don't drive like a maniac all the time, and who'd give me a ticket with a priest in the car?"

Father James looked over his shoulder. He hooked a thumb toward the rear window. "I think you're going to find out."

Emmy glanced in the rearview mirror and saw flashing lights. "Shoot! I wasn't going that fast." She slowed down and started to pull over.

The squad car roared past and made a left at the next intersection.

"Must be your lucky day, Emmy," he said with a chuckle. "Did you get scared he was after you?"

"I've been pulled over before. It doesn't scare me, but I did feel my heart racing for just a second," she admitted.

Ten minutes later they sat in a booth and Emmy poured ketchup over her fries.

"Hush!"

Father James shrugged. "I didn't say anything."

"You were going to comment about how much ketchup I use."

"You do use a lot. Would you hand me the salt, please?"

She handed him the salt shaker. "Ketchup isn't as bad for you as salt. There's already enough salt on the fries. Why do you have to add more?"

59

"Force of habit. Are you going to pray for the food?"

"Why can't you do it? You're a priest, remember?"

He glanced at a family with four kids walking past and then shook his head. "Because if I do it, I would have to drag it out. You can say the prayer the girls use."

Emmy rolled her eyes and then prayed.

"Are we good on the communion thing?" she asked after stuffing three fries into her mouth.

"Just don't do it again if you come back," he said. "Are you going to come back?"

"I don't think so. I know there are plenty of Catholics who are very serious about their faith, but I'm not going to leave my church."

"Even if the new worship leaders don't like you?"

She made a face. "Not everyone at church gets along. We're not all best friends, you know."

"Your church is like your family," he said. "You don't always get along, and you don't get to choose who's in your family."

"Did I tell you that I had my first communion thing at St. John's?" Emmy asked.

"No, you didn't. Are you serious?" He asked and then took a bite of his chili dog. "So good."

"I was eight, and I had to wear the same white dress Diane wore for her first communion. It didn't fit right so Grandma Colasanti had to alter it. She had to hem it up because Diane was a lot taller." Emmy paused to take a drink of her root beer.

"Why didn't your parents, or your grandparents, buy you a new dress?" Father James asked. "Your first communion is a big deal."

"Daddy didn't see the need to buy new dresses for us. Any new dresses they did buy were for Diane. They always figured I could wear them after she either grew out of them or they fell out of fashion and she refused to wear them."

Father James chuckled and said, "Diane was into fashion even then, huh?"

Emmy nodded. "Always. When I was old enough for my

first communion, I remember Grandma and Grandpa coming over so she could fix the dress. They both offered to buy a new one, but Daddy refused. He said he would support his family without any help from his parents or anyone else."

Father James pulled on his ear and sipped his root beer as he listened.

"I remember they argued over the dress. Daddy used to argue with his parents a lot."

"It sounds like you inherited your stubbornness from him."

"I am not stubborn," Emmy insisted.

"Yeah, right," Father James said, laughed and then asked, "What about your other grandparents? They could have bought you a new dress."

Emmy glanced around Darby's as she tried to remember. "I think they might have been in Florida or something. But even when they were in SoHam, they didn't come around much. Grandpa Sandusky never really approved of Daddy."

"I can kind of understand why he would feel that way," Father James said. "He had a habit of getting girls pregnant and fathers don't take that lightly. I've dealt with situations like that too many times over the years."

"Our father would have gone ballistic if Diane had gotten pregnant at the same age as Mom did. She was pregnant when she married Craig, but at least she was older."

"What about you?" he whispered.

"What about me?"

"How would he have reacted if that had happened to you?"

"He would have found out who the father was and then killed him," Emmy answered.

"But not Diane?"

Emmy shook her head as she chewed on her chili dog.

"I wonder if he would have had a different reaction."

"Like what?" Emmy asked. "I can't picture him doing anything other than exploding in a rage."

"You were his little angel, so I think he might have been shattered and not been able to express his anger in the way you assume."

61

Emmy stared at Father James and could imagine their father so clearly. "I suppose it's possible, but he would have eventually exploded."

"You've said he was never violent even when he was drunk, right?"

"I never saw him use physical violence on Mom. They yelled at each other all the time, but they always made up. He spanked me and Diane when we were little, but I never felt he did it while he was enraged. He used to kinda apologize if he had to spank me. I think it really hurt him to have to do that. Like that old saying, you know."

"Did he ever get into fights down at Miller's Bar? He might have been different there."

"I'm sure there were times when fights broke out there," she said and then laughed. "Daddy would take me to Miller's, and I would set on the bar and drink chocolate milk and eat peanuts. I would ask for chocolate milk and he would say I had to drink regular milk. His friends would get on his case and offer to buy me chocolate milk. I probably used that look you mentioned to get my way."

"I can see that," Father James said and then laughed.

"Oh, hush," Emmy said as her eyes sparkled and she bit her lip. "You make it sound like I was spoiled rotten."

"If the shoe fits, or in your case." He pointed to her foot.

"These shoes are comfortable," she replied.

"Have you ever been back to Miller's Bar?"

Emmy shook her head. "Not since I had to pick Daddy up when Mom threw him out of the house."

"Want to check it out sometime? They might still have chocolate milk," Father James said.

Emmy shrugged, but then shook her head. "I don't think so. The original owner passed away, and the area isn't as safe as it used to be."

Chapter Six

"I found this firetruck in my closet. I thought it was lost." Kevin Michael held up the firetruck as he stood a few feet from the large screen TV in the family room. "Can you see it, Daddy?"

Kenny sat in front of his laptop in a hotel room as he Skyped with his family. "I can see it, buddy. Maybe you should clean up your closet more often."

"We want to talk to Daddy, too, Kevin. You've had your turn. Now it's ours. Move back and sit down." Heather pulled on her brother's arm.

"I will. You don't have to yank on my arm," Kevin made a face at his sister but didn't hit her.

Heather and Isabella sat on ottomans in front of the TV.

Emmy patted the space next to her on the couch. "Sit with me so the girls can have a turn."

"Where are you today, Daddy?" Isabella asked.

"I'm in Providence. Do you know where that is?"

The twins shook their heads.

"It's in Rhode Island. Do you know where that is?"

Emmy sighed. *Enough with the geography lesson.*

"Where is it, Daddy?" Heather asked.

Kenny explained the location. "And it's the smallest state in the whole country."

"Is it bigger than SoHam?" Heather asked.

"Yes, but SoHam has almost has many people living there as the actual city of Providence. I read somewhere that South Hampshire will pass the two hundred thousand mark in population in the next few years. It could end up being the second largest city in the entire state."

Emmy shook her head. *Such a dork.*

"Are you coming home tonight?"

"Yes, but not until you are asleep. I'll see you in the morning for church."

Kenny talked to the girls for several minutes.

"I need to talk to your mother now. Would you let us have some privacy, please?"

Heather and Isabella grinned at each other and then giggled.

"Are you going to tell Mommy how much you love her?" Isabella asked with a smile.

"Yes," Kenny answered. "Do you know what day this is?"

"It's the day you and Mommy got married," Isabella answered. "Mommy showed us some pictures. She was wearing her special dress."

"We'll let you talk to Mommy," Heather said as she blew a kiss to her father.

"Take Kevin Micheal upstairs with you, please," Emmy said as she sat on one of the ottomans.

"Do we have to play with him?" Heather frowned.

"I can play in my room," Kevin insisted and then dashed up the stairs.

Emmy waited until the girls were gone and then smiled at Kenny. "Will you be home before I'm asleep?"

"Only if you stay up real late," he said. "Happy anniversary, Em."

"Happy anniversary to you, too, my dorky husband," she said then laughed.

"Why am I so dorky now?"

"The girls don't care how many people live in SoHam or Rhode Island," she explained.

"I know, but it was something to talk about. Sometimes I feel so disconnected from them. I can't keep up with the latest trends and movies and stuff."

Emmy chuckled. "Wait until they get a little older."

"Can we lock them in their rooms until they're thirty?"

"I'm pretty sure that's not legal. Did I mention I wrote another short story?"

He shook his head. "What about this time?"

"Do you remember the time we helped my father paint the garage?"

"Vaguely," he answered. "Why? Did something special happen? Something really worth writing about?"

She rolled her eyes. "No, I wanted to write a boring story.

64

You don't remember, do you?"

"That was a long time ago, Em. Are you going to refresh my memory?"

"It was August and close to ninety degrees. Daddy wanted to get the garage painted over the weekend. I wanted to play over at your house, but he made me help."

"How old were you?"

"I had just turned ten, so you were thirteen. You came over and helped. We worked on the side in the alley because it was in the shade. Daddy wanted a beer, so he sent me in to grab two of them."

"Oh, I think I remember that day now," Kenny said.

Emmy licked her lower lip. "When he wasn't looking, I stole one of the cans..."

"Yeah!" He pointed at her. "You started drinking it. Then you handed it to me."

"You said you had never tasted beer before, so I dared you to try it."

"I only took a little sip..."

"Ha! It was more than that. You drank enough to get a little buzz."

"Did not," Kenny argued.

"Anyway, Daddy asked for his second can, and I gave it to him. He saw that it was opened and looked at me. I admitted to taking a sip, and he thought about swatting me, but then he laughed and said something to the effect he knew it wasn't the first time."

"Are you sure you want to put this in a book?"

She shrugged. "It's nothing scandalous. Diane drank a lot more than me."

"You never got caught," Kenny reminded her. "What else have you written about? Anything I should know?"

"I'll let you read them before I give them to Denise."

"You can wake me up when you get home."

"I'll try, Em."

"Promise?"

He grinned. "I promise, sweetie."

65

After she dropped the kids off at school Monday morning, Emmy went into the den, sat in her recliner, got comfortable and opened her laptop.

"Hey, Em, I'm gonna run over to my parents' house for a while. Want to join me?"

Emmy looked to see Kenny staring down at her. "I'll pass. I want to look at these stories while the kids are at school."

He kissed the top of her head. "I'll be back after lunch. Dad wants me to sort through some old Fridays At Five merchandise he bought last week. He thinks there might be something of value he can sell on eBay."

"See you when you get back."

Emmy reviewed the stories and then called Denise Bartell.

"How are you, Emmy? What have you been working on?" Denise asked as she closed the door to her office on the fourth floor of the building which now housed the offices of the *South Hampshire Herald*. "Have you spent any more time on your autobiography?"

"Not really. I've kinda put that on hold for now, but I do have some stories that might interest you."

"Tell me more," Denise said and then took a sip of her tea.

Emmy explained the theme of the stories and read a few snippets.

"Pardon my laughter, but that sounds hilarious. Did you really do that?"

Emmy bit her lip. "I didn't know any better. I didn't think it mattered how you did laundry."

"What would you like to do with the stories, Emmy?"

"I'd like to let you read them and see if they're any good. If they are, I was thinking about self-publishing them. You told me that would be possible and wouldn't cost too much."

"Your timing is perfect. I have to work today, but then I have a week off. I'm not going anywhere, and don't have any projects of my own at the moment," Denise said.

"Could I run these over to your office?" Emmy asked.

"Sure. Whatever time works for you. Do you know where we're located?"

"Yes, I've driven past it before. Would it be all right if I stopped by in thirty minutes?"

"I'll be waiting," Denise said and then finished her tea.

An hour and a half later Denise convulsed with laughter again. "These will make a great book, Emmy. Especially for people who know you now. They will be amazed."

"Could you help me edit them?"

"Absolutely! I'll go over them for you, and I can have my daughter do the formatting. She can design a cover if you'd like."

"Oh, yes, please. I've seen the covers and artwork she did for you. She's very talented. I have a photograph I kinda like. Maybe she could make it work as a cover. I will pay you whatever you need."

Emmy and Denise agreed on some numbers and a timetable to finish the work.

"Did you have a chance to look at the artwork, Emmy?" Denise asked a little over a week later.

"I did, and I love it!" Emmy exclaimed. "I have read all of your edits, and they make the stories flow better. What else do I need to do to make this an actual book?"

Denise explained the next steps.

"That sounds so easy," Emmy said.

"It is easy," Denise said and then laughed. "That's why so many people are self-publishing now. You have an advantage though."

"What's that?" Emmy asked.

"You already have name recognition and your lion book is fantastic. This book is for an older reader, but I think teens and young adults are going to love it."

"I'll be happy if I sell ten copies, Denise," Emmy said.

Chapter Seven

"Sloane, are you sure it's all right to bring the kids?" Emmy called Easter Sunday afternoon.

"Absolutely, Emmy. Mama wants all the kids there," Sloane answered. "It's Easter break, so there's no school this week."

"Did you guys ever find seats?" Emmy asked. "I couldn't believe how many people were there."

"It is Easter, Emmy. We should have known better and arrived earlier. Did you hear an actual number for the attendance?"

"No, but Liz said it was a record. I couldn't believe how many people were baptized. I think Pastor Tyler did twenty-five and Pastor Jake baptized seventeen teens. I counted," Emmy said.

Sloane chuckled. "I enjoyed the story of the older lady Pastor Ausland baptized."

Emmy adjusted her position on the family room couch. "You mean Frieda Johnson. She was funny."

"How old did she say she was?" Sloane asked. "Isn't she like ninety?"

"I think so. She said she figured she better get baptized before it was too late," Emmy said. "What about gifts?"

"Mama said she will throw any gifts in the trash."

"Do you think she would really do that?" Emmy asked.

Sloane laughed. "How long have you known Mama? She may act tough at times, but she would never do that."

"I hope so. The girls insisted on buying presents."

"Tony had to hide the gifts our kids bought at Kristen's house because Mama kept insisting she didn't want anything. She even tried to cook all the food. I practically had to yell at her to stop. You know how she is."

"Where did you order the food from?"

"Most of it is from Kerry Lynn's Pizza and Pasta, but I also ordered some from Darby's. Mr. and Mrs. Sabatino are bringing some desserts from Ciao Bella. Mama doesn't know that, but she knows they are coming."

"They've been friends for a long time. I remember going to

Ciao Bella with my grandmother Colasanti when I was a little girl," Emmy mentioned. "It's still the best Italian restaurant in the area."

"We're going to eat at seven, but the church is ours after six. Oh, there'll be a bouncy house for the younger kids."

Emmy giggled and then asked, "Can I use the bouncy house?"

Sloane laughed. "Yes, but you have to take off your shoes."

"We'll see you tomorrow."

Kenny backed the Odyssey out of the garage the next evening. "We're on our way," he said as he drove down the winding driveway.

"Mom, I have a question," Isabella hollered.

"Everyone shush. Isa has a question," Emmy said and then turned to face Isabella. "What, sweetie?"

"Is Mama Bertucci older than Me-maw and Gra? She looks older."

Emmy looked at Kenny. "Your dad's older, right?"

"Dad will be seventy-two in September, so he's older."

Emmy turned back to Isabella. "Mama is older than Me-maw, but not as old as Gra. Don't say anything about her looking older, okay?"

"I won't," Isabella promised.

"What about Grandma?" Heather asked. "Is she lots of years older because she can't remember anything?"

"Your grandmother will be seventy-two next week, so she's a little bit older than Gra," Emmy explained.

"Will Gra will lose his memory soon?" Heather asked.

"No, Grandma doesn't remember things because she's sick."

Kevin Michael hollered from the back row, "I was sick, but I still remember stuff."

Kenny looked in the rearview mirror. "Your grandmother has a different kind of illness, buddy."

The kids entered the all-purpose room at the church and immediately saw the two bouncy houses.

"You can play, but you have to take off your shoes," Emmy said. "Watch out for smaller kids, okay?"

"We will, Mom." Kevin Michael pulled off his shoes and threw them in the direction of the bouncy house that resembled a castle.

Kenny carried the bags of gifts inside. "Where should I hide these?"

Sloane pointed to two tables along the far wall. "We're not hiding them. I hope we have enough room."

"We've got more tables," Kenny said.

"Mom, did you see how high I jumped?" Kevin Michael asked.

"I saw. Please remember to look out for the younger kids when they arrive."

"I will. Are you going to play with us?"

Emmy glanced over her shoulder. "Maybe I will, but just for a few minutes." She removed her tennis shoes and joined the kids.

A minute later Kristen and Sloane walked over to the bouncy house castle and stared at Emmy.

Emmy saw them looking. "What? Sloane said I could."

Kristen looked at Sloane and raised her eyebrows.

"I didn't think she would take me seriously," Sloane said and then shrugged.

"I better stop now, but you can keep playing," Emmy said to Kevin and then slid out of the inflatable castle. She saw Tony and Kenny approaching. "I had to try it."

"Wouldn't have expected otherwise," Tony teased.

"You know you want to try it." She poked him in his side. "Don't do it. There's a weight limit."

Kristen checked a text on her cell phone. "John, Mom says they are on their way with Mama."

"She will be early, but I guess it doesn't matter. It's not a surprise party," John said.

"The food is here," Sloane said as she walked over to Kristen and John. "I hope we have enough."

"How many people are we expecting?" Kristen asked.

"Close to two hundred if they all show up. The hospitality committee set the room up for more than that." Sloane counted the tables again. "We should be all right."

"I wouldn't worry about it," John said. "The kids will be more interested in playing."

Kristen put her hands over her ears. "We will have to shut those down to eat. It's way too loud in here."

"What?" John asked with a straight face.

Thirty minutes later the majority of the guests had arrived. Mama's siblings made it to the celebration with all of their children. The entire Lombardi family had not been together since Howard Lombardi passed away in June of 1998.

Kristen walked to where her brother Derrick and his wife Amber stood talking to Tony. "About time you guys got here."

Derrick put an arm around his sister's shoulders and hugged her. "We got here as soon as we could. I was stuck with a client who couldn't decide on his beneficiaries, and Amber was with a patient."

"How do you ever manage to combine research on Parkinson's with maintaining a private practice?" Kristen looked at her sister-in-law. *And how do you still look like a supermodel?*

"I limit my patients," Amber replied. "Is that Marco and Nancy?" She pointed across the room.

"It is and all of Nancy's boys are with them," Tony said. "I should go talk to him."

Tony headed across the room to talk to his brother.

"Derrick, is that Bobby and Brian?" Kristen whispered.

"I believe so, but I might not have recognized them had I seen them in another situation."

"They have both added a lot of weight, and Bobby is practically bald like his father."

"Is that Charlotte?" Amber asked. "Wasn't that her name?"

"Yes, that's Bobby's wife, and I'm pretty sure her name is Charlotte," Kristen replied. "She's gained weight, too. Do they still live in North Carolina?"

"As far as I know," Derrick said as he waved at Emmy and Kenny. "I haven't seen them for three or four years."

71

"Kenny, I want to say hi to Derrick and Amber. I'll be right back," Emmy said.

"I'll be here, Em."

Emmy scurried across the room, dodging people and skidded to a stop in front of Derrick. "Hi," she said while looking up at Derrick and Amber.

"Hi, yourself," Derrick said and then briefly hugged Emmy. He looked down at her feet. "Are we supposed to remove our shoes?"

"No, I was in the bouncy house and forgot to put mine back on," she answered.

"Have you been keeping busy now that you are a famous author?"

"I'm not famous, but I have been busy. How are you, Amber? Is this guy treating you all right?" Emmy asked. *You still look as glamorous as when I first met you.*

Amber smiled at her husband. "I try to keep him in line."

Karla Keasling took over the organization of the food on the tables.

"Can I help?" Mama asked.

"Maria! This your party. I don't want to see you lifting a finger unless it is to eat," Karla insisted. "You should talk to Carmen and Vincent and the rest of the family and guests. Sloane and I will handle this. Now shoo." Karla waved her hands. "We will be ready to eat in fifteen minutes."

Mama looked around the large room. "I didn't expect so many people."

"Hmmmph! If we hadn't limited the invitations, the whole city would have shown up," Karla said.

As promised, fifteen minutes later Karla held a microphone and got everyone's attention. "We are ready to eat." She gave a few instructions about where the family should sit and how the tables would be dismissed. Then she looked at Sloane, who was standing a few feet away. "Should we say a prayer? Is your pastor here?"

Sloane nodded and then pointed to one of the tables in back where families with small children were sitting. "He's back there."

Everyone kept quiet long enough for Pastor Tyler to pray.

72

"Maria, you are first in line, and don't argue with me."

Emmy whispered to Kristen, "How much younger is your mother than Mama? I forgot."

"Mama's fourteen years older, and she practically raised Mom. She helped Grandma Dorothea a lot."

"How is your father doing? Is he going to need more surgery?"

"He probably should get both knees replaced, but he's too stubborn," Kristen said and then grinned at Emmy. "He's like someone else I know."

"I am not stubborn," Emmy insisted.

"I suppose John and I can get in line now, huh?" Tony asked Sloane thirty minutes later.

Sloane smiled, "Yes, the other guests have gotten their food, but that doesn't mean you can take whatever is left."

"We wouldn't think of it," John said and then patted Tony on the back.

"Are you still hungry? There is more food," Emmy said when she saw Heather's and Isabella's clean plates.

"We want to wait for the cake. Will Mama have to blow out her candles?"

"I'm not sure, Isa. That would be a lot of candles."

Heather looked at the deflated bouncy houses. "When do we get to play some more?"

"I'm not sure. Those make so much noise, and I think Mama will need to open her presents and the adults will want to talk to each other."

"Could we go upstairs and play in Noah's Ark until Mama gets ready to open presents?" Heather asked.

Kenny said, "I saw some of the church ladies take their kids upstairs, Em. It should be all right."

"Okay, you can go play, but only if there's an adult upstairs," Emmy said. She looked around the room and noticed most of the guests had finished eating and were mingling. "Kenny, I want to talk to Marco. I haven't had a chance yet."

"Go ahead, Em. I might run upstairs to help watch the kids," Kenny said and then kissed Emmy's cheek.

Emmy spotted Marco talking to Tony a few tables away. *Who are those humongous men with you? They can't be his stepsons.* Emmy made her way over and tapped Tony's shoulder.

He turned around. "Hey, Em. Did you get enough to eat?"

"I had enough. I don't need as much as you." She bit her lip and then looked at Marco. "Hi, how have you been? You still living in Baltimore?"

"Yes, we are, but we have an empty house now," Marco replied and then glanced up at the three men who towered over him. "Do you remember the boys?"

Emmy stared at the three men who were all taller than Tony. "You've got to be kidding."

Marco smiled. "This is Travis. He's in med school at Johns Hopkins. The short one is Bryan, who is working on his masters at Harvard." Marco moved over to the biggest one. "You might have seen Dwight on TV. He plays for Notre Dame."

"Holy... crap!" Emmy swore. "I knew you guys were all grown up, but I didn't realize how grown up you were."

She talked to the men for a few minutes and then Travis and Bryan excused themselves to talk to other guests.

Tony put his hands on Emmy"s shoulders. "Dwight, have I ever told you I used to hang Emmy from the ceiling at home?"

"Not that I remember, Uncle Tony."

"Don't you dare pick me up like that," Emmy warned.

"I wouldn't dare try. I might throw out my back because you aren't as tiny as you once were."

Emmy put her hands on her hips and glared at him. "Are you saying I've gained weight?"

"Maybe a couple of pounds," Tony said. "I bet Dwight could pick you up with one hand. They do a lot more weight training now."

Emmy looked up at Dwight. "I'm sure you could."

Tony grinned at Dwight and said, "Go ahead. Just don't drop her."

Dwight shifted his weight back and forth and shook his head. "I'll pass."

"Yeah, I'm getting too old to be picked up," Emmy said.

Karla and Florentina Sabatino brought out the desserts.

Karla started lighting the candles and announced, "We will be cutting the cake in a few minutes, but we have to sing 'Happy Birthday' first."

Emmy texted Kenny and told him to bring the kids downstairs. They arrived in time to sing.

"Maria, you should make a speech," Karla said and handed her the microphone.

"I can't make a speech in front of all these people, Karla." Mama tried to hand the mic back, but Karla backed away.

"You can do it, Mama," Peter Bertucci, Mama's oldest grandchild, said with a smile.

"I will if you and Dotty help me," Mama replied.

Peter and Dotty stood on either side of Mama as she looked around at everyone.

"Go ahead, Mama. We want some cake," Benjamin said.

"Benjamin Alexander Bertucci!" Sloane shouted.

"It's okay," Mama said. "I will make this short." She paused for a moment and closed her eyes. Her thoughts turned to her late husband, her parents and then her daughter Heather. She opened her eyes and looked at the microphone.

"You have to hold it close to your mouth," Peter said.

"I want to thank all of you for coming out tonight." She glanced to the far wall. "And I see many of you have ignored my instructions about gifts. I'm grateful to have my whole family with me. That doesn't happen often. I don't mean to sound foolish, but I remember a movie Peter liked to watch over and over. It was about a baseball player named Lou Gehrig. He was dying and he still considered himself the luckiest man alive."

Some people in the room gasped and Mama heard them.

"No, I'm not dying as far as I know, but I do consider myself to be the luckiest grandma in the world. Thank you and now let's let the children have their dessert."

Emmy leaned back against Kenny. "Thank God! For a minute I thought she was going to tell us something else. How would we ever get by without Mama Bertucci?"

"Don't know, Em," Kenny whispered into her ear.

75

Later Emmy walked up to Mr. and Mrs. Sabatino. "The desserts were as scrumptious as ever."

"Thank you, Emmy. I hope we brought enough," Mr. Sabatino said.

"We haven't seen you in the restaurant for too long a time, young lady," Mrs. Sabatino admonished Emmy.

"I know. I'm sorry, but we've been so busy. I promise to bring the kids for lunch soon."

"Come and see us when you have a chance."

"I will," Emmy promised.

"Maria, you need to open the gifts now," Karla said a few minutes later.

Mama looked at the tables. "There are so many. It will take me all night."

"Then we had better get started," Karla insisted.

Most of the adults stayed to watch. Some of the people with young children left. Karla had Mama sit in a comfortable chair and Sloane and Kristen took notes as Mama opened her gifts.

"Mama, if you don't speed up, we will be here all night," Kristen whispered.

"I'm trying to go fast, but these are nice gifts, and I want to let everyone see."

"They can see them after you're done."

Mama managed to speed up and finally opened the last gift. "Where will I put all these nice presents?"

"We will make room, Mama," Sloane said.

"I really don't need all this stuff," Mama whispered.

"I know, but there are some really nice gifts."

"I do like to read, and I have several new books now."

Tony and John loaded the gifts in the minivan. Several of the ladies from the church worked to clean the kitchen. Other people put away tables and chairs. Many hands were making the work go quickly. Peter and Dotty sat on either side of Mama on a couch in the hallway outside the multipurpose room.

"What are you thinking about?" Dotty asked while holding Mama's hand.

Mama opened her eyes and peered intently into Dotty's

76

eyes for a moment and then slowly smiled. "You have your mother's eyes, sweetie."

Dotty squeezed Mama's hand more firmly. "Do you mean my first mother?"

"Yes."

"Do I look like her at all?" Peter asked.

Mama turned to look at Peter. "You have her nose and the same shape face."

"We know you still miss her, Mama," Dotty said. "I don't really remember her, and I don't know how her voice sounded."

Mama grinned. "You only have to listen to yourself, Dotty. You sound so much like her."

"Can you tell us a story about her while we wait?" Peter asked. "A story when she was our age."

Mama tilted her head back and stared at the white ceiling. She didn't speak for a moment and then laughed quietly. "I remember she loved to read books. When she was about five she would pretend to read books to her brothers, and they would sit beside her and listen. Your papa was just a baby, but he would listen to her and smile. After she learned how to read, she would read real books to them. Marco would sit still and listen, but Tony always wanted to play."

"Did she ever get in trouble like we do?" Peter asked.

"I'm sure she did, but I don't remember ever having to discipline her as much as the boys."

Dotty released Mama's hand. "How old was she when Grandpa Peter died?"

Mama's expression started to show surprise for just a split-second before she caught herself.

"I know about Grandpa Peter, Mama," Dotty said. "He got sick and went to heaven."

"Well, Heather must have been eight when she lost her father."

"So, she got to know him for a few years," Peter said and then thought about something for several seconds. "What was her middle name? I don't think I know. Papa Tony's middle name is Peter just like mine and Grandpa's."

77

"Catherine," Mama answered. "My middle name is Catarina and that is like Catherine."

"What's Uncle Marco's middle name?"

"Edward."

"Where did my middle name come from?" Dotty asked. "And will I have to use Dorothy when I get older? I know that's my real name. Dorothy Jane Bertucci. It used to be different, but Papa and Mommy changed it when they adopted us."

"You can call yourself whatever you want." Mama squeezed Dotty's shoulders.

"Did you ever see Grandpa Peter's parents?" Peter asked. "Were they really old?"

Mama chuckled. "They were quite a bit older than my parents. Grandpa Peter had four older brothers and sisters, but I can't remember their names. There must be a record somewhere," Mama said as she thought about it.

"Are they still alive?" Dotty asked.

"Oh, no. His parents passed away before he did. Must be over thirty-five years ago."

"Are any of his brothers and sisters still alive?"

"I think there might be one brother and maybe a sister still alive, but they live in Italy. I haven't seen them for close to fifty years. None of his family came to the funeral," Mama said without bitterness. "We lost contact over the years."

"I always want to see my brothers and Noemi," Dotty said. "Even if boys are yucky."

Peter jumped up, stood in front of Dotty and smiled. "But there are more of us than you and Noemi."

"Mama, was my first mommy sick for a long time?" Dotty asked. "There's a girl at school whose mother had cancer for a long time, but she finally died."

Mama clenched her mouth for a moment before shaking her head. "No, sweetie, your mother didn't suffer very long."

Dotty turned to look at Mama. "I'm glad," she said after wiping away a tear.

Mama opened her arms, pulled Dotty close and whispered, "Me, too."

Chapter Eight

"Hey, Kenny, I got an email from Ryan Lederer just now," Emmy hollered as she dashed into the family room from the kitchen. She plopped down onto the couch next to Kenny.

"Did they have the baby?" Kenny muted the TV. "Silly question. They must have to get you so excited."

"They had a baby girl, and guess what," she grinned.

"What?"

"They named her Emmy Rose."

"For real?"

Emmy nodded.

"Aw, that's so sweet." Kenny put an arm around her and pulled her close. "They named their baby after you."

"She said they were going to as soon as they knew the baby was a girl because of that minivan we bought for her band. I figured they would change their mind. If I remember right, she was born at five this morning. Five-five-five."

"What do you mean?" Kenny asked.

Emmy explained, "She was born at five o'clock on May fifth. Get it?"

"Got it. Do you know the details?"

"She weighed..." Emmy put a finger to her mouth. "I forgot. Let me grab my laptop. Be right back." Emmy raced back to the kitchen and returned with her laptop. "She weighed six pounds and nine ounces. It doesn't say how long she was, but Ryan says she has some brown hair and red cheeks and chubby legs."

"Does it say how Jennifer is doing?"

"She and the baby are both doing great. Ryan says he will send photos soon."

"Do you remember when you met Jennifer? Was it before or after we got married?"

"It was before. We met at that festival in Carbondale," Emmy answered. "The final show of that first tour. She and her band were there."

Kenny laughed. "I remember it now. That was the one with the water fight, right?"

"Yeah, someone bought Super Soakers, and the guys ganged up on me."

"You probably enjoyed it, Em."

She poked him in the side. "It was fun. I remember Ryan shooting me at point blank range. He had a crush on Jennifer as soon as they met."

"I wonder if Jennifer will resume touring at some point, or will she decide to call it quits and become a stay-at-home mom?"

Emmy shrugged. "Don't know, but they will have to make some money somehow."

Diane picked up the kids from school the next day, and she came inside with the kids. "Emmy, where are you?"

Emmy carried a basket of clean clothes out of the laundry room when she heard Diane calling from the kitchen. "Doing laundry. What's up?"

"Carson was playing some new songs on the way home on that iPad thing of his. I asked what they were, and he said it was some new tunes by you. Did you release a new CD or whatever?"

Emmy set the basket of freshly folded clothes on the kitchen island. "Heather, would you take this up to your room, please?"

Heather tossed her backpack in the general direction of where it belonged, grabbed the laundry basket without commenting and headed upstairs.

"What is wrong with your sister?" Emmy asked Isabella.

Isabella hung her backpack up and then put Heather's where it needed to go. She shrugged and then said, "Miss Redmon said something to her about talking in class, so Heather said she was never going to talk again. I think she will, so you don't need to worry, Mom. I'm hungry. Can I have a snack, please?"

"We have grapes and some seedless tangerines that need to be eaten." Emmy scooted out of the way as Kevin Michael and Caden raced past. "Where are you going in such a hurry?"

"Hi, Mom, I have to show Caden the new fort I built. He doesn't believe I have a real cannon," Kevin slowed down just long enough to set his backpack on the island and grab an apple.

Diane tilted her head. "Tell me he doesn't have a real cannon."

"It doesn't shoot real cannonballs. They're foam. Like nerf balls. They can't hurt anyone."

Diane sat down at the island. "So did you release a new CD, or just some tunes on Amazon and iTunes?"

"It's available as an actual CD, too, but CDs don't sell like they used to. Kids don't want to be bothered with them now. They want instant downloads."

"Do you still make money on downloads?"

"Yeah," Emmy answered. "You thirsty? I'm going to make some tea."

"Thanks, but I'm good. Did you have a press conference thing today?"

Emmy poured some water into her new teapot and selected a bag of Lemon Zinger from her tea caddy. "No, I told Steward Music I didn't want a big fuss about it and they agreed."

"What's it called? Carson probably told me, but I forgot." Diane checked the fruit in the wicker basket in front of her. "You should buy some pears. I like those little apple pears."

"They're expensive. I only buy them when they're on sale," Emmy said and then checked the landline. She ignored the call.

"Maybe if you sell enough downloads and CDs, you can splurge on some full-price apple pears," Diane teased.

Emmy ignored her sister's jab.

"Since the boys are playing, can I leave them here until dinnertime? I need to relieve Mona. She's watching Lily and Conor, and Conor is probably hungry by now."

"How long have you been gone?" Emmy asked.

"I did some shopping before I picked up the kids. I bought two pairs of shoes to go with that new outfit I found last week."

"You have more shoes than some South Pacific islands," Emmy said and then rolled her eyes.

Diane laughed. "And what do you mean by that?"

Emmy waved dismissively, "Nothing. I watched a documentary on Netflix about remote Pacific islands."

"You're a goof, Em," Diane grabbed her purse and keys.

81

"Call me when you get tired of the boys."

"If they like taco pie, they can eat here."

Diane shrugged as she disappeared out the mudroom door. "Ask them. They can be picky at times."

Emmy woke up as soon as Kenny slipped into bed next to her on Sunday morning. "What time is it?" she asked.

"It's a little after four, Em." Kenny brushed her hair out of her face and kissed her nose. "I tried not to wake you up."

Emmy swiped at her nose as if tickled by a feather. "It's all right. Are you going to get up in time to take the kids to church? I have to leave by ten."

"I set an alarm. Are you all packed?"

"Uh-huh. I just have to throw my toothbrush and toothpaste in with the rest of my stuff. All my clothes are gone already."

"All of them?" Kenny grinned as he put an arm around her.

"You know what I mean. They left on the plane."

"You are going to be so spoiled by the time this tour ends. You would have never agreed to fly everywhere in the beginning."

Emmy snuggled closer to Kenny. "I didn't have kids back then. Go to sleep, so you don't sleep through your alarm."

"I guess the honeymoon is really over now," Kenny sighed.

"Mommy, why can't you go to church today?" Isabella asked as Emmy prepared to leave for the airport later.

"Because I have to fly to Seattle, and it's a long way away. I will be back on Wednesday," Emmy patiently explained again.

"How many nights is it until Wednesday?" Kevin asked.

"Sunday, Monday, Tuesday, Wednesday," Isabella counted on her fingers. "Four days."

"I'll only be gone for three nights and Daddy will be here with you. That's how we planned this tour."

"Have fun singing, Mom," Heather said. "Is Uncle Rory going to play in the band?"

"Not on this trip, sweetie," Emmy answered and then looked at Kenny. She remembered the hard feelings it caused when Rory Porter had joined her on tour for a week in 2011.

Kevin Michael hugged Emmy's legs. "Do a good job at work, Mommy. Make lots of money because I need some new toys. The ones I have are for little kids."

"Kevin Michael! You just had a birthday two months ago. You have plenty of new toys," Kenny said and then shook his head. "We need to get going if we want to make it to Sunday School on time. Everyone out to the van." He shooed the kids out the door and then kissed Emmy. "Call me when you get there."

She poked him in the chest. "I will, but you better do the same. You only called me once last week when you were gone."

"I'll do better. Last week was rather hectic." Kenny grabbed his wallet and keys and looked back at Emmy. "Does it bother you that the Schulenbergs are recording the service today?"

Emmy tilted her head back and forth. "I was disappointed at first, but I'm over it. I hope it turns out all right."

"I'm sure it would sound better if you were there," Kenny said and followed the kids out to the garage.

Chapter Nine

"Hello, Sacramento! How's everyone doing tonight?" Kenny shouted into his microphone ten minutes after opening the show. The guys played for another half hour and then Kenny got the crowd to settle down. "I'm going to bring out a friend who was a big influence on me. I was ten-years-old when I picked up their album on Island Records. I wore it out and bought three more." He motioned to the side of the stage and a man walked out carrying a guitar. "Please welcome Michael Rowell of The 88s!" Kenny shook hands with Mike. "I hope I didn't make you seem old," Kenny said off the mic.

"Not at all. Did you really buy that many copies?"

"At least, and then I found your first two records." Kenny stepped up to his microphone. "We're going to play a couple of Mike's songs." He waited for a response, but the audience seemed indifferent.

They played two songs off of the self-titled 88s Island recording and Mike stayed onstage for two Fridays At Five songs.

"Give it up for Michael Rowell!" Jeff hollered into his mic.

The crowd applauded politely if without much enthusiasm as Mike waved and then walked off the stage.

"Can you believe it?" Kenny shook his head as he took his guitar from his cousin and guitar tech Frankie Hanna. "That guy has one of the best bands in the country, and most people have never heard of him. It almost makes me want to puke."

Frankie nodded and helped Kenny adjust the guitar strap.

Kenny walked back to center stage and motioned for Dave Persching to wait a second before he counted off the next song.

Jeff looked at P.J. and whispered, "He's pissed because of the crowd's indifference."

"Should we do something?"

Jeff shook his head. "Naw, he'll count to ten and then get a drink of water to cool off. Just watch."

Kenny waited for a time and then did just as Jeff predicted before continuing with the show. To show his disgust he left the stage after doing only one song for their encore.

"I'm sorry the crowd didn't show more appreciation," Kenny said to Mike backstage. "I can't believe how people can ignore your music."

Mike shrugged. "We're used to it."

Kenny talked to Mike about life in general and then the subject of recording came up.

"You guys are doing the independent thing, right?" Kenny asked.

"Yeah, we've got another Kickstart project going. Our goal is to raise thirty thousand to cover expenses."

Kenny paused for a moment. "Tell you what. If you reach your goal, I'll double it for you."

"You don't have to do that," Mike said.

"Hey! I might never have been so serious about playing the guitar if I hadn't heard your music. It's the least I can do."

"Deal!" Mike shook Kenny's hand.

"Are you guys ready to see Europe?"

"You better believe it. We're grateful for the opportunity."

The 88s would be the opening act for Fridays At Five on the upcoming tour of Europe.

"Thanks for saving me a seat," Emmy said as she scooted past Kristen and sat down. "I was late getting the kids up this morning. We missed Sunday School." She nudged Tony in the seat next to her. "Hey! Can you give me some room."

"Sure, brat." Tony leaned closer to Emmy and pinned her between himself and Kristen.

Sloane poked Tony in the ribs. "Leave her alone and stop calling her a brat. It's childish."

"I thought the worship band was recording the service again. Why aren't you on the platform?" Tony asked as he gave Emmy some room. "Did they finally realize you can't sing?"

"Yeah, I've been faking it all these years," she answered. "Are you getting fat? You look heavier, and you're taking up more room than ever. Move over." She pushed against his shoulder but couldn't budge him.

"FYI, Mrs. Colwell, I'm fifteen pounds under my playing

85

weight. I'm not eating as much as before," he explained.

"Could've fooled me," she teased.

"Why aren't you singing? I'm serious."

"Because I haven't been able to rehearse. I have been on tour, remember?"

"But only part of the week." Tony shrugged.

"I wasn't here for the first Sunday they recorded, so I guess they didn't need me for today's session."

"Too bad," he said. "The Schulenbergs do sound good together. Maybe they didn't want to change the dynamics of that."

"What do you know about dynamics?"

"I listen to music. I know stuff," Tony put an arm around the back of Emmy's chair and pulled on her hair.

Sloane rolled her eyes.

"I bet you need Peter's help to play a CD," Emmy said and then made a face at him.

"Will you guys knock it off," Kristen said. "Riordan is trying to explain something about the recording.

"It's his fault," Emmy whispered.

After the service Emmy walked out of the sanctuary with Kristen.

"I thought the worship team sounded pretty good today. They had more musicians on the stage than normal. I suppose that was for the recording, huh?" Kristen asked.

"Yeah, they added more percussion and an extra guitar. Four guitars is a little much if you ask me."

"And there were three people playing keyboards if you count Cam on the grand piano."

"Adam and Quinten are better musicians, so Riordan used them on the other keyboards. Not that Cam is bad, but he doesn't have the studio experience."

Kristen grinned. "I do know some stuff, Em."

Emmy looked up at Kristen and made a face. "You're getting as bad as Tony."

Emmy felt a hand on her shoulder and turned around. "Oh, Hi, Liz. I'm sorry we didn't make it for Sunday School. Did you have many kids in your class?"

"There were only eight. Lots of people are on vacation since school got out early this year," Liz said as she braided her hair out of habit. "I heard the school needs three more teachers for next year. You should look into it. You'd make a great teacher."

"I try to help as much as my schedule allows, but I would have to go back to school if I wanted to be a real teacher," Emmy said.

"I better round up the kids."

"I saw Phoebe earlier. I can't believe how much she's grown in only five months, and I love her hair. It's getting long."

"She's got thicker hair than Natty or Grayson," Liz mentioned her other kids. "I'll talk to you later. When do you have to leave?"

"I have to be at the airport by two. We're going to..." Emmy paused and shrugged. "Can't remember. Somewhere in Kentucky, I think."

"The places all start to blend together after awhile, don't they?" Liz walked along with Emmy. "Dany is getting nervous about the wedding. You are still coming, right?"

"I'll be there, but Kenny will be out of town."

"We understand. They can't cancel a show at the last minute."

"He feels bad about it, but..." Emmy shrugged. "Are Dany and Darian spending their honeymoon in the same place you and Tyler did?"

"Yes! You aren't going on vacation, too, are you?" Liz teased.

Emmy bit her lip. "That was just a coincidence. We didn't plan to go on vacation until the last minute. Did we interrupt your honeymoon too much? I know we did some things together."

"We weren't together that much," Liz whispered. "We had lots of time to ourselves."

Chapter Ten

"Are you going to celebrate when you get to Hillsdale?" Jake Boyter asked after Tyler prayed to end the short staff meeting in the conference room at the church.

Tyler chuckled and then answered, "I don't know if my mom or Liz has anything planned. My preference would be they didn't."

"But you only turn thirty once." Darren Eaton pushed backed his chair and stood up. "I survived it."

"I don't consider turning thirty an accomplishment," Tyler said. "Now if this was my hundredth birthday like Elmer Burrington celebrated last week, that would be worth celebrating."

"Enjoy your weekend of vacation." Dr. Ausland patted Tyler's back and smiled. "We will manage to muddle through somehow."

"We are leaving right after lunch and plan to return next Tuesday," Tyler explained. "I will have my phone, so if you need to reach me, I am available. Just don't call during Dany and Darian's wedding."

"What about Derby?" Jake asked.

"She's going with us," Tyler said.

"Happy birthday, boss. I'll see you when you guys get back," Jonah Galves said as he shook hands with Tyler. "Mary is still a bit upset I won't be there for the wedding."

"I'm sorry I won't be here Saturday to help with the softball tournament," Tyler said.

Jonah waved a hand dismissively. "We got it covered. I've got extra volunteers, and I'm going to umpire all the games."

Tyler pictured the barrel-chested man in his umpire uniform and chuckled. "No one will dare argue with you."

"I hope not," said Jake, the diminutive youth pastor who looked like the teenagers he and his wife Maddy mentored. "It is a church-league event."

Darren laughed. "I've been surprised a few times by the language and anger expressed by some of the players on the other teams."

"Certainly not the players on our team," Dr. Ausland said hopefully.

Emmy returned to her seat in a pew near the back of Hillsdale First Nazarene after singing for Dany and Darian at the wedding ceremony. Kevin Michael patted her hand.

"Did I do all right?" Emmy whispered.

"You did a good job, Mommy," Isabella said as she beamed with pride.

"Thank you, Isa," Emmy said.

After a final prayer to end the ceremony, Tyler chuckled as he introduced the new couple to the gathered crowd. Dany and Darian began their exit down the center aisle. Heather and Isabella scooted past Emmy and stood just inside the pew.

"Hi, Dany," both girls said as they giggled.

Dany waved and smiled. "I'll talk to you later."

Heather and Isabella rushed out of the sanctuary a few minutes later and rushed over to where Dany and Darian stood while waiting to greet everyone.

"You look so beautiful, Dany!" Isabella gushed.

"Like a real princess!" Heather added.

"What about me?" Darian asked as he scooped both girls.

"You look very handsome, but Dany looks better," Isabella said.

Darian set the girls down. They spotted Mary Galves and rushed in the direction of their former nanny and kindergarten teacher. "Mary! We remember when you and Jonah got married. Are you going to have a baby someday?"

Mary held the girls' hands and smiled. "We might one of these days, but not yet."

"That's okay," Isabella said. "You can wait until school starts."

Three hours later Emmy and the twins watched as Dany and Darian got into her Prius and drove away.

"Is Dany still going to live in the guesthouse when they get back from Hawaii?" Heather asked.

"Yes, they will live in the guesthouse, but you need to let

them have some privacy. You can't stop over there every day to see them," Emmy explained.

"Is it all right if we call Dany on the phone sometime?" Isabella asked. "Can we ask her to go swimming with us?"

"Yes, but only once in a while," Emmy said as she saw Tyler and Liz approaching.

"Thank you for singing for the ceremony," Liz said as she hugged Emmy.

Tyler carried six-month-old Phoebe Grace. "She's awake. Do you want to hold her?" he asked Heather and Isabella.

"You need to sit down to hold her," Emmy said. "She is awake and she's smiling. Did I hear her during the ceremony?"

Liz laughed. "She was trying to sing along with you, Emmy."

Heather and Isabella each took a turn holding Phoebe. Natalie joined them.

"We asked Mommy if she was going to have another baby, but she said she can't," Isabella whispered. "Me-maw said it was because of a medical problem inside her. You are so lucky you get to have a baby sister."

"You can come over, and we can help take care of Phoebe," Natalie said as Phoebe grabbed hold of Natalie's finger and made happy noises.

"Sometimes we help Aunt Diane take care of our cousin Conor. He's only a little older than Phoebe, but he's a boy," Isabella said. "He won't play with us like Lily does. She's two now and runs all over."

"Mom said it will be several more months before Phoebe learns how to walk."

Eli Michaelis walked up to Tyler, shook hands and said, "Nice ceremony. Did it feel weird to be marrying your sister-in-law?"

Tyler chuckled and shook his head. "Not nearly as weird as when Jake married his mother a few months ago."

Emmy poked Tyler's side. "He didn't marry his mother. He performed the ceremony. You always make it sound weird."

"Where are you heading this Sunday?" Tyler asked.

90

Emmy made a face as she looked up at him. "You know where. We're playing at the high school tomorrow night."

"How did you work that out?" Tyler asked. "Did Dany and Darian change their date to match your show?"

"FYI! I added this to my schedule as soon as she told me the date."

"Where will your plane land? I've flown out of Hillsdale Municipal Airport on some of my training flights, and the two runways are not quite long enough for a jumbo jet."

"You are so funny," Emmy said. "We will be in Detroit on Monday. That's where the plane is."

"How will you get from Hillsdale to Detroit? Are you going to charter a small plane?" Tyler teased.

"I'm going with the band in a rental van. It will be like the old days," Emmy said.

"I shouldn't tease you so much. Liz and I have close to thirty tickets for the show. We passed them out to family."

"Do you think ten dollars was too much to charge?" Emmy asked. "It's a scaled back concert."

"What!? Does that mean we won't see the fancy light show?" Liz asked.

"There will be lights. Just not the whole thing. I guess there wasn't enough room. I'm sorry," Emmy said and then bit her lip.

"Don't be silly. We're teasing," Liz said and then hugged Emmy again.

"Daddy, will you show us on the globe where you are going to be working, please?" Isabella asked on Wednesday morning to delay Kenny's departure a few more minutes.

Kenny set his briefcase on the kitchen island and looked at the plastic globe in Isabella's hands. "Let's set this on the island, and I will show you."

Heather, Isabella and Kevin climbed onto the barstools for a better look.

"This is England," he said as he pointed to the spot on the globe. "I'm flying into London today, and on Friday we will play a show at this big stadium." Kenny stretched his arms as far as he could. "We will be in England for a few days and the go to Ireland..."

He showed the kids the different countries where Fridays At Five would perform.

"Are you going to Skype with us?" Heather asked.

"Yes, and I will call you on the phone."

"Who's going to watch us when Mommy is working?" Kevin asked as he smashed two cars into each other.

Emmy stood with her hands on her hips and glared at her son. "Kevin Michael! How many times have I asked you not to play with your toys on the island?"

"Lots of times," he said as he grinned.

"Then do as I ask, please."

"Gra and Me-maw are going to watch you guys when Mommy is gone," Kenny explained. "Do you promise to behave?"

"We will behave, Daddy," Isabella said.

"Your ride is here," Emmy said. "Let's go outside and wave goodbye."

"Why can't we take Daddy to the airport? It's not that far away." Isabella clung to Kenny's arm.

"I'm not going to the SoHam airport, sweetie. I'm going into O'Hare and that's much farther away."

"And the traffic will be brutal if you don't get going." Emmy led the way to the limo. "Do you have your passport?"

"It's in my briefcase," he assured Emmy. "Don't worry. Elden and Freya will take care of me."

"Why did you need to hire two assistants to take Jana's place? Emmy asked.

Elden Lanier jumped out of the limo and held the door open for Kenny while Freya Mendel sat in the backseat talking on her cell phone.

"They are recent college grads, and Andy isn't paying them as much as Jana. We hired them both because they are engaged, and they each speak several languages. Between them and Charles, I won't have to worry about any language barriers," Kenny said and then laughed.

"Call me when you get to the hotel. I don't care what time."

92

"I will." Kenny kissed Emmy, gave the kids a hug and got into the limo.

"Bye, Daddy!" The kids hollered as they waved.

Kevin Michael ran down the winding driveway but returned quickly. "I tried to race the car because I can run as fast as Luke Skywalker."

Kenny had been watching Star Wars movies with his son.

Twelve hours later Kenny called home.

"Are you settled in the hotel?" Emmy asked.

"All checked in. The flight was uneventful, and we made it through customs in a flash. Charles took care of that."

"It's probably better for you guys to have Charles with you instead of Andy. Charles is more familiar with Europe since he's lived there so much."

"He has taken care of all our European tours over the years, Em," Kenny reminded her.

Andy Walker and Charles La Rosse, lifelong friends who grew up together in San Diego, were partners in Walker Management. The company handled Fridays At Five along with a few other bands. Charles moved to Germany after his wife Carol passed away several years previously. Now he split his time between Germany, Tennessee, where his mother lived, and South Hampshire.

"I know. What I meant is you know how much Andy hates to travel now. It's easier for him to stay home. He should retire and promote Nelson Grapella. He would be better suited to managing you guys."

"He isn't as intimidating as Andy," Kenny said. "Nelson wouldn't intimidate a small child."

"It's not like the old days, you goof. Everything is done by the lawyers now."

Emmy and Kenny talked for an hour.

"I'll try to Skype in the afternoon. Maybe around four. The kids should be up by then."

"They might be, but I was hoping to sleep until noon."

"Heather and Isa know how to Skype. I caught them using your laptop the other day."

"I let them use it. They have a user account or whatever it's called. Do you think we would spoil them too much if I bought them their own laptop or tablet or something?"

"If you do that, they will want their own cell phone, too."

"We can talk about it when you get home. Are the 88s excited to be in Europe?"

"I really didn't have a chance to talk to them, but I'm pretty sure they've been to Europe before," Kenny answered.

"Call me if you need anything, and make sure Elden and Freya take good care of you." Emmy waited a few seconds and then laughed.

"What is so funny, Em?" Kenny asked.

"Those two must go to the same hair salon. They have the same hairstyle. Short on one side and longer on the other. Same color. Blonde on one side. Black on the other. Should I get my hair cut like that?"

"I'd prefer it if you keep your style. You could even let it grow long if you want. You haven't had a ponytail for a while."

Emmy ran a hand through her hair. "I love having it shorter. I wouldn't want a ponytail anymore because Tony would pull on it. He pulls on Isa's ponytail now. Should I get a ring in my nose like Elden and Freya?"

Kenny laughed again. "It took you forever to get your ears pierced. I can't see you getting a nose ring."

"I could get something else pierced," Emmy said.

"No piercings and no tattoos! You need to set a good example for the girls."

"So, Kevin Michael could get a tattoo if he wants?"

"Not until he's older, and don't let the girls wear earrings to church again. They can wear those little stud things."

"You are going to struggle when they reach puberty."

Kenny shook his head and then sighed. "I don't even want to think about that. Thank God it's years away."

Emmy smiled. *It will be here before you know it.*

After the show in Madrid the band had three days off. Kenny took advantage of the break to go sightseeing with Charles.

They headed south out of Madrid and ended up in Granada.

"Have you ever been here before?" Kenny asked as he and Charles walked up one of the hilly streets.

"Once several years ago. I didn't have much time to check out the sights," Charles answered. "I would like to visit The Alhambra while we're here."

"I will defer to you. You know the area better than me." Kenny glanced at the buildings as they walked past. "This reminds me of Istanbul or somewhere. The buildings don't look Spanish. Do you know what I mean?"

Charles nodded. "There is a definite Moorish and Arabic influence."

Kenny called Emmy the next afternoon. "I didn't wake you up, did I?"

"No, I've been up for a couple of hours. Where are you?"

"I'm with Charles in Granada, Spain. You should see this place, Em. It's beautiful. There are some mountains. Foothills. It's definitely not flat around here. We've been walking everywhere and I haven't seen a flat street at all."

"Sounds interesting," Emmy said as she filled her coffee cup again.

"It's an old city, and the buildings are cool."

"I thought it was hot in Spain."

"Not temperature cool. They look neat but old. We've done the tourist stuff and seen all the sights. Lots of them, I mean. We took a taxi into the mountains. There are some large houses outside of the city. We saw one that was for sale. I was tempted to see how much it would cost."

"Why? We have a house, and we don't live in Spain."

"Yeah, but I could see myself living here someday. The climate is pretty mild and the people are really nice."

Emmy took one last sip of coffee and poured out the rest. "I might want to visit Europe someday, but I can't see myself ever living there. I can't imagine living anywhere other than SoHam. This is home and always will be."

Chapter Eleven

"Why did you order a copy, Kristen? I would have given you several," Emmy said over the phone.

"I know, but I thought it would help if I bought one on Amazon. You do get royalties, right?"

"Yes, but I didn't write it to make a ton of money. How did you even know it was available? I didn't mention it."

Kristen sat down on the couch in her family room and turned on the TV. "Isabella told Gracie about it. Grace asked me to buy it so she could read it."

"No way, Krissy!" Emmy shouted into the phone. "It's not a fairy tale like the Lion stories. There are things in there that aren't for kids."

"Oh, like what?" Kristen asked as she grinned. "Do tell."

"No, you will have to read it."

"I can't wait," Kristen said. "Oh, by the way, did you hear who is expecting?"

"No, who else is having a baby? It seems like everyone I know is pregnant," Emmy sighed.

"I'm not," Kristen replied. "Do you want to know or not?"

"Fine! Who?" Emmy plopped into her recliner in the family room and put her bare feet on the coffee table. "I'm going to take a nap this afternoon. I didn't get home until three in the morning, and I need to pick up the kids sometime today. They wear Gra and Me-maw out."

Kristen told her the name.

"Lori Crowell, huh? I don't even know her. Who is she? How do you know her?"

"She works in the office at church. You'd recognize her even if you don't know her name."

"Whatever! Have you talked to John about the progress on the new sanctuary?"

"We talked about it at dinner last night. According to Garrick Winston... Do you know who he is?"

"I know who he is," Emmy lifted her knee and ran a finger over the small scar she received from playing in Kenny's yard as a

96

kid. "He's the computer geek in charge of the project."

"Garrick said the work should be finished before the end of September."

"From what I've heard about him, he can probably tell you what time it will be finished down to thirty minutes or so."

"He is usually very precise with his schedules once the weather variables are out of the equation," Kristen said.

"I snuck a peek in there after church on Sunday," Emmy said and then giggled.

"You aren't supposed to go into the work site without supervision. Did you wear a hardhat?"

"No, but I didn't stay long. It's going to be so big."

"Duh! What would be the point of building a new sanctuary if it wasn't larger than what we already have?"

Emmy yawned and didn't respond.

"Are you still there? Did you fall asleep?"

"I'm here, but my eyes are closed."

"I'm hanging up. Take a nap and call me later. I have more stories to tell you."

Five minutes later Emmy's cell phone woke her up. She heard the ringtone and knew Father James was calling. "This better be important because I was taking a nap," she snapped.

"Why are you taking a nap at ten in the morning? Who's watching the kids? You do remember the kids, right?"

"I didn't get home until late, and the kids are still with Gra and Me-maw. Could you pick them up for me, please? I'll owe you one."

He shook his head. "Not a chance. I don't have car seats."

"They use booster seats now. Pretty please," she begged.

"No," he said emphatically.

"I hate you. Why did you call, anyway?"

"I was browsing through Barnes and the other guy and saw a book that looked interesting, so I ordered it."

"Get out! You never buy books. You steal them from the library."

"I do not steal from anyone," he asserted. "I might have borrowed one or two for an extended length of time, but I plan to

97

return them when they have one of those amnesty days."

"What day?"

"Once a year or so the library has a day when they will forgive overdue fines. I plan to take advantage of their generous offer."

"You need to go to confession. What book did you buy?" Emmy stretched her legs and shifted her position in the recliner.

"*Adventures In Raynor Park*. Have you heard of it?"

Emmy jumped off of the recliner and banged her shin on the coffee table. "Crap!" She swore while hopping on one foot and trying to rub her shin.

"Are you all right? I heard a noise."

"I banged my shin on the table. Why did you buy my book? I would give you one." She sat on the coffee table and examined her leg. "I'm bleeding."

"Should I call for an ambulance?"

"Very funny."

"I thought you wanted people to buy your books. Most authors do like to get paid for their work." He paused. "Does the library have a copy I could borrow?" He drew out the word borrow.

"They don't have one yet. You're the second person who's called this morning to tell me they bought the book online."

"Who else was gullible enough to buy a copy? Your mother-in-law?"

"No, she knows better. Kristen bought a copy because Gracie wanted to read it. It's not a book for kids," Emmy explained as she wiped some blood off her finger using her t-shirt.

"Really? Is it suitable for men of God?"

"There aren't any stories for dirty old men," she said.

"There better not be, young lady. Do you really need me to pick up the kids? I will if you want."

"No, I'll get them after lunch," she said and then paused. "There might be some things in the book that surprise you. I wasn't always a perfect angel like I am now."

Father James coughed several times.

"Fine! Be that way," she said and ended the call.

98

A week later Kristen heard the doorbell ring and saw a Fed Ex truck in the driveway. She opened the door and waved to the driver as she left. *This has to be Emmy's book because I haven't ordered anything else.* She opened the package and headed to the family room.

"Did you get something in the mail?" Grace glanced away from the TV for a moment.

Kristen held up the book. "Emmy's new book arrived. Will you and Zachary play so I can spend some time reading?"

"We will let you have some quiet time, Mommy," Grace grinned. "Can I see the book when you finish?"

"I'll see, but I don't think there are any pictures like in her book about the lions."

Grace and Zachary amused themselves while Kristen relaxed and read the book.

Fifteen minutes later Kristen sat up with a start. "No! Tell me you didn't," Kristen shouted.

Grace walked over to the couch and sat next to her mother. "What is it, Mommy? Did Aunt Emmy do something bad in the book?"

Kristen closed the book so Grace couldn't see the pages even though Grace couldn't read an adult book yet. "Maybe you and Zachary should run upstairs and play in your rooms."

"That means you don't want us to know what's in the book," Zachary said as he picked up his trucks. "Come on, Gracie. We can ask Heather about the book."

Kristen waited until Zachary and Grace left the room and then opened the book again. *Why on earth would you do such a thing with Rory Porter? I wonder if Kenny knew it at the time?* She continued to read and occasionally shook her head. *Well, that's not so bad.* Kristen finished a chapter. *I'm sure plenty of other girls did much worse.*

Sloane called an hour later and asked what Kristen was doing.

"I got Emmy's book today, and I've been reading it. I'm halfway done, and I want to finish it. You aren't going to believe some of the stuff in here."

"Like what?" Sloane asked. "I thought it was about her childhood."

"It is, but there are stories from junior high and high school. Things I never knew about her, and I thought I knew everything."

"Dotty heard about the book and wants to read it."

"Don't let her," Kristen said. "She's too young for some of this stuff."

"She'll be ten in a month," Sloane reminded Kristen.

Kristen got up and walked into the kitchen. "I won't let Gracie read this until she's a teenager. Maybe not until she's in high school." Kristen opened the fridge and took out a bottle of Perrier water.

"Are you guys going to the concert or the fireworks tomorrow?"

Kristen opened the bottle and took a sip of water. "I didn't know there would be a concert since Kenny and the guys are in Europe."

"Tony said the city booked a different band and there will be fireworks. They always do the fireworks at the stadium," Sloane said.

"John hasn't mentioned it, so I doubt if we will go. I'll talk to you later. I want to finish the book."

"It must be pretty good. I might need to borrow it."

Tony walked over to Kristen's house the next morning to drop off some files from work. "John needed these, so I thought I would bring them over," Tony explained. He set the files on the kitchen desk.

"Did you walk or jog all the way?" Kristen teased. "We live so far apart."

"I didn't run, but I might go for one later. Where is he, anyway?"

"He ran to the store. I'll make sure he gets these."

"Why didn't he drive?" Tony joked and then saw Emmy's book on the desk. "Sloane was telling me about this. Did you finish it? Can we borrow it? Sloane wants to read it."

"Go ahead, but you might be surprised."

Tony picked up the book. "Nice cover. That's Kenny and Emmy in his backyard, right?"

"Yes, and that's a tent in the bottom right corner." Kristen pointed out.

"Yeah, so what?" Tony shrugged.

"You'll have to read the book," Kristen said.

"Sloane told me to tell you we aren't going to the stadium tonight. I picked up a few fireworks from one of the guys at work."

"You better be careful. Don't set them off in the woods or you might start a fire," Kristen warned.

Tony chuckled. "Mama said the same thing."

"Mommy, is Daddy coming home tonight?" Heather asked as she searched through the fridge for something to eat.

Emmy pulled a package of chocolate pudding from the fridge and handed it to Heather. "Daddy is in Europe, sweetie. He won't be home for about six weeks. Why are you asking?"

"Because he always plays at the stadium and then we get to see the fireworks. Can we still see the fireworks?" Heather opened the package and licked the foil lid.

"Do you really want to go?"

"We like fireworks," Heather said as she nodded.

"I'll see if anyone else is going."

Emmy called Kristen a few minutes later.

"We're not going, and neither is Tony. He does have some fireworks. He's going to shoot them off as soon as it gets dark."

"I don't want to fight the crowd at the stadium. I guess we'll stay home."

"I read the book," Kristen said.

"You did, huh?" Emmy bit her lip. "Were you shocked?"

"A little bit. I'll talk to you about it later. I need to get dinner ready."

Tony saw Emmy's book on the kitchen counter later and picked it up. He found Sloane sitting on the couch in the living room and held out the book. "Are you going to read this?"

101

"I am," she answered.

Tony looked at the book and tilted his head.

Sloane held up her Kindle. "I like reading on here better."

"Is it all right if I read this later? Maybe after the kids are in bed."

"Sure, go ahead. I liked the part about you guys playing football when you were three."

"We only knew each other for a couple of weeks, and we didn't meet again until high school."

"Mama showed me that photo. It's cute. You were so much bigger than Emmy even though she was a few months older."

"She's always been a pipsqueak."

"I'll tell her you said so. Now go away and let me read." Sloane waved a hand to shoo Tony away.

After shooting off his fireworks in the driveway later that night, Tony walked over to Emmy and nudged her side. "I hear your book is rather shocking. Is there anything in there about us?"

"Just the part about Mama taking that photo of us."

"The one she took in front of that apartment building?" Tony asked.

"Yeah."

"Nothing about high school?"

She shook her head. "No, the book ends after my first year at Roosevelt High. I didn't know you then. Were you afraid I would embarrass you?"

"I never did anything to be ashamed of," Tony answered. "How about you?"

Emmy's eyes sparkled like the stars in the clear sky. "I'll never tell."

Tony helped Sloane get the kids in bed and then headed to the basement to begin reading. He brought along a bag of mustard-flavored pretzel sticks and a cold, two-liter bottle of Dr Pepper. He poured himself a tall glass of pop, ripped the bag of pretzels, settled into his recliner and opened the book.

He came back upstairs two hours later, tossed the empty pretzel bag into the garbage and put the half-empty two-liter in the fridge. He checked the alarm system, headed upstairs to the master bedroom and saw Sloane propped up in bed with three pillows holding her Kindle.

She glanced at Tony and then turned her attention back to her reading. "Did you finish it?"

"I'm about halfway through. I'll finish it tomorrow. How far along are you?" He got ready for bed and slipped under the sheet next to Sloane.

"Fifty pages to go. Will it keep you awake if I keep reading?"

Tony kissed her cheek and then turned on his side. "Won't bother me." He turned off the light above his side of the king-size bed and felt the breeze from the ceiling fan. "We better not let Dotty read it."

"Ya think!" Sloane exclaimed. "I might never let her read it. I don't want her to get any ideas."

Sloane and Tony finished Emmy's book on Saturday. Mama saw the copy sitting on Tony's desk after lunch on Sunday. Mama held the book and checked with Tony and Sloane. "Did you finish this?"

"Yeah, I actually read the whole thing, and it's not about sports," he said as he grinned. "Do you want to read it?"

"Is it as good as her book about the lions?" Mama asked.

"Oh, yeah! It's better."

Sloane rolled her eyes. "Do you want to read the book or use my Kindle?"

"I like reading books the old-fashioned way," Mama said. "I'll be in my room if the kids need me." Mama headed to her rooms in the back part of the house beyond the kitchen.

Sloane looked at Tony. "It's a good thing Emmy is gone until Wednesday. Mama might get a bit upset with her."

"Ya think!" Tony grinned.

"Who wants to go for a bike ride with me?" Emmy asked the kids Wednesday afternoon.

"Where are we going?" Heather asked without taking her eyes off the TV.

103

"I need to take some Tupperware back to Mama. You could play with Dotty and Noemi," Emmy answered.

"Can we go swimming again when we get back?"

"Sure, I think we can all use the pool."

Isabella put on her shoes. "Can we see if Dany wants to go swimming?"

"You can ask, but she might be busy," Emmy said.

"We don't get to see her as much as before," Heather whined.

"That's because she and Darian are married now. They spent all their time together," Isabella said.

"Kevin Michael! You need to come with us," Emmy hollered up the stairs.

He stomped down the stairs carrying two trucks. "Can I take these? I want to show them to Ben and Taylor."

"You have to carry them. I'm not going to." Emmy grabbed the bag with the Tupperware as the kids raced through the mudroom, into the garage, put on their helmets, and jumped on their bikes. "Wait for me by the gate!" Emmy hollered as she put the bag in the basket on the front of her mountain bike.

Kevin raced his sisters down the driveway, and waited for Emmy. "I couldn't carry my trucks," he said.

"I've got them. This basket might look dorky, but it comes in handy at times."

They crossed the street and made their way up the winding, hilly driveway to Tony and Sloane's house. Kevin and Heather jumped off of their bikes and let them fall to the ground by the side of the front sidewalk. Isabella used the kickstand on her bike.

"Knock first!" Emmy yelled.

Kevin bounded up the front stairs and pounded on the door. Emmy shook her head and rolled her eyes.

Peter and Ben checked the sidelights on either side of the heavy, wooden door and opened it. "Hi, we thought you would be in the pool."

"We went swimming this morning. I brought some new trucks to show you."

The boys disappeared through the house and went outside

104

to the backyard. Heather and Isabella went upstairs with Dotty and Noemi.

Emmy found Sloane and Mama in the kitchen and set the Tupperware on the counter. "I brought these back."

Mama pointed a finger at Emmy. "Happy belated birthday, and I need to talk to you, young lady."

Emmy bit her lip as Sloane chuckled. "You are in big trouble, Emmy."

"Why?" Emmy shrugged.

"I read the book," Mama motioned for Emmy to follow her.

"It wasn't that bad," Emmy looked up at Sloane. "Was it?"

Sloane grinned. "You surprised Mama."

Emmy followed Mama to the sitting room.

"Have a seat," Mama said as she took a seat in her wooden rocking chair and began to rock back and forth.

Emmy sat facing Mama with her hands in her lap. "I can explain."

"I'm listening," Mama frowned.

"Which part didn't you like?"

"Did you have to tell the whole world you went swimming with Rory Porter?" Mama asked.

Despite having turned thirty-four years old the previous day, Emmy blushed. "I don't think the whole world will read my book."

"No, but the people who do will know you went swimming in your underwear," Mama said and then closed her eyes.

"But the underwear was navy blue. It's not like he could see anything," Emmy insisted. "I didn't know we were going swimming. I would have worn a bathing suit otherwise."

"Will Kenny be surprised if he reads the book?"

Emmy shook her head emphatically. "There's nothing in the book he doesn't already know about. In fact, I told him I went swimming with Rory a couple of days after it happened. He didn't seem to mind."

"What about the time you and Rory snuck onto the football field with those older kids? They were smoking marijuana and drinking beer." Mama rocked back and forth faster now.

105

"I shouldn't have done that, and I made sure I emphasized that in the book. I certainly don't condone my behavior, or the actions of the other people."

"Did you smoke any of the marijuana?"

"No way, Mama!" Emmy placed a hand on her heart. "I did drink some beer, but I've never smoked anything in my life."

"Did you really climb in and out of your bedroom window?" Mama's frown slowly dissolved and turned into a grin.

Emmy giggled and then said, "I used to do that all the time in the summer."

Mama's grin turned into a laugh. "Didn't you have any girlfriends? You hung out with Kenny and Rory all the time. No wonder you were such a tomboy."

"I hung out with Barry in grade school," Emmy said nonchalantly. "There weren't any girls my age on our street, and I wasn't allowed to leave our block. I don't remember any kids at all on the other side of the street. It was all old people. The other kids on our block were even older than Diane. I did play with Amy Porter a few times, but she was into weird stuff even as a kid."

"You shouldn't talk about her like that," Mama said. "God rest her soul."

"Didn't you ever do anything wrong when you were growing up?"

Mama stopped rocking. "I made mistakes. I am human, Emily, but I would never tell anyone much less write about it in a book."

"You never did anything like I did, huh?" Emmy asked. *I would be shocked if you did.*

"Certainly not. I did not play with any boys in the neighborhood, and I never went swimming with anyone other than my brothers."

"Do you hate me now?"

"Of course not, child," Mama answered. "Did you leave out anything that would shock me even more?"

Emmy bit her lip.

"It's all right. You don't have to tell me," Mama said.

"Mom, is it all right if Dany and Darian come over after dinner to go swimming?" Heather hollered from the kitchen.

Emmy walked down the stairs and frowned at Heather. "Did you call Dany and pester her?"

Heather shook her head. "She's on the phone now. I didn't call her."

Emmy took the landline from Heather. "Hi, Dany. You are always welcome to use the pool. I could make dinner if you want to come over earlier."

"Thanks, but Darian is using the grill. Could I come for dinner if he turns the steaks into charcoal?"

Darian walked past Dany with the platter of steaks. "I didn't turn them into charcoal the last time. I just left them on for a couple of minutes longer than I needed."

"I'll see you after dinner, Emmy," Dany said.

"How were the steaks?" Emmy asked later that evening as she gathered up the paper plates from the picnic table on the deck. "We had our own cookout."

"Not bad," Dany answered and then confessed. "Better than the brownies I tried to make last night."

"Can we go swimming now?" Heather asked as she and Isabella appeared in their bathing suits.

"You can go if Dany and Darian are ready. I need to change into my suit and check on your brother. He's still over at Diane's with Caden and Carson," Emmy said. "It still feels like it's in the nineties, and there's no breeze at all. I'm so glad we have a pool."

"So are we," Dany said with a smile. "Give us five minutes, and we'll be ready. I'm wearing my suit already."

Isabella looked up at Darian. "Mom said we went to Hawaii with Miss Liz and Pastor Tyler on their honeymoon, but we couldn't go with you."

Darian smiled.

"Isa! We didn't go on their honeymoon. We happened to be on vacation at the same time. It was just a coincidence, and you were only six months old," Emmy explained.

"Did you have fun in Hawaii?"

Darian picked up Isabella. "We did have fun. We saw a real volcano and an amazing sunset."

"Did you guys go to Haleakala?" Emmy asked.

"We did, but that was for the sunrise," Dany said.

"Oh, right. We did that with Tyler and Liz. It was amazing. Did you go zip-lining?"

"We did, but we didn't do the pig roast like Lizzie and Tyler," Dany said.

"Who's ready to go swimming?" Darian put Isabella over his shoulder and headed to the in-ground pool.

By the time Emmy changed and joined everyone, Darian was tossing Heather and Isabella into the air and splashing water everywhere.

"Mommy, you should let Darian throw you in the air. It's fun," Isabella said as Darian tossed Heather over his head.

"I'll swim with you, but I don't want to be thrown around like that. I'm too old," Emmy said as she walked into the pool from the shallow end.

"You're not as old as Aunt Diane or Grandma," Isabella said.

"No, but I'm not a kid anymore." Emmy swam over to where Dany tread water. "This feels so good. I was sweating like a pig before. I had to shower before I could swim."

Darian swam over and pushed Dany and Emmy under the water. They popped back up and looked at each other.

"Should we gang up on him?" Emmy asked.

"Yeah," Dany replied. "Between the two of us we almost weigh as much as him."

Dany and Emmy swam after Darian. They caught him and managed to dunk him. He stayed under the water and pulled both of them down by their legs.

Heather and Isabella watched and laughed as Emmy, Dany and Darian goofed around like kids.

"It's a good thing Mommy isn't really old," Isabella said.

Chapter Twelve

"Do you have everything?" Diane asked Brady as he zipped his suitcase closed. "Did you remember some pajamas this time?"

"I packed two pairs," he said, laughed and then added, "If I've forgotten anything, I can always buy it when I get to Tokyo."

Diane sat on the edge of the bed with her shoulders slumped.

Brady noticed. "What's wrong? You know I have to travel at times."

"I understand you want the business to succeed and expand, but why does it always have to be you doing the traveling? Bennett doesn't have little kids at home."

"True, but he does have a school to manage," Brady said as he sat next to Diane and put an arm around her shoulders. "It won't be forever, but it is important that I be there."

"It's summer. Why can't Bennett go now?"

"He does have responsibilities even in the summer," Brady said.

"I understand your desire to create new challenges for yourself, but we have plenty of money already."

"I'm not doing this only for the money. You do realize that, right?"

Diane stood up. "I know. You better get going. Call me when you get settled. I won't be able to sleep until I hear from you." She waved a finger at him. "No texts! I want to hear your voice, so I know you're safe."

Brady kissed her cheek and then laughed. "Have you been watching those movies about Americans getting kidnapped again?"

"It does happen," Diane said softly.

"It won't happen to me," Brady said confidently. "I will have Roscoe along."

"He's only one man, Brady," Diane said.

Diane called Emmy after lunch. "I need to talk to you."

"Okay, what's up?" Emmy asked.

"Not on the phone. Can you come over here?"

"I suppose. Is it all right if I bring the kids?"

Diane sighed. "Yeah, but I'm putting Conor and Lily down for naps."

"No problem. The kids can play outside. It's only in the eighties today. We'll be there in a few."

Emmy and the kids walked through the woods to Brady and Diane's house.

"There's Carson and Caden," Emmy said as she spotted the boys. "The younger ones are sleeping, so play outside and try to be quiet, okay?"

"Do we have to play with the boys?" Isabella asked.

Heather yanked on her sister's arm. "Come on, Isa. We can play with them and pretend to be princesses."

Emmy headed inside and found Diane in the family room.

"Did you get the little ones down already?"

Diane nodded and patted a spot on the couch beside her. "Lily volunteered to go down. She has been doing that lately. Conor only fussed for a minute."

Emmy plopped down next to Diane. "What's so top secret that you can't talk about it on the phone?"

"How often do you have sex?" Diane blurted out.

Emmy bit her lip for a moment but then grinned.

Diane sighed and then rolled her eyes. "Don't be so immature."

"You are aware Kenny is in Europe, right?"

"I know, and I didn't mean right now. I mean on an average week when he's home."

Emmy shrugged. "I don't know. I don't keep score. Maybe twice a day," she said with a straight face.

"Really?"

"I wish," Emmy said and then laughed. "Maybe when we were first married. Why? What's going on?"

Diane took a deep breath. "Brady is losing interest in me. He hasn't... you know... for about a month."

"A month! How can you stand it?"

"For crying out loud, Emmy. We aren't kids anymore," Diane said with a frown.

110

"Exactly!" Emmy grinned.

"Why did I even mention anything?" Diane started to get up, but Emmy pulled her back down.

"Sorry. I'll be serious now. Tell me what's happening."

"He's still nice and all. He gives me kisses and hugs, but at night if I'm even awake when he comes to bed, he turns away from me and goes to sleep. He tries to at least. Sometimes he gets up and doesn't come back to bed at all."

"Is it because of the new company? You said he's been traveling a lot and working long hours when he's home."

"I'm sure that's part of it," Diane said and then looked at Emmy.

"Why are you looking at me like that? Are you hiding something?" Emmy grabbed both of Diane's shoulders and twisted her so she could look directly into her eyes. After a pause, Emmy asked, "Are you seeing someone on the side?"

"No! Why would you think that? Are you still seeing Rory?"

Emmy released Diane and stood up. "That was uncalled for."

Diane looked up at Emmy. "Sorry. Sit back down, please."

Emmy hesitated but then sat down. She crossed her arms over her chest and stuck out her lower lip.

"Oh, quit pouting. That doesn't work anymore."

"Rory and I are friends," Emmy insisted.

"Yeah, whatever. It doesn't matter. I'm worried about Brady."

"You didn't answer my question."

"No! I am not seeing anyone else," Diane said slowly with emphasis on each word.

"Then it's probably just the stress of the new business. I can't picture Brady doing anything," Emmy said. "Sure, he had relationships before you guys got together, but that's all in the past."

"I can't tell Brady, but sometimes I wish he had never started the new company. We don't need the money. Not that the company's not making a ton of it right now."

111

"Really?" Emmy interrupted. "Tons of money?"

"Oh, like you guys are on the verge of bankruptcy," Diane said sarcastically. "It's not like some companies that take years to show a profit. With his new contracts, the company is returning a healthy profit."

"Do you think Brady and Bennett will sell it in a couple of years?" Emmy asked.

"It wouldn't surprise me," Diane said. "They could make enough to either buy an island or start another company of some kind."

Emmy giggled and then said, "I hope they buy a small island. Kenny and I can build a grass hut and live there. We could run around naked all day..."

Diane poked Emmy in the side. "Will you ever grow up?"

Emmy grinned while shaking her head. "Not planning to."

Brady set his briefcase down in the entryway and hollered, "I'm home. Is anyone here?" He waited for a response but didn't hear an answer.

The driver brought the luggage from the car. "Where would you like these, Mr. Robertson?"

"Please, leave them there, and I will take them upstairs later," Brady said, paid the man and over-tipped him.

Emmy approached down the hall from the back of the house. "Hey, Brady. I thought I heard someone. Did you just get home?"

"Yes. Where are Diane and the kids? Are they here?" Brady asked while trying to look past Emmy. He ignored the bikini top and jean shorts she wore.

Are you afraid she's left you? Are you feeling guilty about something, Brady? Emmy looked up at Brady for a moment before she turned and pointed. "They're out back. I came inside to get some water for Lily. How was your trip?"

"Exhausting, but I'm home early," he answered. "Would you not tell Diane I'm home, please? I want to run upstairs and change into something more comfortable."

Emmy ran a hand over the jacket of his designer suit. "You

112

got five minutes to change," she said and then giggled.

Brady hurried and came outside ten minutes later with a bottle of water in his hand.

Emmy looked at him and laughed. *For cripes sake! Will you get rid of those black socks and wear a shirt that doesn't have a collar. It's summer. You need to chill. No one wears socks with sandals. At least no one with any sense of fashion.*

"I'm home!" Brady announced.

"Daddy!" Lily squealed as she ran to him.

Brady picked her up and smothered her with kisses as he hugged her.

Diane got up from the patio table and walked up to Brady. "You're early."

"I am, and I don't feel jet-lagged for some reason." He stared at his wife. "Is that a new swimsuit?"

"Yes, do you like?" Diane put her hands on top of her head and posed for him. "It's a Christopher Milani original, and I paid way too much money for it."

"I think it's money well spent." Brady set Lily down and opened his arms for Diane. "I missed you," he whispered.

Emmy smiled as Brady kissed Diane. "Carson, will you watch Lily while I get the stroller for Conor. I think we should all go for a walk. Maybe we could go swimming at my house."

"But we can go swimming here, Auntie Em," Carson said as he pointed to the pool.

"Yes, but I don't have my bathing suit with me," Emmy said.

Caden walked over to Emmy. "It's under your shorts, Auntie Em. You were sitting in the sun earlier."

Diane turned to look at Emmy. "It's all right. You don't have to take the kids to your house."

"Are you sure?"

Diane glared at Emmy. "We're not horny children like someone else I know. We can wait until tonight."

"I won't wait when Kenny gets home," Emmy said and then giggled.

"And how long will that be?" Diane asked.

"A month," Emmy sighed.

"Just make sure you wait, and don't forget about next Saturday," Diane said.

"I won't forget. It's Mona's birthday, and the party is at their house."

"I think the steaks are ready," Bill Robertson said as he stabbed one of the rib-eyes and turned it over.

Brady held a platter. "The kids ate all the hot dogs already. Mona sent out another package. I'll cook them if you want to take the steaks inside. Tony and John are looking hungry, and I'm worried they might starve to death."

Emmy ran up to Bill and Brady. "Tony said he was about to pass out unless he gets some meat soon."

"He's in luck," Bill said. "I'm bringing in the rib-eyes now." He handed the platter to Emmy and loaded up the steaks. "Can you carry these without dropping them, little lady?"

Emmy wrinkled her nose. "I'm not a child anymore even if Carson is taller than me."

"One of these days all the kids will be taller than you, Emmy," he said as he touched her nose and grinned. "Thanks for coming over early and helping in the kitchen. Mona would have done all the work herself otherwise."

"She shouldn't have to do anything today. It's her birthday," Emmy said as Bill set another steak on the platter.

"That one might be too well done."

"I'll give it to Tony. He'll eat anything," Emmy said and then bit her lip.

"What, Emmy?" Bill asked.

"How old is Mona? I'm too shy to ask her."

Bill laughed. "That'll be the day."

Emmy made a face. "I'm still shy at times."

"Don't tell her you heard this from me, but she is sixty-six today."

"It will be our secret." Emmy held the platter with one hand as she zipped her mouth closed.

"Careful there, Em."

114

"Where is Spencer?" Marissa Robertson whispered to her husband Bennett later as the adults sat in the family room. "He was supposed to be here by one o'clock. It's nearly two."

Bennett pushed his glasses back up his long nose and checked his watch. "He will be here soon. He said he might run a little late because Mackenna had to work this morning."

"I want him to introduce her to Mother and Father and Mona and Bill."

"Do you think that's necessary?" Bennett asked as he watched his daughter Abigail talking to Emmy in the corner. *I wish you would let your hair grow longer, Abby. You look so pretty with long hair.*

"They are getting rather serious. Mother would be horrified if she knew they were spending so much time together without a..."

"People don't need chaperoning nowadays, Marissa. He's twenty-three. Your mother still lives in her interpretation of the old South. I'm surprised she deigns to grace us with her presence."

"It's not easy for them to travel," Marissa said.

"It would be if she would fly. No one travels by train these days."

"My brothers have given up trying to convince her flying is safe," Marissa whispered. "Did I tell you how shocked Mother was earlier to see those grown men in their swimming trunks and no shirt?"

"I'm amazed you and your brothers even exist," Brady mumbled.

Marissa frowned as she stared at him.

Winston and Abigail Hartley sat stiffly upright on the couch as they talked with Bill and Mona.

"Bill could always send the plane for you, Abigail," Mona said.

"Thank you, but no. I have never flown, and I will not start now." Abigail Havilland Hartley used a small paper fan to give the appearance of keeping cool.

Winston Hartley adjusted his tie and then smoothed out his white mustache but didn't speak.

"Is that one of Abby's friends from college?" Abigail asked

while looking at her granddaughter.

"Don't you remember Emmy? You have met her before," Mona said.

"I can't be expected to remember everyone who is introduced to me," Abigail said haughtily.

Bill choked back a laugh.

Mona nudged Bill and then said, "The twin girls and the little boy Kevin Michael belong to her. They live down the road."

"I see," Abigail said with obvious disapproval.

"Kenny is in Europe now with his band. He is a very famous rock star."

Abigail fluttered her fan. "I never listen to that horrid music."

"Emmy is also a singer, and she writes books," Mona said in a last effort to impress Abigail. It failed.

"How do you like Stanford?" Emmy asked Abby.

"I like the school, but I love being away from home," Abby said while smiling. "I hated the Barclay Academy, but I tolerated it. At least it is finally a coed school. I could have never gone to North Park like Spencer. I would have died."

"I got my degree from North Park," Emmy said. "But I didn't live on campus. Where is Spencer anyway?"

"He should be here soon. He had to pick up Mackenna from work. Mother doesn't know, but he and Mackenna are living together. She can be as clueless as Grandmother at times."

"Do you want to go outside with me? I need to check on the kids. Tony is supposed to be watching them, but they can be a handful."

"Sure," Abby said. "He's still a hunk, huh?"

"He's actually lost weight since he retired from the Bears. Don't tell him I said so, but he looks better than ever."

"Too bad his wife is getting rather heavy. Didn't she used to be much slimmer?"

"She has had trouble losing weight after having four babies," Emmy said in defense of Sloane.

"You and your friend Kristen still look amazing," Abby said as she spotted Kristen sitting at one of the patio tables under

116

an umbrella with John and Sloane.

"Everyone is different," Emmy said.

"I don't plan to have children until my career is well established. I will only have two at the most. A son first and then a daughter."

You are rather naive. It doesn't always work out the way you envision. Emmy stared at Abby.

"Hey, Em!" Tony hollered as he walked out of the oval-shaped pool carrying Noemi and Grace on his shoulders. "Are you coming in the pool?" He set down the girls, and they scampered to their mothers.

"Would you mind if I use the pool, Abby?" Emmy asked after making sure Heather, Isabella and Kevin Michael were occupied.

"Go ahead," Abby grinned. "I'll sit on the edge and keep an eye on Tony."

"Be right there, creep," Emmy told Tony as she slipped off her top and shorts.

"Hurry up, brat. I want to show Peter and Carson how far I can throw you."

"Are you going to let Uncle Tony throw you?" Carson asked as Emmy dove into the pool.

"He'll have to catch me first," Emmy said.

She managed to stay out of his grasp for a time.

"Let me go," she squealed as Tony put his hands around her waist and lifted her up.

Isabella stood at the end of the pool with her hands on her hips. "Uncle Tony, you better not hurt my mommy!" she ordered.

Tony let go of Emmy and smiled at Isabella, who was still in her bathing suit. "I wouldn't dare hurt your mommy. Should I see how high I can toss you instead?"

Isabella grinned and jumped into the water. Soon all the kids were in the pool with Tony. They climbed all over him and tried to dunk him under the water. They didn't realize he was standing on the bottom.

Emmy pulled herself out of the water and sat on the edge next to Abby.

"He's so strong. The kids are having a blast with him," Abby said.

"He's gentle with the girls, but he can be a bit rough with the boys at times. Especially Caden. Caden is kinda sensitive and shy."

"If I wasn't dressed, I would let him toss me around the pool," Abby sighed.

Emmy waited until the sun dried her skin and then put on her shorts and t-shirt.

"Hello, everyone," Spencer said as he walked into the family room. "This is Mackenna Barlow." He introduced his grandparents and Mackenna smiled charmingly. Even at Grandma Abigail.

"Goodness gracious," Abigail murmured softly. *How many piercings does she have in her ears and what is that in her nose?*

"Are you hungry?" Mona asked. "We have leftovers and maybe even a steak or a burger or two." *I love your hair, Mackenna. I'm sure Abigail is shocked. No one in her family would dare have pink and purple highlights.*

"Thanks, Mona. We stopped and grabbed some lunch. Happy birthday, by the way."

"I wish Bill wouldn't make a fuss about it, but he does. Can I get you something to drink?" Mona offered. "There is beer in the cooler by the pool."

"That sounds good."

Spencer and Mackenna stayed inside to let Grandma Abigail interrogate both of them for several minutes.

"Mother, I believe you have asked enough questions," Winston said to his wife. "Let the kids go outside and have some fun."

"Thanks, Grandfather," Spencer smiled and escaped with Mackenna in tow.

Mackenna glanced over her shoulder as they headed outside. "Are your grandparents always so formal?"

Spencer laughed. "Ha! That was them being casual."

"Are you going to tell your mother about our living situation soon?"

"Not unless I have to. I'll tell Father first. He is more understanding, but even he doesn't know about Abby's boyfriend."

Spencer and Mackenna walked out onto the deck and saw some people in the pool and others sitting at the tables.

"Where should we sit?" Spencer asked.

"There's Abby with someone," Mackenna pointed to one of the tables on the far side of the pool. "I want to talk to her. Will you grab a beer for me, please?"

"Sure. That's Emmy Colasanti with Abby. You do know who she is, right?"

"I've heard about her," Mackenna said.

Abby spotted Mackenna and waved. "Come and talk to us."

"Hi, Abby, I met the grandparents," Mackenna said as she sat next to Abby.

"Did Grandmother Hartley give you the third degree?"

"A little, but I think she was in shock. She kept staring at my hair and my ears and nose. I'm Mackenna Barlow." Mackenna extended a hand to Emmy.

"I'm Emmy. I love your hair, but Kenny would kill me if I did that."

"I change it every month," Mackenna said as she flipped her mostly black hair around.

Spencer arrived with two beers, handed one to Mackenna and sat beside his sister.

"Thanks, Spencer. I am thirsty." Abby grabbed Spencer's beer and took a long drink.

"Would you like a cool beverage, Emmy?" Spencer asked as he stood up.

"Thanks, but I'm sticking to water," Emmy said and took a drink of her Ice Mountain.

Spencer returned and sat next to Emmy and out of reach of Abby.

"What have you been doing this summer? You did graduate, right?" Emmy asked.

"I'm taking a class and working for my father and Uncle Brady," he explained. "How are you? Are those your girls?"

Emmy grinned and nodded. "They are getting big, huh?"

119

Spencer looked around the deck area. "Where is Kenny?"

"Still in Europe. He won't get back until mid-August."

"I listened to your new CD. I like it. Are you still on tour?"

Emmy explained the logistics of her current tour.

"So you are only gone part of the week. That probably works best for the kids," Abby said.

"I do take them with me in the summer a little. The girls are to the point where they want to sing with me."

"Are they talented?" Spencer asked.

"They are. Go figure," Emmy said and then laughed. "Speak of the devil," Emmy said as Isabella rushed over.

"Mommy! Can Heather and I change clothes and play inside with Dotty and Noemi and Grace?" Isabella asked as she dripped water on Emmy's legs.

"Okay, but you need to dry off before you go inside," Emmy said. "Use the bathroom just inside the patio door." She looked up just in time to see Tony coming with one of the kids red plastic bucket. "That better not be full of water, you creep!" She tried to get away, but didn't have time.

Tony turned the bucket upside down over her head. "See. Empty."

"You're a creep."

"Hi, Tony," Spencer said. He and Tony shook hands.

Emmy noticed Abby staring at Tony. *Someone has a crush on you, Tony. You better be careful.*

"Sloane is going to take the younger kids home, but I'm going to stay here with Noemi, Peter and Dotty," Tony said as he stood behind Emmy while dripping water on her.

"Will you stop that!?"

"Sorry, brat. Are you through swimming?"

"For now," Emmy answered. "Are Kristen and John leaving, too?"

"Yeah, is it all right if Kevin Michael goes with Sloane? He wants to play with Ben's new trucks. I'll bring him home later," Tony said.

"You can keep him overnight if you want. Bring him back before church in the morning. Why didn't Mama come with you?"

"She complained about her back. I told her to stay home and relax."

"She works hard taking care of all the kids," Emmy said. "Sometimes I think she should move into Hampshire Glen. It would be easier on her."

"You mean the place your parents moved to?" Tony asked. "That senior citizen place?"

"It would be a lot quieter."

"Maybe you should mention it sometime. She won't listen to me."

"Would you like to go outside and sit by the pool?" Mona asked Abigail and Winston.

"No, thank you. I burn easily," Abigail answered. "Would you mind if Winston and I return to Marissa's home. I feel a headache coming on."

Winston and Abigail left with Marissa and Bennett. Bill and Mona walked them to the front door.

"Thank you for coming. Come back and see us anytime," Mona offered.

Abigail didn't reply.

Bennett shrugged. "Sorry, Dad. You know how she is."

"Don't worry about it. I might go for a swim myself. I'm pretty sure Emmy and Tony are still here. I heard some of the kids upstairs a few minutes ago."

"Send Spencer and Abby home sometime," Bennett said and then hurried to open the car doors for his wife and in-laws.

"I'm going to upstairs to see what the children are up to," Mona said. "Thank you for a beautiful birthday." She kissed Bill and then headed upstairs.

Bill walked outside in time to see Tony toss Emmy into the deep end of the pool in her clothes.

"You are going to die, Tony Bertucci!" Emmy hollered after coming back to the surface.

Bill walked over to the edge of the pool and offered a hand to Emmy. "Did you slip, Emmy?"

She pointed to Tony and stuck out her tongue. "I'm going to kill him as soon as I catch him."

Abby rushed over and stood in front of Tony. "I'll protect you, Tony."

Spencer laughed. "I wouldn't get in Emmy's way, Abby. She might be small, but she sounds serious."

"Would you like a towel, Emmy?" Bill offered.

"Thanks, Mr. Robertson, but I'll take these wet things off and dry off soon enough. Some people never grow up!" she made a face at Tony and then dropped her shorts. Her feet got tangled up and she fell back into the pool.

Tony ran toward the pool and dove headfirst in Emmy's direction. He pulled her head out of the water and she coughed out some water in his direction. "Are you all right?"

"I tripped," she said and then wrapped her arms around his neck.

Tony carried her out of the water as easily as he would carry one of the little kids.

Abby stood at the edge of the pool with her arms folded across her chest and a frown on her face.

"Should I push you in, so he can rescue you, sis?" Spencer stood behind Abby with his hands on her shoulders.

He received an elbow to the stomach as an answer. "Not if you want to live," Abby said and then sat down next to Mackenna.

"Are they related, or having an affair? What is going on?" Mackenna asked while watching Tony carry Emmy to a table on the other side of the pool and set her down.

"How the hell should I know?" Abby spat viciously.

Bill walked over to Tony and Emmy after hearing Abby's remark. "Are you all right, Emmy?"

"I'm fine. I got my shorts tangled up and fell in. No big deal. I would have surfaced sooner or later." She bit her lip and looked at Tony. "Thank you."

"No problem, brat," he said as he pulled her shorts off from around her feet. "I shouldn't have thrown you in the pool."

She smiled and kicked him in the shin. "You will pay for that later, creep."

Spencer walked over and smiled at Emmy. "Here's your Ice Mountain, Emmy." He handed her the bottle of water.

"You are so funny, Spencer. I think I've had enough water for now."

"Would you like a beer?" Spencer asked.

Emmy thought about it. "Normally I would, but not today. Thanks, Spencer."

Bill and Spencer sat down and Spencer waved to Mackenna and Abby.

"It looks like the party is over there, Abby. Should we join them?"

"I guess we should be sociable," Abby answered. She hurried past Mackenna and took the empty seat next to Tony. "That was such a brave thing to do," Abby said as she placed a hand on Tony's bicep.

"It was my fault in the first place and Kenny would have been upset if I let her drown. At least for a few minutes," Tony joked and ignored Abby's hand.

"You're still a creep," Emmy said and stuck out her tongue.

They sat at the table and talked for nearly an hour.

"Spencer, I should get home. I have laundry to do, and I need a ride," Mackenna said.

"I need a ride, too," Abby said. She had long given up trying to throw herself at Tony.

"Will you say goodbye to Mona for us, Uncle Bill," Spencer said. "Nice to see you again, Emmy."

"You, too. I should round up a couple of kids. I'm sure Mona must be tired of them by now."

Tony shook hands with Spencer and smiled at Mackenna and Abby. "Thanks for the steaks." Tony rubbed his stomach. "Mine was excellent."

"Which one?" Emmy asked. "You ate three of them."

"Did not," Tony said. He held up two fingers. "I need to take some kids home."

Spencer, Mackenna and Abby left. Emmy walked up the stairs with Tony.

"I didn't realize she had such poor taste in men."

"What or who are you talking about, brat?"

"Abby has a crush on you. What poor taste," Emmy teased

123

and then raced ahead of Tony. "It's time to go home, girls."

"But, Mom!" Heather whined. "We are having a tea party. We need more time."

"You have two minutes. Say thank you to Mona and give her kisses and hugs."

"Happy birthday, Grandma Mona," Isabella said as Heather pouted. "Thank you for playing with us."

"It was a most wonderful tea party. Thank you for coming."

Heather broke off her pout and hugged Mona.

"Are we keeping Kevin Michael?" Tony asked.

"Yes! You can keep him and Dotty and Noemi can move into our house," Heather said.

"Meant overnight, Heather. You would miss your brother if he moved away."

Heather shook her head. "No, I wouldn't."

"It's all right with me if Dotty and Noemi spend the night. I don't have to leave until two," Emmy said.

"I'll bring them some clothes," Tony said.

Tony walked into Emmy's room an hour later and sat down on the couch. "I brought clothes for the girls, and Kevin needs pajamas and clothes for the morning. What are you watching?"

"*The Iron Throne*, but I don't understand it. Have you ever seen it?"

He shook his head. "Sloane won't allow it because there's too much nudity. Why are you watching it?"

Emmy laughed. "I'm a girl. Naked women don't bother me and how much nudity is too much?"

"You'd have to ask Sloane," Tony said and pointed to the TV. "She would consider that too much."

Emmy paused the DVD. "I guess that didn't help," she said and then giggled.

"Where are the girls?" Tony asked to change the subject.

"In the twins' room. They are playing dress-up. Are things under control at your house?"

Tony shrugged. "Just the normal chaos with five boys in the house. Are you going to play the DVD?"

"Why are you tired of looking at..."

124

"Nothing I haven't seen before."

"You are such a creep," Emmy smiled.

"I heard there's a lot of violence in this show."

"Not as much as at a football game," Emmy said. "But they do kill a few characters in every episode."

"Good to know," Tony said as he pulled his phone out of his pocket. He read the text from Sloane. "Sloane wants to know if you want to keep me overnight."

"What does she really want?" Emmy asked without taking her eyes from the TV.

"She said Noemi has to be in bed by ten."

"What about Dotty?"

"Ten thirty."

"What difference does a half hour matter?"

"Got me." Tony shrugged and then pointed at the TV. "Ouch! I bet that hurt."

Emmy laughed. "Only temporarily."

"Were you serious about Abby earlier?" Tony asked.

"You couldn't tell? Are you blind? She was fawning all over you," Emmy said and then laughed.

"I don't know what fawning means," he confessed.

"You are such a dope. Remember when she said 'Oh, Tony, you are so strong' and crap like that? She was touching you."

"Not really. I wasn't paying her any attention. Did you do that when we were dating?"

She threw a pillow at him. "No! I always thought you were a creep," she said but then giggled. "I might have been like that with Christopher but never you."

Tony covered his ears. "I don't want to hear about you and anyone."

"You will have to read the book if I ever get it finished," Emmy said.

"No chance." He stood up. "The clothes are on the island. I'll let myself out, brat." He left the room just as another character bit the dust.

Chapter Thirteen

"Mommy, are we going to sing with you today? You promised we could." Heather asked backstage at the Willis Insurance outdoor pavilion.

"I will let you sing one song with me. You and Isa can choose the song."

Heather looked at Isabella. They whispered back and forth for a moment.

"We want to sing 'Christmas All Year Long,'" Heather announced.

"It figures," Emmy said and then laughed. "Okay, but you better remember the words. I don't think I do."

"Mommy, you can look at the computer screen. It has all the words."

Emmy slapped her forehead. "Of course. How could I forget that?"

"You are so silly, Mommy," Isabella said.

Emmy and the band were headlining the daylong festival in Villa Glen. She had two hours to kill before going onstage. She made sure the kids ate something healthy and then handed them over to Kristen.

"Thanks for agreeing to watch the kids, Krissy. I need to get ready."

"Not a problem, Em. Gracie wanted to watch you at work. I don't think she's ever been backstage at a big concert."

"This isn't anything like a Fridays show," Emmy reminded Kristen.

"It's still a big deal to Gracie. She has been talking about hearing the girls sing all day."

"I gave Kevin Michael the choice of coming to the show or playing with trucks at Tony's house. He didn't hesitate. He wanted to play with Ben. He's going to stay with Tony and Sloane until Wednesday. I will be so glad when Kenny gets home, and my tour is over. I'm tired."

"You look tired. Zachary and John are probably over there, too," Kristen added.

126

Emmy hugged the girls. "I will come and get you when it's my time to sing. You can listen from the side of the stage, but you have to obey Aunt Kristen."

"We will, Mommy," Isabella promised.

Emmy headed to her dressing room and picked out a clean pair of jeans and a new white top to wear. She met with the band in the green room.

"I need to tell you guys something, and I hope you don't think this is a rash decision on my part."

"What is it, Emmy?" Bobby O'Connor asked. "I think we have a pretty good idea but go ahead and tell us."

"We have a little over two weeks before the end of this tour," Emmy said and then sighed. "I am beat. Between touring, taking care of the kids and house, and working on my books, I am just wiped. I don't feel like I'm doing justice to any part of my life. So, after we finish, I have decided to take a break from touring for at least two years. Do you guys hate me?"

Bobby walked over and put his hands on her shoulders. He kissed the top of her head and smiled. "We don't hate you. We could tell how much this tour has affected you. We can always find someone else to sing," he joked. "That's the easy part. Singers can be found under every rock."

Emmy made a face at him and then looked at the other guys. "Do you agree with Bobby?"

Micah smiled. "Do you mean the part about finding singers under rocks, or the other thing?"

"You know what I mean," Emmy said.

The rest of the guys assured Emmy they understood her decision.

Quinten Matthews shrugged and said, "We might have to get real jobs for a while, but we might decide to carry on. Who can tell at this point?"

Christian Becton checked his hair in one of the mirrors. "I should have told you guys before, but I had already planned to head back to Los Angeles after we finished the tour. I've been offered a gig with a local band and have lined up some studio work. I won't have to wait on tables anymore."

"What about the crew, Em?" Bobby asked.

"They can find jobs with other bands if they want to travel. Nelson will still be my manager, and Tobias can pick up a gig mixing FOH for any number of bands. Same with most of the other tech guys." Emmy looked at Miles Goossens. "You are always so quiet. Do you have anything to say?"

Miles stood up. "I love playing in this band. If you guys decide to forge ahead with new members, I'm willing to go along. When Emmy decides to tour again..."

"If she decides to tour again," Bobby corrected Miles.

"If Emmy needs us, we can be there for her. Right, guys?" Miles glanced at the other musicians.

"Sounds like a plan to me," Micah said. "Are Heather and Isabella really going to sing a Christmas song tonight?"

"I let them choose, and that's what they chose."

"Do we have a chord chart for it?" Christian asked.

The guys looked over the arrangement.

"No biggie. We can handle it," Quinten said.

Later, Emmy brought the twins out to sing. Heather counted off the song for the band, and she and Isabella sang it without much help from Emmy.

"Great job!" Micah high-fived the girls after they waved to the crowd.

"You guys did all right," Heather said, "but I heard someone hit an A instead of an E."

Micah stared at Heather.

Isabella tugged on his arm. "Mommy told us to say that. We think you played it the right way."

"Thanks, Isabella." Micah looked at Emmy and laughed.

Emmy needed to hang around after the show to fulfill an obligation, so Kristen offered to take the girls home.

"Thanks, Krissy. I'll come and get them when I get home," Emmy promised.

"Don't worry about it. They can spend the night with us. We're going to watch them the next three nights anyway. Gracie wants to camp out in her room," Kristen said.

"That sounds like fun. I used to do that when I was a kid."

Kristen stared at Emmy.

"At Kenny's house. We would turn the third floor into a fort and stuff."

"Whatever, Emmy," Kristen said.

"It was fun," Emmy whispered.

Two hours later Emmy and the guys boarded the leased bus for the short trip back to SoHam. They would fly out the next morning on another leg of the tour.

"Do you know of any musicians looking for a gig?" Micah asked the guys.

"Hey! Are you replacing me already?" Emmy plopped down one one of the couches.

"Not for a couple of weeks, Emmy," Bobby teased.

"I know this guy who sings and writes some decent tunes," Quinten said. "They're rock songs, but we can handle them."

"We need someone to replace Christian," Micah reminded them. "I can play some lead, but not enough to carry the band."

"I know this guy who plays guitar," Miles said softly. "A couple of them, actually."

"Who?" Bobby asked.

"Freddie and Marshall Bender from the worship team," Miles answered.

"Of course!" Micah said. "Why didn't I think of them. I heard them talking about maybe getting a band together to play some local gigs. They would be perfect. They both can play lead. I've heard them jamming together. It's awesome."

Emmy coughed to get their attention. "Have you forgotten that Freddie is married with three kids. I don't think Marika will want him touring all over the country."

"Who's talking about touring all over?" Micah asked. "We are only thinking about playing locally to start. We might attract the attention of a record label and sign a big contract like someone else we know. Then the record label will pay us big money to be rock stars."

"You are hilarious, Micah," Emmy said and then grinned.

"We don't have to decide tonight, but I might talk to Freddie and Marshall about the possibility," Micah said.

Emmy leaned against Bobby. "I'm not even gone, and you guys are replacing me already."

Bobby put an arm around her shoulders. "No one will ever replace you, Emmy. You are one of a kind."

Emmy made a face at him. "You are just saying that to tease me."

"Yeah, so."

"Hey! I know two other singers we could hire, but they won't work cheap," Micah said.

"Who?" Christian asked.

"Heather and Isabella."

"No way!" Emmy said as she straightened up. "I'm their manager, and you guys can't offer them enough money."

Emmy Skyped with Heather and Isabella on Tuesday afternoon from a hotel in Buffalo, New York.

"What did you do today?" Emmy asked.

"We played with Gracie in the morning, and after lunch we went swimming with Dotty and Noemi and Uncle Tony. Aunt Sloane made us stop because today is Dotty's birthday. She's ten now."

"Shoot! I forgot about Dotty's birthday. Will you tell her happy birthday for me?"

"We will, Mommy," Isabella said. "How much longer before Daddy gets home?"

Emmy checked the calendar on her phone. "He will be home in twelve days. That's less than two weeks."

"We know how many days there are in a week, Mom," Heather said and then rolled her eyes. "We're not babies anymore."

"Believe me. I know that all too well," Emmy said and then sighed.

Chapter Fourteen

"Emmy, we just landed. We need to pass through customs, and I should be on my way home. Call me back if you get this message." Kenny waited a few more seconds and ended the call.

"Still sleeping, huh?" Jeff asked.

"Understandable. It is two in the morning."

The guys cleared customs and departed O'Hare in limos. Kenny arrived home just after four. He left the luggage in the garage and raced inside and up the stairs to his bedroom. There was enough light for him to see Emmy sprawled across the bed. He undressed quietly and slipped into the small space along one edge. He kissed her forehead. Then her nose. He heard her sigh, so he quickly kissed her mouth.

"Are you awake, Em? I'm home."

"I'm still sleeping. Who are you?"

"Have I been away that long? Have you forgotten me?"

"I might like to get to know you again," she whispered. "But it will have to be quick because my husband is supposed to be coming home today."

She tried to stop but she started to giggle.

"You are such a stinker, Em. Move over so I don't fall off the bed."

She moved the wrong way, and he fell on the floor.

"I'm all right."

She leaned over the edge of the bed. "Ooops! Sorry. Wrong way."

He sat up and smiled at her as he rubbed his head.

"Are you going to stay down there, or are you coming to bed?"

"Are you going to push me out again?"

"It depends," she said while biting her lip.

"On what?" He moved his face closer to hers.

"On what you try to do to me." She inched her mouth closer to his.

"Can I get back in bed if I kiss you like this?" He kissed her mouth a little longer this time.

131

"Not sure. Try again."

He pressed harder on her lips and kept his lips there even longer this time.

She put a finger to her mouth. "That was better, but my husband is a real good kisser."

He put his hands to her face and opened her mouth wider.

"Are you trying to use your tongue?"

"Maybe."

"Try again."

He did and Emmy sighed.

"Em, my leg is starting to cramp. Can I get back in bed?"

She patted the spot beside her. "If you insist."

Kenny came downstairs just in time to say goodbye as Darian and Dany took the kids to church.

"I need coffee," he said.

"I made a fresh pot."

He put his arms around Emmy. "I missed you."

She leaned back against him. "I missed you more."

"You're supposed to say 'Oh, were you gone.' You used to say that all the time when I would come home."

"Sorry, I forgot." She turned around to face him. "I should tell you about this dream I had last night."

"I'm all ears," he said.

"Yes, you are, but I love you anyway." She touched his funny-looking ears. "So, last night I had this dream. A strange man crept into my bedroom. He tried to kiss me and I think he might have..." She pulled him closer and whispered into his ear.

"That sounds serious. Do you remember what he looked like?" Kenny asked with a straight face.

"No, it was dark, but I do remember he kissed me and I could tell he needed a shave." She rubbed her hand over Kenny's cheek. "Kinda like you. You need a shave."

"What else do you remember?"

She whispered several things.

Kenny straightened up. "Ummm. That might be illegal. Should we report him to the police?"

132

"No way! If we do that, he might not come back tonight."

"We aren't going to make it to church this morning, are we?" Kenny asked an hour later.

"I don't think so. I don't think I can move."

Kenny grinned. "I'm going to take a shower. What time do you have to be at the airport?"

"I forget. Do I have to leave?" She tried to sit up but fell onto her back.

"I'm pretty sure you need to be there, Em. You only have three more shows to do."

"I think we have to leave at one. What time is it?"

"Almost eleven."

Kenny showered, headed downstairs, made more coffee and looked in the fridge for blueberries. "Ah! We have some."

By the time Emmy came downstairs, Kenny had a stack of pancakes ready.

"Did you use the blueberries?" Emmy asked as she slipped onto one of the island barstools.

He handed her a cup of coffee. "I did. Would you like me to fix you a plate?"

"Yes, please," she took a sip of coffee, set the cup down and rested her chin on her arm. "I am so wiped out. When I get back on Wednesday, I want to sleep for a week."

By the time she finished her pancakes and a second cup of coffee, she felt much more alert.

"What were you saying about Charles staying in Europe?"

Kenny carried their empty plates to the sink. He leaned against the counter. "He decided to stay in Germany with friends."

"When will he be back in the States?"

Kenny shrugged. "Who knows? He might stay for a month or as long as a year. You never know with him."

"Are you going to surprise her?" Andy Walker asked as he dropped Kenny off at the SoHam airport Tuesday morning.

Kenny grabbed his duffel bag and shook his head. "She knows I'm coming. She asked if I would be there because she's thinking this might be her last show ever."

133

"I can see her taking time off, but I can't see her retiring. If you want to call it that."

"We'll have to see. Thanks for the ride, Andy." Kenny got out but paused as Andy leaned over toward the open door.

"Do you guys need a ride home tonight. Tomorrow morning. Whatever. Do you?"

"If I say yes, will you pick us up personally, or will you send a limo?"

"The girls and Kevin like to ride in limos."

"Thought so. I'm sure Nelson has made arrangements for us to get home, but thanks."

"You are definitely coming home tonight, right?"

"Yes, why?"

"What the heck! I might as well come with you. I would hate to think I missed her last show. Not that I believe this will be her last concert, but just in case."

Andy parked the car next to the hanger where Mr. Robertson parked his Gulfstream and joined Kenny.

"Do you always carry a change of clothes with you?" Kenny asked as he noticed the carry-on in Andy's hand.

Andy nodded. "It pays to be prepared."

The plane landed at Lambert International Airport. Andy and Kenny took a cab to the hotel.

"Do you think she's still here?" Kenny asked as walked up to the registration desk.

"It's too early to head to the venue," Andy answered.

"May I help you gentlemen?" the clerk asked with a practiced smile.

"Emmy Colasanti's room, please?" Kenny asked as he smiled back

"I'm sorry, but we have no one registered under that name," she answered but this time a hint of recognition crossed her face.

"He means Olivia Porter's room," Andy said with authority.

The clerk smiled. "I know who you are."

Kenny explained the reason for them being there.

"So, Ms. Porter is expecting you, correct?"

"She's expecting me but not him," Kenny answered.

134

"And you are?" the clerk turned her attention to Andy.

"I'm their manager."

That failed to impress the clerk.

"I'm her cousin," Andy said.

"Of course you are, sir."

Eventually, Kenny and Andy made their way to room 6011 and knocked on the door.

"Who is there, please?" a young voice asked. "My mommy said not to open the door to strangers."

"It's Daddy and Uncle Andy."

The door opened about twenty seconds later. Kenny and Andy stared at Emmy.

"What? You never seen a lady in a towel."

"Daddy, are you going to play your guitar for us tonight?" Heather asked as she brushed past Emmy. "Hi, Uncle Andy."

"You have terrible timing," Emmy said as she stepped aside to let Kenny and Andy into the room.

"I think my timing is perfect," Kenny said with a grin.

"This isn't a suite!" Andy raised his arms in exaggerated annoyance. "I better have a talk with Nelson."

Emmy walked up to Andy with her hands on her hips. Her hair dripped onto her bare shoulders and her wet feet left marks on the carpet. "I do not need a suite. I'm not a diva."

"And where do you plan to get dressed?"

"I didn't expect you."

"Should we wait downstairs?" Kenny asked.

"The kids are ready. Andy can take them downstairs and you can stay with me," Emmy said as her towel slipped just a little.

Kenny kept his eyes on Emmy's eyes. "I better wait downstairs, Ms. Porter, or else you might be late for the show."

Emmy waved to the crowd and left the stage. A couple of minutes later she brought the girls back out for the last song. Kenny had been on stage the entire show.

"Do we get to sing again, Mommy?" Heather asked. "We already sang our Christmas song."

"Daddy and I are going to sing 'I Will Be True To You.'"

135

"Mommy!" Heather said with hands on hips. "That's one of Daddy's really old songs."

"I know, but he still likes to sing it," Emmy teased Kenny with a grin. "He's kinda dorky, you know."

By the end of the song Emmy's tears flowed. She hugged Kenny and the girls. Andy Walker brought Kevin onto the stage.

"Is the show over, Uncle Andy? Can we go eat now? I really need some ice cream."

"We can have some ice cream in a few minutes. Your mom and dad are about finished," Andy explained.

"Should I say anything about this being my last concert?" Emmy held Kenny's hand as she waved again to the crowd.

"I wouldn't, Em. I can't believe you won't feel differently after a year or two."

The band played softly as Emmy and her family left the stage. The house lights came up and the band rushed backstage.

Bobby O'Connor embraced her and whispered into her ear, "I know how you feel right now, but I refuse to believe I will never play the drums behind you again."

"I don't know what to think right now, Bobby. We've been working together my whole career. I need to take time to think and pray about the direction of my life."

The rest of the guys hugged Emmy and the girls.

Kenny heard a commotion, looked around and spotted a lady running awkwardly in their direction with two young girls.

Two security guards appeared and moved in between Emmy and the intruder. "Stop!" one of the guards shouted.

"I need to talk to her. She knows me!" the lady shouted.

Andy and two other security people began to hustle Emmy and the kids out of the room.

"Come on, Em. We need to go," Andy said as he picked up Heather and Isabella.

Kenny grabbed Kevin Michael and began to follow Andy.

"Wait, Emmy! It's Jackie! The taxi driver's daughter! I still have the note you gave my father," the lady shouted.

Emmy stopped in her tracks and turned. She looked up at Kenny. "The taxi driver?"

Kenny looked at the lady and shrugged. "I remember the taxi ride and a photo. Don't remember a note."

"Em, come on. We have to go," Andy repeated.

"Wait! I think I know her."

"Em, are you sure?" Kenny asked.

Emmy stared at the lady who appeared to be about her age. Emmy looked at the two girls who bore an obvious familial resemblance to the lady. "Jackie? Jackie? I'm sorry, but I don't remember your last name," Emmy said as she began walking toward the lady.

"It's Jackie Wainwright now, but it used to be Tomkins. Jackie Tomkins. My friend Naomi Belton and I came to see you years ago at the New Horizon Methodist Church. My husband is the pastor there now."

The entire security team looked at Andy, Kenny and then at Roscoe Sandchek, who appeared as quickly as if he were a ghost.

"It's all right," Roscoe said quietly.

The security detail stood down, and Emmy and Jackie approached each other... slowly.

"I'm sorry for sneaking back here, but I had to see you, and I didn't know how to reach you. I'm sorry for causing so much trouble," she said. "I'm not usually like this."

"It's all right. Are these your daughters?" Emmy asked. *I vaguely remember that church.*

"We want down, Uncle Andy!" Isabella squirmed.

Andy set the girls down. Kevin Michael clung to his father.

"They are mine," Jackie said.

Heather and Isabella approached the two young girls, who held onto their mother.

"I'm Isabella and this is my sister Heather. What are your names?"

The girls let go of their mother and stood before Heather and Isabella.

"I'm Abriana and this is Calneshia. She's younger than me," Abriana said losing a bit of her shyness.

"Those are beautiful names," Emmy said. "Tell me about what's happened to you, Jackie." *I don't think I would have ever*

137

recognized you. You look a lot older than the girl I kinda picture. A lot heavier, too.

"You don't look any different than the last time I saw you, and I know he's your husband. The famous rock star," she said while pointing at Kenny."

Emmy looked over her shoulder and harrumphed, "He's a dork."

"I tried to come to your concert several years ago, but I was pregnant with Abriana and went into labor." Jackie laughed and then continued. "You won't believe this but the same thing happened again. I was in the hospital giving birth to Calneshia when you were here."

"That's amazing," Emmy looked down at Jackie's stomach.

Jackie waved her hands and shook with laughter. "Don't worry! I'm not even pregnant now. Just fat."

Emmy and Jackie talked for several minutes before Emmy needed to leave for the airport.

"Can you give me your number or email or something?" Emmy asked.

Jackie gave Emmy the information. "Oh, Emmy, I'm so glad I got to see you again. I look forward to hearing all your music, and I promise I won't miss another of your concerts because I'm having a baby."

"Let me know if you're ever near Chicago. We could get together and do lunch or something."

"Oh, sweetie, I never travel much. That's why I love it when you come to St. Louis." Jackie smothered Emmy with a hug.

On the plane ride home Emmy sat quietly with Kenny.

"I bet I know what's on your mind, Em."

"Am I that transparent?" she whispered. "Am I being selfish for wanting to stay at home and not having to travel?"

"I wouldn't call it being selfish, but I think God might disagree."

"I'm sorry I told Jackie you were a dork."

He laughed. "It's all right. I don't mind being your dork."

Chapter Fifteen

"Thanks for letting us meet here, Emmy," Bobby said as he sat in the control room of Kenny's basement studio Friday night. "We didn't know where else to meet. We didn't want to bother Pastor Tyler about using the church."

"It's all right. You guys are always welcome here." Emmy sat in one of the chairs by the mixing board and spun around with her feet in the air.

"Will you stop that?" Bobby stopped her with his foot.

"Is Kenny here?" Micah asked.

"No, he left yesterday. He won't be back until Sunday. They're still touring."

"Right, I was hoping we could record some stuff."

Emmy grinned. "I know how to do that. Nothing real fancy with effects or fancy plug-ins, but I can do basic recording. Are you waiting for Christian?"

"He headed back to LA this morning. He loaded up his van and took off for Holly-weird," Quinten said as he moved his hand indicating forward motion.

"I could never live in California," Emmy said as she moved her hands up and down like an earthquake. "Have you guys decided about your future?"

Micah looked at the guys. "I guess the guys are letting me speak for the group. We want to forge ahead and see what happens."

"Who's going to sing? Who will replace Christian?" Emmy asked.

"Miles and I talked to Freddie and Marshall last night at worship band rehearsal," Micah said.

Emmy looked at Miles.

"Okay, I did the talking, but Miles was there for support," Micah said.

"What did they say?"

"They are willing to give it a shot. They should be here soon."

"Oh, I hope they don't have any trouble getting past the

security shack. They probably aren't on the list," Emmy said.

Quinten nodded. "They do look rather suspicious with their long, wiry, black hair and swarthy complexions. I would bet they have some Hispanic blood in their ancestry."

"They are originally from El Paso," Miles added.

"You guys are still going to play on the worship team, right?"

"Yes, Emmy, we aren't quitting," Bobby said with an accusing look.

Emmy frowned at Bobby. "Hey! I haven't quit, but Sadie kinda said they don't need me that often, and Kenny doesn't have time."

"Sorry, Em. I didn't mean to insinuate you guys have quit."

Emmy's phone rang, and she talked briefly to the guard at the security gate.

"Freddie and Marshall are on their way," she told Bobby.

A couple of minutes later the doorbell rang.

"I'll get it, Em. It's probably Freddie and Marshall." Bobby jumped off of the couch, dashed through the door and raced up the stairs to the garage service door. "Hi, guys. Come on in."

Freddie and Marshall followed Bobby.

"Have you guys ever been here before?"

"Never had the pleasure." Freddie glanced around the huge, finished basement.

"Everyone is in the studio over there." Bobby pointed. "I like the cowboy hats. Where are your long coats?"

"Too hot," Marshall answered.

"Have you guys ever seen *The Long Riders*?"

"A couple of times," Freddie said while admiring the flat screen TV that nearly filled a wall.

"Your coats remind me of the ones those guys wore except yours are black."

Emmy walked out of the control room. "I didn't know you were coming. I would have let the guard know."

"No trouble," Freddie said.

"Well, come on in. Everyone else is here. I assume you know everyone, right?" Emmy asked.

140

Freddie and Marshall nodded and shook hands with the guys.

"Have a seat," Micah said as he pointed to the couch.

"Do I need to leave while you guys discuss band stuff?"

"You can stay, Em," Bobby said. "We're not discussing anything top secret."

Emmy sat on the arm of the recliner Bobby occupied.

"Okay, we kinda discussed our plan for the band yesterday. I know both of you guys can sing. I've heard you do some blues and Allman Brothers covers." Micah took charge of the meeting.

"I like the idea of two lead guitars," Quinten said. "We are going for a harder edge to the music."

"I don't mind singing some, but you've heard my voice. I sound like Gregg Allman with a sore throat," Freddie said. "Marshall sounds a bit better than me. We used to split the vocals in our band back in Texas."

Emmy leaned against Bobby and whispered, "That's the most I've heard him say."

"Hush." Bobby poked Emmy in the side. "Are we going to jam on some tunes?"

"We didn't bring our guitars because Miles said there would be several here," Marshall said.

"Kenny keeps a few at the house even when he's touring," Emmy said. "I'm sure he won't mind if you use them."

Fifteen minutes later Emmy had the board set to start recording. She did some level checks, and the guys sat in a circle in the studio.

"Do you need chord charts?" Miles asked.

"No, we can follow along."

"I made a list of cover songs that everyone should know. Should we start with those, or do one of the songs the worship team uses?" Micah asked.

"Let's do 'Sweet Home Alabama,'" Bobby suggested.

"Are you going to sing, Micah?" Quinten wondered.

"I'll give it a shot. If I sound too awful, just tell me."

They extended the jam to nearly ten minutes as Freddie, Marshall and Quinten traded solos. Micah played his acoustic

Gibson and did a decent job on the vocal.

"Did you get that, Em?" Micah asked as they discussed which tune to do next.

"Got it. Did you want to hear the playback?"

"Maybe later," Micah said. "Bobby wants to do 'La Grange.' He claims he can sing better then Billy Gibbons."

Emmy laughed. "I doubt it. I've heard him sing before, but let's give him a chance to embarrass himself."

The guys jammed for an hour before taking a break.

"Who's watching the kids, Em?" Bobby asked.

"I put them to bed before you guys arrived. They were wiped out from swimming all day. Want to run upstairs with me and check on them?"

"Sure. The guys are discussing goals, and I told them I would go along with whatever they decide."

Emmy and Bobby headed upstairs to the bedrooms.

Emmy peeked into the girls' room and then checked on Kevin Michael.

"How can they sleep with a band rocking out downstairs?"

"Kenny planned ahead. There's lots of soundproofing," Emmy answered. She leaned against the hallway wall.

Bobby put his hands on either side of her on the wall.

She looked up at him. "Am I making a mistake by not touring for... who knows how long?"

"That's for you to decide, but I know this last tour wore you out."

"How could you tell?" Emmy asked and then laughed. "Could it be because I would sit next to you on the plane and lean against you and fall asleep?"

Bobby grinned. "That would be part of it."

They talked for several minutes.

"Maybe we should go back downstairs before they send out a search party," Bobby suggested.

"They might think we're..." she paused.

"What?"

"Never mind." She ducked under his arm and started to head down the stairs.

142

Bobby grabbed her hand. "What would they think, Em?"

"I heard Micah and Quinten talking one day," she said and then looked into Bobby's eyes. "They were wondering if you and I had ever let our relationship get more serious than it should be."

"Shoot! I'll set them straight, Em."

"No, Bobby, that might make things worse. Let it go. Forget I ever said anything. We know we've never... you know."

"They should know it, too."

"Please, Bobby. Don't say anything."

He looked into her eyes for a moment. "Okay, I'll keep my mouth shut for you."

They headed back downstairs, and Emmy played back some of the jam session.

"Micah, you sound a lot better than I expected," Quinten said. "Of course, I assumed you would sound like Alvin."

"Alvin who?" Miles asked.

"You know. Alvin and the Chipmunks," Quinten said and then laughed.

Miles sat stoically.

"No clue, huh?"

"Never heard of them."

"Never mind," Quinten said and then shrugged.

"Should we talk about a name?" Micah asked.

"I've got a suggestion!" Emmy bounced on her toes.

"What would you call the band, Em?" Bobby asked.

"You guys like southern rock stuff, so how about The Bender Brothers Band? It would be like a tribute to The Allman Brothers Band."

The guys looked at each other for a moment without speaking. Then they all began to laugh.

"Thanks, but I don't think so, Em."

Emmy made a face at the guys. "Well, I like it."

The guys discussed names for a while. Several were suggested, but they couldn't come up with one they all liked.

"We could call ourselves Emmy's Old Band until we come up with something better," Bobby suggested in jest.

"We need to figure out when we can practice," Micah said.

143

"And where," Bobby added as he grinned at Emmy.

"I suppose you guys could use the basement as long as no one needs if for recording," Emmy said. "Of course, you have to call yourselves The Bender Brothers Band in exchange for the privilege of using it."

"Where else could we practice?" Micah asked.

"Fine! You guys can call yourselves whatever you want. Let me know when you want to practice."

The guys decided on a time that worked for everyone.

"I gotta skate," Quinten said and took off with Freddie and Marshall.

"Thanks for letting us jam tonight, Emmy," Micah said as he opened the door to leave. "You coming, Bobby?"

"In a minute. I need to make sure everything is shut down."

"Talk to you later. Thanks again, Emmy." Micah glanced at Bobby and then left.

"I can shut everything off, Bobby. You don't have to stay."

"I don't mind. I don't need to be anywhere, and no one is waiting at the apartment for me," Bobby said as he walked into the studio and checked to make sure everything was off.

Emmy stood in the doorway and waited. Bobby turned off the lights and tried to get past Emmy, but she didn't move.

"You should find someone."

He put his hands on her shoulders and looked into her eyes. "I haven't met anyone lately, and I didn't exactly made a wise choice the last time I was involved with someone."

"Pardon me, but Maria DeGott was the worst possible wife for you."

"Are you trying to tell me she was a bitch?"

"Yeah, but you couldn't see it."

"I can now," Bobby said and then chuckled. "The last I heard she was shacking up with Pedro from the band."

"Yuck! He's not nearly as hot as you," Emmy said as she turned around and walked back into the control room.

Bobby grinned. "You still think I'm hot, huh?"

She turned around and said, "I meant for a punk."

"You just wish..." he paused.

144

"Wished what?"

"Nothing."

"If you're going to hang around, you want a pizza? I'm kinda hungry. All I ate for dinner was some salad. I have to watch my figure, you know."

"Yeah, you look like you've gained a couple of ounces. What kind of pizza? Delivery?"

"I have some mini Home Run Inn pizzas in the freezer. That enough for you?"

"Sure. I have to watch my figure, too."

She poked him in the belly. "You are still as skinny as when we first met. You just didn't have tattoos back then."

"Hey! I'm not covered like some guys. I saw this guy at church who was inked all over."

"How could you tell?" She grabbed his hand and led him toward the stairs.

"He was wearing shorts and a t-shirt."

"I should show you my tattoos one of these days."

Bobby stopped suddenly and pulled Emmy toward him. She put a hand on his chest to keep her balance.

"Get out! You're yanking my chain, right?"

She shrugged and grinned before racing up the stairs.

I've seen you in a bikini, and I never noticed any ink. He walked slowly up the stairs.

She used the microwave and then the toaster oven to heat the pizzas while Bobby sat at the island and drank a Dr Pepper.

"You want the sausage or the cheese?" she asked.

"Sausage," he said.

"Sausage, please," she corrected as she cut the pizza into quarters.

"Yes, Mommy."

She tore off some paper towels and joined him at the island.

"Thanks, Em," he said as he looked at her hip.

"Still trying to guess where they are, huh?"

"You don't have any. You made a big fuss about getting your ears pierced. No way you've got any ink." He took a bite of pizza. "Shoot! This is hot."

145

"Ya think," she said and then giggled. "You made such a big deal over your first tattoo. You whined about how much it hurt for a week."

"Some hurt more than others. Have you ever thought about getting a tongue stud or a nose ring?" he asked and then blew on his pizza. "I'm kidding. I can't see you with a bunch of piercings."

"Do you think I would look good if I added purple highlights to my hair?"

He looked at her.

"I'm asking a serious question. Don't stare at me like I'm crazy," she said as she nudged her leg against his. "Would I?"

"You could probably pull that off. Your hair is dark enough. It might be too curly, though." He tugged on her hair. "Have you ever thought about a reverse perm?"

"Just a thought, and, no, I've never thought about getting it straightened."

"Ask Kenny about the piercings."

Emmy shook her head. "He would say no."

"He might surprise you. You got another Dr Pepper?"

She pointed to the fridge. "I'll take one, too."

Booby got up, grabbed two cans from the fridge and returned to his stool.

Emmy tried to grab one from his hand, but he jerked it back.

"What do you say?"

"Please, may I have a Dr Pepper, kind sir," she used her childish voice.

He handed her one.

"You're a punk," she said as she made a face at him.

"And you are a brat," he replied.

"Do you remember the water fight we had in Houston?" she asked.

"Was that Houston, or San Antonio?" Bobby asked while opening his pop. "I can't remember."

She swallowed a bite of pizza. "Somewhere in Texas. It had to be over a hundred in the shade. There were fans onstage that blew water on us to keep us from melting."

146

"After the show we used our Super Soakers and someone used a garden hose."

"Was that you?"

He shook his head. "It might have been Boyd or Perry. Whoever it was, you ended up soaked to the skin."

"And I was wearing a white t-shirt."

"I remember Adam got after the guys."

They reminisced about things that happened on tour for close to an hour.

"Can you imagine what it must be like for rock bands who don't go to church? They probably get even wilder."

"Only if they have a female singer on the bus, Em," Bobby said. "We were pretty mean to you at times."

"I let you guys tease me."

"You were a good sport. Most of the time anyway." He smiled at her and checked the time on the microwave. "I better go. Thanks for letting me hang out."

"Hey! I thought of another name for the band!"

He rolled his eyes. "What now?"

"Okay, Marshall Tucker got their name from a janitor's key or something like that. I mean there isn't anyone named Marshall Tucker in the band. Like no one is Jethro Tull. Anyway, I use Olivia Porter as a fake name..."

"We are not calling ourselves The Olivia Porter Band."

"No!" she swatted his shoulder. "I was thinking of The Oliver Porter Band. Oliver. Get it? How about that?"

Bobby shook his head. "I'd rather go with The Bender Brothers Band."

"You guys wouldn't know a good name for a band if it bit you in the butt." She slid down from the stool and walked toward the mudroom.

He followed. "Thanks for everything, Oliver. See you later."

"Wipe that stupid grin off your face and go away, punk." She opened the door into the garage for him. "The Oliver Porter Band rolls right off the tongue."

Chapter Sixteen

Emmy drove the kids to school Monday morning and waited in line with the other vehicles. The new sanctuary construction necessitated a different traffic pattern temporarily.

"What is our teacher's name? I forgot," Heather asked.

"Her name is Trina Payne, but you need to call her Mrs. Payne," Emmy said.

"She teaches Sunday School, Heather. How could you forget her name?" Isabella asked as she checked her backpack for her lunch. "Mommy, we've never had a black-lady teacher before, but Mrs. Payne seems nice."

"Of course she is. Why would you think she wouldn't be nice?" Emmy asked as she moved ahead in the line.

"Because you said Pastor Williams was scary."

Emmy hit the brakes hard and turned to look at Isabella. "I did not!"

"Yes, you did, Mom. Don't lie."

Emmy bit her lip and thought about it. "Okay, I might have said that, but I meant something different. Pastor Williams is big like Tony and John and he can be very serious at times. I didn't mean he was scary like..."

"Like Darth Vader?" Kevin Michael asked.

"He's not scary," Heather said. "He just breathes funny."

"Mrs. Payne is a very nice lady, and it doesn't matter how she looks."

"Is she as old as Me-maw?" Heather asked.

"I don't think so, but she is a grandmother."

Emmy made it to the front of the line and the volunteers helped get the kids out of her BMW.

"I will park and come in to make sure you know where to go," Emmy said.

"Mom! We know where to go," Heather rolled her eyes. "We are big girls now."

"I need to take Kevin Michael to his class."

"Mom!" Kevin Michael protested.

"Don't argue. I'm coming in."

148

Emmy parked and made her way inside. She said hi to Mary Galves and stopped to talk to Sloane Bertucci.

"Hi, Emmy, did you drop off the kids already?"

"I did, Sloane. I wanted to make sure Kevin Michael got to his class all right."

"I saw him with Ben, Gracie and Natalie earlier. They're all in Helen Chilton's class."

"She's the teacher who replaced Liz, right?" Emmy asked.

"Yes," Sloane said as she waved to some of the students.

"There's no way she can be as nice as Liz. I know Natty was disappointed Liz wouldn't be her teacher this year."

"Someone told me she's selling a brand of specialty fragrances and natural makeup to earn some income. Have you heard about that?"

"Jane Lorraine. I bought some perfume and makeup," Emmy said. "They're nice. I never used stuff like that before, but I do now."

You never wore makeup. I can't tell if you wear any now. Must be nice. Sloane directed some kids to the right classroom.

"I better let you do your job. Talk to you later." Emmy started to walk away but stopped. "Oh, what is Mama going to do now that all the kids are in school at least part of the time?"

"She wants to read more books and maybe help out at St. John's. Your brother has started a new project for the seniors."

"He never mentioned that to me," Emmy said.

"It just started," Sloane replied and then turned her attention to a couple of boys. "Slow down! No running!"

"See ya, Sloane." Emmy walked down the hall to Kevin Michael's class. *Father James didn't mention anything to me. I better call him later.* She peeked into the classroom and saw Kevin with his friends. She checked on the girls and saw them talking to Noemi, Zachary and Caden. I love how all the neighborhood kids are in the same class.

"Hello, you look a little old to be one one my students."

Emmy turned and smiled at Mrs. Payne.

Mrs. Payne hugged Emmy. "How are you, honey? I'm going to have a wonderful class this year."

"I just wanted to make sure the girls got to the right class," Emmy said as Mrs. Payne squeezed her tightly.

"I saw your name on the volunteer list. I appreciate you taking the time to be involved."

"I wish I could help more often."

"I understand. You are busy with your career. Stop in and see us whenever you have the time."

On her way out Emmy stopped to talk to Mary Galves.

"Hi, Emmy, can you believe school is starting already?" Mary asked.

"I'm ready for the kids to go back." Emmy looked around the classroom.

"I only have one student from the neighborhood." Mary pointed to Taylor Beckett Bertucci. "Soon all the kids from Bristol Ridge will be past kindergarten."

"Coby, Lily and Conor will start school in a few years. Of course you might not be teaching by that time," Emmy said as she waved to Taylor Beckett and some of the other kids.

"Why would you say that, Em?"

Emmy grinned. "Because you might have kids of your own by then, silly. See you later."

As Emmy was heading out, she saw Pastor Tyler talking to Pastor Darren Eaton. She walked up to them.

"Morning, Emmy," Tyler said. "Did you get the kids to school all right?"

"I did, and I saw Natty. Why aren't you down at Olivet? Kenny said you were teaching a class."

Tyler chuckled. "Because the class I'm teaching is only on Tuesday and Thursday mornings."

"Oh," she said. "Do we have to call you Professor Hammond now?"

Darren's green eyes sparkled. "He might end up being the college president one of these years."

"No way! We already lost Dr. Behren that way. We want to keep all of you guys for a long time," Emmy said as she walked away.

"Mommy! Mommy!" Heather and Isabella shouted as they rushed into the kitchen from outside.

"What is it? Where have you been? Your clothes are muddy. Take those shoes off before you track mud everyone." Emmy pointed to the mudroom. "Shoes off! Now!"

The girls returned a moment later.

"It's a good thing you changed clothes after school," Emmy said while shaking her head. "Now tell me your news."

"You tell it," Heather nudged Isabella.

"We were playing in the woods over that way. We went all the way to the road that curves around and guess what we saw."

"I give up. What did you see?" Emmy pulled two chicken breasts from the fridge.

"You didn't even guess, Mommy," Heather complained.

"Okay, did you see an elephant?"

"Get serious!" Heather sighed.

"We saw a moving van pull out of the driveway across the road. That means the new neighbors have moved in. We should go over there and see if they have any kids our age," Isabella said.

"Right now might not be the best time if they are just moving in. We should give them time to settle in," Emmy said.

"Can we go tomorrow?" Heather asked.

"Maybe we could go on Saturday. What would you like with chicken breasts for dinner?"

"Mashed potatoes and corn," Kevin replied as he walked into the pantry searching for a snack. "Gravy, too."

"Can we Skype with Daddy before dinner?" Isabella asked.

"We might talk to him tomorrow. He said he would be busy tonight." Emmy checked the fridge for some microwavable mashed potatoes. She pulled out a package and checked the date. "I love how easy these are." She watched as Kevin dashed out of the kitchen with a bag of pretzel sticks. She started to holler but didn't. *At least pretzels are healthier than chips.*

Emmy called Mona Robertson the next morning. "Hi, Mona, what can you tell me about the new family? The kids saw a moving van there."

151

"I haven't met them, but I know some details. Their names are James and Paige Plant. They have five kids. James is a neurosurgeon and Paige is an accountant who works from home. Bill was relieved when they purchased the property a couple of years ago. All the estates have homes on them now except for the land Bill gave to Bennett. I don't know if he will ever build a home here. Marissa doesn't like the woods at all."

Sounds like Marissa. Emmy laughed quietly. "Heather wanted to know if they have any kids her age. Do you know?"

"The oldest is in college. Princeton, I believe. The other children attend The Barclay Academy. One is in high school, and I think there might be one in junior high. The two youngest must be in elementary school."

"I didn't know Barclay had an elementary school. When did they start that?"

"Years ago, but it's really a separate school," Mona explained. "I was going to have lunch with Paige on Saturday. If you're not busy you could meet her."

"Where?"

"Over here. Bring the kids. I think Paige is bringing her two youngest," Mona said.

"I'll let you know later. Thanks, Mona."

"Is it still all right if I bring the girls over?" Emmy asked Mona shortly before one on Saturday. "We already ate."

"Yes, dear. Paige is here with her two youngest. Come on over."

Emmy used Kenny's Civic to drive over to the house. She dropped Kevin Michael off at Tony's because he wanted to play with Ben.

"Why did we use Daddy's car, Mom?" Heather asked. "Are your cars broke?"

"I drove your father's car because he doesn't drive it enough," Emmy said. *That's true, but I actually drove it because I didn't want to use either of mine. I didn't want Paige to think we spend money on fancy cars.*

Emmy pulled up to the front of Bill and Mona's and the

152

girls jumped out and ran to the front door. Emmy walked past a large black car parked by the portico. *I know that's a Mercedes, and they're more expensive than my BMW.* By the time Emmy reached the front door, Bill had opened it to let the twins inside.

"Nice car, huh?" Bill said with a smile.

"Yeah, but I bet I get better gas mileage in my Civic Si."

Bill glanced at the parking area and noticed Kenny's Civic. He looked at Emmy.

She shrugged. "It needs to be driven once in a while."

Mona introduced Emmy to Paige and the twins to Paul and Brienna.

" Grandma Mona, can we go upstairs and play with the big dollhouse,?" Isabella asked.

"Of course, dear. Go ahead," Mona said.

"Brienna, would you like to play with us?" Isabella asked.

Brienna looked at her mother who nodded. The three girls chattered as they ran out of the room and up the stairs.

Emmy sat on the love seat with Mona across from Paige and Paul, who sat on the couch.

"I was telling Paige about the history of Bristol Ridge," Mona said.

Emmy nodded. She looked mostly at Mona but would sneak glances at Paige. *I love that hairstyle and the blonde highlights. I know you have a son in college, but if I didn't know that, I would think you were only about forty. Your son looks bored to death, but he must have good manners because he's pretending to be interested in what Mona's saying.*

"There was nothing but woods when Bill purchased the property. He originally envisioned a golf course, but changed his mind. Kenny and Emmy were the first ones to build a home here."

Mona tried to get Emmy involved in the conversation without much success.

"Mona mentioned that Bill is your godfather," Paige said to force Emmy to talk.

"He knew my grandpa a long time ago."

Mona looked at Emmy after she didn't elaborate. "Emmy is too shy to mention her grandfather was one of the original

153

investors in Robertson Industries. He put the investment into a trust for Emmy and her sister until they turned twenty-five."

Paige knew enough about Robertson Industries to realize Emmy must have a rather sizable trust fund.

"It was a pleasure to meet you, Emmy," Paige said as she got ready to leave with her kids. "We should get together sometime so the girls can play."

"They would like that," Emmy said.

Near the end of the board meeting on Monday Pastor Tyler informed the board of a change in the office staff.

"Mrs. Millner has decided that since her husband is going to retire next month, she will retire also."

Jim Rosek shook his head. "All righty then. I never thought I'd live to see the day Harriet would retire. She and her family were original members of the church, and she's been managing the office for as long as I remember."

"Do you have a replacement?" Dylan Michaelis asked.

Tyler nodded. "We do. Lois Crawford has been Harriet's assistant for almost ten years. She has agreed to take over the position."

"We will save about a thousand dollars a month," Roger Goldman said with a smile.

As Emmy entered the foyer on Sunday morning she saw some people gathered around a table in the corner. She walked over to see what attracted everyone's attention and saw a poster of the Schulenbergs and a picture of the new CD.

"*Restoration*. I like that name," Emmy said to one of the other ladies.

"Fifteen dollars is too much for a CD," someone said.

"I thought this was supposed to be the worship team's CD. They aren't even mentioned," one lady said as she put the CD down and walked away.

I'll buy one after church. Emmy decided.

During the service Riordan mentioned the new project. "We have our brand new CD just released this last Tuesday on sale in the foyer for fifteen dollars. Sadie and I will be more than happy to autograph a copy for everyone."

Kristen turned to Emmy and whispered, "You never did that when your CDs came out. I don't think you ever brought CDs to church to sell."

"I brought my lion book to church," Emmy said.

"True, but you gave them away," Kristen replied. "People are not going to appreciate them selling their CD like this."

"I was going to buy one after church, but I don't need their autographs," Emmy said.

Pastor Tyler dismissed the congregation and Emmy and Kristen slowly made their way to the foyer. Emmy glanced at the table.

"I'm surprised they aren't selling t-shirts," Kristen said under her breath.

"If you look closely, I think there are t-shirts," Emmy said. "Notice there aren't any of the older people trying to buy anything. It's all teens and kids."

"It's like the merchandise table at one of your concerts, Em."

"Yeah. Maybe I shouldn't sell merchandise if I ever go on tour again."

Niles Talford called Emmy in the afternoon nine days later.

"Do you have good news?" Emmy asked with obvious glee.

"I do," he answered. "Sofia insisted I call you before you heard the news elsewhere. We have a son and his name is Landry Carl. Carl is my father's name."

"I like that name. Landry is cool. He'll probably grow up to be a football player. I want to hear all the details."

Niles told Emmy everything.

"I'm glad everyone is doing good. I can't wait to see him."

"I'm sure we will bring him to church as soon as we can, Emmy."

Chapter Seventeen

Garrick Winston led the way out of the new sanctuary and into the foyer. Daniel Keasling followed along with Roy Posey, Tyler Hammond and Reed Shafer.

"The guys did a great job of cleaning up," Tyler said. "We could set out the chairs and have a service this Sunday."

"The gray carpet allows the color on the walls to pop," Garrick said. "I was concerned at first, but it was the right choice."

"Waste Management picked up the dumpsters this morning," Reed added. "Now we can have the parking lot repaved and re-striped."

"I will call them later today," Roy said.

Garrick checked a text on his phone. "The final inspections are set for Wednesday. I don't foresee any issues, so you will be able to move into your new sanctuary starting Thursday."

Tony Bertucci and John Randolph trotted down the stairs at the far end and joined the group.

"I forgot how much room there was up there," Tony said while pointing up.

"Did you check out the tech room?" Tyler asked.

"Yeah! It looks like Kenny's recording studio," Tony said with a huge smile. "I'm glad we have people who know how to use all that new gear."

Tyler nodded. "We can now stream our service live and feed it to all parts of the old building and the school. I lost count of how many TV monitors we have."

Mr. Keasling shook his head. "I can't believe all the systems can be controlled on an iPad or a phone. All this new technology is beyond me."

"It's not that complicated," Garrick said. "Everything is smart-wired. If I open the app, I can tell you which lights are on. What the heating and cooling systems are doing. I can even play music throughout the building or in certain areas."

"What happens if the power goes out?" Mr. Keasling asked.

Roy pointed to the second floor. "The generators will kick

in after a few seconds. They're designed to run for a week if needed. They're the same kind we installed in the new hospital."

"With all the utilities now underground, I doubt if you will have any issues with power interruptions," Garrick reported.

Tyler shook hands with Mr. Keasling. "I can't believe we held the groundbreaking ceremony at the beginning of last November, and it looks like we will be able to have the dedication service almost exactly one year later. I never would have thought that possible."

"Anything is possible with a large enough crew," Garrick said.

"I think God had a part in it, too," Tony added with a smile.

Pastor Tyler unlocked the front door of the new sanctuary building Thursday morning. He held it open for Dr. Schofield and they stepped inside.

"I am impressed," Dr. Schofield said as he gazed upward and then around the large foyer. He walked over to the center of the foyer and looked back. "I love the glass wall. It lets in so much light."

Tyler turned off the alarm and then chuckled. "According to Mr. Tomanek it is strong enough to withstand a severe tornado."

"That's good. This is Illinois," Dr. Schofield said. "I like the welcome center, and is the coffee bar over there?"

"Yes. We have a much larger foyer than before, and we still have the coffee shop in the other building," Tyler said.

"Any complications with the inspections?"

Tyler shook his head and smiled. "We passed with flying colors. I admit to being nervous yesterday, but we are good to go."

"Isn't it amazing how God can provide?" Dr. Schofield patted Tyler on the back. "You have a new sanctuary and the church is debt free. That is fantastic!"

"We have some very generous people in the church. Did I tell you about our summer camp fund?"

"Not that I recall," Dr. Schofield said as he left the foyer and entered the sanctuary. "What is the capacity?"

"Right now it's limited by the number of chairs we have,"

Tyler answered. "We could squeeze fifteen hundred in here if we had to."

"And the camp fund?"

"We have close to ten thousand set aside for next year. Our goal is to send over a hundred kids to camp. We could send more, but the campground is limited."

"Perhaps some of our more affluent churches could start an expansion project," Dr. Schofield suggested.

Tyler chuckled. "I assume you mean us, right?"

"You do need to have something for your generous people to support."

"I could bring that up to the finance team."

Dr. Schofield walked up the steps onto the platform. He spread his arms wide. "There are some churches smaller than this. I suppose you need the room for Emmy to wander around."

"She doesn't dance around as much now," Tyler said.

"How are things going with your class? Is it taking more time than you expected?" Dr. Schofield asked about the Christian Faith class Tyler taught at Olivet Nazarene University.

"Not really. Pastor Herb helped me get started. Dr. Quanstrom did ask if I would consider teaching two sessions next semester."

"Will you have enough time? Is Liz going to start teaching again soon?" Dr. Schofield glanced at the ceiling. "Are all the lights LEDs?"

"I believe so," Tyler said after looking at the ceiling. "We haven't decided about Liz teaching. She would like to stay home, but we have to check the finances."

"I am a firm believer in stay-at-home moms, and I also believe God takes care of all our needs. How is your healthcare plan?"

"The church makes sure all the staff members are covered and pays all the costs."

"Good. I would have been surprised to hear otherwise," Dr. Schofield said as he walked down the steps and toward the back of the sanctuary. "If you have the time, I'd love to take you and Liz out to lunch."

"I'll text her and see what she and Phoebe are doing."

"Are you planning to use the new sanctuary this Sunday?" Dr. Schofield stopped in the middle of the sanctuary and looked up. "I wouldn't want to have to climb up there to change a light bulb."

"Neither would I," Pastor Tyler said. "We decided not to push it this week, but we will move into the new building the following Sunday. The dedication ceremony is still set for the first Sunday in November as long as you are still available."

"I believe that is on my calendar."

Saturday morning the members of the tech team met with representatives from DelSasso Sound and Stadius Acoustic Works to dial in the new audio and video gear. Sean DelSasso introduced the guys to the crew. Mitchell Gallagher, Nate Burkett and Donte DiVirgilio, the owners and founders of Stadius Acoustic Works, shook hands with everyone.

"I want to thank you for allowing us to provide the gear for your beautiful new building," Mitchell said.

Nate Burkett pulled Sean aside to ask, "Has everything arrived and been installed?"

"We are waiting for some of the TV monitors, but all the audio gear has been installed. We did have an issue getting all the wireless gear to sync, but one of your technicians took care of it," Sean answered. "All the LEDs are working. Jeff and Josh Morrissey have already programmed some scenes. They love the moving fixtures. We didn't use anything like that in the old sanctuary."

Mitchell continued to talk to the people on the tech crew. Many of them worked professionally for Steward Music Group, or some of the local bands.

"How do you like the new Avid VENUE boards?" Mitchell asked Stuart Lederer the senior engineer at Steward Music Group.

"It took me a while to really learn the full capabilities, but I love the clean sound. It might take some time to train all the techs here at the church, but most of them work for me," Stuart said. "Bruce Sutherland is the lead engineer for the church, but he's working for Fridays At Five at the moment. He's familiar with the Avid boards."

"The boards work well with the new Martin Acoustic Pro speaker arrays, and the Anacrusis subs are amazing."

"I agree," Stuart said. "I'm eagerly anticipating the rehearsals next week. I think the worship team will love the new system."

Mitchell nodded. "The new personal monitor system will allow each musician to mix up to forty-eight channels. That is quite an advance over the older systems."

"The new software is incredible. I can see exactly what frequencies need to be adjusted throughout the building."

Donte DiVirgilio walked onto the platform with Robby Collins. "Are you going to isolate the acoustic drums?"

"Since the sanctuary is so large, and the platform is enormous, we want to try something different. We will have the kit on a riser with some Plexiglas in front, but nothing on the sides or the top," Robby explained.

"I still play drums at my church," Donte said. "It's a much smaller building, so we use a Roland TD-50KV to control the sound level on the stage."

"We've never used e-drums in the sanctuary, but the teens use an older Roland set. I've played it, but I'm an acoustic guy."

"You should try the TD-50s. The feel is amazing," Donte said.

"Do you use a regular kick drum?" Robby asked.

"Yes, there's a pad that goes over it," Donte said and then explained more about the latest e-drum kit from Roland.

"I'll have to stop by DelSasso Sound and try one."

More of the worship band arrived, and Stuart and Mitchell headed upstairs to the sound booth. For the next couple of hours the various tech people had a chance to play with the new toys.

"We will be here Tuesday," Mitchell said. "We will stay in town until all the bugs are worked out."

Stuart shook his hand. "Maybe we'll be fortunate and there won't be any glitches."

Chapter Eighteen

"Emmy, I'm glad I caught you," Diane said around noon on Monday.

"What's up? I was just about to head to Sainsbury's to do some grocery shopping," Emmy said.

Diane wasn't sure how to tell Emmy what had happened, so she just blurted out, "Mona is at St. Bart's. She had open heart surgery..."

"WHAT!!!???" Emmy screamed loud enough to hurt Diane's ear. "Tell me you're kidding."

"Sorry, Em, but she was having chest pains during the night yesterday so Bill called 9-1-1. They rushed her to the hospital, did some tests or whatever and told them she needed the surgery right away. I should have called you earlier, but I knew how you'd react." *Crap! I know you're crying. I should have come over and told you in person.* "Are you okay?"

"Is Mona all right?" Emmy finally calmed down enough to ask.

"Well, Brady said she's resting as comfortably as possible. I'm sure she's on a bunch of pain meds and stuff. I just dropped Lily and Conor off with Kristen, and I'm on my way back to St. Bart's..."

"I want to go with you. Pick me up! What do you mean by back to...?" Emmy asked, but Diane had already hung up.

Diane picked Emmy up and headed to the hospital.

"You mean she's be in the hospital for over a day and you didn't tell me! I absolutely hate you, Diane!"

"Em, I know how much you care for Bill and Mona, but they are my in-laws. Not yours. Besides, there was nothing you could do, and she was in intensive care."

"Can't this car go any faster?" Emmy complained.

"I'm going ten over the limit. We will get there as soon as I can. You need to learn to be patient."

Emmy jumped out of the BMW 5 Series before Diane came to a full stop in the parking deck.

"Emmy! You are going to get hurt one of these days,"

Diane hollered as she got out of the car.

"Hurry up, Diane! I'll hold the elevator for you," Emmy shouted.

They rushed into the hospital, got their visitor passes and headed upstairs. Even though only family was supposed to be allowed to see Mona, Emmy walked right in.

Diane followed. *I actually am family, so I suppose since Emmy is my sister, she is kinda like family, too.*

Emmy saw Mr. Robertson sitting in a recliner next to Mona's bed. She rushed over and looked at Mona, who was sleeping.

"The doctor said she's doing great. They've already moved her into a regular room." Bill stood up and put his hands on Emmy's shoulders. He felt her quivering and knew she was crying. "It's all right. She will be as good as new in a couple of weeks." He kissed the top of her head. "The surgery was a complete success."

Diane walked over to Brady. "Any change?"

"Not really. She is supposed to sleep for several hours," he answered.

"Where are Bennett and Marissa?" Diane asked.

"They went out to grab some food. They were here all night."

"So were you, and I only went home to change clothes and check on the kids."

"Did you explain everything to Carson and Caden?"

"Yes, and I'm not sure if they realize how serious this is. They think of my mother as being sick and she looks fine."

Emmy turned to face Mr. Robertson. She bit her lip and looked up into his eyes but couldn't say anything.

"You can pull up a chair and sit by me, or you can sit in the recliner."

Brady moved one of the chairs for Emmy.

"Thank you, Brady," she whispered as she sat down. "I don't want to wake up Mona."

"You could hold a concert in here and she wouldn't wake up, Emmy," Brady said trying to be funny, but he saw the horrified expression on Emmy's face. "I only meant because of the meds.

162

She will wake up without any trouble."

Mr. Robertson held Emmy's hand. *You still have small hands, Emmy.* He smiled at her and squeezed her hand. *I remember sitting in my recliner at home with you on my lap. You must have been about two. Maybe younger. Lily and I were watching you for some reason that I can't remember. You knew how to play patty-cake or whatever it was called and were trying to teach me how to clap. You would laugh and giggle. Eventually you fell asleep on my chest and I took an hour long nap with you.*

"What are you thinking about, Mr. Robertson?"

"I was recalling one of my favorite memories," he said with a smile.

Two days later Emmy stopped at the house to visit Liz and Phoebe after seeing Mona and Bill at the hospital.

"How are they doing?" Liz asked. "We have been praying for them a lot. Natty prays for them at night. She calls them Aunt Emmy's other grandma and grandpa."

"Aw, that's so cute. Heather and Isa have always called them Grandma Mona and Grandpa Bill."

Emmy mentioned a few products she needed. Liz checked her Jane Lorraine stock and placed the items in a gift bag.

"Oh, did you check your email this morning?" Liz asked as she sat down with Phoebe.

Emmy reached out and Liz handed Phoebe to her.

"I just fed her, so she should be good."

"You are as cute as ever," Emmy grinned at Phoebe who smiled back. "What about email?"

"Regina had the baby last night."

"She did! I didn't hear anything."

"They knew they were having a boy but wouldn't reveal a name."

"What did they name him?" Emmy asked while making funny faces at Phoebe.

"D'Andre Sahil."

"What?"

Liz spelled the name for Emmy.

163

"Oooh! I'm not sure I like that name," Emmy said and then put a hand to her mouth. "Please don't tell anyone I said that."

"I'm not overly fond of it, either, to be totally honest," Liz admitted. "Do you have any idea how long Mona will be at St. Bart's. Tyler and Pastor Ausland talked to her and Bill yesterday."

"Mr. Robertson thought it would be another week. They try to send patients home as soon as possible."

"Are you going to help take care of her when she gets home?"

"You know the answer to that," Emmy said as she handed Phoebe back. "I think she is poopy."

"Em! How can you say my precious Phoebe is poopy?" Liz teased.

"Not her! Her diaper, and when did you switch to disposables?"

"Last week. The cloth diapers were starting to smell no matter how often I washed them."

"I never used cloth diapers. My mother used them on me and Diane, but I don't remember wearing them," Emmy said.

Liz spread a changing mat on the couch and changed Phoebe. "You are such a goof at times, Em."

"I should run. I have to stop at the store to get something to make for Mr. Robertson's dinner. Kenny left this morning, so I have to be back in time to pick up the kids."

"Mr. Robertson is coming home at night, right?"

"Yes, the doctor convinced him it wouldn't be good for his health to stay overnight."

"Is anyone?"

"Not now. I plan to see Mona every morning until she comes home. I'm going to spoil her when she gets home. I may not be a nurse, but I certainly know how to clean a house and cook meals," Emmy said and then giggled.

"What's so funny?" Liz asked.

"I probably should have been a maid."

"You can come over here and clean to your heart's content, Em."

Eight days later Diane called Emmy's cell phone and it went directly to her voicemail. "Where are you, Em?" Diane didn't leave a message but dialed the landline instead.

"Hi, Kenny, sorry to bother you because I know you have to leave soon, but where is Emmy? I need to talk to her."

"She's over at Bill and Mona's cleaning the house again. She wants it to be spotless when Mona comes home," he answered.

"Good, because she's coming home today. In a couple of hours actually. She won't need to come to St. Bart's today. She's been here so much the nurses think she works here."

"That's quick. It's been less than two weeks, right?"

"Ten or eleven days. I can't remember exactly," Diane said. "She didn't answer her cell phone."

"She might have mine. You could try it. Do you have the number?"

"I think it's in my contacts list. I'll try it."

Diane eventually reached Emmy and told her the news.

"That's great. I'm about finished here. What should I make for dinner? I made lasagna last night for Mr. Robertson. There is some left, but I don't want Mona to have leftovers on her first night back home."

"Lasagna is better the second day. That's what you always say."

"I could make a fresh salad."

"The doctors have put Mona on a strict diet for now."

Diane explained what she knew about the foods Mona should eat.

"I can fix fish for her, and let Mr. Robertson have the lasagna."

Diane laughed.

"What's so funny?"

"You've known Bill all your life even if you don't remember it, and yet you insist on calling him Mr. Robertson. You are supposed to be an adult now. He won't mind if you call him Bill."

"Do you remember that dinner party we went to with Fernando and Ethan?"

165

"I remember," Diane answered.

"He asked me to call him Bill that night, but I just couldn't," Emmy said.

Diane laughed again. "Em, you were fourteen."

"Was not! I was almost twenty-one," Emmy insisted.

"Okay, you only acted..."

"I'm hanging up. Call me back when Mona and Mr. Robertson are on their way."

Three hours later Emmy saw Brady's black Mercedes E-Class pull into the parking area in the front of the house as she finished cleaning the sidelights on the front door. *About time!* She quickly gathered the paper towels and Windex and put them back into the cleaning supplies closet. She took one last look around before she hurried outside and raced down the steps and over to Mona.

"I have heard you've been working too hard," Mona said.

Mr. Robertson walked by her side as she carefully climbed the stairs.

"Shouldn't you be in a wheelchair?" Emmy asked.

"The doctors insist I get more exercise," Mona replied. "They made me walk five miles a day before they would release me."

Mona looked around as she entered the wide hallway. "The house has never been this clean, Emmy. Thank you."

Emmy beamed with pride. "You are most welcome, m'lady." She even curtsied.

"You're a goof, Em," Diane said as she wiped a smudge of dirt from Emmy's cheek.

Diane, Emmy and Mr. Robertson helped Mona get settled while Brady carried in her suitcase and other items from St. Bart's. Mona and Mr. Robertson sat in their leather recliners in the front parlor.

"Would you like something to drink?" Emmy asked. "You are supposed to drink lots of water."

"A glass of water would be very nice. Thank you, Emmy."

Emmy scurried away to get the water.

Mona shook her head and looked at Diane. "I'm not going

166

to let her wait on me all the time."

Diane laughed. "She will spoil you rotten if you let her get away with it."

Emmy returned with a pitcher of ice water and a small plate of sliced lemons on a silver serving platter.

Diane rolled her eyes. Mr. Robertson grinned. Mona thanked Emmy.

"Em, who is that sitting in the recliner?" Diane asked as she pointed to Mr. Robertson deliberately trying to embarrass her sister.

Emmy frowned at Diane. "You know who." *What are you doing?*

"What is his name?" Diane asked.

"Mr. Robertson. I know what you're doing. I can't help it if I need to call him that."

Mr. Robertson spoke up to defuse the situation. "I think it's very sweet that Emmy calls me that. I don't mind in the least."

Emmy grinned at him and then stuck out her tongue at Diane.

"Such a baby," Diane muttered. "I'll take Brady home. We will check on you later. I need to wrap some presents for Conor."

Emmy put a hand to her mouth. "I almost forgot. He turns one today."

"We will have a party for him on Saturday. He won't know the difference," Diane said.

"Thank you, Diane. I'm sure we will be all right with Emmy here," Mona said. "Please give my love to all the kids."

Later, Emmy returned to the living room, noticed Mona's eyes were closed and whispered to Mr. Robertson, "I have some leftover lasagna and garlic bread for you if you're hungry."

Mona opened her eyes. "I'm not sleeping, Emmy. Just resting my eyes."

"I have a fresh garden salad with lots of veggies for you. I baked some fish, and I can mix some vinegar and oil for the salad."

"That sounds delicious, dear, but I would love a small portion of lasagna. It's always better the next day, you know."

167

Chapter Nineteen

Andy Walker handed his corporate Visa card to the shocked ticket seller. "Yes, I want to pay for all the tickets. I called earlier and talked to Alan Freedman in the group sales department. He said he would meet us."

She flipped her long platinum hair over her shoulder, looked at the credit card and noticed the corporate name. She looked back at Andy with wide open eyes. "Is this real?"

He laughed. "I've been using it for years, so I hope it's real."

She called group sales and Alan Freedman appeared in a matter of seconds.

He walked up to Andy, shook his hand and said, "Welcome to the Rock and Roll Hall of Fame!"

Four hours later the buses departed the Hall of Fame. One of the buses headed to the hotel while the others headed to the Quicken Loans Arena where the crew would finish preparations for the final night of the tour.

Kenny walked down the hotel hallway with Andy to his room. "I could spend an entire week going through all the exhibits at the Hall of Fame."

"I was bored after a few minutes," Andy said but then laughed. "Gotcha!"

"Maybe I shouldn't tell you, but I've always dreamed we would make it to the Hall one of these days."

"You mean as inductees, right? I don't think they make inductees pay to get into the building," Andy joked.

"Crazy dream, huh?" Kenny shrugged.

Andy slapped him on the back. "I'd say you guys are a solid bet. Unless they change the rules, you guys should be inducted in 2021. That's twenty-five years after your first recording."

"I wish I had your confidence, Andy," Kenny said.

The band played the final show of the tour. Kenny walked off the stage, handed his guitar to Frankie and accepted a clean towel from him. "One more for the books, huh, Frankie?"

"Here's your cell phone, boss. Emmy called earlier. She wanted you to wake her up when you get home," Frankie said.

Kenny laughed. "If I wake her up, I get yelled at for disturbing her sleep, and if I let her sleep, I get yelled at for not waking her up. What should I do?"

Frankie wiped off the guitar and shook his head. "Never been married. Don't know what to tell you. I'll bring the guitars over on Monday if that's all right."

"Frankie, if you ever decide you don't want to travel anymore, I think I'll call it quits, too."

"What would I do if you guys didn't tour?" Frankie asked.

Kenny slipped into bed just after four in the morning. He nudged Emmy, and she rolled over and opened her eyes.

"Hi, I'm home," he said while grinning.

"So I see."

"The tour is over. I'll be home with you every day now."

"That's good," she said and then yawned.

"Do you want to hear about the show?"

"Yes, tell me all about it."

He lay on his back and told her about the show. He turned on his side and mentioned the visit to the Rock and Roll Hall of Fame.

"Did you see Elvis?"

"We did," he answered. He moved onto his back again and rambled on for several minutes before he looked over at Emmy. He smiled and watched her chest rise and fall as she slept. "I'll tell you more in the morning, Em."

Emmy walked into the new sanctuary building with the kids after Sunday School.

"Mommy, why are there so many people here, and why are we going to this new building? Don't we have children's church today?" Kevin Michael asked as he tried to loosen the tie Emmy made him wear.

"This is a special Sunday, so you won't have children's church," Emmy explained for the third time that morning.

169

"Do we have to sit with you and Daddy, or can we sit with Noemi and Gracie?" Heather asked.

"I think families are supposed to sit together today," Tony Bertucci said as he walked up behind them.

"I asked Kristen if she could save some seats," Emmy said as she zigzagged her way through the crowded foyer.

Tony followed as best he could.

Emmy entered the spacious new sanctuary of Crest Ridge United Nazarene and looked to the left where Kristen said she would be sitting with her family. "I see John and Kristen," Emmy grabbed Tony's arm and pointed. "Let's grab those seats while we have a chance."

"Sloane is heading that way, too." Tony watched as his kids followed Sloane into the row of chairs in front of John and Kristen.

Eventually, Kenny made his way into the sanctuary along with Andy. They spotted Emmy and sat beside her.

"I wonder how many chairs they have available?" Emmy asked.

"Don't know for sure, but it looks like they've used every available space to put one," Kenny answered.

"It won't be this packed next week when they go back to two services," Tony said as he turned to face Emmy from his seat in the row in front. "How will they ever cram all these people into the gym for the potluck?"

Emmy giggled and tapped Tony's arm. "Are you worried you might not get fed?"

"Not at all. Haven't you ever heard the story in John about the fishes and loaves of bread?"

"I hope we have a better variety," Emmy joked.

"What did you think of the service?" Emmy asked John Randolph after Pastor Tyler dismissed the congregation with a prayer and instructions for the potluck.

"I liked it, but I kept waiting for someone to use incense," he joked. "Why don't your priests wear robes?"

Emmy made a face at him and poked him in the arm. "You know they're not priests."

Heather tugged on Emmy's dress. "Mommy! We need to go

170

to the gym right now! Pastor Tyler said families with small children can go first."

"Shush, Heather," Kenny said. "He meant families with babies and real little kids. You guys aren't considered little anymore."

"But I am starving," Heather said as she rubbed her belly. "I haven't had anything to eat since breakfast, and that one man talked for hours. It was way too long. We need food before we starve to death."

"If it's all right with everyone, I'll take all the kids to the gym," Sloane offered. "The older ones can fix their own food, and I'll help the younger ones."

"Are you sure, Sloane?" Kristen asked. "You don't have to do that."

"I don't mind. That will give you a chance to mingle."

The kids followed Sloane as if she were the Pied Piper of Hamelin.

Emmy stood on her tiptoes and looked around the still crowded sanctuary. All of a sudden she hollered, "Lynette!" She waved and then told Kenny, "I see Lynette and Paul Jefferson over there. I absolutely have to talk to her. I'll find you in the gym. Save me a place, please."

"Okay, Em," Kenny answered.

Emmy weaved her way through the crowd and eventually made her way to Paul's side. She waited patiently as Lynette talked to one of the older ladies.

Lynette ended the conversation, turned to Emmy and held out her arms. "Let me have a hug."

Emmy began to cry. "I haven't seen you in like a million years," Emmy whispered.

After a long hug Lynette let go. "Let me look at you." Lynette checked Emmy out. "You haven't gained a pound, and you don't look any older. How did you manage that?"

"I look older," Emmy insisted.

"Maybe a year at the most. I look twenty years older than when we left, and I've gained a few pounds," Lynette admitted. "That's from having teenage girls. Your time will come."

"Hi, Paul. I didn't mean to ignore you," Emmy said as she hugged him.

He smiled. "It's good to see you, Emmy. Lynette, I think I will start heading to the gym. I have a few people I need to talk to." He left the ladies alone.

"Where are your girls?" Emmy asked.

"Back in Iowa City with their grandparents."

"How old are they now?"

"Fourteen, but they think they are eighteen," Lynette said and then laughed. "I'm not complaining. They are great kids. I never have any trouble with them. Not serious trouble anyway. They are bigger than you, Emmy."

"I'm afraid Heather and Isa will be bigger than me in a couple of years. I know Kevin Michael will be."

"We have to catch up with each other. I want to know everything the church is doing," Lynette said.

"When do you guys have to head home?" Emmy asked.

"Tomorrow morning. Paul has to get back to work."

"We have to talk again after we eat, okay?" Emmy asked. "I have to let you see the kids."

"I promise, Emmy. Let's find each other later."

"I'm full," Kevin Michael said. "Can I go play?" He showed Emmy his empty plate.

"Okay, but do not go outside." She looked at the twins. "Are you finished? I want you to meet someone."

Heather jammed the rest of her hot dog into her mouth and nodded. Isabella drank the last of her milk and said, "We're ready."

Emmy stood up and glanced around the room. She spotted Paul Jefferson, because he stood taller than most people, talking to Herb and Carolyn Ausland. *There you are.* She caught sight of Lynette with her back turned as she talked to Lenore Toth. "Follow me, girls," Emmy said and led the way across the gym.

Emmy waited until Lynette finished talking and then introduced the twins.

"You were still babies when we left," Lynette said. "Well, not exactly babies, but you were only a year old."

"We will be nine in January," Heather said.

"I have twin girls, Ruth and Esther, but they're quite a bit older," Lynette said. "They were in your mother's wedding."

Heather and Isabella looked at each other with obvious confusion.

"They were the flower girls," Lynette explained.

After a couple of minutes Emmy let the girls find their friends and grinned at Lynette. "Can we find a place to talk? I have so much to tell you."

"Give me a minute, and I'll join you," Lynette said.

"I'll wait over there with Kenny," Emmy said.

"I'm all yours," Lynette said a few minutes later. "Hi, Kenny, it's good to see you again."

"And you, too," Kenny said.

"We'll be back."

Emmy and Lynette sat on a couch in the teacher's lounge.

"Oh, Lynette, do you remember how much I pestered you with my problems with men? I must have been such a nuisance."

Lynette laughed. "You were rather confused about your feelings toward certain people, but I never considered you a pest."

"Did I ever tell you that Tony proposed to me?" Emmy asked.

Lynette tilted her head. "If you did, I have forgotten, and I doubt I would have forgotten something like that."

"We didn't tell a lot of people because I said no. Obviously, since I married Kenny," Emmy said as she rolled her eyes. "I kinda gave him the wrong message about how I felt one night, and he bought a ring and he and Mama took me out to Ciao Bella. He was supposed to ask me there, but he kept getting interrupted. We can laugh about it now, but he was frustrated that night."

"So where did he propose?" Lynette asked.

"In the living room," Emmy said.

Lynette held out her hands. "Whose living room?"

"Oh!" Emmy giggled. "My living room. The house I shared with Kristen. I felt so awful that night because it was all my fault he bought a ring." Emmy glanced at her finger. "Oh! This is the actual ring he bought." She held out her hand to Lynette.

"What!?" Lynette did a double take. "Isn't that the ring

Kenny gave you? It looks like it. You showed it to me when you got engaged. Why are you still wearing it?"

"I should explain something," Emmy said and then bit her lip.

"Yes, you need to explain."

Emmy tried to scoot back on the couch as if she wanted to hide.

"Explain!" Lynette insisted.

"Okay," Emmy said but then she wouldn't continue. She put her arms over her chest and sat quietly.

"What did you do to cause Tony to buy a ring? I know you didn't sleep with him. What did you do?" Lynette asked softly.

"We went farther than ever before that night and again the next day. I knew it was wrong, but I couldn't help myself," she paused. "I might have said something about if he wanted more I would need to get engaged." Emmy took a deep breath. "I never admitted that to anyone. Not Kristen or Kenny or anyone. It was wrong, but I wasn't thinking straight."

"Oh, Emmy," Lynette said and then sighed. "You should have known better, but you were still pretty young."

"At least Tony got his money back, and now we're best friends. He's like my big brother."

Lynette held Emmy's hand and looked at the ring. "I've never heard of anyone buying an engagement ring from someone whose proposal was turned down."

"I know, but there's more. I saw this ring about a month earlier when I was shopping with Kristen. I once told someone that God had Tony buy it because it wouldn't have been there when Kenny needed it. Does that make any sense?"

Lynette laughed. "Coming from anyone else, no. It would not make a lick of sense, but from you, yeah. I get it."

They hugged and spent several minutes talking about the church. Lynette asked about several couples she had known. Emmy caught Lynette up on news.

"So you think Pastor Herb will officially retire soon, huh?" Lynette asked.

"I'm pretty sure. Tyler and Darren are doing a great job. No one thinks of them as being too young anymore."

They talked about other old friends and then Emmy paused.

"I can tell you have something to ask, or confess. You used to always bite your lip like that when you wanted to talk about guys. Spill it!"

"Have I ever mentioned Rory Porter?"

Lynette thought for a few seconds. "The name doesn't ring a bell. Who is he?"

Emmy explained how Rory lived in the same neighborhood. She mentioned Rory's reputation with the ladies and how he disappeared from her life for many years. She explained how she reunited with him at the nursing home.

"Did your father ever remember him?" Lynette asked.

Emmy shook her head. "He never gave me that impression. He would talk about Rory but only as his therapist. Rory and I spent a lot of time together. We talked about the old days back in Raynor Park. I put some of the things Rory and I did in my book."

"What book? I bought the one about the lions, but there's nothing about growing up in it."

"Oh, I wrote another one. I called it *Adventures In Raynor Park*. It's about me growing up. There are stories about me and Kenny and a couple about Barry Newton," Emmy said but then paused.

"And some about this Rory character, huh?" Lynette asked. "Tell me more."

"There are some about me and Rory, but not everything. We did some stuff that weren't the best choices." Emmy waved her hands. "Nothing too terrible, but stuff that I would never let Heather or Isa do."

"Did your parents know what you were doing?" Lynette asked.

"I'm not sure. At the time I didn't think they knew I would sneak out of the house, but I've since learned that Mom knew. She didn't tell Daddy because he would have grounded me for life, and he would have killed Rory."

Lynette stared at Emmy for a moment. "That would have been a rather strong reaction for doing some not so terrible stuff,"

Lynette said using air quotes. "What exactly did you do? Or can't you tell me?"

"I suppose it's all right to tell you now," Emmy said while staring at the floor.

Lynette waved a hand. "No, don't tell me. But I will say parents often know more than we think."

"I plan to keep a closer eye on my girls. We live in a different type of neighborhood. The girls won't have as many chances to... do stuff like I did."

"Are you and Rory still friends?"

Emmy explained how Rory now lived in Florida.

"That's not what I asked."

"Yes, we are still friends, but just friends," Emmy said and then bit her lip.

Lynette laughed and grabbed Emmy's hands. "You are a terrible liar. Don't ever try to bluff anyone."

"I'm not lying. We are just friends." Emmy took a deep breath and held it.

Lynette stared into Emmy's eyes. "I can still tell if you are holding back."

Emmy's shoulders slumped as she let out her breath. "Fine! I had a crush on Rory when we were kids because he was one of the bad boys in the neighborhood. That attracted me to him, but he never even kissed me back then."

"Back then?"

Emmy put a hand to her mouth. "Crap! I shouldn't have said that. But I did kiss him just to see how if would feel. Nothing more."

"Even though you had Kenny?" Lynette asked.

Emmy nodded. "Does that make me a bad person?"

"No, it means you are human."

"We should get back to the gym. Kenny and Paul are probably wondering where we are," Emmy said and then hugged Lynette again. "I'm so happy to see you again."

Chapter Twenty

Two weeks later Emmy and Liz were walking along the corridor leading from the educational unit to the new sanctuary talking about Phoebe when Kenny and Tyler joined them. Emmy heard Tyler mention something about three years.

"I can't wait until she's walking," Liz said as she carried Phoebe on her hip. "She likes to crawl, but I'm afraid to let her go in here. There are too many kids running around. She might get trampled."

"I can't believe Tyler has been senior pastor for three years already. The time has flown by," Emmy said as she grinned at Phoebe. "I'll carry her if you want."

"Amazing, huh?" Liz mentioned as she passed Phoebe over to Emmy.

"How's your class doing, Pastor Tyler? Are they learning anything from you?" Emmy asked. She smiled at Phoebe and said, "You are such a cutie."

Phoebe jabbered and made happy noises at Emmy.

"I'm doing my best to make things easy for them to absorb the knowledge," Tyler answered with a chuckle.

"Have you ever thought about teaching another class?" Kenny asked.

"I'm not sure I have the time."

Liz said, "He wants to start working on a doctorate in religion."

"For real?" Emmy asked.

Tyler nodded as he scooted out of the way as three ten-year-old boys scampered past. "Slow down!"

"If you get a PHD, will we have to call you Dr. Hammond?"

"You may still call me Professor Hammond," Tyler answered with a straight face.

"Emmy, when is your book coming out?" Liz asked. "I thought you said you finished it."

"I did and it's supposed to be released in a couple of weeks. I doubt if anyone will buy it because it isn't a kids' book," Emmy said. "There's nothing about talking lions or cats in it. It's definitely for mature, older people."

"I think you might sell a few copies, Emmy," Tyler said and then chuckled. "Especially if you reveal any secrets."

Emmy made a face at Tyler. "It's not that kind of a book, and I don't have too many skeletons in the closet."

Kenny coughed and Emmy tried to kick his shin.

"You're lucky I'm carrying Phoebe, or else you would both be in big trouble."

A few minutes later Kenny and Emmy found seats on the aisle for the service and she asked, "Are you going to take some more classes now that you're finished touring?"

He looked at her and shrugged. "I'm not sure, Em. I have kinda lost interest for the time being," he admitted.

"You don't have to be in a hurry to get your degree. You could spread it out over a few years. Who knows? Maybe you and the girls could graduate from college at the same time," she teased.

Kenny glanced down at the aisle and grinned. "Phoebe, where are you going?"

"Come back here!" Liz shouted as she chased after Phoebe.

"Pastor, I'm sorry to bother you on a Saturday morning, but I just talked to one of my college friends from Olivet," Roger Goldman said over the phone. "He and his wife are members of SoHam First Nazarene, and he's on the board. They met last night and Pastor Mauston shocked them by tendering his resignation effective in two weeks. Did you know about this? I know you keep in contact with him."

"No inkling whatsoever. What happened?" Tyler asked. "I talked to Tom earlier in the week, and everything seemed to be all right."

"According to my friend, Pastor Mauston is leaving the ministry completely. He said he had a business opportunity that he had been exploring for some time."

"He never mentioned anything about a business opportunity to me. I've known him for several years. Wow! This is a total surprise to me."

178

"I'm assuming the church might need to provide someone to fill the pulpit for a time," Roger said. "The only other member on staff over there left a couple of months ago. He started that church for motorcyclists."

"I'm sure we can help out for as long as needed. I'll call Tom and talk to him today."

Tyler left a message for Pastor Mauston and called again five hours later after not receiving a return call. Pastor Mauston answered and they chatted for a few moments before Tyler brought up the real reason for his call.

"Is this something that has been in the works for a long time?" Tyler asked.

"I have thought about it over the years, but an opportunity presented itself that I cannot ignore."

Tyler wondered if the declining attendance and loss of revenue might be a major part of the reason for leaving, but he didn't ask.

"I know what everyone must be thinking," Pastor Mauston said. "I will admit the declining attendance played a part in the decision. I feel the time has come for a change in the leadership of the church. I would hate for it to suffer the same fate as some of our other small churches and have to close completely."

They talked for a few more minutes before Tyler brought up the subject of pulpit supply. "I'm sure we can help for as long as needed," Tyler offered.

"I appreciate that, Tyler. I will let our board know. They will make the decision."

The Crest Ridge church board met Monday evening and after going through the various team reports and other monthly business, the next item on the agenda involved Pastor Tyler and his staff.

"Do I need to leave the room for this discussion?" Pastor Tyler asked.

Roger Goldman smiled and suggested, "It might be easier if you were not present. We might need to discuss some of your weaknesses."

"We will find you when we need you again," Dylan Michaelis said.

Tyler left the large conference room and headed to his office.

"All righty then," Jim Rosek said with a chuckle. "What weaknesses? Do we even need to discuss this?"

"I talked to Dr. Schofield, and he suggested we do a full review of Tyler and the staff," Roger said.

The board talked for ten minutes and failed to come up with any glaring weaknesses of Tyler and the entire staff.

"He has shown remarkable improvement in regards to delegating responsibilities," someone mentioned.

"He realizes he can't do everything in a church of this size," another board member added.

Bill Griffith added, "I think we have a great staff."

"I move we extend Pastor Tyler for three more years," Jim Rosek said.

The motion was seconded and quickly passed.

"Do we need to have the congregation vote?" Lenore Toth asked.

"I don't believe we do," Carol Wisnewski, the board secretary, said as she typed on her laptop. "But I will double check with the district office."

"We need to discuss raises for the staff," Dylan Michaelis mentioned. "Correct me if I'm wrong, but hasn't it been over a year since we raised their salaries?"

After some discussion Roger Goldman, who chaired the finance team, suggested a ten percent raise for Tyler and a seven percent raise for all other staff members. The board unanimously approved the motion.

"I don't want to bring this up prematurely, but Dr. Ausland did confide in me," Roger Goldman mentioned. "He will probably announce his official retirement after the new year. We might want to begin a preliminary search for a replacement. We have a large group of seasoned members, and Pastor Herb has been assuming the responsibility for them."

"Are we ready to bring Tyler back?" Bill Griffith asked.

They brought Tyler back into the room, and Roger went over the board's decision.

"I want to thank you for your vote of confidence in me and the staff. Liz and I are very grateful for the kindness and generosity of our church. I can't imagine going to another church at this point."

"Good!" Jim Rosek said and then laughed. "Because we have you under contract for a full forty years."

Tyler brought up the resignation of Pastor Mauston. No one had been aware of his pending decision.

"I offered to help fill the pulpit if needed," Tyler said.

The board discussed the situation for a couple of minutes.

"I took the liberty of asking Pastor Darren if he would be willing to serve for a month if needed. He agreed, but insisted he would not accept the position of senior pastor if offered."

After concluding their other new business and reviewing the calendar, Dylan Michaelis brought an idea to the rest of the board. "There are other large churches in the Chicago Central District that have more than one campus. I'm thinking of Chicago First, and I believe the Wheeling Estates church has two campuses. If necessary, should we need to consider making SoHam First a satellite campus in order to keep the church open?"

"Would the people over there be interested in becoming a part of this church? They are an older congregation," Bill mentioned. "I realize we are much larger, but there might be some resistance. I've been to services at both churches, and SoHam First is definitely more conservative musically."

"My wife and I attended there when we were first married," Jim said. "It was a very conservative church back in those days."

"It's not real common in the Nazarene denomination, but some of the independent mega-churches have several campuses," Dylan Michaelis said.

"We certainly don't need to decide tonight," Tyler said. "We don't need to worry about that until the need arises. We have enough issues of our own."

Chapter Twenty-One

"What will I do for three hours if no one shows up?" Emmy asked Kenny as he drove her to downtown SoHam for her book signing at Paul's Bookstore. "I don't want to waste his time. Do you think I should have changed the title?"

"No, I still think *But God! I Write Songs* is a great title," Kenny said as he rubbed his jaw and felt his two-day-old beard. "You could always help organize some books, Em. You know he is always buying old books by the hundreds."

"I suppose." She closed her eyes. "Lord, please don't let me be too disappointed because no one shows up."

Kenny shook his head as he listened to Emmy's prayer.

Paul Tockstein maintained his store in a five-story building on Polk Street in the old downtown section of South Hampshire even though most other booksellers had gone to an online format to reduce overhead. He specialized in rare and valuable first editions and his business now occupied the entire building.

"Will you buy a copy, so the day's not a total waste?" Emmy asked.

"Do I have to pay full price?" Kenny teased.

"You are such a dork."

Kenny and Emmy arrived at the bookstore, parked on the third level of the deck across the alley and walked into the store through the entrance in the back.

Denise Bartell, who edited all of Emmy's books, and Ophelia Sturges, Emmy's newly hired literary agent, spotted them and rushed to greet Emmy.

"Where have you been? I've sent you three texts." Denise asked. "There are over two hundred people waiting in line outside just to buy your book."

"Get out! Are you kidding?" Emmy's mouth dropped. "It's cold outside."

"It is December," Ophelia added in a high, squeaky voice.

"No, I'm not kidding. Come with me." Denise said leading the way to a table set up for the event.

Emmy followed while staring over her shoulder at

Ophelia's flaming red hair. *When did you change your hair color? You were blonde the last time I saw you.*

"Meet you in a bit, Em," Kenny said. "I need to talk to Mr. Tockstein first."

Denise hustled Emmy along. "You have bottled water, several Sharpies and a stack of books. There are more once those are sold."

"I can't believe this," Emmy said when she saw the people waiting outside.

"They started lining up an hour ago," Ophelia said.

"How soon will the store open?" Emmy asked.

Paul Tockstein checked his watch. "Ten minutes."

"Oh, hi, Mr. Tockstein. Thanks for letting me do this," Emmy said. "Kenny was looking for you."

"I'll see if I can find him," Mr. Tockstein said and then walked away. He nodded to one of his employees, who then walked over to the front door with a set of keys.

"Emmy, one of these days you have to realize people regard you as a celebrity," Denise said and then adjusted her floppy hat. "There is a display of your other books over there. People might want to buy those as well."

Emmy looked up at Denise and bit her lip. "Why would people be so interested in my book? You've written several books that are way better than mine."

"I'm not famous. You are," Denise said. She put her hands on Emmy's shoulders. "Are you ready? This will be like work."

"I guess I'm ready. Could I use the bathroom first?"

Denise rolled her eyes. "Please do."

Emmy looked in the mirror as she washed her hands. "Lord, please help me get through this. Don't let me get a big head. I will never think of myself as a celebrity no matter what anyone says." She took several deep breaths and walked out and over to the table. "I'm ready."

"Have a seat, Emmy. Ophelia and I will be right here with you," Denise promised.

"Is that so I don't get up and run away," Emmy joked but actually thought about escaping.

"You will be fine. Here they come." Denise pointed to the customers who followed the employees to a roped-off area.

"God, this is all your fault," Emmy whispered as she looked up.

Denise and Ophelia kept the employees busy opening boxes of new books as the customers talked briefly to Emmy. She made sure she spelled everyone's name correctly as she signed the books.

"Why do I have to sign each book on the same page?" Emmy asked Denise.

"It's customary for authors to sign on the title page," Denise said.

Emmy kept working for two hours without a break.

Denise opened a bottle of water. "You need to take a drink."

"Thanks, Denise. I've been too busy to even think about water."

"You can take a few seconds to take a sip of water every once in a while," Denise said and then laughed. "Think of it as my Christmas present."

After the three scheduled hours passed, Denise and Ophelia looked at the line of customers.

"I know I'm supposed to stop, but I can't disappoint anyone," Emmy said.

"Your call, Emmy," Denise said.

"I'll keep going."

Seventy minutes later Emmy signed the last copy of her book in the entire store, stood up and shook her hand. "It's numb. I can't feel a thing."

Kenny approached with Mr. Tockstein.

"Emmy, you sold every single copy," Paul smiled.

"I'm sorry," Emmy apologized.

Paul laughed. "That's a good thing. I have more on order. I've had plenty of book signings over the years, but I can't remember one that sold out my entire inventory. There's not a single copy of any of your books to be had."

"Even the other two?" Emmy asked.

Paul pointed to the empty display. "All gone. I should have ordered more CDs. They disappeared in the first hour."

"I need a break," Emmy said. "I'm wiped out and I could eat a horse."

"We could order lunch," Paul suggested. "My treat."

He ordered sandwiches, chips and drinks from the Jimmy John's down the street. Jimmy John's delivered in a flash, and they ate in the break room on the fourth floor.

"Have you thought about your next book?" Ophelia asked sipping her drink.

Emmy froze with her sandwich halfway to her mouth and stared at Ophelia.

"I'm only asking as your agent."

Denise laughed. "You can take a few months to decide, Emmy. I know how much you struggled with this one."

"Ya think," Emmy replied. "I did love writing the other two, but this one was a struggle," Emmy sighed. "I remember when I was sitting in Kenny's recording studio minding my own business and listening to some tracks. I remember praying for the people on my prayer list and then stopping to listen like Pastor Tyler teaches us when the Holy Spirit told me God wanted me to write a book. I fought it and then I wrote the other books. From now on I think I'll stick to shorter books. Maybe more fiction."

"You could create a fictional series based on SoHam and the Raynor Park neighborhood," Denise suggested. "You could use some of your memories as a starting point."

Emmy grinned. "If I create a fictional version of SoHam, I could tell some of the stories I didn't dare use in my book about the real neighborhood."

Kenny stopped sipping his Dr Pepper and stared at Emmy.

She noticed and patted his arm. "If I create fictional characters, I could pretend you aren't such a dork."

Denise doubled over with laughter.

After they finished eating Emmy reminded Mr. Tockstein of the books he found for Kenny over the years.

"I remember the book your great-great-grandfather wrote. Have you ever read it?"

Emmy shook her head. "Not completely. I had a friend who is fluent in Italian read some of it to me, but it's rather boring. It's like a technical manual about woodworking."

"I assume you still have your music box, correct?" Mr. Tockstein asked.

"I do." Emmy thought about the music box her grandmother Mary Colasanti presented to her on her ninth birthday. "It still plays flawlessly."

"My offer still stands if you ever decide to sell it," he said.

"I appreciate that, but I could never sell it," Emmy said.

"I totally understand. I would never sell it if I were you."

Later Emmy rode with Kenny to the school to pick up the kids.

"Did I make you mad when I mentioned leaving out some stories about Raynor Park?"

Kenny shook his head. "God has forgiven you for anything you might have done with Rory, so I can forgive you, too."

"It wasn't just with Rory," Emmy said and then put a hand to her mouth. "That didn't come out right."

Kenny stared at her as he waited for the light to change.

"Aw, come on. I didn't mean it like that. I never did anything much worse than play tackle football with a bunch of guys when I was in junior high."

"We played football, Em."

Emmy bit her lip. "They were rougher than you."

"Whatever," he said as he punched the Odyssey's accelerator and roared through the intersection. "Would you really considering writing a whole series of books about characters you create?"

She shrugged. "Maybe. I haven't given much thought to my next book. I'll wait for the Holy Spirit to tell me what to do."

"Look what happened the last time you did that," Kenny said and then grinned.

Chapter Twenty-Two

"I think you've practiced your song enough times," Emmy said after listening to Heather and Isabella rehearse the song they would sing in the Christmas program an hour later.

"Do we sound good, Daddy?" Isabella asked.

Kenny turned off of Canton Lane and into the church parking lot. "You sound just like angels, sweetie."

"When I get older, I want to sing, too," Kevin Michael said as he unbuckled his seatbelt.

"You have to sing with Ben and Zachary," Heather told him. "You can't sing with me and Isa because we want to make real CDs like Mommy and Daddy."

Kenny waited in the line with other vehicles waiting to drop off passengers. He looked at Emmy and said, "I have a great idea."

Emmy smiled at him. "That's good, dear. Try not to forget it this time so you can tell me later. You don't have many good ideas."

He shifted to park, and stared at Emmy.

"See you later," Heather said as everyone exited the van.

Kenny shook his head and found a parking spot. He got out, closed the door, stood next to the van and tilted his head. *Shoot! It was a good idea, but I can't remember it now.* He sighed and walked into the church.

Emmy waited inside for him. "What is your idea?"

"I'll tell you after church."

Emmy rolled her eyes. "You forgot it already, didn't you?"

Kenny shrugged.

"We saved two seats for you," Kenny told his parents later as he helped hang up their coats. "We're up close to the platform."

"Are they really singing a solo?" Mr. Colwell asked.

"It's actually a duet, Dad," Kenny replied.

Mr. Colwell stared at his son. *I can see why Emmy calls you a dork.*

They followed the crowd and entered the sanctuary.

Mr. Colwell looked around. "You said it was big, but this is amazing. It almost looks like The Center except more modern."

Kenny thought about the abandoned warehouse he and some other partners had converted into a state-of-the-art concert venue several years prior. "I suppose it does in a way."

Mrs. Colwell waved as she spotted Emmy standing in the third row. "There's Emmy, but we have to find a way to get to her."

They slowly threaded their way through the crowd.

"The girls and Kevin Michael will be on this side of the stage," Emmy said.

"Does Kevin have a speaking part?" Mrs. Colwell asked.

"He has one line of scripture to say along with some other kids. I hope he doesn't freeze up. He knows the line."

About halfway through the thirty minute program Heather and Isabella sang their song. After the applause died down, Mr. Colwell leaned close to Emmy and asked, "Wasn't that one of your songs?"

"It was on the Christmas CD," Emmy answered.

"They did a great job. Did you teach them to use the microphones like that?"

"I told them to hold them close enough so the sound guys could do their job," Emmy said.

Mrs. Colwell smiled and waved to Heather and Isabella as they took their place with the other children. "I'm not surprised they sound good together. You and Kenny used to sing together at their age. You knew how to harmonize even then."

Emmy whispered, "God gave me that talent."

Mr. Colwell joined the other parents and grandparents taking pictures of the kids after the program.

"Did you like our song, Gra?" Heather asked.

"I did," he said as he hugged both girls.

"Mommy wrote it, but she said we could sing it," Isabella said.

Mr. Colwell smiled. "That was very generous of your mother. Did I ever tell you that she used to sing Christmas songs and other songs with your father when she was your age?"

"Did she really?" Isabella asked.

188

Mr. Colwell nodded. "She did. I wish we had a recording of them singing together. I would love to hear that again."

Kenny listened to his father and that cemented his idea in his head. *I'm going to do it. I don't want to have the same regrets Dad does when I get older.*

"Is that the last of them?" Emmy asked Kenny late on Christmas Eve.

"That's all from the closet. Did you stash some upstairs?" He handed Emmy a stack of presents.

"I brought them down earlier." She knelt in front of the floor-to-ceiling Christmas tree and found a place to put the gifts.

Heather and Isabella peeked around the corner of the family room and giggled. Kenny and Emmy heard the sound and turned to look.

"What are you doing out of bed?" Kenny asked.

Emmy stood up with one present still in her hands. "You are supposed to be sleeping."

Heather and Isabella rushed into the room and sat down in front of the tree.

"Mommy, did Santa come early?" Heather asked and then both girls giggled again.

Emmy looked at Kenny and shrugged.

Kenny coughed and then said, "Yes, Santa needed to drop these off early because he needed to rush over to China and deliver some presents to all the good boys and girls over there."

"China?" Emmy rolled her eyes. "Such a dork."

"Oh, Daddy," Isabella looked up at her father. "We know the truth about Santa Claus."

"And what might that be?" Kenny asked.

Heather had been checking the tags on the presents, but she stood up and put her hands on her hips. "Santa isn't a real person. He's a made up story like the Easter bunny and the tooth fairy. We know you and Mommy buy the presents."

"Maybe Santa tells us what to buy and gives us the money," Kenny tried one more time.

The girls shook their heads.

189

"Does Kevin Michael know?"

"Don't worry," Heather said. "We aren't going to say anything to Kevin Michael. He still thinks Santa is real."

Isabella looked at Emmy and then grinned. "Daddy, how old was Mommy before she knew Santa wasn't real?"

Kenny tilted his head and thought about it for a moment. He rubbed his jaw and looked very serious. "Well, as best I can remember, I think she was thirteen."

Emmy frowned at Kenny. "Was not!"

"How old were you, Mommy?" Isabella asked.

"I was twelve," Emmy said and then grinned. "Your Uncle Rory told me Santa wasn't real."

Kevin Michael woke up just after six in the morning. He rubbed his eyes and remembered what today was. He threw off his police car blanket, jumped out of bed, raced from his room and took the stairs two at a time. He nearly tripped but regained his balance. He dashed around the corner and peered into the family room. He raised both hands over his head like he was signaling a touchdown. "Yes!" he shouted. He turned and sprinted back up the stairs and into his parents bedroom. He launched himself and landed in the middle of the king-size bed. "Mommy! Daddy! You need to wake up. I checked under the tree and guess what?" he yelled.

Kenny opened his eyes as Emmy pulled the sheet over her head. "What, buddy?"

"Santa has been here. There are a thousand million presents under the tree," he said as he held his arms out wide. "We need to get up now and open them. I think he might have left some for you, too, Mommy."

"Do you really think so?' Kenny asked.

"I'm pretty sure he left one or two for Mommy," Kevin said as he nodded vigorously. "Even if she has been naughty at times."

Emmy threw back the sheet and sat up. "I have not been naughty."

Kenny smiled as he nodded at Kevin Michael. "She's been very naughty."

190

Heather and Isabella walked into the room looking half asleep with their hair sticking up all over.

"What's going on?" Heather asked.

Kevin Michael looked at his sisters and threw his hands up. "Don't you know? It's Christmas! Santa was here, and he brought tons of presents. Come on! We have to go downstairs." He scrambled off of the bed, scooted past his sisters and hurried down the stairs.

"Are you awake enough to open presents?" Kenny asked the girls.

"I don't think I can go back to sleep," Isabella said.

Heather yawned and asked, "Do we have to wait until after breakfast?"

Kenny looked at Emmy. "Your call."

"Give me a minute to pee, and I'll meet you downstairs. I want to read the Christmas story at least before they open everything," Emmy said.

"What about my parents?" Kenny asked.

"Shoot! I forgot about them. What time are they coming over?"

"Not until nine or ten," Kenny answered and then thought about it. "Let's go ahead. They won't mind. The kids can show them their presents later."

Emmy made it downstairs a few minutes later. She got the kids to settle down long enough for her to read the Christmas story from the Book of Luke.

"Now can we open presents?" Kevin Michael asked.

"Can Isa and I be Santa?" Heather asked and then added, "I mean, can we pass out the presents Santa brought us?"

"Yes, you may be Santa's helpers," Kenny said with a grin.

Kenny's parents arrived around nine and stayed for brunch. They were delighted to see the presents Santa Claus brought without having to sit through the two hours it took to open them.

"Are you sure you don't mind?" Kenny asked his mother. "The kids were up early."

She patted his arm. "It's all right. Maybe next year we can get here earlier."

By three o'clock the kids were content to play in their rooms with their new toys, Kenny's parents left to visit other relatives and Kenny had taken all the garbage bags full of wrapping paper and boxes out to the garage.

"Would you mind if I took a nap?" he asked Emmy.

"Go ahead. I'm going to relax and maybe read for a while. I might join you later," she answered.

He grinned wickedly.

"Only for a nap. Now who's being naughty?"

Kenny wrapped his arms around her waist and pulled her close. "Have I told you lately how much I love you?"

She tilted her head back and forth. "It's been a few hours." She sighed contentedly as he kissed her.

An hour later Emmy listened at the bottom of the stairs. *I can't hear a peep from anyone. I know Kenny and Kevin Michael are probably asleep, but should I check on the girls?* She listened a while longer and thought she could hear the twins playing with their new dolls. *I'll let them be.* She went back to the den, sat down in her recliner and picked up her book. She opened it, but then closed it right away. *I wonder what Rory's doing? I haven't talked to him all month.* She glanced at her cell phone and bit her lip. *He might be busy.* She picked up the phone and dialed his number. *If he's busy, I won't talk long.*

Rory heard the phone ring and checked to see who might be calling. He grinned and answered, "Did Santa make it to your house, little girl?"

"How do you know it was me and not one of the kids?" she asked.

"They have their own phones, Em. So, did Santa make it through the snow?" Rory asked.

"It's in the forties here, and we don't have any snow at all. Are you busy? Should I call later?"

Rory plopped down on the couch and put his bare feet on the coffee table. "Not doing a thing. I worked a few hours this morning and then went for a run. Did I mention it's about seventy-five and sunny?"

"I hate you. Where's your girlfriend?"

"I thought you were my girlfriend," he teased.

"In your dreams," she teased back.

"She's working a double shift today. We were together yesterday."

"Oooh! Is it getting serious? What was her name? Rachel, or Rosanna? I can't remember."

"You know her name, and Rochelle and I are just friends," he claimed.

"You shouldn't ever lie and especially not on Christmas," Emmy said. "You don't have to tell me how often she stays at your place, or how often you spend the night at her apartment."

"Nice try, but not even close to working."

They spent thirty minutes talking about Christmas and catching up on the latest things happening in their lives.

"So, they caught you guys putting out the presents. I wish I could have been there for that," Rory said as he chuckled.

"Oh, Rory, they are growing up so fast. It seems like they were just learning how to walk a couple of years ago."

"At least you aren't getting any older, Em," he teased.

"You are so funny. I have something serious to ask," Emmy said.

"Okay, fire away."

"Do you remember when you told me Santa wasn't real?"

He started to make a joke but stopped. "I never told you that, did I?"

"Yes, you did, and I didn't want to believe you."

"I'm sorry. How old were you, Em?"

"I was ten, and you made me cry," she whispered.

"I shouldn't have been so mean to you. I'm sorry," he said.

"It's all right. I was pretty sure Santa wasn't real. You took me over to Darby's and bought me a hot dog and root beer to make up for it."

"I'm surprised Diane didn't tell you just to be mean," Rory said.

Chapter Twenty-Three

Dr. Ausland walked slowly onto the platform of the new sanctuary, turned and faced the congregation. He closed his eyes for a moment, and then smiled. "Since this is the second service, I suppose by now some of you might have heard what I am about to tell you. Today I am officially retiring. Again, and this time I vow to make it stick," he paused as some of the people laughed. He started to speak, but nearly everyone in the sanctuary began to clap as they rose to their feet. He bowed his head and waited until he could continue. "Thank you," he whispered.

Emmy leaned close to Kenny and whispered, "Should we have bought them another new minivan?"

He whispered back, "Dr. Ausland specifically requested that the church not make a big deal about this. Tyler said the board wanted to do something, but Dr. Ausland convinced them otherwise. Tyler said the board agreed to respect his wishes."

"Is that why there's no potluck or anything?"

"Yes. Dr. Ausland's only wish was to be able to preach one final time."

Once again, Dr. Ausland amazed Emmy with his ability to recite all his scripture passages from memory. He didn't use notes as he spoke and surprised nearly everyone by making it through the entire service without becoming emotional. That is until he made the mistake of looking directly at Emmy. Tears filled his eyes as he watched Emmy's tears cascade down her face. He closed his eyes and paused momentarily until he could continue.

"I'm sorry for that," he said after using his handkerchief to dry his eyes. "You can blame Emmy for tripping me up."

Emmy tried to hide as everyone around her turned to look at her.

"Way to go, Em," Tony said as he turned around and touched her knee.

"I couldn't help it," she said and then bit her lip.

Dr. Ausland finished his message and then prayed for the congregation. He and Carolyn walked out to the foyer where they spent the next hour talking to everyone. Kenny had taken the kids home because Emmy needed to stay for a meeting. After the meeting she waited in line to say goodbye to Dr. Ausland. She hugged Carolyn and then looked up at Dr. Ausland.

"Give me a hug, Emmy," he said as he held out his arms.

"I'm sorry I made you lose your concentration. I tried not to cry, but I kept thinking about everything you've done for me over the years." She rested her head against his chest. "I'm going to miss you so much."

"We will still see each other. Carolyn and I plan to visit our children and grandchildren more often, but we will still be living in the area. Our home will be here."

Emmy waited a few seconds before asking, "How many miles are on your Odyssey?"

Dr. Ausland chuckled softly. "Not as many as you might think. We have a Toyota Corolla that we drive to save on gas."

"I was just wondering," Emmy said.

"The Odyssey will last for many more years," he said.

"Are you still awake?" Emmy asked as she cuddled against Kenny that night. "I can't get to sleep."

He put an arm over her. "I'm awake now. Why can't you sleep?"

She turned onto her stomach and looked at him. "I've been thinking about my music box."

Okay?" he asked after she didn't elaborate.

"Tomorrow is the girls' birthday and they will be nine. I was nine when Grandma Colasanti gave the music box to me. I want to continue the tradition, but on the other hand, I don't want to give it up."

"There's no law that says you have to give it away, Em."

"I know."

"How do you plan to give it away? Why did your grandma give it to you instead of Diane? Do you know?" Kenny asked.

"I think Grandma gave it to me because she knew I would care for it more than Diane. Diane probably would have trashed it."

"Heather would trash it," Kenny said and then chuckled. "I can see that. Isa would treasure it like you have."

195

Emmy flipped over onto her back and accidentally elbowed Kenny's jaw. "Sorry. Did I hurt you?"

He rubbed his jaw. "I don't think you broke it."

"You would know it if I did," she teased. "What should I do?"

He turned on his side. "Okay, let's assume you are going to give it to Isa because she will appreciate it. Heather might want something else. Maybe not. You could always wait until Isa is older. Your grandmother didn't give it to your mother..."

"She wouldn't give it to a daughter-in-law, you goof. It had to stay in the blood family, and I highly doubt Daddy would have wanted it."

"Right. Did you promise to give it to Isa tomorrow?"

"Not that I remember, but I might have told her Grandma gave it to me when I turned nine."

"That doesn't mean you promised to let Isa have it on her ninth birthday," Kenny said as he fluffed up his pillow. "I wouldn't worry about it, Em. You could talk to Isa about it tomorrow and tell her that it will be hers at some day in the future."

"I could. I just don't think I'm ready to move my treasures to another place. I could keep the CDs and the note you wrote on my twentieth birthday in my dresser, but the purple ribbon is rather fragile now, and the baggies with the kids' hair is too valuable to take a chance with. It's silly, but knowing they're in the music box is comforting."

Kenny held her close and they didn't talk for a moment.

"Do you still have your plane ticket, Em?" he whispered.

She thought about the plane ticket she didn't use, and the fact the plane crashed killing all aboard including a man she knew from Robertson Industries. She shook her head. "I got rid of it last year. It didn't belong. Everything else is a good memory. The plane ticket reminded me of something awful. I decided it was time to look to the future and forget about that event."

He kissed her tenderly. "Do you think you can get to sleep now?"

She scooted even closer and whispered, "I might need a little help."

196

Kenny picked up the kids from school and after they were settled he asked, "Did the kids enjoy the cupcakes you made?"

"They ate all of them," Heather said.

"Even the extra ones we made," Isabella added.

Kenny pulled the Odyssey onto Canton Lane and headed home. "Your mother and I didn't buy you many birthday presents this year, but I have an idea that could be a lot of fun."

"What?" Heather asked. "Is it something dorky?"

"I don't think so. I thought of it Sunday but then forgot it."

"What is it, Daddy?" Isabella asked.

"Hey! There goes a police car with its lights flashing," Kevin Michael said as he squirmed around to follow the car. "I bet he's after bank robbers."

"He's probably chasing a speeder," Heather said.

"I hope it wasn't your mother," Kenny said.

"What is your idea?" Isabella asked again.

Okay, you both like to sing together, so I recorded some tracks, and I want to record you singing to them."

"You mean like a real CD?" Heather asked.

"Yes, I can make a CD for you with your picture on the front..."

"Can we sell them to our friends?" Heather asked.

"I don't think you should sell them, but you could take it to school. Maybe Mrs. Payne would let you play it for the class sometime."

The prospect of recording excited the girls. Kenny produced the session for them just like he would for a real band. He had chosen five songs for the session from his and Emmy's back catalog and recorded new tracks over the last month to fit the girls' vocal range. The girls knew the songs and quickly learned the different arrangements. Kenny had them rehearse each song until they knew it well enough to record. They nailed four of the songs on the first take, and only needed to replace part of the other song. He took pictures of them in the studio and used one of them from the Christmas program for the cover. He used printable CDs and burned three copies. One for each of the girls and one for himself. He showed the girls and Emmy the finished CDs after dinner.

"Thank you, Daddy," Isabella said as she examined her copy. "It looks like a real CD."

"It is a real CD," Heather said. "Look! It even has the name of the record company. Bristol Ridge Records."

"Can we play these in our room?" Isabella asked.

"Okay, but you still have to do your chores before you go to bed," Emmy said. "Tomorrow is a school day, so you have to be in bed by nine."

The girls played the CD as they cleaned their room.

Just before nine Emmy made sure Kevin Michael was tucked in bed and then checked on the girls.

"Does our room look clean?" Isabella asked.

Emmy inspected the twins' large bedroom. "It looks a lot better. You didn't throw everything in your closet did you?"

Heather and Isabella looked at each other and giggled.

"Tomorrow night you will have to clean the closet," Emmy said with a sigh.

"Can we take our CD to school tomorrow. We want to show it to everyone," Heather said.

"Okay, but if Mrs. Payne says there isn't time to play it, you have to listen to her and not be disappointed."

"We will, Mommy," Isabella promised.

The next day Mrs. Payne made time near the end of the day to play the thirteen-minute-long CD for the whole class.

"Is that really you?" one of the kids asked.

Heather showed everyone the cover and read some of the liner notes.

Mrs. Payne listened along with the kids. "That was very good," she told Heather and Isabella. *I shouldn't be surprised because of who your parents are. You have inherited your mother's ability to sing right on key.*

The Crest Ridge church board met the last Monday of the month. They discussed the staff position recently vacated by Dr. Ausland.

"We've only talked to one person about the position,"

Pastor Tyler said. "Dr. Ausland recommended Rev. Harold Milhuff. Most of the seasoned members know him. He was on Pastor Herb's staff years ago and served until 1997 when he left to pastor one of the churches in Chicago."

Roger Goldman asked, "Did Rev. Milhuff give you any indication as to how long he would serve? He's in his seventies, I believe."

"As far as I could tell, he wants to keep working as long as his health permits," Tyler answered.

After a short discussion the board decided to add Rev. Milhuff to the staff.

"I will send out an email to let everyone know," Tyler said.

Before the meeting adjourned Jim Rosek asked, "How much did it cost to replace the heating and air conditioning unit on the north side of the roof?"

Bill Griffith responded, "We got it for $11,000. Reed Shafer tried his best to repair it, but he ended up calling Polar South Heating and Cooling. One of their guys came out and tried. He said it was time to replace it, so we did."

"We do have to heat the old sanctuary even if we're not using it at the moment," Tyler said.

"We need to decide how we want to use it. It's too large to hand it over to the teens," Dylan Michaelis said as he glanced around the table. "We have a large group of teens, but that sanctuary can hold over a thousand people."

"The school is still expanding," Lenore Toth said. "We will need more classrooms next year unless we want to limit the enrollment."

Jim Rosek added, "Maybe we should talk to Carl Tomanek about an addition to the education building."

"We've got the space for an addition," Marley Menconi, who headed up the Women's Ministry, said.

"We don't have to decide anything tonight, and we've gone past eight thirty. Let's pray about this, and maybe we can appoint a committee to study it over the next few months," Tyler said and then closed the meeting with prayer.

Chapter Twenty-Four

As Emmy waited for her coffee to brew Sunday morning, she sang "Love Come To Life" and danced around the kitchen. *Only six more days before Big Daddy Baker comes to town.* She heard her cell phone chirp and danced over to where it lay on the counter. Without breaking her rhythm she checked the text. *It's from Heidi Knapp. Oh no, she's sick and wants to know if I could fill in for her.* Emmy quickly texted back that she could and then poured some coffee into an insulated cup. She raced back upstairs and told Kenny the news.

"Are you leaving right away?" Kenny asked as he searched for a clean pair of jeans.

"I need to hurry if I want to make it to practice before the first service. Will you make sure the kids are presentable?"

"I'll try," he answered.

Emmy grabbed her purse, the coffee, the keys to her Civic Si and ran out to the garage. She made it to the church a few minutes before the time the worship team gathered to rehearse. She parked behind the new sanctuary and hurried to the door that led directly into the music suite.

Riordan Schulenberg spotted her just as he took a sip of his water. *Why are you here so early? You're not on the schedule.*

Emmy saw Riordan and headed his way. "Heidi texted me this morning. She's sick."

"Yes, I received the same message," Riordan said.

"I know all the songs and I can fill in for her."

Riordan paused. *Aw, that's why you're here.* "That's very thoughtful of you, Emmy, but we have three singers already. Sadie, myself and Regina. We should be able to get by."

Sadie walked over to see what Riordan and Emmy were talking about.

"That's very kind of you to offer to fill in, but you and Heidi don't sing the same part," Sadie said as she took Riordan's hand and smiled at Emmy.

"Oh," Emmy said as her shoulders slumped. "So you don't need me, huh?"

200

"You are so busy with your career. We will survive somehow," Sadie said.

Emmy clenched her jaw for a brief time but then managed a small smile. "Okay, I can sit back and listen. I am on the schedule for next Sunday."

"Thanks for the offer though," Riordan said with a smile and then waved to some of the other worship team members. "Excuse me. I need to talk to Robby and Regina about the order of service."

Emmy took a deep breath and thought about talking to some of the team, but she turned around and walked out of the building and back to her car. She sat in the car and cried. *Lord, am I being selfish? I want to sing for you, but are you trying to tell me something?* She dried her eyes, started the car and moved it to the parking lot in the front. She walked inside with a group of people, found a seat near the back and waited for the service to begin.

"Let me open this service with a Psalm and a prayer," Pastor Tyler said.

Emmy closed her eyes and prayed briefly. Then she listened quietly to Tyler and allowed the Holy Spirit a chance to talk to her. When Riordan asked the congregation to stand and sing, Emmy joined in. By the time the worship team finished, her attitude changed. I can still sing and worship from here. I guess I don't need to be on the platform.

She met Kenny and her friends for Sunday School and explained what happened.

"So you hurried over here for no reason, huh?" Tony asked. "Too bad no one texted you back and told you to stay home."

"Does that mean you aren't singing in the second service either?" Kenny asked.

Emmy shrugged. "Guess not."

"Are you going home, or will you stay?"

"If I go home, I could make lunch, and we could eat on time," she said. "Would you mind if I didn't stay?"

"Depends on what you make for lunch," Kenny teased.

She made a face at him and decided not to stay after the Sunday School class.

"Is lunch ready?" Kenny asked as he followed the kids inside.

Emmy turned from the stove and smiled at him. "I made a pot of chili using Andy's recipe. I texted him after church, and he's coming over. Do you think you can handle his firehouse chili?"

"I can handle it, but what about the kids?" Kenny asked as he walked over and sniffed the open pot of chili. He kissed Emmy, pulled her close and whispered, "If it makes you feel better, I didn't think the worship team sounded great today. They were missing a little something."

She looked up at him. "Are you just saying that to make me feel better?"

"Did it work?" he asked while he grinned.

"A little, and I made some mild chili for the kids."

The kids changed clothes and made it downstairs just as Andy walked into the kitchen.

"Uncle Andy! I have some new cars," Kevin Michael said as he held a car in each hand.

"All right, buddy!" Andy inspected the new cars. "And how are my princesses today?"

The girls hugged him.

"Do we have any oyster crackers, Em? I know you made cornbread, but I like crackers in my chili." Kenny asked as he helped the kids get situated in the breakfast nook.

"We have some in the pantry," she answered. "Don't you like my cornbread? I made it from scratch."

"I like it, but I'm not going to put it in my chili."

Kenny prayed, and Emmy set a bowl of chili in front of everyone. She sliced the cornbread and buttered several pieces and let everyone take what they wanted.

"Are you going to sit down and eat with us, cuz?" Andy asked as he pulled out a chair for her.

"Yes, but I wanted to serve you guys before I sat down."

Andy looked at Kenny.

Kenny shrugged. "Your guess is as good as mine."

"What's the big deal?" Emmy sat down. "I serve you sometimes."

"Is the chili hot, Mommy?" Kevin Michael asked.

"If you mean temperature hot, yes, but your chili is not spicy hot like ours."

Kenny took a bite of his chili. "Not too hot." He spoke too soon. His eyes began to water and his tongue burned. "Maybe it's a little hot."

Andy laughed, so the kids laughed along with him.

Tony called around five. "Hey, brat, are you coming over to watch the Super Bowl?"

"No, I'm going to stay here and watch it with Kenny and Andy," she answered.

"Okay with me. You just don't want to see your beloved Broncos get annihilated by the Seahawks again," Tony teased.

"This year will be different."

Tony laughed. "Care to make a little wager?"

"Name your price?" she responded.

"How about fifty bucks?"

"Cheapskate! A hundred."

"Deal! I should feel bad for taking money from you so easily, but I don't. You can pay me right after the game."

"You should make a quick run to an ATM because I know you don't have that much cash on you," she said.

"Don't send one of the kids over with the money. I want to tear it from your hand," Tony laughed. "I know how much you hate to part with your money."

Emmy called Tony immediately after the game ended.

"I can't believe they tried to pass," Tony said. "They could have rammed the ball up the middle they were so close."

"I'll take my money in crisp new twenties," she said with obvious delight.

"Fine," he sighed. "I guess I'm not too disappointed. I've always respected Manning as a player and as a person."

"Is he better than Brady?" Emmy asked.

"Who knows? Brady's meaner, and so is his coach."

"You can pay me tomorrow. I gotta go."

"Will you take a check?" Tony asked.

"Cold, hard cash, creep," she insisted.

203

Emmy heard her cell phone later that night, checked the caller ID and answered.

"Aha! This phone does still work. I was starting to think you forgot to pay your bill," Father James said.

"I'm sorry. I've been rather busy." Emmy walked into the den and plopped into her recliner.

"That's a load of bull. You've been ignoring me. Did you watch the game?"

"I did, and I won a hundred bucks from Tony. We never actually pay each other, but it's fun anyway."

"I lost fifty because of that stupid call at the end, and I did have to pay."

"That's what you get for using a bookie."

"If I owned the Seahawks, I would fire the entire coaching staff. That was the dumbest call in history." His voice rose in fury.

"It's good to know the game meant nothing to you as a member of the clergy dedicated to the service of our Lord."

"He would be upset too if he had money riding on the game."

Emmy sighed. "I have something serious to talk about."

"What might that be, my child?"

"Will you stop patronizing me?"

He chuckled. "All right, I will talk to you as your brother and not in my official capacity as a representative of His Holiness."

"Do you even know who the pope is?" Emmy laughed back.

"I would probably recognize him if he was wearing his hat."

"Are you ever serious?" Emmy asked.

"Usually only for funerals, but I'll make an exception for you."

"Thank you. I need to vent. Will you listen and not interrupt?" She asked and then waited several seconds. "Aren't you going to answer me?"

"I didn't want to interrupt," he answered.

"You are hopeless."

"Okay, I'm comfortable now. Please vent away."

"Are you going to fall asleep?"

"I'm going to try very hard to stay awake and listen to every word you say."

"The worship team leaders don't want me anymore. Heidi Knapp texted me this morning..." Emmy explained what transpired at church. "We've had more than three singers plenty of times. We need more musicians in the new sanctuary because it's so big. I understand that Riordan and Sadie are the leaders and they are the focus of the team..."

"Pardon me for interrupting, but isn't Jesus the main focus?"

"Yes, but I'm not talking about that. I'm talking about stage presence, or whatever you want to call it. Riordan and Sadie stand in the center of the stage. That way everyone can see them. The other singers are on the sides or the edges. Wherever. Do you get the picture?"

"I can picture it," he answered.

"So, like I said, I offered to fill in for Heidi and rushed to get there on time. Don't say a word about my driving." She heard him chuckle. "I made it there early, and they blew me off like I wasn't needed. I'm on the schedule for next week, and I'm tempted to not show up. It's obvious they don't want me around," she stopped and caught her breath. "Okay, I'm done."

Father James sat up on his couch. "First of all you aren't going to blow off church next Sunday. That's so not you. Second, I would think you would enjoy taking a break from the team. You've been singing there for over ten years."

"I get a break! We have four teams, and I'm only singing once a month. We even booked my last tour so I could be there every Sunday. I want to sing more often."

"Have you ever thought about joining a smaller church where you could sing every week?"

"No! I'm not switching churches just because I can't sing every week. How silly would that be?"

"Exactly," he said.

She rolled her eyes. "You're no help."

"Anything else on your mind, little sister?"

"We should do Darby's this week," she answered.

"Sounds good to me as long as you're buying."

"Whatever! Call me and let me know what day works for you." *Danny Darby never lets you pay for anything.* She hung up and smacked the arm of her recliner.

"I've listened to the last CD you produced, and I loved it," Jeremiah Tolla said as he relaxed on the couch in Kenny's basement studio. "I'm not sure we can compete with that group."

Kenny tilted his head. "Which CD do you mean?"

"The one you did for that new recording duo," Jeremiah said with a straight face.

Kenny caught on and laughed. "Did they bring their CD to church and make you listen to it?"

Jeremiah smoothed out his heavy, full beard and smiled. "They are so proud of it, and it really does sound good. Did you do the tracks yourself?"

"I had a little help," Kenny said.

Cecil Harden and Warren Dewar the other two members of BearFace entered the control room and greeted Kenny.

"I can still hear your accent," Kenny said to Warren. "Do you ever get back to New Zealand?" Kenny's hand was swallowed up in Warren's enormous paw.

"It's been a couple of years, but I did spend a week in Wellington visiting old friends," Warren answered.

Kenny shook hands with Cecil, who played bass, and noticed some gray streaks in Cecil's red, bushy beard. "I listened to the demos Jeremiah sent over. You've really improved your playing."

"I actually broke down and took some lessons from Jackson Brewster at church. Jeremiah threatened to replace me if I didn't," Cecil joked.

They talked about the first CD Kenny produced for the band.

"I think the new songs are even better. I liked the piano. Who played it?" Kenny asked.

Jeremiah put a finger to his chest. "It's nothing too complicated."

"None of our music is very complicated," Cecil said and then laughed hard enough to make his belly jiggle.

"We have the whole month to work on the new CD," Kenny reminded the guys.

"Mom, will we get to meet Big Daddy?" Heather asked Saturday afternoon as she stepped into the bathtub and sat down.

"I'm not sure. You might, but there isn't one guy called Big Daddy. The name of the band is Big Daddy Baker," Emmy explained.

"Why?" Kevin Michael asked as he walked into the girls' bathroom.

"Kevin! Get out of here! I'm taking a bath," Heather yelled.

"Why what?" Emmy asked as she scooted Kevin into the twins' bedroom.

"Why is the band called Big Daddy Baker?"

"Well, there are two brothers named Baker, and one of them is pretty big."

"So they should call the band Big Daddy Baker Brothers," Kevin said and then shrugged. "Makes sense to me."

"That's because you're only six," Heather hollered from the tub.

"I'll be seven pretty soon. I'm not a little kid anymore."

Isabella walked into the room. "Mommy, are you going to sing tonight?"

"No, sweetie, but Pastor Jeremiah and his band are going to play some songs," Emmy said.

"Are they the opening act?" Isabella asked.

"Yes, they are."

"Can Heather and I be the opening act one of these days?"

"We will have to see, Isa."

Earl and Rose Wheeling's M&R Productions had been chosen to be the first company to use the new sanctuary as the venue for a concert. They scheduled Big Daddy Baker and sold all the tickets. Tyler and Earl walked out onto the stage to survey the situation an hour before the doors opened.

"The band did their soundcheck, and I think they're eating now," Earl Wheeling said. "Don't let anyone know I said this, but I don't think the lead singer misses too many meals."

"You may be right," Tyler chuckled. "Jeremiah wanted me to thank you for letting them open. They don't get many chances to play in front of a large crowd."

"I understand you probably need to talk to your church board, but assuming all goes well tonight, I would be interested in using the building two or maybe three times a year. It's obviously a great venue and the location works," Earl said.

Tyler nodded. "You would need the board's approval, but we built this with events like this in mind."

Earl shook hands with Tyler and smiled. "Let's head backstage and talk to the band."

Kenny led the way to their seats in the middle section close to the front. He walked into row nine and counted to ten. "These five seats are ours."

Heather and Isabella took their seats and looked at the stage.

"I don't see Pastor Jeremiah," Heather said. "How long do we have to wait?"

"About thirty minutes," Emmy answered.

Kevin Michael carried one of his firetrucks and placed it on the back of the empty chair in front of him.

"You can play there for now, but you will have to stop when someone sits there," Kenny said.

Thirty-five minutes later the pre-show music stopped in the middle of a song and Earl Wheeling walked to the center of the stage. He talked for a couple of minutes and thanked the church for the use of their sanctuary. "I believe the guys are about ready, so please get ready to welcome BearFace to the stage." Earl waved to the crowd and walked off.

The house lights dimmed within a few seconds and many in the crowd began to holler and clap and stomp their feet. Jeremiah, Cecil and Warren moved into position.

"I think I see Pastor Jeremiah!" Heather yelled.

"You better cover your ears, kids, because I think Mommy is going to whistle." Kenny covered his ears and the kids followed his example.

Emmy whistled and then the band started the first song.

"I see Pastor Jeremiah!" Isabella shouted as she and Heather jumped up and down in time with the music.

"Crap! Now we can't see," Heather shouted as the people sitting in front of them stood up.

"Heather! That's not a word we use," Emmy said.

"I hear you use it, Mom. Is it a swear word?" Heather asked.

Kenny grinned at Emmy. "She's got you there."

"Please, try not to use that word," Emmy said to the girls. "And I promise to try better to only use good words."

Kenny looked at Emmy's hands. *No fair crossing your fingers, Em.*

Emmy held out her hands to let Kenny see them. "I really will try. I promise."

Most of the people in front sat down which let Heather and Isabella see Pastor Jeremiah performing.

Despite the threat she voiced to Father James to not show up for church the next morning, Emmy arrived early and with the proper attitude. She sang and helped the congregation worship from her position on the side and near the back of the stage without a complaint.

"Nice job, Em," Kenny whispered when she sat next to him. "Too bad you were on the other side of the stage. I should have brought binoculars."

"I am not going to let Riordan or Sadie dictate my attitude no matter if they fire me."

You're a volunteer. Why would they fire you? Kenny thought as he held her hand.

Chapter Twenty-Five

"I think we're finished," Kenny said after recording a vocal overdub by Jeremiah Friday afternoon. "Do you guys have time to listen to the rough mixes?"

The other two members of BearFace nodded.

Jeremiah removed his headphones, left the vocal booth and walked into the control room. Kenny double-checked to make sure everything was saved and backed-up to multiple hard drives before he started playing the tracks for the new CD.

"I have time," Jeremiah said.

"Did you ever decide on the official title?" Kenny asked. "I've been calling it BearFace II."

Jeremiah looked at Cecil and Warren, who both nodded. "We made a list of possible titles, but the one we like the best is *Relentless War*. That comes from the lyrics to 'The World Is Burning' in the second verse," Jeremiah explained. "Mia painted a picture for the cover that fits the title."

"She's doing all the artwork, right?" Kenny asked.

"She liked doing the first CD, so we're letting her do this one too. She's got a gift that none of us have."

Cecil and Warren nodded in agreement.

Kenny punched a button on the computer keyboard and the first track began to play.

"It's rougher and punchier than the first CD," Kenny said before the second track started.

The guys listened to all nine tracks without much comment. Kenny stopped the playback and spun his chair around to face the guys. "What do you think?"

Cecil and Warren stood up together.

"Sounds like our job is finished," Cecil said.

Warren extended his hand and Kenny shook it. "We're going fishing in Canada for a week. Will the final mix be finished by the time we get back?"

"Jeremiah and I have all of next week to work on it," Kenny said as he removed his hand from Warren's grip.

"I think we're done," Jeremiah said a week later.

"Are you sure? We did kinda rush through that last track. We could come back and finish it tomorrow," Kenny said. "We would have to finish this weekend because Fridays At Five is heading to the Steward Music studio on Monday."

Jeremiah shook his head. "No, I can't be here tomorrow." He paused and then added, "Mia and I are flying down to Birmingham, Alabama, in the morning."

Kenny waited as Jeremiah fought to compose himself.

"We are interviewing for the position of senior pastor at one of the satellite campuses of Trinity UMC in Homewood. That's just outside Birmingham. The church board knows."

"That's great," Kenny said. "Have you been there before?"

"We've been to the area, but not that specific church," Jeremiah said. "We aren't going to let the children know until we know for sure."

"I understand. I won't tell anyone."

"I'm praying for a good fit. I want to be a senior pastor."

"This sounds like a step in the right direction," Kenny said. "The kids will be sorry to see you go."

"Cecil and Warren know about it, and they're both willing to relocate."

"Good. You'll be able to keep BearFace together," Kenny said.

The members of Fridays At Five gathered in Steward Music Group's Studio Four shortly after ten Monday morning. Will Consoli and Stuart Lederer would be working in the control room for the sessions which could last up to a year.

"Can we listen to some of the demos, Will?" Kenny asked.

Will played a minute or so of ten demos as the guys listened.

Jeff shook his head. "We've got twenty demo songs that are decent, but I don't think there's one of them that blows me away."

"I've got a song that needs some work with the lyrics," Adam said.

"Let's hear it," Jeff said.

211

"Okay, Dave and I worked on the music," Adam said. He played the song on his keyboard and sang the lyrics he and Dave had written.

By the end of the day, nothing had been recorded. The guys spent the entire afternoon working on lyrics for two new songs.

"We've been struggling for two weeks without a lot to show for our effort," Jeff said around four o'clock. "Let's call it a day."

"Let's listen to these tracks, and then head home. I'm mentally wiped," Kenny said.

"I hear ya," Dave said.

They listened to the tracks.

"They're well recorded," P.J. said. "But they sound like filler to me."

"Let's come back Monday and listen again," Dave said.

As Kenny was leaving he mentioned to Will and Stuart, "Save the tracks. We might need to use them in the future."

"Are you sure you don't mind if I go to the show by myself?" Emmy asked Kenny Saturday afternoon.

"I'd rather not go, Em. I will have other chances to see them. I really don't feel like fighting the crowd. You know it's general admission, and everyone stands for the whole show, right?"

"I know," she said. "I went to your show there back in 1998. I doubt if the place has changed much."

The Spencer Auditorium opened in 1971 and still hosted shows on Friday and Saturday nights. Most of the bands were relatively new with maybe one CD released. Occasionally, a well-known band past its prime would use the venue.

"Who is the headliner?" Kenny asked.

"Do you remember that band from Milwaukee called The Imaginations? They had a couple of hits about ten years ago. Kind of new wave stuff."

"Are you going to stay for the whole show?"

She shrugged. "I might see if I can sneak backstage to see

212

the guys and blow off the other band. They aren't really my style."

"Do they know you're going to be there?"

"No, I told Nelson I wanted to surprise them. He said he wouldn't tell them, but he would try to find me after the show and bring me backstage."

Nelson Grapella, who managed Emmy, now also managed her old band.

"Try not to get trampled by the crowd. That place can get a little out of control at times," Kenny reminded her.

"I don't plan to get involved with a mosh pit or anything," she laughed and then ran upstairs to shower and get ready.

The doors would open at eight and the twenty-one and over show would start at nine. She wanted to leave around seven thirty.

"Mommy, why can't we go to the show?" Heather asked as Emmy brushed her hair.

"Everyone has to be older than twenty-one to get in, sweetie. I will bring you to one of the shows they do closer to home, okay?"

"Okay, but tell Bobby not to play too loud," Heather said and then ran back to her room to play with Isabella.

Kenny walked out to the garage with Emmy. "Will you call me when you're on your way home?"

"Are you sure you'll still be up? I might hang out with the guys until after eleven."

"Very funny, Em. Call me." He kissed her and she got into her Civic Si. He watched until she disappeared down the driveway.

Emmy made it to the venue a bit earlier than she expected. She pulled into the VIP lot and gave the security guard her name.

"You can park over there by that red Corvette, Ms. Colasanti. I'll make sure you will be able to get out easy enough."

"Thank you," Emmy said. She spotted the van and the U-Haul truck the band used to haul their gear into the city. She parked and walked around the building. She joined the other people waiting in line to enter the venue. She wore a baseball cap, her old army coat and faded jeans. No one recognized her.

When her old band took the stage, Emmy whistled as loud as she could. The guys couldn't hear her, but it didn't matter. She

213

stayed at the edge of the crowd to the right of the stage. During one song she even danced with two college-age guys. As the band left the stage, she called Nelson.

"Where are you, Emmy?" Nelson asked from the side of the stage. She told him and he spotted her. "Come up to the front, and I'll take you backstage. Did you like the show?"

"I loved it. They really rocked the place. Too many times the crowd ignores the opening act, but I think they made a lot of new fans tonight."

Nelson met her at the front and helped her climb onto the five-foot-high stage. He checked out her old army jacket and grinned. "Are you trying to be incognito? You look like a college student."

"I didn't want to attract any attention. I saw some fans in the crowd from my last tour, and I didn't want to detract from the new band. You know what I mean?"

Nelson put an all-access pass around her neck. "Keep that on, and let's find the guys."

He held her hand and led her to a noisy, cream-colored room crowded with people.

Emmy put a hand on the wall. *This is the same color as when I was here sixteen years ago. I wonder if its been painted since then.* She scooted between people while holding onto Nelson.

"There they are!" he pointed.

"I see them." Emmy dodged past some people and ran up to the guys.

Bobby spotted her and smiled. "Hey, guys! Look who's here. Do you want an autograph, young lady?"

She poked Bobby in the chest. "I thought you guys hated my suggestion for the band name."

"We couldn't think of anything better, so for tonight we were the Bender Brothers Band," Micah said as he hugged Emmy.

She hugged Quinten and Miles and shook hands with Freddie and Marshall Bender. Even though they were part of the worship team, she didn't know them all that well. "I like those long coats," she said to Freddie and Marshall.

"We used to wear these back in the old days," Freddie said.

214

"Where's Kenny?" Bobby asked.

"He's at home with the kids," Emmy answered. She stepped back as some fans tried to get autographs from the guys.

"So, you're here all by yourself, huh?" Bobby asked while signing his name for two female fans.

The two fans stared at Emmy, but didn't recognize her.

"Why didn't you come backstage before the show?" Micah asked.

"I didn't want to bother you. This was your first big gig."

"We did play at Larry's Uptown Grill three nights. That showcase got us this gig. That plus our association with you and Kenny," Micah said.

Two fans bumped into Emmy from behind and she fell into Bobby. He grabbed her and kept her from losing her balance.

"Thanks, Bobby," she said.

"This place is a zoo. We were heading to catering. Are you hungry?" Bobby asked.

"I could eat, and I want to talk to you guys."

Emmy told Nelson where she would be, and followed Bobby through the crowd to a smaller room with three buffet tables covered with food.

"Is this for the other band?" Emmy asked.

Bobby shook his head. "No, they have their own room. We haven't even had a chance to meet them, but we might later. Did I tell you we're opening for them three more nights?"

"You didn't tell me. Where?"

"Not sure, but we'll take the exposure. Are you getting warm? Should I take your jacket?"

"Thanks, but I can hold it." Emmy removed her army jacket.

Bobby grabbed two plates. "Tell me what you want. I know you like fresh fruit."

"That would be enough for now," she said. She followed Bobby through the line and to a table along one wall.

"We can talk here without having to shout."

She grinned at him. "I can't believe you're using that name."

215

"I wanted us to be the Bobby O'Connor Band, but the guys threatened to fire me," he joked. "Did you like my drum solo?"

"Not bad for a punk," she teased. "I did like the show. Have the guys at Prater-Saylor got anything booked for you?"

"They're working on a summer tour. We would open for some alternative country bands in small venues. Mostly in Texas and the Southwest," Bobby explained.

They finished eating and Bobby tossed the trash. He came back and sat close to Emmy.

She leaned against him. "Did I ever tell you about the night I came here to see Fridays At Five?"

"If you did, I don't remember it. Tell me again."

"I was kinda dating Tony Bertucci because Kenny didn't want me to wait for him because they were gone for over a year. I didn't see him for so long. I'm rambling, huh?"

"How did you survive?" Bobby asked with a grin.

"We weren't... never mind. Diane got tickets for the show, and I rode in a limo with Kenny's parents, Tony, and Diane and Craig. I saw Kenny in that other room. It was packed with people just like tonight. He saw me and picked me up and hugged me."

"In front of Tony and everyone? Did he kiss you?"

"No, but I think he would have if Tony hadn't been there. I would have let him."

"I bet you would have," Bobby said. "I know how much you missed him on our tours."

"Hush! I'm not that bad, am I?"

"You get kinda..."

"Shush, someone might hear you."

"Don't look now, but some people are staring at you."

"Shoot! I don't want to be recognized hanging out with you."

"Are you worried people might get the wrong idea?" Bobby asked with a grin.

She poked him in the side just as two female fans walked over.

"You're the drummer, right?" one asked.

Bobby smiled and said, "I am."

216

"Is this your girlfriend?" the other one asked.

Bobby put an arm around Emmy and grinned. "No, she's just a fan who follows me around."

The fans left and Emmy elbowed Bobby with considerable force. "Why did you say that? They probably think I'm your groupie."

"Aren't you? I have seen you at a lot of our shows."

"You are such a punk. If I ever get the band back together, remind me to fire you."

Emmy stayed at the venue until midnight.

"I better get home. I need to be at church tomorrow," Emmy told the guys.

"Hey, could I catch a ride with you?" Bobby asked. "I want to make it back for church, too."

"I could drop you off, but it'll cost you," Emmy said.

"I'm willing to pay," Bobby said.

Emmy said goodbye to the guys. "You should pay me for coming up with the name for the band."

"Uh, we're changing it after tonight, Emmy," Micah said. "We're going to call ourselves the Oliver Porter Band."

"Very funny." She stuck out her tongue at Micah.

"Where's your car?" Bobby asked as he handed the army coat to her.

She led the way outside to the VIP lot. "You wanna drive?"

"Sure! Do you trust me not to wreck your car?"

She laughed. "Did you really think I would let you drive my baby?"

She drove Bobby back to SoHam and dropped him at his apartment.

"Thanks for the ride, Em. See you in the morning."

She headed home and slipped into bed next to Kenny just after two.

"How was the show? Did you stay for the Imaginations?"

"No, I wasn't interested in them. I hung out with the guys, and I gave Bobby a ride home. They were really good. I think they will do all right without me."

217

Chapter Twenty-Six

Pastor Darren Eaton walked into Tyler's office Monday morning and took a seat.

Tyler looked up from his iPad. "Did you give them an answer?"

"I did. I declined the offer. Jody and I prayed for days about it. I do want to be a senior pastor one of these days, but this wasn't the right time or place."

"How so?" Tyler asked. He got up, walked around his desk and closed the door.

Darren waited for Tyler to sit down. "When I filled in for that month, I saw some people from this church."

"That doesn't surprise me. You do have people who like to hear you preach," Tyler said and then chuckled. "I can't understand why, but they do."

Darren laughed along. "Hey! Some of them even like to hear Jake preach."

Tyler turned around and looked at the large map of SoHam and the surrounding area on the wall. "Most of our members live in this area." Tyler make a sweeping gesture over the west side of SoHam and the cities that bordered it. "We have a few who drive over from the east-side and even south of the river, but not a lot. I can understand if some of them would want to switch churches. SoHam First would be a lot closer."

Darren tapped his jaw. "How can I say this without it sounding egotistical?"

"Just say it, and I will understand," Tyler said.

"One of the reasons I turned down the offer was because I thought it might pull some of our people away. They might follow me to SoHam First, and I didn't want that to happen."

"Please don't take this the wrong way because I care deeply for each person who comes here, but I think we could afford to lose a few people to SoHam First. It might be just the spark that church needs to regain some momentum."

Darren shook his head. "That wasn't the only reason I declined. Jody has expressed a desire to move back to the

Columbus area one of these days."

"I can understand that. Liz used to feel that way every time we would go back to Hillsdale."

"I was going to give Pastor Williams a break, so he could teach his Sunday School class, but under the circumstances, maybe I should see if Jake or Rev. Milhuff would handle it."

"I'm sure either one of them would be willing. Jake loves getting to preach to adults, and Rev. Milhuff would be a perfect pastor for them if he was twenty years younger. He mentioned he has filled in over there in the past."

"I'll talk to him first," Darren said.

"I'm sure Emmy will be thrilled to have Pastor Williams return to his class," Tyler said and then chuckled.

"Why is that?"

"Don't tell anyone, but Emmy told Liz she didn't care much for Dennis Orman as a teacher. She said he was too boring."

Darren grinned. "He does speak in a monotone at times."

"I've been in the class. He's not that bad, but he's not Pastor Williams. Don is rather serious most of the time, but he can let his sense of humor out occasionally."

"Emmy doesn't hide her feelings, does she?"

"She can be brutally honest at times," Tyler said.

Two days later Diane lit the candles on Lily's birthday cake and then sighed. "Can you believe she's already three? It feels like yesterday that I was nursing her and she was so tiny. Now she talks constantly and plays with her dolls by herself."

Emmy nodded. "She does seem mature for her age. Heather and Isa let her play with them."

"Sometimes I wish she had a sister," Diane said as she took a picture of the cake.

"Are you seriously thinking about having another baby?"

"Lily mentions a sister about once a week, but we're not trying to have another," Diane admitted.

"I'll bring everyone in here. We can sing and watch Lily blow out her candles," Emmy said.

Caden Garrett stood alone against the building watching some kids playing games during recess. A soccer ball came flying toward him and hit him in the chest. Two seventh grade boys rushed toward Caden.

"Little help, toad breath," one of the boys hollered.

Caden picked up the soccer ball and threw it in the general direction of the boys. It landed short.

"Hey! Don't you know anything? You're supposed to kick it," the taller boy said as he picked up the ball.

The other boy approached Caden and grabbed his arm. "What's wrong with you? Can't you talk? Are you in the retard class?" The boy pushed Caden to the ground.

The other boy threw the soccer ball at Caden and hit him in the back. "I bet you love to play dodge-ball. You make a perfect target."

Both boys stood over Caden and laughed.

"Come on! Get up so I can knock you down again," one said.

Carson Garrett plowed into the back of both boys and caused them to fall against the building. "Leave my brother alone!" Carson balled his hands into fists and stood ready to throw a punch.

The two boys used their hands to cover their face up and stumbled as they tried to get up.

"Don't you ever pick on him again!" Carson shouted.

The two boys scrambled away on their hands and knees.

Carson threw the ball at them. "Take your old ball with you."

Heather and Isabella appeared and squatted in front of Caden.

"Are you all right?" Heather extended a hand to her younger but bigger cousin. "Your elbow is bleeding."

Caden sniffled and used a hand to wipe away some tears. Heather and Isabella helped Caden to his feet.

Carson turned as he heard Mrs. Payne approaching. "Here comes your teacher, Caden."

"What is going on? Caden, are you hurt?" Mrs. Payne

220

picked up Caden with ease and held him to her chest.

"He's bleeding, Mrs. Payne," Isabella said.

"Some big boys were trying to hurt him," Heather added. "But Carson made them stop."

Carson explained to Mrs. Payne what he saw. "I'm sorry for pushing those boys, but they were hurting my brother."

"Let me see where you're bleeding," Mrs. Payne said as she set Caden down. She checked his elbow. "It doesn't look too bad, but let's take you inside to the nurse's office. You probably need a Band-Aid." She pointed a finger at Carson. "You better come with me. I want to hear more."

Isabella came inside with Caden, but Heather stayed outside to play with her friends.

"Does it hurt?" Isabella asked.

Caden nodded. "Is it still bleeding?"

Isabella checked. "Just a little."

"I don't want to see it," he said. "I don't like blood."

Isabella patted his shoulder. "It's okay. I don't like blood either."

"You won't tell anyone I was crying, will you, Isa?"

She crossed her heart. "Our secret."

Mrs. Payne talked to Carson about the incident. He explained what happened but did not divulge the names of the two boys.

"I understand your reluctance, but I will need to call your parents," Mrs. Payne said.

Carson nodded. "My mom is home but my stepfather is on a business trip."

Mrs. Payne reached Diane an hour later and explained the situation.

"He's never gotten into a fight before," Diane said.

Mrs. Payne chuckled. "From what I've learned it wasn't much of a fight. These two boys were bullying Caden and Carson simply reacted. He pushed the boys, but I don't think he even had to throw a punch. They cowered against the building and then ran away. Carson wouldn't tell me their names, but I found out. This isn't the first time they have picked on one of the younger boys."

"Are my sons all right? Do I need to come over to the school?" Diane asked.

"Caden needed a Band-Aid, but he's all right now."

"Is Carson in much trouble?"

"No, he's not in any trouble as far as I'm concerned. The other boys are another story. I'm sure Mrs. Toth called their parents again."

"I will have a talk with Carson," Diane said. "I certainly do not condone any type of fighting."

"One more thing," Mrs. Payne whispered. "Caden was a little embarrassed about the whole incident. I don't think too many of the other children witnessed the incident, but Heather and Isabella did. He felt ashamed about crying in front of them."

"He is more sensitive than his brother," Diane mentioned.

"I thought as much. I've noticed he doesn't talk much to the other students. He plays with Zachary, but not many of the other boys. He has opened up since the beginning of the year."

"Do you think I have anything to worry about?"

Mrs. Payne smiled over the phone. "Not at all. He's a little smaller than most of the boys, but Caden is very intelligent. I can't see him becoming a football player, but I could see him as a college professor or a doctor."

"Please, let me know if anything else happens, Mrs. Payne."

Emmy heard about the fight from Heather and Isabella and decided to run over to see Diane after dinner.

"Did he get in trouble?" Emmy asked.

"Not really," Diane said and then explained what Mrs. Payne had said.

Carson came into the kitchen to get a glass of milk and heard his mother and Emmy talking.

"I don't condone fighting, but I'm kinda proud of what you did," Emmy said.

"Aw, it wasn't a fight, Aunt Em. I saw them hurting Caden, so I just reacted. I don't think I even hit them. I pushed them down, and they ran away."

"Did I ever tell you about the time I punched Barry

222

Newton?" Emmy asked.

Carson took a drink of milk and then shook his head.

"I was ten, and I got in trouble for riding my bike across the street in front of Darby's. Your grandfather had warned me not to cross that street, but I did because Barry did. Anyway, he took my bike away for a week."

"That's when he painted it that hideous purple color, right?" Diane asked.

"I loved that bike," Emmy responded. "It was green when Mom first bought it.

Diane laughed. "An ugly green if I remember right."

"It wasn't that bad," Emmy said.

"Is that why Isabella has a purple bike now?" Carson asked.

"I let the girls choose their own bikes, and she picked that color. Heather didn't want the same color, so she chose a red one."

Caden walked into the kitchen and saw Carson drinking milk. "Can I have some, too?"

Carson filled a glass for Caden and even added some Hershey's chocolate sauce for him.

"So what about Barry Newton?" Diane asked.

"Okay, so I followed Barry to Darby's and I guess Daddy saw me. He asked me about it at dinner, and I didn't lie to him. I admitted crossing the street, and he took my bike away."

"I remember that," Diane said. "What else happened?"

"After the week was up, I got my bike back and rode right over to Barry's house. He was playing in the yard, and I walked right up to him and slugged him in the belly without any warning."

Carson didn't say anything for a moment before asking, "Did he hit you back?"

"No, because he was taught to never hit a girl."

"Did you hurt him?"

Emmy shook her head. "Not really. I think I surprised him more than anything."

"What happened after that?" Carson asked. "Were you still friends?"

"Oh, yeah. We rode our bikes around the neighborhood all

223

the time," Emmy paused and bit her lip.

"What's wrong, Auntie Em? Are you crying?" Caden asked.

Emmy wiped her eyes with the back of her hand. "I was thinking about your grandfather's funeral. There was a picture of me and my old bike." She looked at Diane. "Do you still have the photographs from the wake?"

"I think I have them somewhere. Why? Do you want them?" Diane asked.

Emmy nodded. "I'd like to see them again. I could scan them into my computer and make copies for you."

"I'll try to find them someday, but I don't need copies. They don't mean as much to me as they do you, Em," Diane said as she turned and walked out of the kitchen. She didn't let Emmy or her sons see as tears filled her eyes.

"Why are we going to the mall, Mommy?" Isabella asked. "I was going to play with Noemi and Grace."

"You've been asking for phones, and I had a talk with your father last night. We decided to buy you each a basic cell phone."

"I want a new iPhone!" Heather shouted.

Emmy shook her head. "You are not getting an iPhone. They are too expensive. We're going to buy basic phones."

Heather and Isabella started texting each other on the way home. They dashed inside after Emmy parked in the garage.

"Daddy, thank you for letting us have cell phones," Isabella shouted as she held her phone out to show him. "I got a purple cover."

Kenny set down his magazine. "I see."

"I got a pink cover," Heather said. "Thanks, Daddy."

"Did Mommy explain the rules?" he asked.

Heather rolled her eyes. "Yes! We are not supposed to call our friends all the time. We have to text Mommy when we go over to our friends' houses. We can't take them to school. Can we buy better phones when we turn ten?"

"We will see how well you follow the rules," Kenny said.

Chapter Twenty-Seven

"Hey, what are you doing this morning? You busy?" Emmy asked Father James the Saturday before Easter.

"I am contemplating my message for mass tonight and tomorrow. If you recall, this is an important time of the year," he answered. "I am fasting and spending most of the day in prayer."

Emmy laughed. "What a load of... Never mind. You use the same message every Easter. Don't you have it memorized by now?"

"What's on your mind, my child?"

"I'm taking the kids to church in an hour for the Easter egg hunt. It starts at ten and lasts for about five minutes. Wanna go with us?"

He didn't hesitate. "Absolutely! Will you pick me up?"

"Sure," she answered. "Oh, I promised we would go to Darby's for lunch. I guess I'll have to drop you back at the rectory since you're fasting today."

"Hold on! I started my fast yesterday. I could use a chili dog."

Emmy laughed. "I'll be there soon."

Later, Father James stood at the back of Noah's Ark with Pastor Tyler and watched as over two hundred children eagerly gathered up the carefully-hidden-in-plain-sight Easter eggs.

Tyler chuckled. "Hours of preparation and planning and it's all over in a few minutes."

"It looks rather chaotic, but I noticed the younger ones have a section of their own," Father James added.

"We have to keep the older kids separated."

"Are there a lot of neighborhood people here?"

Tyler looked around the large room. "We are attracting more and more every year."

Kevin Michael rushed up to Pastor Tyler and Father James. He held out his basket. "I found lots of eggs, but Ben and I helped Lily and Phoebe find some. They're little so they need help. I gotta go find more eggs." He rushed off.

Emmy walked up holding Conor in her arms. "Would you

hold him for a minute while I help Lily?" She handed Conor to Father James. "He kept getting knocked over."

"Conor, were the big kids getting in your way?" Tyler said as he grinned at Conor.

Conor, who at eighteen months old hated to be held, squirmed to be let down.

"Okay, I'll let you go, but you better be careful." Father James set Conor down, and he and Tyler watched Conor run in a jerky manner after the other kids.

"Have you talked to Emmy about the worship team?" Tyler asked. "She hasn't said anything to Liz as far as I know."

"She has mentioned it a time or two," Father James watched as Isabella helped her little cousin find an egg.

"I don't mean to pry if it's something she said in confidence."

"It wasn't a confession." Father James laughed. "She did express some feelings of not being wanted by the new worship leaders. I'm not saying that's true, but it is how she feels."

"She hasn't said anything to me, but I could sense a change."

"It can't be easy for the new couple to accommodate her schedule. She does travel quite often at times."

"True, but she didn't miss too many Sundays," Tyler said.

"She did mention when she first joined the team she sang every week. Now the team has more members, and they rotate the schedule. I'm sure that is part of the reason she feels unwanted. I've only known Emmy for close to three years, but I feel I know her pretty well," he said. "You've known her longer."

"Yes, but I have a feeling she confides in you more," Tyler admitted.

Father James scratched his nose and then made direct eye contact with Tyler. "I hope that doesn't bother you."

"Not at all. I'm glad she has a real brother. She treats Tony like a brother at times, but I think she's doing that less and less." Tyler chuckled as he saw his son Grayson's joy over finding a special egg. "Has she ever talked about her childhood with you? I know some details about it."

Father James got Emmy's attention and pointed to where Conor and Lily stood trying to open the plastic eggs. "One day we spent the whole afternoon talking about it. She told me how she met Kenny and some of her other friends."

"Rory Porter?" Tyler asked.

Father James hesitated.

Tyler shook his head. "I'm not trying to pry. I know she and Rory are close friends."

Father James rubbed his jaw. "I don't think Emmy knows when she and Rory first met. It's more like he was around the fringes. She told me how Kristen introduced her to Tony in high school."

Tyler laughed. "I've heard that one. Then she realized they lived in the same apartment building as kids."

"Yes, but only for a short time. No longer than a month."

They watched as the Easter egg hunt came to a close. Pastor Jeremiah and Mia got the kids' attention.

"Do you have to talk to the children?" Father James asked Tyler.

"No, this is Jeremiah and Mia's specialty. We can slip away and talk if you'd like."

They left Noah's Ark and walked down the hall of the education building.

Father James glanced at a plaque on the wall and paused to read it. "So this building is named for the former senior pastor, right?"

"Yes, it's fitting because he's the president of a college now."

They walked out of Behren Hall and into the foyer of the old sanctuary. They took seats in the Coffee Corner.

"Emmy admitted she didn't have many friends in high school. Not close friends," Father James said. "She claims she was rather shy."

"It's hard to believe," Tyler chuckled. "But I can still see it. She's shy around people she doesn't know."

"Until you hand her a microphone and put a band behind her," Father James added. He laughed at the image in his head.

227

"Dr. Ausland told me Emmy created quite a stir when she joined the worship team. He said she brought a breath of new life to the group."

Father James laughed. "I can imagine the looks of the older people as Emmy danced around the stage. Too bad there's no video of that."

"Oh, but there is," Tyler said. "I found a DVD of a service from 2002. I think it might have been transferred from a tape because the quality isn't all that great, but the audio is all right. It's the first Easter Emmy was part of the team."

"I'd love to see that sometime."

"Let's go to my office. I'll make a copy for you."

Tyler looked at Father James. "It's probably none of my business, but how old are you?"

Father James laughed. "Heather and Isabella tease me that I'm older than dirt, but I was born in 1955. That makes me old enough to be Emmy and Diane's father."

"I didn't know their father, but everyone tells me you look just like him."

"I like to think I'm more handsome," Father James joked. "Diane was more reluctant to accept me into the family, but Emmy opened up to me immediately." He paused and glanced around the office. "Emmy has dealt with friends abandoning her over the years. Kenny's band traveled for over a year at a time when she could have benefited from him being here with her. She told me Rory left SoHam and they didn't see each other for over ten years."

"She told me they reconnected in the nursing home," Tyler said.

Father James laughed. "She worried what our father might do if he recognized Rory from the old neighborhood. Not that he could have done anything."

"I get the impression Emmy didn't have many female friends growing up."

"Yeah," Father James tilted his head. "She said there weren't many girls her age in the neighborhood. She told me how she met Kristen in a school restroom."

"Emmy and Liz are good friends now."

228

"It's good for her to have close friends in the church. I'm not a psychologist, but it's not difficult to sense her feelings of insecurity."

Tyler nodded. "She has admitted feeling guilty about their material gain if you want to call it that."

Father James grinned. "She said she would be happy living in their guesthouse, so I told her I would move into the main house."

"This church has been blessed with many generous members."

"Maybe I shouldn't tell you, but they did contribute when St. John's needed to replace the roof."

Tyler waved a hand. "I don't mind in the least. I am concerned about the worship team. Emmy is a big part of the team. People notice when she isn't on the platform, and they let me hear about it. I get emails and texts."

"She doesn't think anyone misses her."

The DVD finished copying. Tyler placed it in a jewel case and handed it to Father James. "We will have to remind her how much she is missed."

"Thanks for the DVD. I can't wait to see it."

Father James left the office with Tyler following.

"There you are," Emmy said. "I've been looking all over for you. I need to run Conor and Lily home before we do lunch." Emmy noticed the DVD in Father James' hand. "What have you got there?"

Tyler explained.

"Why did you give him a copy? He's just going to watch it to make fun of me." Emmy put her hands on her hips, but then she tried to snatch it from her brother.

He held the DVD behind his back and wagged a finger at her. "No, you don't. This belongs to me."

You are both creeps," she said while making a face. "Were you talking about me?"

"Your name did come up in our conversation, my child," Father James said very seriously.

Emmy rolled her eyes. "Will ya listen to him. One minute

229

he thinks he's some kind of priest, and the next minute he's calling his bookie to bet on the horses."

"I never bet on the horses," Father James said. "I'm sticking to football and a few baseball games."

She tried once again to steal the DVD without any success. "Do you still want to go to Darby's for lunch? It's a long walk from here."

"We could do Darby's another day if you have stuff for lunch at home. I would really like to watch my new DVD. I might be able to get some new ideas for Easter mass."

Tyler laughed. "I'm not getting in the middle of this." He shook hands with Father James. "I'll see you at the next meeting." He smiled at Emmy. "Will I see you tomorrow in church?"

She stuck out her tongue. "I'm going to pray for both of you."

Father James helped get all the kids into the Odyssey and Emmy drove back to Bristol Ridge.

Kevin Michael showed everyone his stash of candy. "I found so much. I'm going to eat it all today."

Emmy shook her head. "As soon as we get home that candy is going to get locked away. I will dole it out as I see fit."

"You're no fun, Mom," Kevin Michael complained until he spotted a SoHam squad car with its lights flashing.

Emmy dropped Conor and Lily off and then pulled into her garage.

"What would you like for lunch?" she asked everyone.

"I thought we were going to Darby's," Heather said.

"A change of plans. We're eating here," Emmy explained. "We eat too much fast food."

"Sandwiches are okay," Isabella said.

An hour later Emmy joined Father James and Kenny in the family room.

"Are you ready to watch?" Kenny asked.

"I will clobber you both if you make fun of me," she said as she plopped down on the couch since Father James was sitting in her recliner.

Kenny popped the DVD into the player and then returned

to his recliner. "This should be interesting," he said smiling at Emmy.

"Would you like to sit on the couch?"

"No, I'm good here," Kenny answered.

"I'm only offering so you could get used to where you'll be sleeping tonight," she said with a sweet smile.

"Hush! I want to hear this," Father James said. "Could you turn it up a little?"

Kenny turned up the volume as the worship team started playing.

Emmy covered her eyes. "I look hideous. I look like I'm twelve."

"Not at all, Em. I'd say you look at least fifteen," Kenny teased.

They watched in silence through two songs.

"I didn't know the Nazarene church allowed dancing like that," Father James said.

"I'm not sorry I poisoned your sandwich now," Emmy said as she leaned back and crossed her arms over her chest.

They listened to the rest of the worship band before fast-forwarding to Dr. Ausland's message.

"I can't believe how young he looks," Kenny said.

"Are you saying he looks a lot older now because he's had to deal with Emmy all these years?"

Emmy rolled her eyes.

Kenny nodded. "I think you've got a valid point there, Father James. It's kinda like the President always looks about twenty years older when he leaves office because of the stress."

"If I had to make a guess, I would say that Pastor Ausland looks about twenty years older now," Father James said.

"Go ahead! Take your best shots," Emmy said. "I hope you enjoy sleeping on the couch, and it's quite a long walk back to St. John's." She jumped up and stormed out of the room. She walked into the den and slammed the door behind her.

"Do you think she's really mad?" Father James asked. "Did we go too far?"

"I'll talk to her, but I think something else is bugging her,"

231

Kenny said as he stopped the DVD. He popped it out, put in back in the jewel box and handed it to Father James as he headed to the den.

"Go away!" Emmy yelled after hearing Kenny knock on the door.

"Are you all right, Em?" Kenny opened the door slowly. "Can I come in?"

"I left the door unlocked, didn't I?"

He entered cautiously, stood behind Emmy's recliner and kissed the top of her head.

She looked back at him. "I'm not mad at you guys. Seeing that DVD reminded me of how much I used to love singing with the worship team. It's different now."

"What can I do to help?"

"Since you don't have a time machine, I can't think of anything," she answered.

Father James entered the room. "Should I call a cab, or will someone run me home?"

"I'll take you home. I might stop at Darby's for a root beer and a slice of chocolate cake," Emmy said.

Kenny rubbed his stomach. "A slice of cake sounds good."

"I hear ya," Father James agreed.

Emmy shook her head. "Men! Such a waste of space."

Pastor Jonah Galves gathered his volunteer attendance-takers in the library near the end of the second service. They sat around the conference table in the middle of the room and opened their iPad tablets.

Jonah opened his laptop. "I haven't checked the records, but I have to believe today's attendance is an all-time high."

They took a few minutes to go over the numbers.

"So, we had 754 in Sunday School. In the first service there were 1136 people and 1412 for the second service," Jonah said as he entered the numbers into his laptop.

"We need a new way of keeping track of everyone," Mary Galves said.

Dylan Michaelis rubbed his jaw. "I wonder how much it

would cost to get facial recognition software like the government uses."

"Oh, Da, be reasonable," Mary said.

"We could build our own database and use cameras at every entrance to track who enters the building," Jonah added.

Dylan mentioned, "People opposed online giving at first, but now the percentage of people using it continues to go up."

"At least we don't have to go around and count heads the way we used to. That would take forever," Kate Cordell sighed.

Two weeks later Emmy joined her kids in Noah's Ark for the final Sunday with Jeremiah and Mia Tolla. She found a seat in the back next to Liz Hammond and Kristen Randolph.

"We are going to need more space real quick," Liz whispered as she surveyed the room.

"Has the board decided how they want to use the old sanctuary yet?" Emmy asked. "I heard the teens are going to take it over."

"That's one plan, but I don't think they've made any decision."

"Is it always this crowded in here?" Kristen asked. "I haven't been in here in months."

"It has been lately," Liz answered. "The kids love Jeremiah and Mia. They will be missed."

"I remember when they started here," Emmy said. "The twins thought he looked like Jesus because of his beard."

"Mia told me they want to start a family," Liz mentioned.

"I'm surprised they've waited this long. Do you know how old they are?" Emmy asked.

Liz thought about it. "Mia is a few months younger than me. I knew her at Olivet."

"I didn't know she graduated from Olivet," Emmy said.

"She started there but transferred to somewhere closer to home, and Jeremiah is just a couple months younger than Tyler," Liz said.

"I hope the board hires an older couple to replace Mia and Jeremiah," Emmy said.

233

"Why?" Kristen asked. "The kids relate to young pastors."

"Every pastor on the staff is young except for Rev. Milhuff, and he's here to take care of the old people."

Kristen grinned at Emmy. "How does it feel to be older than everyone on the staff?"

"You're older than me, Krissy." Emmy tried to think of the ages of all the staff members. *Tyler, Darren, Jonah, Jake, Jeremiah. Shoot! They're all younger than me.* "I can't think of anyone who's older."

"I'll pass your suggestion along to Tyler," Liz teased.

Jeremiah and Mia stayed to say goodbye to all the children and parents who weren't staying for the potluck.

"Mommy, Pastor Jeremiah said we could come to Alabama to visit them sometime. Can we go next week?" Kevin Michael asked.

"We might have to wait until after they've settled in at their new church," Emmy answered.

"I'm sorry for calling this late, Em," Liz said.

"It's not that late. It's only a little after ten. What's up? Is everyone all right?" Emmy asked. She threw the faded green dishcloth at the kitchen sink.

"I thought I would tell you about the couple the board interviewed tonight."

"Did you meet them?" Emmy asked. "Are they nice?"

"I did meet them earlier, and guess what?" Liz asked while picking up some of Phoebe's books.

"What?" Emmy asked.

"They are older than you," Liz said joyfully.

"For real!? Like real old?"

"Almost ancient," Liz said while picking up one of Derby's chew toys.

"What are their names? Did the board hire them? Or Tyler, or whoever makes those decisions?" Emmy asked while walking down the hallway.

"Tyler said the board made them an offer. I have their names and details if you're interested."

234

"Tell me! I have to know." Emmy plopped down on the couch and put her head on a pillow with her feet on the back of the couch.

"Okay, their names are Wade and Blaine Dickinson. They're from Ohio. They have two boys. Damian and Donavon, who were born in 2004 and 2006." Liz deposited the chew toy in the trash and walked back into her kitchen.

"One of them is the twins age. How old are the parents? They can't be that old if their kids are that young."

Liz stifled a laugh while leaning against the counter. "Trust me, Em, they are ancient."

"Tell me, Liz," Emmy insisted.

"Okay. Wade was born in 1978 and Blaine in 1980. March 13 to be exact, so she's four months older than you. Happy?"

"You're a stinker, Liz," Emmy said. "Are you trying to tell me I'm an old woman now? Should I join Mrs. Thompkins and her group of old biddies?"

"Maybe not this year," Liz teased.

"Well, at least they're not younger than me," Emmy sighed. "Tell me more about them."

"Well, Wade doesn't have a beard, and Blaine is a teacher."

"Will she be hired to teach at the school? What grade does she teach?"

"Not sure, but we will need teachers for next year. You should go back to school so you could teach."

"I might just do that."

Chapter Twenty-Eight

Pastor Tyler missed the early morning call from Wade Dickinson, but he listened to the message and returned the call.

"I'm glad you have decided to take the position," Tyler said. "When will you and Blaine be able to start?"

Wade answered in a deep bass voice, "I resigned my position here three weeks ago. Yesterday was our last official Sunday. Would you mind if we take a couple weeks of vacation?"

"Not at all," Tyler answered. He checked the calendar behind his desk. "You could take the entire month of May if you desire and start here the first Sunday in June. When does school end?"

"Blaine has been homeschooling the boys, but we want to enroll them in the church's school for next year." Wade checked his schedule. "We would like to start before June. Would it be all right if we start on May 24?"

"Certainly. Now about the housing."

"The place you described sounds perfect," Wade assured Pastor Tyler.

"Bill Griffith and his team have done some remodeling. He updated the kitchen. They painted everything a neutral color and should be installing the new carpet before the end of the week. The backyard is fenced in, and you will only be a half mile from the church."

"We couldn't ask for more."

"If you let us know when you will be arriving, I can make sure there are some guys to help you move in," Tyler said.

"We don't have a lot of stuff."

"That will make it an easy job for the men," Tyler said and then chuckled.

"Thank you. I will stay in touch and let you know when we will be there."

Emmy wiped her sweaty brow with her red bandana and inspected the kitchen again.

Liz laughed as she looked at Emmy. "You have dirt all over

your cheek and that rag isn't helping." Liz wet a Handi Wipe and handed it to Emmy. "Try this."

Emmy wiped her face. "Is that better?"

"Yes, you don't look like a homeless person now."

Emmy threw the Handi Wipe in the garbage and retied the bandana around her head. "I don't think we can get this place any cleaner."

Tyler heard the comment as he walked into the kitchen with Darren Eaton and Jake Boyter. "This house looks brand new. The only room that hasn't been changed is the second bathroom, and it was done before Jeremiah and Mia moved in."

Darren smiled at Emmy. "This is one advantage of having a young staff."

"What's that?" Jake asked while knowing what Darren would say.

"Young guys like us can do a whole lot more physical work than older pastors."

Emmy made a face at Darren. "Just because all you guys are younger than me doesn't mean I'm getting old."

"Of course not, madam," Jonah Galves said as he entered the room. "The garage is all clean."

Emmy turned to Mary Galves. "Would you mind if I slug him?"

"Go ahead, Em. He shouldn't be teasing you like that." Mary grinned and then added, "He knows to respect his elders better than that."

Emmy was spared further teasing by the arrival of Jess and Joe Zawaski.

"All the yard work is finished, Miss Emmy. Is there anything else you need done?"

Emmy smiled at the two brothers who worked on her tour crew. "I can't think of anything. Would you like some lemonade or ice tea?"

"Yes, please," Joe answered.

"Ice tea sounds good," Tyler said.

Emmy stuck out her tongue. "I'm only taking care of Jess and Joe. The rest of you mean guys are on your own."

237

An hour later Wade Dickinson parked the U-Haul truck in the street, and an older model Dodge Grand Caravan parked behind him.

"They're here!" Emmy hollered. She walked out the front door, and everyone else followed.

Wade jumped down from the truck, walked around the back and saw a dozen people walking in his direction. "Wow! I didn't expect such a large reception."

Blaine, Damian and Donavon exited the minivan and joined Wade in the asphalt driveway.

Tyler walked up to Wade and extended a hand. "How was the trip and your vacation?"

"Relaxing and much needed. The trip was easy enough," Wade said and then sighed. "So this is the house, huh?"

Damian looked up at his mother. "Can we check it out?"

"Go ahead," Blaine said.

Tyler introduced everyone to Wade and Blaine. He saved Emmy for last.

"This is..."

"Hello, Emmy. It's a pleasure to see you again. How have you been?" Wade asked as he and Blaine hugged her.

"I'm fine," Emmy stammered.

Tyler looked at Darren and then Emmy. He asked Wade, "Do you know her already?"

"Of course!" He looked directly at Emmy. "We saw you in concert on the last tour and probably every time you appeared in Ohio. You might not remember us because you meet so many people on the road, but we did talk to you."

"Several times over the years," Blaine added.

"Thank you," Emmy said. She bit her lip and tried to remember meeting Wade and Blaine. *They are kinda memorable. Wade is tall and has that deep voice. Blaine's long hair reaches to her butt.* She looked at Liz and shrugged.

"Let's go inside and you can check out the house," Liz said. "Emmy has been cleaning like a whirlwind."

Wade and Blaine stopped. "Emmy has been cleaning our house?" Blaine asked.

238

"We tried to help, but she's done most of the cleaning," Liz said.

Damian and Donavon ran out of the house, shouting, "It's a brand new house! It's so clean!" They ran up to Emmy and grinned.

"We know you," Damian said. "We have all your CDs. I'm taking piano lessons, and Donnie wants to play the guitar or maybe drums. We want to start a real band when we get older. We want to be singers and write our own songs like you."

"Do you really go to the same church where Dad will be working?" Donavon asked. "Please say you do."

"Yes," Emmy said.

"That's awesome!" both boys yelled. "Do you ever sing on Sunday? Will we get to see you sing in person again?"

Tyler whispered to Darren, "Have you ever seen anyone treat Emmy like this before?"

Darren scratched his head. "Well, kinda, but not to this extent. I remember the teens in our church asking for autographs years ago, but the boys are so excited."

Emmy bit her lip before answering, "I do sing at our church when I can."

"We can't wait to hear you. You want to come inside? We need to pick out our rooms."

Wade and Blaine walked up to Emmy. "Please forgive their exuberance. They have been so excited about the move ever since they found out this is your church."

Everyone headed inside except for Jess and Joe. They opened the back of the truck and got it ready to be unloaded.

Wade and Blaine followed Emmy through the house.

"Everything is just perfect," Blaine whispered to Wade. "We've never lived in such a fancy house before. I bet it has central air."

"All the appliances look brand new, and I even saw a built-in dishwasher and microwave," Wade whispered back.

"Hey! There are two bathrooms," the boys hollered. "Can this be our bathroom?"

"I suppose," Blaine followed the boys into the bathroom.

239

"You've got your own tub and shower. You will have to keep it clean."

"This is the master bedroom," Emmy said as she stepped inside the fifteen by fifteen foot room. "I hope it's big enough."

"Oh, it will be plenty big," Wade assured her.

After showing the Dickinsons around the house, Tyler prayed for the family.

"Are we ready to unload?" Jess asked.

"I think we are," Tyler said.

Two hours later Wade and Blaine stood in the living room and admired their new home.

"If you give us the keys to the U-Haul, we'll take it back," Darren said.

Wade handed him the keys. "The rental agreement is in the truck."

Darren whispered, "Make sure you give your receipt to Lois Crawford. She's the new church secretary. She will make sure you get reimbursed."

"Thank you all for your help," Wade said. He shook hands with everyone. Blaine hugged the ladies and struggled to keep her emotions in check.

"Liz and I would like to take you out for lunch if you're hungry," Tyler said.

"You don't have to do that," Blaine whispered.

Liz smiled. "We might convince Emmy to go with us."

Damian and Donavon beamed with the prospect of having lunch with Emmy.

"Can you go with us, Em?" Liz asked.

"I guess so, but I should call home first."

"What would you like? We have just about every chain you can imagine here. Some great local restaurants, too."

"Can we go to Darby's Dogs?" Damian asked.

Tyler looked surprised. "How do you know about Darby's?"

Damian pointed to Emmy. "Because that's her favorite restaurant. It says so on her website. Can we go there, please?"

"Em, are you up for a trip to Darby's?" Tyler asked.

"I'm always up for that," she shouted. "Let's all go to Darby's."

Everyone else used an excuse of some kind not to go.

"It looks like it will just be seven of us going," Tyler said. "I'll drive."

"Emmy, you can take off your bandana now," Liz said. "We are through with the cleaning."

"I should leave it on because I look awful."

Emmy sat in the middle row with the boys as Tyler drove through SoHam.

"Have you really always lived here?

"Can we see where you went to school?

"Are there still pictures of you hanging up in Darby's?"

"Can we see where you grew up?"

The boys asked a thousand questions.

"How do you know so much about SoHam?" Emmy asked.

"We've read all your books," Damian answered.

"We got them from the library," Donavon added.

Tyler pulled into Darby's parking lot. "We're here."

Emmy got out with the boys. They waited for their parents and then stood in front of them as they stared at the entrance to Darby's Dogs.

"Are we going inside?" Tyler asked after a moment.

Liz grabbed his arm. "Maybe we should take a picture first."

"Yes, please!" Damian hollered. "Could you take a picture of all of us with Emmy by the door?"

"Okay," Tyler chuckled. He took three pictures with his phone.

Once inside the boys stopped and gawked.

"I can smell hot dogs," Damian said.

"Can we get hot dogs and fries?" Donavon asked his mother.

"You can order whatever you want," Tyler said.

The boys grabbed Emmy's hands and pulled her in the direction of a certain booth. They stopped and looked at the photographs.

241

"This is your booth, right?" Damian asked. "And that's you and your husband, right?"

"Yes, it is," Emmy whispered.

Blaine motioned to the boys. "Come and tell us what you want to eat."

They rushed over to their mother.

"Do we have to share our fries?" Donavon asked.

Liz said, "You can each have fries and whatever. The church is paying for lunch."

"Hot dogs with everything, fries and a root beer!" They both shouted.

As everyone placed their order, Emmy waved to Danny Darby.

He walked up to Emmy and looked at the Dickinsons. "Hi, how are you. I got your text. This is your new pastor, huh?"

"Children's pastor. I'm buying and don't give me any flak."

"You're the boss, Em." Danny grinned.

Since Kenny and Emmy's booth wasn't big enough for seven, they sat at a nearby table. The boys pointed out the photographs to their parents.

"Can we have more root beer?" Donavon asked.

"One should be enough," Blaine said.

"They have free refills," Liz said to Blaine.

"Oh, I didn't know."

"Can we, Mom?"

"Okay, but just one more cup."

Emmy sat quietly and listened to everyone as she ate.

"You all right, Em?" Liz whispered.

Emmy nodded. "I feel weird. Why are they treating me like someone special?"

"It's because you are." Liz put an arm around her. "Special, I mean."

Tyler took a couple of pictures of the boys sitting in the booth with Emmy before they headed back to the house.

"We bought a few groceries," Liz mentioned. "Just staples and stuff. If there's anything you need, please let me know. I know where to get the best deals."

"Thank you, Liz. We appreciate everything you've done for us. We are so blessed to be here. This is where God wants us. I am positive."

Emmy said goodbye to the boys and walked back to the Flex with Tyler and Liz. "I left my car at church. Can I have a ride?"

Tyler chuckled, "No, you need to walk. It's not that far."

Liz shook her head. "Don't listen to him, Em."

Emmy made a face and got in the car. She waved at the boys and smiled as Tyler backed out of the driveway.

"All right! Tell me what's going on. No one has ever been so excited to move into a small three bedroom ranch before. What gives?" Emmy looked back and forth between Tyler and Liz.

"You tell her," Tyler said.

"I couldn't help notice some of their furniture is older than me, and they're not antiques."

"Wade and Blaine grew up in West Virginia in a rather poor area. After college they served as missionaries in Africa in one of those poor countries. I don't remember the name. The church they came from in Ohio couldn't afford to pay them much."

"So coming to SoHam must be quite a shock to them, huh?" Emmy asked.

"You could say that," Tyler chuckled.

"Why did the board hire them? If you say it was out of pity, I will scream."

"We hired them because of their love for children, and the fact they are the couple God chose," Tyler said.

Emmy bit her lip. "I'm sorry for doubting that."

"I can think of someone else who was excited to move into a small house, and from what I've learned it was in a lot worse condition than where the Dickinsons will live," Liz said.

"Who?" Emmy asked.

"You, you goof!" Liz shook her head. "Have you forgotten what you wrote in your own book about your parents buying a house?"

Emmy's shoulders slumped. "Oh, I forgot about that. I was excited about that house. I didn't know it at the time, but it needed

243

a lot of work. The toilet didn't work right, and it had those cheap metal kitchen cabinets," Emmy said and then paused.

"You all right, Em?" Liz asked.

"I loved that old house," Emmy whispered.

"Mom, is the new guy going to be at church today?" Heather asked as they ate breakfast.

"Yes, they are going to start today, and I want you to be extra nice to them, okay?" Emmy said as she set a plate of pancakes on the table.

"I saw them at the church last week," Isabella said. "They have two boys, right?"

"They do, and I believe they will be going to school with you in the fall. Now eat your breakfast, so we can make it to Sunday School on time for once."

"Mom! Mom!" Isabella hollered to get Emmy's attention after the second service.

Emmy waved and the girls dashed toward her.

"Mom, you are never going to guess what the new people can do," Isabella said as she tried to catch her breath.

"What can they do, Isa?"

"They know how to sing songs in African."

"In African? Do you mean an African language? They are lots of different languages," Emmy said.

Heather and Isabella nodded.

"They told stories about living in Africa and living in a house with a dirt floor. It was so cool!"

Emmy laughed. *Somehow I think it might have been rather hot, and I can't imagine you living in in a place with no floor.*

"Can we invite them over for lunch sometime? The boys said they learned how to swim in a lake with wild animals," Heather gushed.

"We can have them over someday," Emmy said. "Where is your brother?"

"Oh, he's talking to Pastor Wade. He was showing some boys pictures of elephants and stuff. He said we should call him Pastor Wade because his other name is too long."

244

Emmy saw Kevin Michael and Ben Bertucci walking with the Dickinson brothers and waved at them.

"I gotta go. That's my mom waving at me," Kevin Michael said. "I'll see you next week. Come on, Ben. I want to see if we can play in the woods and hunt for wild animals."

Kevin Michael and Ben raced up to Emmy.

"Slow down," Emmy said. "Why are you so excited? I bet I can guess."

"Mom, can Ben and Taylor come over to play? We want to search the woods for wild animals. I bet we can find some bears and maybe mountain lions," Kevin said.

"They need to ask their mom first."

The boys sprinted away to find either Sloane or Tony. Kevin spotted Tony at the edge of the crowd and ran up to him.

"What's up, Kevin?" Tony asked.

"Uncle Tony, can Ben and Taylor come over to my house? We want to hunt for wild animals in the woods."

"It's all right with me, but what will you do if you find one?" Tony asked seriously.

"We will capture them and bring them home," Kevin answered while Ben nodded.

"Okay, but try not to scare your mother," Tony said as he saw Emmy approaching. "On the other hand, she might like it if you find some snakes and lizards and stuff."

"We're not hunting for them," Ben said. "We want to find real wild animals like Pastor Wade saw in Africa."

"Did they ask?" Emmy looked up at Tony. "I'll feed them if it's all right."

"It's okay with me. Are you taking Taylor Beckett with you?"

Emmy glanced at the boys. "Maybe they should change clothes first and then come over."

"Good idea."

After changing clothes at home, Ben and his brother Taylor Beckett rode their bikes over to Kevin Michael's house.

"Mom says we have to eat lunch before we go hunting," Kevin Michael said. "She made sandwiches and we have some chips. Did you bring your guns?"

Ben and Taylor held up their plastic guns.

The kids sat in the breakfast nook to eat. Kevin told his sisters about his plan.

"There aren't any bears or lions in the woods, you goof," Heather said. "You might see some deer or rabbits, but nothing like Pastor Wade talked about."

"How do you know?" Ben asked.

"Because I'm older and smarter," Heather replied.

"Well, we're going to go hunting anyway," Kevin insisted.

"Can I go with you?" Heather asked.

"No way! Girls can't be wild animal hunters. You have to be a warrior to do that."

Emmy heard that part of the conversation. "Let the boys have their fun, Heather. I invited Dany and Darian over to show us their new kittens."

"I didn't know they had kittens!" Isabella exclaimed. "I love kittens."

"Can we buy some kittens?" Heather asked.

"I don't think so because your brother is allergic to cats and dogs," Emmy said.

"Then can we get rid of Kevin Michael? He could live in the woods," Heather teased.

"I'm not real bad allergic. I pet Scout."

"Yes, and you sneeze and your eyes get red whenever you're around her," Emmy reminded him.

The boys finished eating and raced outside and into the woods. Dany and Darian arrived a few minutes later with a cat carrier. Heather and Isabella put their fingers inside the carrier to play with the kittens.

"Can we take them out of the cage?" Heather asked.

Emmy nodded.

"Where should we put them?" Isabella asked.

Dany suggested the laundry room. "They're not totally house broken."

"Good idea. It will be easier to clean up if they have an accident," Emmy said.

246

Darian kissed Dany on the top of her head. "I'm going to find Kenny."

Emmy followed Dany, the girls and the fluffy kittens into the laundry room. She closed the door behind her as Dany set the carrier on the floor and opened it.

"Are they afraid to come out?" Isabella asked.

Dany sat on the floor. "Give them a chance to check out their surroundings."

One kitten poked its head out of the cage and took a couple of steps toward Dany. The other kitten attacked the other's tail, and both kittens tumbled over in a ball of fluff as they wrestled.

"Do they always play together?" Heather asked.

"Were there more kittens?" Isabella tried to pet one but it scurried away.

"There were six in the litter, but other people took the rest," Dany said.

Isabella managed to pick one up and held it in her hands. "Do they miss their brothers and sisters?"

"I don't think so." Dany looked up at Emmy. "You aren't a cat person, huh?"

Emmy wrinkled her nose. "I've never had a pet."

"Not even when you were a kid?" Heather asked.

"No, Mom would never allow animals in the house. There were dogs and cats in the neighborhood. Some of them roamed free, but I didn't play with them like other kids."

"Could we get a kitten or a puppy?" Heather asked.

"I don't think so, sweetie."

"What about a goldfish?" Isabella asked.

Emmy shook her head. "I'll have to talk to your father." *He can be the bad guy who says no pets.*

"Do they have names?" Heather managed to capture the other kitten.

"The one in your hand is Mittens because of her white paws, and that is Cracker."

Heather and Isabella giggled.

Dany looked up at Emmy again. "Darian named her."

"Does your mother still have a lot of cats?" Emmy asked.

247

"There were nine the last time I counted. She names all of them."

"Doesn't your father mind?" Emmy asked.

Dany shrugged.

Heather stood up and handed Mittens to Emmy. "You can hold her, Mommy."

Emmy held onto Mittens.

"Let her lick your face," Heather said.

Emmy let Mittens get close to her face and then sneezed. She sneezed again. And then once more.

"Emmy, your face is turning red," Dany said as she stood up and took the kitten from Emmy. "Have you ever been checked for pet allergies?"

"Maybe when I was little. I vaguely remember going to the doctor after getting a rash."

"I think I should put the kittens in their carrier," Dany said. "I think your mother might have an allergy, and we don't want to make her sick."

The boys returned from their adventure just as Dany and Darian walked out of the house with the girls and Emmy.

"Did you capture any wild animals?" Darian asked.

Kevin Michael shook his head.

"We saw a bunch of squirrels, a rabbit and a skunk, but nothing else," Ben said.

Taylor Beckett walked over to Darian. "Are those kittens?"

"These are Mittens and Cracker."

"That's a silly name for a kitten," Taylor said.

Darian laughed. "I agree. Maybe I should think of a better name. What would you name her?"

Ben walked over to the kittens as Kevin Michael walked over to Emmy.

"I would name her Tonto," Ben said.

"That's an even sillier name," Heather said. "I would name her Fluffy because she is so fluffy."

"I like that name," Darian said. "From now on we'll call her Fluffy."

Emmy looked at Dany and rolled her eyes.

248

Emmy heard the front doorbell Tuesday morning and went to check. She picked up the package and brought it inside.

"What was it?" Kenny asked.

"UPS. It's from Jeremiah. I bet it's CDs."

Kenny took the package into the kitchen, set it on the island and opened it with a knife. "It is CDs."

"Duh! How many?" Emmy asked.

"A whole bunch, and here's a note." Kenny read the note to himself.

"What does it say?" Emmy asked. When Kenny didn't answer, she tried to grab it out of his hand. "Let me read it."

"It's just a thank you note for helping with the CD," Kenny said. "He says they like their new church, and they are getting used to the hot weather in Alabama." He handed the note to Emmy, picked up one of the CDs and inspected the cover.

Emmy quickly read the note and waved it at Kenny. "He's also invited you to come down and see them play sometime. He's invited you to sit in with BearFace. Would that interest you?"

Kenny thought about it. "It could be fun."

Chapter Twenty-Nine

"What time is the reporter from that cheap tabloid supposed to be here?" Emmy asked while checking email at the kitchen island. "Could you warm this up for me, please?"

Kenny added some coffee to her cup. "It's not a cheap tabloid. It's *The Rock Seen* and it's a very reputable magazine."

"If you say so. I've never read it myself."

"She's supposed to be here at ten, and her name is Gloria Ronstadt."

"Is she related to Linda?" Emmy asked without taking her eyes from her laptop.

Kenny shrugged. "I'll ask her. Do you want to meet her?"

"Gloria or Linda?"

"Gloria. I don't think Linda is coming," Kenny said and checked the time on the microwave. "It's ten now."

"So I see," Emmy said as she looked up. "Will you settle down? It's just another interview. You've done a million of them."

The landline rang and Kenny answered it. He listened and said, "Thanks." He hung up and headed toward the mudroom. "She just passed through the gate."

Emmy yawned. "Can you tell how excited I am?"

"Are you going to be civil? I don't often do interviews for magazines, and she came all the way from San Francisco."

"Then why do this one? Did they offer a lot of cash?"

Kenny shrugged. "Some money. I'll bring her in here so you can meet her."

"But I look a mess," Emmy ran a hand through her curly, dark hair.

"You look perfect. Be nice. I heard a car."

Kenny went outside and greeted Gloria. They shook hands and he brought her inside to the kitchen. "Em, this is Gloria Ronstadt from *The Rock Seen*."

Gloria removed her shoes, put the strap of her large bag on her shoulder, walked over and offered a hand to Emmy. "It's a pleasure to meet you, Emmy. Thank you for letting me steal some of Kenny's time."

Emmy shook hands and noticed Gloria's hairstyle. "It's nice to meet you, too. Where do you get your hair done?"

Gloria ran a hand through her dark, curly hair. "Nowhere special. It's always been like this."

"Mine too," Emmy said and smiled. "Can I offer you some coffee, or water? We have orange and apple juice."

Gloria waved. "Thanks, but I'm good." She turned to look at Kenny. "Where should we do this? I would like to see your studio."

"We could use the control room. There are comfortable chairs."

"Sounds good to me," Gloria said. "Lead the way."

Emmy watched as Gloria followed Kenny. *You must either be part Mexican, like Linda, or else you have some African American ancestry. I love your light chocolate skin. You never have to work on a tan.* Emmy took another sip of coffee and turned her attention back to her laptop. *I wish I looked that good in black jeans. I wonder how much you struggled to get them on.*

Kenny opened the door to the control room. "This is it." He waved to include the twenty-five foot wide room.

"This is amazing." Gloria walked over to the mixing desk and looked into the studio. "That's where you guys record, right?"

"Yes, it's divided into some recording booths, but we use the open area most of the time." Kenny picked up a newspaper from Emmy's recliner and put it in the trash basket. "We can sit here if you'd like."

She sat and pulled out a small notebook and a recording device. "You don't mind if I use this, do you?"

"Go ahead," Kenny said and then grinned. "We are in a recording studio."

Gloria smiled and then looked at her notes. They went over some biographical details.

"I pulled this from Wikipedia. I wanted to verify the accuracy."

Kenny nodded.

"Okay, first question. How would you describe your high school experience? Were you popular? Did you do most of the

251

usual things? School dances, prom, homecoming, ditch classes? Did you spend a lot of time smoking in the boys' room?"

Kenny laughed. "You aren't old enough to know that song."

"My father used to play it," she said and then waited.

Kenny sat back and looked at the ceiling. "I wasn't really one of the popular kids. I was somewhere between a geek, or a nerd, and one of the lesser popular kids."

"Did many of the other kids know you sang and played guitar?" Gloria asked and then leaned back in the recliner which released the foot support.

"By the time I was a senior, most of them knew. I played with a couple of high schools bands very briefly."

"Briefly? Why?"

Kenny scratched his jaw. "I don't want to make this sound egotistical, but..."

"They sucked as musicians?"

Kenny chuckled. "You could say that."

"I've never seen a photograph of you with really long hair. Why is that?"

"Mom and Dad wouldn't have allowed it," he answered. "They were very supportive of my desire to be a musician, but drew the line at long hair."

"Okay, back to the popularity."

"I felt like an outcast at times because I wasn't interested in the usual social stuff."

Gloria shifted her position so she could look directly at Kenny.

"I knew I wanted a career in music, and I was very focused on that. I practiced several hours a day. Time that other kids would spend at the mall, or hanging out at Darby's."

"I want to talk more about Darby's later, okay?"

"Sure." Kenny put his feet on the coffee table.

"Did you date often?"

"Not really," he answered.

"Was that because you and Emmy were a couple?"

He hesitated. "Not really. Emmy and I never really dated in high school."

252

Gloria tilted her head and wrote something in her notebook.

"I should explain. Emmy was my best friend growing up. She still is, but that's different." He waved a hand. "You've probably read how we met. She was seven at the time and I was ten, I think. Anyway, in high school... I was a senior and she was a freshman. I graduated early like she did, so we were only together for half a year."

"You lived on the same street. Did you walk to school together?" Gloria asked.

"We did," Kenny said. "I remember her first day. She was a little nervous, so I held her hand."

"That's sweet."

"I suppose, but it wasn't romantic."

"Please, explain."

"She was too young for us to romantically involved. She was still a tomboy, which I liked, but I didn't have time for that kind of social life."

"But you did date occasionally, right?"

He looked at the ceiling again. "I might have had four or five dates before my last year at Roosevelt. After that I concentrated on my music almost exclusively."

"You were still friends with Emmy though," she said.

"Oh, yeah. She was a part of the music."

"Is it true she sang with the band at your first gig, or is that an urban legend?"

He nodded. "She sang with us at all the local gigs. Of course she couldn't travel with us because of her age."

"Do you remember the girls you dated?"

"I remember their names. They're probably married now. I won't give you any details because I don't think they ever went on a second date with me."

"Why not?"

"Because I was a dork, and probably bored them to death talking about guitars and songwriting and stuff like that."

"I see. Were certain types of girls attracted to you because you played guitar?" she asked with a grin.

Kenny laughed and looked away. "Yeah, there were those

253

ladies. They would hang around at our gigs."

"I'll get back to that later. Did you have a favorite subject in school? I'm assuming you and Emmy never shared a class, right?"

He shook his head. "Never shared a class. We almost never saw each other during the day. If you've ever seen, or heard about Roosevelt High, you'd know it's a huge building. Our classes were on different floors. We would walk to school, or I would drive us. We tried to meet for lunch, but that wasn't always possible."

"You were never in the marching band. Why?"

He laughed. "Because they didn't need a guitar player. Have you ever seen the Woody Allen movie where he plays a cello, or was it a tuba, in the marching band? I think it was a cello."

She laughed. "I have seen that."

"I would have had to carry an amp. It wouldn't have worked."

"Did you take music classes at school?"

"We did have music classes, and I got good grades. I wasn't like Einstein flunking math and physics."

"That's an urban legend," she said with a quirky laugh.

"The teacher knew I played guitar and wrote songs, so she asked me to play in front of the class," Kenny mentioned.

"Was that your first public appearance?"

"No, I played at church during my first year at Roosevelt," he said and then waved a hand. "I remember the really popular guys were the jocks. Football players especially. They were treated like gods. They got all the popular, pretty girls."

"Were you jealous of that?"

"I suppose I was to a certain extent. I remember a few athletes who took advantage of their popularity to... attract girls."

"Girls use their good looks to attract certain guys, so it works both ways," she said with a sly smile.

"There was one girl I dated. She might have been the only one I went out with more than once."

"So you really liked each other, right?"

Kenny nodded. "Anyway, this football player asked her out. He got her pregnant. She dropped out and moved away."

"Have you ever been in contact with her?"

"No, I've never really tried."

"High school can be cruel."

"It can be," he said. *Just ask Emmy.*

"According to the official story, the band's first gig was..."

"April 21, 1995. The Christian Youth Center on Douglas Street. They didn't often have secular bands, but my dad knew someone." Kenny shrugged. "There were about three hundred people there, but I've heard that several thousand people claim to have been in the audience that night. Emmy did sing with us. She was fourteen."

"How long did it take to get the band together?"

"I knew Jeff and Jeremy. I'd met them a couple of years earlier. They were in a band together. We spent about a month auditioning drummers and other musicians. Paul Joseph was almost a part of the original band, but he decided to stay with The Notable Exceptions. We tried out a few guys to be the second guitar player, but no one really fit. Other than Paul. Once we found Dave Persching, we were set. We rehearsed for like six months before we played a gig. We wrote a ton of songs and made cheap demos on my recorder. There are some that were awful. My father still has those early demos somewhere. We didn't want to do many covers. We didn't want to be known as a cover band. You know what I mean?"

"I understand. Were any of the band members working day jobs?"

"Everyone but me. I was spending a year at Paul Frank Junior College. I promised my parents I would go to college for at least a year before I devoted myself to a music career. The other guys worked part-time to pay the rent. Jeff and Jeremy shared an apartment for a time. Once we signed with Steward Music, they quit those jobs."

"So you've never had any other job than the band, right?" she asked checking her notes.

"Right."

"The band played gigs in the area for a while. I read you traveled in a minivan."

255

"Dad bought a Honda Odyssey for us. We hauled our gear in a trailer. There were six of us. We hired Frankie Hanna as our road crew." Kenny used air quotes. "Andy Walker became our manager, and he traveled with us. After we signed with Steward Music and released our CD, we started renting U-Haul trucks for the gear. We eventually bought a bus. Well, I guess we leased one first. I can't remember. We traveled by bus. We hired more guys for the crew and over the years it became a circus. We've cut it down now, and we fly as much as possible."

"You are working in the studio now, right?"

"We are, but it's a struggle. I'd rather not talk about that."

"So back in high school. Did you go to the prom? Or homecoming? Any of those special events that mean so much at the time?"

"Nope! I thought about it my junior year, but I chickened out."

"Why?" Gloria asked. "You must have had plenty of girls willing to hang out with a guitar hero."

"Yeah, I guess. I almost asked this one girl, but then I heard from a classmate she already had a date."

"You didn't go your senior year either?"

"No, I had graduated, and we were playing gigs by then."

"You never took Emmy to the prom or anything?"

He shook his head. "She was too young. We never really dated like I said. We were together a lot, but we didn't... you know. Go places. Her parents didn't allow her to go on solo dates until she was sixteen. I was on the road by then."

"Did she ever feel like a sister?"

He frowned.

"Maybe a cousin or something?"

"Maybe when she was in grade school. We went to the same grade school."

"The one named for your grandfather, right?" Gloria asked while checking her notes.

"Yeah. I was three years ahead of her. We went to different schools for five years and then she made it to high school."

"Did you always love her?"

256

"Wow! That's rather personal."

"Yes, it is. Did you?"

"Okay, I'll answer like this. We loved each other as friends until sometime in high school. Then it changed, but I was gone so much. There was one time when I didn't see her for over a year. I told her to date other guys."

"Why?"

"Because I didn't want her waiting for me to come home. I wanted her to enjoy high school. As much as one can enjoy those years. I guess some people enjoy them more than others. I wouldn't want to go through high school again." *Man! Why am I rambling so much?*

"Did you think of Emmy as your girlfriend after you started touring full-time?"

He thought about it. "That's complicated. Other than that one year, I would get home once in a while, and when I did, I would always see her. We would hang out together. Sometimes with a group of people. Other times just by ourselves."

"Did you take advantage of the groupies who must have followed the band?"

"No comment," he said.

"They were around, right?"

"No comment," he replied with a hint of anger.

She smiled. "Do you remember the first girl you ever kissed? Not when you were a kid. The first girl you kissed because you liked her."

"I was a sophomore, and I kissed this girl after school."

"It wasn't Emmy, right?"

"No."

"Do you remember the first time you kissed her?"

"Yes," he answered and didn't elaborate.

"Oh, come on! Do I have to pry it out of you? It's just a kiss. Or was it?"

"I don't like the implication."

"Sorry. I apologize."

"I remember our first kiss. Most guys would have kissed her a lot sooner, but we were best friends. Kissing each other was a

257

big step. It changed our relationship."

"Were you the first boy to kiss her?"

"I was actually. A couple others had tried without success."

"Can you tell me where it happened?" Gloria asked.

"On the old couch in the carriage house."

Gloria smiled. "I've done some research about the carriage house. That's where the band first practiced. It burned, and your family rebuilt it, right?"

"We did. All that was left after the fire were the brick walls."

Gloria checked her notes. "So how did your relationship change after the kiss?"

Kenny laughed. "We kissed more often."

"How old was she?"

"Fifteen, and I was nineteen. She would turn sixteen that summer."

"So it took you almost nine years to kiss her, right?" Gloria teased.

Kenny grinned. "I was shy."

"Can I ask about Rebecca Morrison?"

"You can ask."

Gloria stared at Kenny for a moment. "I can understand if you're trying to protect her."

"Emmy and I still consider Becky a friend. She's married to a pastor with three children. Her husband's name is Taylor, and he knows about our relationship."

"I won't use their names if that will help you open up."

"I appreciate that."

"Would you consider that relationship to be your first serious one as an adult? Oh, does Emmy know?"

"She knows," Kenny said. "She met Becky at Christmas when I brought her home. She was hurt, but she hid her true feelings. Do you know why Becky ended the relationship."

"I don't, but you can tell me off the record."

Kenny nodded and Gloria paused the recorder.

"We talked about getting married, and were close to buying a ring, but she decided she couldn't live with my lifestyle. We were

258

touring in Europe at the time. Becky needed to get home for the start of school, so she left."

"Did you propose to Emmy soon after that?"

Kenny thought about the time and shook his head. "It was almost two years later."

"While you were with Becky, did Emmy date other guys?"

"Is this still off the record?" Kenny asked.

"It is unless you tell me otherwise."

"Let's stay off the record for now."

Gloria nodded.

"Emmy dated a little, but she only had one serious relationship." Kenny paused. *Should I mention that Tony proposed?* He rubbed his jaw. *I better not.* "It ended, and I flew home one night and proposed during halftime of a Bears' game. She said yes, and we got married the next April."

"Can I ask about Darby's on the record?"

"Sure."

Gloria resumed recording. "The story is you took her to Darby's when she was eight or nine, and you sat in that one booth. Is that true or not?"

"It's true," Kenny said and then chuckled. "I bought her a hot dog and root beer. Might have been a chili dog. Maybe some fries. Mr. Darby put up some photographs by that booth later. Apparently, tourists come in and take pictures of it. We think it's funny because we still go there. We've even seen people taking pictures of the photos with us in the restaurant."

"What? You're kidding. They don't recognize you guys?"

"These days they are more likely to recognize Em than me. I'm not very memorable. I blend in."

"I would recognize you anywhere."

"Thanks, I guess."

"Can you still eat at Darby's without being hassled?"

"Oh, yeah! We could go there today. Emmy meets Father James there a lot."

"Who?"

Kenny explained.

"That's amazing."

259

"They get along great. They tease each other all the time, but they love each other. So do the kids."

"In the beginning, you would be away for months at a time, and now you both are busy touring. How do you manage to maintain a strong relationship?"

"We practice kissing when we see each other," Kenny said and then grinned.

"Ah, I get it. Funny."

"We keep in touch when we're working. Sometimes we get together on the road. We bring the kids along at times. They don't think of us as anything other than mom and dad. We just sing songs for a living."

"Would you allow your children to become professional musicians? Have they expressed any interest in music?"

"The twins love to sing together. Emmy has even brought them out on stage with her. They don't understand the celebrity stuff. To them it's just fun. We try not to spoil them, but it's not easy."

"Could we talk about high school again?"

"Okay."

"How did you manage to..." she paused and tapped her pen against the notebook. "You were rather young when the band became famous. I've seen what can happen to other musicians who achieve celebrity status at a young age. Sometimes they let it escalate out of control. You seem to have escaped the tabloids without any trace of scandal. Didn't you ever trash a hotel room, or spend a fortune gambling?"

"Emmy claims I am the dorkiest rock star in the world. She says I'm more like a Sunday School teacher than a celebrity."

"You both claim your faith in God keeps you grounded. Has it always been like that? Is that why you seem so normal?" she asked.

"I grew up going to church. After I started touring full-time, I wasn't always able to attend church, and that took a toll. While Becky and I were together, I rededicated my life to God. Now the band is able to choose when we tour and avoid being away from home for weeks at a time. The only time we're gong for long stretches is when we tour abroad. Otherwise, we are usually home part of each week."

"Did Emmy grow up like you?"

"Do you mean going to church or what?"

"Yes."

"Her family was, is, whatever, Catholic." Kenny waved his hands around. "You know what I mean. They stopped going when she was... before she was a teenager. She came to church with my family at times."

"I'm surprised your parents didn't adopt her. She spent a lot of time at your house, right?"

Kenny laughed. "She had her own room."

"Really?"

Kenny shrugged. "Not exactly, but our house is pretty big. My parents' house, I mean. She would spend the night occasionally, and she always used the same guest bedroom."

"What did her parents think about this arrangement? I read a book about Elvis and how his future wife came to Memphis at a very young age. You are three and a half years older than Emmy. That's not a big deal now, but when you were in high school it was more significant."

Kenny pointed to the recorder. "Could you pause that thing, please?"

Gloria paused it.

"Off the record?"

Gloria nodded.

"Emmy's childhood wasn't always the best. I don't mean she was abused physically or anything. Her parents fought a lot, and her father drank."

"I understand," Gloria said.

"Emmy would stay at our house at times to escape. Understand?"

"Yes."

"You can turn it back on."

She did.

"Emmy's parents were concerned about her spending time with me after we got older, but they understood our friendship. We

261

both loved music. Emmy took piano lessons as a kid. She would practice at our house at times."

"Would you say your relationship was based on your love of music?"

"Yes, but I always thought she was cute," Kenny said. "Back to your question. Our parents knew we were best friends. My parents thought of Em as part of the family long before we were married. Her parents accepted my relationship with her despite our age difference. Emmy graduated early, got a job and moved into her own apartment. She and her sister both moved out as soon as they could. I lived at home until we got married. Different situations."

"You've written a few songs about Emmy. How does she feel about that?"

"Have you ever listened to her CDs?"

Gloria nodded.

"She has written about our relationship more than me. The whole *Carriage House Sessions* was about us. My songs about her are simple love songs. She's a much deeper writer than me. 'Sweet Girl' was one of the first songs I ever wrote. Maybe the very first. Certainly the first song we ever recorded about her. She's still the sweetest girl I know. When she stayed with us, her parents always knew about it. She even went on trips with us a few times."

"Would you describe Emmy as being naive as a young lady?"

Kenny thought about it. "Yes and no, and I'll explain what I mean. Emmy certainly knew about... stuff. She learned from her older sister, but she was innocent at the same time. Maybe you shouldn't put anything about her sister in the story."

Gloria nodded.

"She struggled with her feelings like any other teenage girl, but she survived relatively unscathed. There are no skeletons in her closet."

"Good! I'm not looking to create a scandal just to sell magazines. I hate that crap." she set her pen down. "It can't be easy for you guys to maintain a normal life with both of you in the public eye."

262

"That's why we still live in SoHam. We don't attract a lot of attention because we grew up here. The people that know us think of us as just another young couple with kids and a minivan in the garage."

Gloria laughed. "They probably haven't seen your home."

Kenny smiled. "We have been blessed. Emmy still feels guilty at times because we do live in a dream house in a rather exclusive area. Most people wouldn't get past the security building."

"I noticed the gate at the end of your driveway was open. Do you ever close it?"

"We do at night, or if we're gone. We have family who live here and good friends, too."

"So you keep it open for them." Gloria checked her notes again. "Can we talk about the early days of the band again?"

"Yes," Kenny said. "But not about..."

"Right. So you never really had any other girlfriends other than Becky."

"And Emmy," he added.

"Yes, but you sort of describe her as your best friend. You didn't really go on dates," she said and then glanced at him.

He nodded.

"I get the feeling you thought of her as family. When did that change? Please don't say the moment you kissed."

Kenny closed his eyes for a moment. He opened them when he heard Gloria turn off the recorder. "You can keep it going."

"Okay."

"I think it changed for good when Andy and I showed up on her porch dressed as gangsters."

Gloria's eyes opened wide.

Kenny waved a hand. "Let me explain. We were doing that European tour. The one with Becky along. Then she left, and you know that story." He paused. "We got back to the States in mid-December. Andy and I headed to Emmy's house. The one she rented with Diane except Diane had gotten married, so Em lived in this big house all alone."

263

Gloria nodded as if she knew the story.

"So Andy rang the bell like he always does. It sounds like a machine gun. Whatever. We were wearing these long black coats and fedoras. Gangsters. Em let us in and she hugged Andy. Did I mention they are distant cousins? Anyway, then we kissed, and she wanted a better kiss. I told her I only had one left. She said to use it, and if she liked it, we could go to the store and buy more kisses. I kissed her... uh... you know how."

"I can picture it."

"From that moment on I never thought of her the same way."

Gloria checked her notes. "Okay, but that was December of 2001, right? Yet you didn't propose until the next October. Why did you wait so long?"

Kenny shrugged. "Because we were on tour a lot of that time, and because I'm a dork."

The interview ended and Kenny led Gloria out through the garage to her car. He watched her drive away and then headed inside.

"Where are you, Em?"

"Family room. Is she gone?" Emmy hollered.

Kenny walked into the family room and sat on the couch next to Emmy. "She's gone. What are you doing?"

Emmy closed her laptop. "Nothing. How did it go? Did you spill all our deep secrets?"

"Not all, but some," he said and then grinned.

She shook her head. "Will I be mad at you if I ever read the story?"

He shrugged. "Do you need a kiss?"

"You're such a dork," she said but then she kissed him.

Chapter Thirty

The members of Fridays At Five stared at each other as they sat in the control room of Studio Four at the Steward Music Group complex.

"That track doesn't do anything for me either," Jeff Rawlings said as he motioned for Will Consoli to stop the playback. "Am I the only one completely bored with these songs?"

"I admit these songs are not the best I've ever written," Kenny said.

Paul Joseph shook his head. "We all contributed to these songs, Kenny. You can't take the blame for this mess."

"Man! We were so hopeful when we started recording," Dave Persching said. "We had twenty demos and couldn't decide which ones to use because we thought they were all good. Turns out they all sucked. Especially mine."

Adam Vicini took a drink of water as he listened to the guys. He finally said, "I confess my songs are not up to Fridays At Five standards. The lyrics need work."

"Your songs aren't that weak," Kenny said. "They need tweaking, but I wouldn't throw them away."

"What are we going to do?" Jeff asked. "I don't want to waste time in the studio if none of these tracks are worth it."

"I think we should take a break and either write some new songs, or else rework the ones we like the best from the demos," Kenny said.

"Are we obligated to release a CD this year?" Paul asked.

"We have a couple of years before we are legally committed," Dave said. "I don't want to wait until the last minute and have to release something not up to our standards."

The men discussed their options for another thirty minutes before deciding to write new songs.

"I want to save these sessions," Kenny said. "We might be able to salvage something for use down the road."

Adam asked, "Would anyone mind if I keep the three songs I wrote on my own?"

The guys didn't object.

"What's on your mind, Adam?" Jeff asked.

"Since these songs wouldn't really work for the band, I was thinking I might try to record them if I ever want to do a solo project. I know we're a band, but."

"Each of us has the option to record a solo project," Dave mentioned.

"How do you know all of this legal stuff?" Jeff asked.

Dave shrugged. "I had our attorney explain the legal mumbo jumbo to me."

Kenny added, "I don't mind if you use your songs for a solo project. You could use my basement if you need a place to record. No one else is using it."

"Thanks, Kenny. I might just take you up on your offer."

Kenny returned home around three and heard the kids playing in the pool.

"You're home early," Emmy said as Kenny walked out to the pool. "How was your day?"

Kenny plopped onto the lounge chair next to Emmy. "It kinda sucked."

"Are you going to elaborate?" Emmy asked and then hollered, "Kevin Michael! Do not run and jump into the pool if your sisters are in the area."

"We listened to tracks for two hours, and everyone agreed they all suck."

"All of them?" Emmy asked.

Kenny sighed. "Pretty much."

"Did you erase them? Delete everything?"

"No, I actually saved everything to a hard drive. There are pieces of music and some of the lyrics worth saving."

"Daddy! Watch me! I can dive into the water," Isabella said. She stood at the end of the diving board, lifted her hands over her head and dove into the water three feet below.

"Good job, Isa," Kenny said and then applauded. "Oh, I offered the basement to Adam."

"What? Is he moving in? Emmy asked. "Did he and Juliana breakup?"

"No. He might start working on a solo project," Kenny said

and then looked at Emmy.

She rolled her eyes.

"Oh, you knew they didn't have a fight, huh?"

"I talked to Juliana and held baby Kinsey on Sunday. Kinsey's three months old already."

"I thought she was just born."

"Are you going to change clothes, so you can use the pool?" Emmy asked.

Kenny looked at Emmy. "Is that a new bikini?"

"I've worn it before."

"If I get in the pool with you, can we have some fun?" Kenny grinned.

She made a face. "You can have fun with the kids. I'm working on my tan. I'm envious of Gloria Ronstadt."

"Why?"

"Because she looks great. Didn't you notice?"

"Not really," he said.

"Then you are either a dork, or else you really love me."

"Guilty on both charges," Kenny said.

Kenny and Emmy dropped the kids off at Tony and Sloane's house the next morning. Kenny parked the Odyssey and Emmy jumped out with the kids. Sloane stood up and wiped her brow.

"I love your flower garden," Emmy said. "I could never grow anything except weeds."

"Mama helps take care of them," Sloane said.

"I love roses." Emmy sniffed some of the flowers and then straightened up. "Thanks for watching them, Sloane," Emmy said as Kevin Michael ran around the house with Ben and Taylor. "We won't be gone for more than a couple hours."

"It's all right. The boys will play outside, and the girls will probably have a tea party or something. Peter is playing with Carson and Caden. He said they were building a new fort."

"At least they're playing outside. Is Tony at work?" Emmy asked.

"He and John are in Peoria," Sloane answered.

267

Mama Bertucci came outside and waved from the porch. Heather and Isabella scampered up the steps and hugged her.

"It's so good to see you. I haven't seen you for so long," Mama said. "Dotty and Noemi are upstairs."

"I have my cell phone if you need to get hold of me. We could bring lunch if you want," Emmy said.

"I've got stuff here, Emmy. Don't worry about stopping."

Kenny headed to the Gordon Hill section of SoHam where the band owned a warehouse they used for rehearsing and storage.

"Kenny, I think someone must have bought that building. They're turning it into condos." Emmy pointed to one of the buildings along Forster Street.

"Do you remember how rundown this area used to be?" Kenny asked.

"Yeah," Emmy answered while staring at another building. "There's a Subway and a new Great Clips in that one. When you guys bought your practice place, my parents were afraid to let me come here. I remember Daddy saying this was one of the highest crime areas in the city."

"It was at one time. Now the younger people are moving back. It's a real melting pot of racial diversity. There are more jobs in the area, and it's close to downtown. Maybe downtown SoHam will pick up."

"We should take the kids to a Hammers game this summer," Emmy said. "We haven't been to a baseball game lately. I wonder if they still have Two-Dollar-Tuesdays."

The SoHam Hammers minor league baseball team played at the newly-renamed Barclay Field located a block east of Roosevelt High.

"Did I tell you Mr. Kesson tried to buy the naming rights for the ballpark?" Kenny asked as they waited at a red light. "There's a taco stand next to that Thai food place. That's new."

"What was he going to name it?" Emmy watched as two young mothers pushed strollers along the sidewalk.

"I heard he wanted to call it Steward Music Field, but the Barclay family has deeper pockets."

Ya think," Emmy said. "They have tons of old money."

A few blocks later Kenny turned onto a side street and parked next to the warehouse owned by Fridays At Five.

Emmy jumped out and ran over to the side entrance. "Is the code still the same?"

Kenny shook his head. "No, we had to change it because too many people knew the code."

"I hope you didn't use your birthday for the code. Please tell me you guys were smarter than that."

Kenny walked up the steps and shielded the keypad with a hand as he punched in six numbers. They heard a click and the metal door unlocked.

Emmy opened it quickly. "Aren't you going to tell me the code? I might need to get inside sometime."

"If I told you, I'd have to kill you, Em," he said with a straight face.

She rolled her eyes. "Such a dork."

"We used your birthday in reverse. 0-8-8-0-7-0."

They entered the 55,000 square-foot building, saw lights flashing on the stage and heard the Bender Brothers Band rehearsing. Emmy walked up to the stage while Kenny headed over to the sound booth. The guys ended the song and Emmy waved.

Bobby O'Connor came out from behind his drums. "Come on up, Em."

She climbed the steps and stood at the front edge of the stage next to a row of stage monitors.

"Hi, Emmy, how did we sound?" Micah Hurst asked as he set his solid-black Fender Telecaster in a stand.

"You guys rock! That song reminded me of the old Allman Brothers Band."

Bobby laughed as he walked up to her. "That's good because it was an old Allman Brothers tune."

"I knew that," Emmy said as she grabbed one of Bobby's drumsticks from him. "It would sound better if you guys had a decent drummer."

"You want to audition?" Bobby handed her the other stick.

"No, I've got a job."

269

Quinten Matthews strolled over from behind his keyboards. "We're leaving in the morning, Emmy. Are you sure you don't want to join us?"

"I'm sure." She smiled at Miles Goossens and then at Freddie and Marshall Bender.

Kenny finished talking to the tech guys and joined Emmy on the stage.

"We were trying to convince Emmy to go with us," Bobby said. "Would it be all right with you if she did? You wouldn't miss her, would you?"

"Nah! I might miss her after a few months, but I think the kids would miss her sooner," Kenny teased.

"Hey!" Emmy poked Kenny in the side. "I've never been gone for over a year like you did that time."

"I don't think we want her along," Bobby said as he grinned at Emmy and then turned to face the guys. "Remember how much she complained on that last tour? She whined about missing Kenny and her comfortable bed."

"You better hush if you know what's good for you, Bobby," Emmy warned.

"Were you still using a minivan and a trailer for that tour?" Marshall asked Kenny.

Kenny shook his head and chuckled. "By that time, we had moved on. We used a bus and several semi-trucks."

"We're not using a bus, but we have two full-size vans and a large U-Haul," Micah said. "We don't have to haul as much gear around since we're not headlining. We don't need a sound system or a light rig."

"Yeah, I'm using a five-piece kit," Bobby said. "I will have to set it up myself, so I might even cut it down to a four-piece."

"I remember the days we had to set up our own gear," Kenny said.

"Oh, please," Emmy drew out the word to several syllables. "You haven't even tuned your own guitars for decades. You never lift anything heavier than a guitar pick."

"I did in the old days, Em. We paid our dues. Literally and figuratively."

"Marshall and I used a van and a trailer back home in Texas," Freddie said.

"Did y'all ever have to ride horses to a gig?" Emmy asked in a terrible southern accent.

"No, but we once we played for a bunch of cows," Freddie said.

"Get out!" Emmy laughed.

"It was a rodeo at a stockyard. The place smelled of manure and hay. The stage was made out of an old wagon bed, but at least the cows wanted an encore."

"You're so funny. What about your jobs at Liberty Manufacturing?" Emmy asked.

"They granted us a leave of absence without pay," Freddie answered.

"Did they fire you?" Emmy asked.

Freddie shook his head. "Not exactly, but they might soon."

"Do you guys have your drivers lined up?" Kenny asked.

Bobby nodded. "We're using a bunch of the Twilleys. Larry, Carl and Sutton, I think. Might be another one."

Leonard Twilley was the original driver for Fridays At Five, and other bands before them. Several members of his family now worked in the business.

"I used to try to get them to let me drive the bus, but they never would," Emmy said.

"Good thing," Bobby said and then grinned. "Those buses weren't meant to go over a hundred."

"Hey! I don't drive that fast," Emmy said.

"Not in town," Micah added.

"Are you guys going to stand around and talk, or are you gonna rehearse? You need the practice," Emmy teased.

She and Kenny stayed for an hour.

"You guys be careful out there," Emmy said as they got ready to leave. "I'll miss you guys."

"You can always surprise us by showing up for a gig, Em," Bobby said.

She put a finger to her mouth. "I'll think about it."

271

Eight days later Emmy sat at the kitchen island checking her email when Kenny walked in with Adam Vicini.

"Hi, Adam, give me a couple minutes, and we can go downstairs," Emmy said. "Kenny, will you make sure the kids don't drown. Kevin Michael needs to change if he wants to go swimming."

"He's playing with Ben and that neighbor boy from over there." Kenny pointed to the west.

"Do you mean Paul Plant?" Emmy asked.

"That's the kid!" Kenny pointed a finger at Emmy. "You are so smart."

Emmy closed her laptop. "I was smart enough to marry you."

Adam smiled.

"Call me if you can't handle the kids."

"I am their father," Kenny said.

"Exactly." Emmy grinned and headed downstairs with Adam.

"I've got five songs I want to play for you, Em. Is that all right?"

"Sure. Do you want me to make demos for you?"

"I've got the tracks we recorded at the studio. They're enough to give you an idea of how I hear the song. I'm not totally satisfied with the lyrics."

"Do you have copies for me?"

He pulled the copies out of his folder and handed them to her. "Could you play the first song?"

Emmy booted up the system and started the song. She followed along with the lyrics.

"What do you think, Em?" Adam asked.

"I like the first verse and most of the chorus, but what's up with the bridge? It's almost like it's from a different song."

Adam laughed. "It was from a different tune."

She tilted her head and stared at him. "Duh! Write a bridge that fits this song, you goof."

"Okay, you have to remember I'm not a professional writer like you."

272

They listened to all five songs and then spent an hour going over the lyrics.

"Just because I make a suggestion doesn't mean you have to change your lyrics, Adam."

"I know, but the changes you've suggested make sense," he said as he looked at his pages.

"Does this mean I get a writing credit?" Emmy asked as she grinned.

"Of course," he answered. "I wouldn't rip you off."

"I'm kidding! You don't have to give me credit for changing a word or two here and there."

"Yeah, but like this one," he said and then showed her one page. "You changed the whole verse and half of the chorus. You deserve credit for that."

They finished and Emmy walked outside with Adam. "Call me when you want to work again."

"I will, Em. Thanks for letting me take up your morning."

Adam left and Emmy walked around the house to the pool. She saw Kenny sleeping on one of the lounge chairs and shook her head.

"We didn't want to wake Daddy up," Isabella said as she got out of the pool and walked over to Emmy.

Emmy sighed and said, "It's a good thing you can swim like a fish."

Chapter Thirty-One

"We haven't talked about a vacation, but this would be the perfect summer to take one," Emmy said to Mary Galves as they waited in the foyer before the second service started. "Neither one of us is going on tour. I'm helping Adam with some stuff, but Kenny and the guys are having a terrible time trying to get anything useful done."

"You should start planning now. You shouldn't wait until the last minute like the Hawaii vacation," Mary said.

"You're right, but I can't think of anywhere the kids would enjoy," Emmy said.

Mary put a finger to her mouth. "Let's see. Maybe Disney World, or England. What about California? Or New England? I hear Maine is nice in the summer."

"I'll see."

Mary looked past Emmy's shoulder and saw some old friends approaching. "Don't wait too long. I'll talk to you later."

Emmy felt a tap on her shoulder and turned around. Her eyes sparkled as she moved into the opened arms of Lynette Jefferson. "I didn't know you were in town. Why are you here?"

"We wanted to surprise you," Lynette said as she hugged Emmy for a moment. "Hi, Mary, it's good to see you, too."

Mary smiled at Lynette and then at two young ladies, who were obviously twins, before she waked away.

Emmy stepped back, smiled at Paul Jefferson and then noticed the two young ladies. She put a hand to her mouth. "Oh my God! How can you be so grown up? This is not possible."

Lynette put an arm around the waist of each of her twin daughters. "They're bigger than me, and won't let me forget it."

"I'm not sure I can tell you apart anymore," Emmy said as she looked back and forth between the two girls. "I used to know, but I can't tell now."

"I'm Ruth," the one to Lynette's right said.

"Then you are Esther," Emmy said. "How old are you?"

Neither girl answered.

Lynette shook her head and frowned. "They're not shy.

274

They just don't like to talk to people they don't know. They're fifteen and will be sophomores when school starts."

"That's so unreal. Are you on vacation?"

Paul noticed some old friends and excused himself.

"Not a vacation," Lynette said.

"You don't have family here anymore," Emmy said.

"No, my parents moved back to Indiana shortly after we took the church in Iowa. Paul is from Iowa in case you forgot."

"What is your brother doing these days?" Emmy asked.

"He lives in Terre Haute and teaches physical education at Terre Haute Central."

"I remember he played basketball in high school."

"Can you keep a secret for a few hours?" Lynette asked.

"If I have to."

Lynette felt a tug on her arm and looked at Ruth. "Go ahead, but you have to sit with us for church."

The girls dashed away to join some high school-age kids.

"I almost didn't recognize them," Emmy said as she watched the girls disappear. She turned back to Lynette. "Tell me the secret."

"We interviewed at SoHam First a month ago, but you can't say anything."

"Oh my gosh, Lynette! Did they offer it to you? Did you accept? I won't say a word, but I will pray that you take the position." Emmy hugged Lynette. "It would be so good to have you back in SoHam. Did they offer it to you guys?"

"Yes, and we accepted. The church is actually voting today."

"They better vote yes." Emmy hugged Lynette again

"The salary is more than we expected. Not that that's the most important thing."

Emmy grinned. "I can't wait for you guys to move back."

"We are staying in a motel until the moving van arrives."

"Do you have a place to live already?" Emmy asked.

"The church owns a parsonage. They have been doing some work on it, but it's supposed to be ready by the middle of the week."

"When will you start?"

"Our first official Sunday is the first one in July, but we will be there next Sunday."

"Good!" Emmy grinned. "That means I get my Sunday School teacher back."

Lynette looked perplexed.

"Pastor Williams has been filling in. Now he can come back," Emmy explained. "Oh, Lynette, I'm so glad you're moving back. I really need to talk to you."

"You can always talk to me, Emmy. I assume it's not about boys this time."

Emmy shook her head. "Not boys, but I have to make another choice, and you remember how much I struggled making decisions."

Lynette chuckled and said, "I remember, Em. I remember."

Emmy checked the list of necessary items for the girls' camp a third time. "You aren't allowed to take any electronics, Heather." Emmy pulled Heather's iPod out of her suitcase.

"But, Mom! How will survive a whole week without it?" Heather pleaded.

"You will survive just like all the other kids," Emmy said. "Where is your toothbrush?"

"It's in the bathroom. I haven't brushed my teeth yet."

Emmy checked the time. "Get your butt in there and brush your teeth. We have to leave in fifteen minutes."

Ten minutes later Kenny and Kevin Michael stood outside the garage and waved as Emmy took the girls to the church.

"Will I get to go to camp next year?" Kevin asked.

Kenny nodded and then picked Kevin up. "Next year you and Ben and and Grace and Natalie will be old enough to spend a week at camp. Carson, Peter and Dotty went to camp and they had a blast."

"Carson told me they got to swim in a lake and go canoeing. Will I be old enough to do that?"

"You might have to wait a few years before you can do all those things, buddy." Kenny set Kevin down and watched him scamper around to the back of the house.

"I'm going to go swimming and pretend I'm in a lake with lots of fish," Kevin Michael said.

Emmy arrived at the church with fifteen minutes to spare. She saw Kristen talking to Sloane and joined them.

"Hi, guys, am I late?" Emmy asked.

Maddy Boyter walked over with a clipboard. She smiled and said, "We are still waiting for five more kids. Can you believe we have twenty-one children going to this camp."

"Peter said there were even more at his camp," Sloane mentioned.

"Tyler had to rent a van," Maddy said and then checked off two more kids from her list.

Jake pulled the church's twenty-five passenger Titan bus to the front of the old sanctuary.

"Does he have to have a special license to drive that thing?" Kristen asked.

Maddy nodded. "He's got a Class C license. So do Tyler and Jonah. The bus has come in handy so many times. It was a wise investment."

Emmy watched as Heather and Isabella talked to Noemi Bertucci. "I can't believe they are old enough to even go to camp. They've never been away for a whole week before."

Sloane rolled her eyes. "Em, your girls are used to traveling all over the world. I think they'll handle a week of camp without any trouble."

"I never went to camp when I was a kid. I think Kenny did, but not me." *My parents couldn't have afforded it even if they would have let me go.*

"Lindsey and I went to camp every year," Sloane said. "Now our kids are going to camp together. I guess that means we are getting old."

Emmy hugged the girls before they got onto the bus. "Have fun and try not to get homesick."

"Mom! We aren't going to get homesick," Heather said. "We have all our friends to play with."

"I will miss you and Daddy," Isabella said.

277

"What about your brother?" Emmy asked.

"I might miss him, but you better not tell him I said so."

Jake turned into the entrance of Nottawaseppi Lake Nazarene Camp and passed under the wrought iron arch formed with the name of the lake and the Native American tribe in large letters.

"Where's the lake?" someone sitting near the front hollered.

"Do we get to go swimming today?"

Isabella looked at Heather. "Do you think it will be harder to swim in a lake than in our pool?"

Heather shrugged. "It's just water, Isa."

Jake and Maddy helped get the kids registered and situated. Since there were more girls than boys at the camp, the girls were housed in the modern dormitory. The large building was divided into quadrants separated by walls and with each quadrant having its own outside entrance. The boys made do with the more rustic cabins. Heather, Isabella and Noemi dragged their suitcases into the area assigned to them.

"Heather, we can use these bunk beds, and Noemi can use this one next to us. It will be like having a sleepover every night," Isabella squealed excitedly.

The girls looked around the large room and couldn't count how many bunk beds there were.

"We have indoor bathrooms," Heather said. "I heard from some of the older kids that whoever gets stuck in the cabins has to take showers in an old building with bugs and maybe even snakes."

Noemi put a hand to her face. "I will scream if I see a snake. Do you think there are snakes in the water?"

"That's just something the boys said to try and scare us," Isabella assured Noemi. "Boys are so gross."

Later that afternoon everyone gathered in the chapel.

A lady with hair so red it appeared to be on fire stood on the stage with a microphone. "I want to welcome everyone to Adventure Camp Week. My name is Beth Qualley, and we have lots of fun activities planned." She introduced some of her assistants and the camp counselors. "I want to thank Olivet

278

Nazarene University for supplying the counselors for all the camps this summer. They've done a fabulous job so far."

Later the 224 kids were divided into eight teams. All the kids from Bristol Ridge ended up on Red Team #1. The kids gathered around the four counselors assigned to their team.

Margaret Adams hushed the kids by waving her hands. "I want to tell you about some of the activities we have lined up." She looked at two boys who were still talking and raised her hand. "Everyone needs to pay attention to us when we are talking. If we raise our hands that means you need to stop talking and listen. Okay?"

The boys stopped talking after some encouragement from the kids around them.

"Today we are going to play water kickball," Margaret said and then explained the rules. She mentioned several other activities.

One of the boys raised a hand and asked, "My brother was here and he said they got to play on the Iceberg. Will we get to play on it, too?"

"Unfortunately, the Iceberg is outside of the area we will use for swimming," Margaret said. "It's for the older campers."

Heather whispered to Isabella, "I saw a picture of it. It looks so cool. I can't wait until we're older and get to play on it."

"What is it?" Noemi asked.

Heather tilted her head and thought about the Iceberg. "It's this thing shaped liked a pyramid out in the water. You climb up the sides and then you can jump off into the lake. It looks like fun."

"It sounds scary to me," Noemi said.

"Heather! Did you hear that?" Isabella nudged her sister. "She said there would be a talent show on Thursday. Maybe we can sing together."

Jake and Maddy met some of the other people who would be staying for the week. They checked into their room at the motel-like building that housed all the adults who wouldn't be staying in either the dorms or cabins with the young campers.

Jake pointed to the name on the door of their room. "We're in the Pocahontas room."

Maddy looked at some of the other doors. "All the room are named after Native Americans or tribes."

"Is there a Geronimo room?" Jake asked.

Maddy shook her head and frowned at him. "That wasn't his real name. That's what the white people called him."

"Who was Towanda?" Jake asked.

Maddy shrugged. "I don't know. Let's unpack and find our kids."

Heather, Isabella and Noemi lined up outside the cafeteria and then followed their leaders into the large area.

"This is almost as big as the cafeteria at school," Isabella whispered.

"I hope the food is good," Noemi said. "Peter said he bought food at the Snack Shack every day."

The campers sat at tables much like they did at school. The dinner was served buffet-style.

"I like the pasta," Heather said as she slurped a strand of spaghetti into her mouth. "But I wish it had more meatballs in it."

After dinner everyone gathered in the chapel for the evening service. A song leader stood on the stage and the kids followed her motions as they sang several songs.

"Heather! We know this one. We sang it at Vacation Bible School last year. Remember?" Isabella grinned.

"I remember it, but these aren't the motions we used," Heather said.

Later, Margaret made sure all the girls were tucked into bed and turned off the lights. "Good night, everyone. I'll see you bright and early in the morning."

Heather leaned over from her top bunk. "See you in the morning, Isa. We can sleep together if you get cold."

Isabella snuggled deeper under her blankets. "I'll be all right, but if you get cold, you can come down here."

After breakfast the campers marched to the chapel with their counselors. The kids from Bristol Ridge sat with the other members of Red Team #1 in their assigned area. Zachary and Caden grinned at the girls.

"Why are you grinning like that, Zach?" Heather asked. "You look goofy."

"I caught a frog in the shower house. Want to see it?"

"No! We don't want to see it," Noemi said to her second cousin.

"I want to see it," Heather said.

"I put it in a box in our cabin. I made holes in it so the frog could breath. I'll show you later."

Isabella frowned. "Hush! Miss Qualley said we need to listen to this man. She said he and his family are missionaries from Africa, and he's going to tell us about living there. Maybe he knows Pastor Wade and Miss Blaine."

Admirando Chambo showed pictures of the mud hut where he lived as a child. He kept the campers attention with his animated delivery.

Zachary whispered to Caden, "We could build a mud hut in the woods. That could be our secret hiding place."

Caden nodded but felt a little afraid of the idea.

The week passed very quickly for the campers. Some of the counselors didn't share the same feeling though. Many of them needed to catch up on their sleep after four weeks of camps. Jake and Maddy helped the kids from church pack up and allowed them a chance to say goodbye to the new friends they made during the week.

"Pastor Jake, if I decide to become a missionary, do I have to live in Africa?" Isabella asked.

"No, the church has missionaries in many other counties. Do you think you might be a missionary when you grow up?"

"Maybe, but I don't want to live in a mud house," Isabella replied.

Emmy paced in front of the church as she, Kenny and Kevin Michael waited for the bus to arrive.

"What time are they arriving?" Emmy asked again.

"Will you relax!" Kenny put his hands on her shoulders. "They won't get here any sooner if you keep pacing."

Kevin Michael pointed to the entrance. "There they are!"

Jake parked the church bus and the kids scrambled off. Heather and Isabella waved and raced over to Emmy and Kenny.

"Mom! We had so much fun. Can we go back next year?" Heather asked.

Emmy hugged her daughters as if she hadn't seen them for a month instead of a few days. "I missed you so much! You have to tell us everything you did."

Kevin Michael walked up to his sisters. "I missed you a little bit. Next year I get to go with you."

Isabella hugged him. "You will have so much fun. We went swimming in the lake."

"Did you see any fish or bugs in the water?" he asked.

"No," Isabella answered.

Kenny placed the girls' luggage in the Odyssey, and they headed home.

"I want to know everything you did from the time you arrived," Emmy insisted.

"Mom! Didn't you ever go to camp? We just did the usual stuff," Heather said.

"I never went to camp. Please, tell me. Did you sleep okay? Where did you sleep?"

Heather looked at Isabella. "You can start."

"Okay, we stayed in this really big dormitory with all the other girls. We had carpet, but Zachary said the floors in the cabins were plain old wood with bugs and spiders everywhere."

Emmy let the girls describe their activities with only a few interruptions.

How big was the chapel?" Emmy asked.

Heather spread her arms as wide as she could. "It was huge. There weren't chairs like at our church. They had these wooden benches to sit on."

"Where was the stage?" Kenny asked.

"Well, you came in the front door and the stage was to the left in front of all the benches. We sat in the same place all the time," Heather said. "We didn't use most of the benches."

"There were these metal rafters in the ceiling," Isabella

added. "And I think the roof was made of metal, too."

"Was there anything you didn't like in the cafeteria?" Emmy asked.

"I didn't like the meat loaf. It tasted funny," Heather said. "I liked the corn dogs. They were yummy."

"Did you spend all your money?" Kenny asked.

"I still have a dollar left, but Heather used all her money," Isabella said. "She bought a lot of pop and candy."

"We sang for the talent show, and won a blue ribbon," Isabella said. "But all the other kids got blue ribbons, too."

"We won the swimming race," Heather said. "We finished way ahead of everyone, but we didn't get to jump off the Iceberg."

"They have a climbing wall, and when you get to the top you go on a zip line, but it's for older kids," Isabella explained.

"That sounds like fun. Can I try it?" Emmy asked.

"Mom! You're too old to go to camp," Heather said and then rolled her eyes.

"I'm going to go on the zip line when I go to camp," Kevin Michael insisted.

"Do you even know what a zip line is?" Heather turned around and frowned at her brother.

"I've seen pictures. It's a line way up in the air and you slide on it."

"You have to be a big kid to go on it," Heather told him."

"Mom! Will I be a big kid when I go to camp next year?" Kevin asked.

"You might be big for your age, but you will still be too young to use the zip line."

"I told Pastor Jake and Maddy that I might be a missionary when I get older, but I don't want to go to Africa," Isabella announced.

"Where would you want to go?" Kenny asked.

Isabella thought about it. "I would be a missionary in Minnesota, but not in the winter."

"I don't blame you, Isa," Emmy grinned.

Chapter Thirty-Two

"Emmy, could I talk to you for a minute?" Mary asked after the second service on Sunday morning.

"Sure. What's up?" Emmy asked and then looked up at Dahlia Michaelis. "Are you ready to start college?"

"I can't wait," Dahlia said as she grinned. "We need a favor, Emmy."

"Okay," Emmy glanced back and forth between the two sisters.

"It's difficult to believe, but Dahlia is turning eighteen on Wednesday, and she wants to have a pool party. I know this is a big favor, and it's the last minute, but..."

"Let's have the party at my house. I know you and Jonah don't have a pool. Your parents don't either, right?"

Mary shook her head.

"We can call it a birthday, graduation and a going-away-to-college party," Emmy bounced on her toes. "Will you invite boys?"

"Would you mind terribly if I did?" Dahlia asked.

"I won't mind. What time should we start the party?"

"Would seven work for you guys?" Mary asked.

"We can start at seven and end whenever. I'll make sure we have plenty of pop and bottled water available. We could order pizzas unless you want something else," Emmy offered.

"Pizza would be great, but you don't have to buy. I have some money saved," Dahlia said.

Emmy shook her head. "You can save your money. Kenny and I will pay for the pizza and stuff."

Kenny walked up behind Emmy. "What are we paying for now, Em?"

"We're throwing a pool party for Dahlia Wednesday," Emmy answered.

"Mom! I'm ready to go over to Ben's house," Kevin Michael announced as he walked into the kitchen on Wednesday. He carried a backpack and a large red firetruck.

284

"Did you pack any clothes?" Emmy asked. She grabbed the backpack, opened it and stared at Kevin. "You can't take all these cars. The backpack is for clothes. You are spending the night at Tony's. Go back upstairs and put some clean underwear, a pair of shorts and a t-shirt in the backpack. Clean clothes from your dresser drawer." She ordered and then pointed upstairs. "Go! Now!"

"Mommy, can we stay up long enough to see Mary and Dahlia?" Isabella asked.

"Yes, they should be here by seven. You can stay up until nine, but you have to play inside. The party is for Dahlia and her friends."

"I could take you and Heather to a movie if you'd rather do that," Kenny offered.

Isabella shook her head. "Thanks, Daddy, but we'd rather see Mary and Dahlia than go to some movie for babies."

"I was thinking of the new Terminator movie. It starts today," Kenny said.

Emmy put her hands on her hips and glared at him. "You are not taking the girls to a Terminator movie."

Heather rolled her eyes. "Mom! We've seen the other ones. They aren't scary movies."

"No way! When did you see the other ones?" Emmy asked.

The twins looked up at their father, but didn't say anything.

Emmy took a deep breath and let it out slowly.

"Are you counting to ten, Mommy?" Isabella asked. "Is Daddy in trouble?"

"I'm always in trouble," Kenny said. He grinned at Emmy, put his arms around her waist and pulled her close.

"Come on, Isa," Heather said as she pulled on her sister's arm. "We better go upstairs so they can kiss."

"We aren't going to kiss," Emmy said.

Kenny didn't listen to her.

The guard in the security shack opened the gate for another car filled with teenagers. *Whoever this party is for must be pretty special. Kenny and Emmy usually don't have people over during the week.* He started to sit down but saw another car coming.

Dylan and Cora Michaelis walked into the kitchen and saw Emmy adding red kidney beans to two large bowls of taco salad.

Emmy looked over her shoulder. "You made it."

Mr. Michaelis smiled. "The security guard gave us a funny look when we said we were here for your pool party. I told him the party was for our daughter, and he laughed and said good luck."

"I'm having a hard time believing Dahlia is eighteen already. She wasn't even ten when Mary became our nanny," Emmy said as she stirred the taco salads.

"The years have flown by," Cora said. "We wanted to thank you and Kenny for letting the kids use your pool."

Emmy waved a hand. "No problem. I told the girls they could use the upstairs if they needed to change, but I think most of the kids wore their bathing suits under their clothes."

"We don't plan to swim, and we won't stay too long. Can I help with anything?" Mrs. Michaelis asked.

"I've got this under control. You should check with Kenny. He's outside somewhere." Emmy poured two packages of shredded cheese into the taco salads. She looked out the window over the sink just in time to see two boys toss one of the girls from church into the pool. "I'm going to have as much fun as the kids."

By seven thirty over forty guests had turned the pool and deck area into a sea of shirtless teenage boys and girls in, for the most part, modest bathing suits. Emmy noticed a few one-piece suits but most of the girls wore bikinis. Several of the girls, including Dahlia, were still wearing shorts. Kenny played classic rock music over the outdoor speakers. Emmy danced to the music as she covered a picnic table with the taco salad, bags of chips and even some veggie trays. She saw Kenny approaching with more pop.

"Will we have enough?" Emmy asked.

"There's more in the garage, but I told Jonah it was his responsibility to keep the coolers full from now on." Kenny set the case of Dr Pepper on the deck next to the coolers. "Jonah wants to set up a volleyball court in the yard. I told him it was fine with me."

A few minutes later Dahlia walked up to Emmy with a soaking wet, tall young man in tow. "Emmy, do you know Kieran Lochlin?"

"I've seen him around church. Why? Is he your boyfriend?" Emmy asked knowing it would embarrass Dahlia. Even under her tan Emmy could see Dahlia blush.

"We're going out, but usually just with friends," Dahlia admitted.

"That's a good way to date." *It's more difficult for things to get serious that way.*

"Are you going to swim with us?" Dahlia asked Emmy. "Kenny is sitting with my parents. We can't convince him to join us."

"I wouldn't mind getting in the pool. I've got my suit on already," Emmy said as she looked up at Kieran. *I like your blue eyes and that California-surfer-dude blonde hair. You remind me a little of Christopher Braun. I hope you're not as much of a player as he used to be.* "Are most of your friends from Lincoln High?" Emmy asked Dahlia.

Dahlia looked around. "I'd say it's half and half. Most of the kids from church attend Crest Ridge Central. Jocelyn and Marcus go to Barclay Academy."

"Did you ever have your father for a teacher at Lincoln?" Emmy asked.

"No! Thank God! I would have died of embarrassment, but some of my friends were in his class. They said he wasn't too boring, but I don't believe them."

"I bet both your parents are good teachers," Emmy said. "I know Mary is a great teacher. All the kids love her. Do you think you will be a teacher?"

"Never in a million years," Dahlia answered.

"What about you, Kieran?" Emmy asked. "You go to North Park, right?"

"Yes, but I haven't decided on a major. It's likely to be something to do with computer systems," he answered with a smile at Emmy.

"The pizzas should be here by eight thirty," Emmy said. "I

287

didn't bother with dessert, but we have some ice cream."

"I don't think anyone will care about ice cream, Emmy. The pizza and the other stuff will be plenty."

"Come on, Dahlia. We're going to play volleyball," Kieran said.

Emmy watched as Kieran led Dahlia away. She saw him put a hand on Dahlia's back. Then she saw another couple from church. She frowned as that boy put a hand on the back of the girl's shorts. Emmy laughed as that girl swatted the boy's hand away. *That's it. Don't let him think he can get away with anything.*

"Mommy, can we have some pizza?" Heather asked.

"If it gets here in time, you may have some, but you still have to be in bed by nine."

"Daddy said we could stay up later tonight because we won't be able to sleep with all the noise," Heather said.

"We'll see," Emmy said. "Be careful if you use the pool. There are lots of kids here, and they might not see you."

"We're not invisible, Mom. We know how to swim better than them."

"Just be careful," Emmy said and then sighed as she saw three boys running toward the pool. She walked over to where Kenny sat. "Should we be concerned about having so many teenagers here? I just saw three boys take a running start and jump into the pool."

Kenny pointed to the pool. "I think Jonah's got it under control, and Jake and Maddy just arrived a few minutes ago. They will keep things manageable. They deal with teenagers all the time."

"I guess I shouldn't worry," Emmy said as she sat on Kenny's legs.

"You will have teenagers of your own to worry about soon enough," Mrs. Michaelis said.

Emmy looked at Heather and Isabella and sighed. *We have a few years before that happens.*

The kids gravitated into groups. Most stayed by and in the pool. Others played volleyball, and a few danced on the deck. The pizzas arrived on time and Emmy gathered everyone together.

"Before we scarf down the pizzas, I would like for Pastor Jake to say a quick prayer," Emmy said and motioned to Jake.

"Lord, we thank you for your blessings. We thank you for Dahlia and her friends. Thank you for Kenny and Emmy allowing us to be here, and thank you for the food. Amen." He finished and smiled at Emmy. "Was that quick enough?"

"I didn't mean you had to say a short prayer. I kinda meant for you to pray quickly while everyone was paying attention."

Jake laughed.

The kids formed a line and filled paper plates with pizza. Some sat at the tables on the deck and around the pool. Others made due by sitting on the ground and others balanced themselves on the deck railing to eat.

Kenny took the twins inside to eat. Emmy looked around for a place to sit. She saw Dahlia, Kieran, and Jake and Maddy at a picnic table situated under a large maple tree and joined them. Jonah and Mary joined them after Mr. and Mrs. Michaelis left the party.

"How much land do you have out here?" Jake asked.

"I think it's between fifteen and twenty acres. Kenny bought one of the original properties before we were married. He even had the house planned. He ended up buying the rest of the land on this side of Springdale Lane a few years ago. Springdale is the main street out here and it's like a horseshoe," Emmy explained while chewing her pizza.

"So you own everything inside the horseshoe," Maddy said.

"Yeah, I guess so," Emmy said. "Sorry for talking with my mouth full. I get on Heather for doing that all the time."

"Dany and Darian live in the guesthouse," Dahlia said as she pointed to the south. "They said they would stop by after he gets off work."

Emmy added, "Darian works at Aberdeen Investments. That's the company that manages our investments." She put a hand to her mouth. "I didn't mean to brag."

Maddy patted Emmy's arm. "You don't have to apologize for being successful."

"I haven't been to a graduation party for a few years,"

289

Emmy said. "This is a combination birthday and graduation party even if no one cares."

"Your birthday is next Wednesday, Em. This could be your party, too," Mary said.

"I've had enough birthday parties already," Emmy said.

"How old are you?" Kieran asked. "You don't look very old."

"Thank you, Kieran, but I'm too old to mention my age," Emmy replied.

"Mary told me about you going to Kristen's and Derrick's parties when they graduated from Roosevelt," Dahlia said. "She said some kids had beer at one of the parties."

"Dahlia, maybe Emmy doesn't want to talk about those parties," Mary said as she frowned at her sister.

"It's all right," Emmy said. She looked at Jonah and Jake, both pastors on the church staff. "What you're thinking off happened at Derrick's graduation party. There were some kids who disobeyed the rules and brought beer to the party. The adults had beer and stuff, but these were high school kids who were underage." She glanced around the table. "It's probably no big secret that I grew up in a family where the consumption of alcohol was the rule rather than the exception. I think I might have been ten when Rory and I stole some of Daddy's beer."

"Do you mean Kenny?" Maddy asked.

Emmy shook her head. "Rory Porter is an old friend from the neighborhood. You've probably never met him." Emmy explained how she and Rory reconnected after not seeing each other for so many years. "Rory and I kinda hung out together."

"Owen and Amy are gone. Rory and his mother are the only ones left," Mary explained.

"So these kids brought beer to Derrick's party. Even though I didn't think it was wrong to have a beer, I didn't drink any at the party. Some of the kids tried to make it seem like I was drinking, I wasn't." Emmy waved both hands as she talked. "One of them was this girl who tried to get me in trouble at school a few times. She even set me up on a blind date with a kid named Jayson. I don't remember his last name, but he looked like Tom Petty." Emmy paused briefly. "I actually ran into Dawn a few years ago, and she's now a Christian. She's a Baptist minister and works as a chaplain for the prison system in Arkansas. She's like the last person in the world I would have ever thought would be a minister. I guess that shows how God can use anyone to further His Kingdom."

Jake and Jonah looked at her.

"Crap! I didn't mean it like that," Emmy said as she turned red.

Jake grinned. "We know what you mean, Emmy. None of us are perfect. We all need God's grace."

"Some of us need it more than others," Emmy said.

"Oh, Emmy," Mary said. "You think you were so bad as a kid, but you weren't. Sure you did some things, but you and Kenny used to sing at church for the youth group."

"Yeah, but that was before I gave my heart to Jesus. I would sing at church with Kenny on Wednesday and sneak off with Rory and his friends on Saturday night to party. Not every Saturday, but a few times." Emmy waved a hand to include the whole area. "And I'm not talking about a party like this. I mean parties where kids would be drinking beer and smoking pot and messing around." She bit her lip and started to cry.

"It's all right, Emmy." Mary said as she and Maddy each put an arm around Emmy's shoulders.

Emmy wiped her tears with the back of her hand. "I remember some of those girls ended up pregnant. I could have ended up like them, but I think even before I knew Him, Jesus was protecting me. I'm not saying I never did anything, but I never..." She bit her lip and looked around the table. "Maybe I should shut up before I say something I shouldn't."

Jake coughed and everyone looked at him. "Talking about sex is not easy. Maddy and I have counseled a number of teens on that subject."

"Our parents talked to us about sex," Mary volunteered.

"Mary! Do you have to tell everyone," Dahlia said. "I never talked to Da about it. Just Ma."

"It can't be any easier for teens now with everything they're bombarded with," Emmy said. "I can't believe movies nowadays."

291

Kieran glanced around the table. "I can't speak for all teens at the church, but I gave my heart to Christ when I was twelve. I didn't know too much about sex back then, but I soon learned more." He turned to look at Dahlia. "Please don't think I'm weird, but I made a pledge not to have sex until I was married. It's not easy because I really like girls. Especially you." He paused then added, "Please don't tell everyone. I don't want them to think I'm gay or something."

Dahlia smiled into Kieran's eyes. "I don't think you're weird."

Dany and Darian walked up to the table behind Dahlia. Darian put his hands on his younger sister's shoulders. "Happy birthday, Dahlia. Did we miss anything?"

"We were just talking about sex," Emmy said. She blushed as everyone stared at her.

"Way to set a good example, Emmy," Dany teased.

"It wasn't like that," Emmy insisted. "We weren't talking about having sex with different people or anything."

Everyone stared at Emmy.

"I just made it worse, didn't I?"

Now, everyone nodded.

"Just throw me in the pool," Emmy said.

"Does anyone need more pizza?" Maddy asked.

Chapter Thirty-Three

"I really don't want to play for more than two hours," Jeff said as Fridays At Five rehearsed in their warehouse for their concert at the SoHam Memorial Stadium the next day. "I'm not sure my fingers will hold up longer than that."

"Have you been slacking off?" Jeremy Lenhart asked. "Are you going to need a music folder with all the chord charts?"

"Hey! Just because you've been trying to remember how to play our old songs doesn't mean I don't remember them," Jeff answered back. "Do you need Adam to show you how to play?"

Jeff and Jeremy's friendship predated the formation of Fridays At Five. Jeremy left the band in 2011 to spend more time with his family. His daughter Jennifer suffered from a form of leukemia.

"What are these black keys for?" Jeremy asked. "Have they always been there?"

Kenny and Dave huddled together on the side of the stage. Kenny held his iPad as they perused a list of possible songs.

"Since this is going to be our only show this year, should we stick to the hits?" Dave asked.

"That would be the easiest. We can play most of those songs in our sleep. If we had more time to rehearse, I would suggest we throw in a few obscure tracks. There are some songs we recorded for a CD and never played them live."

"We could do that sometime."

"I've seen a few bands do one of their CDs from start to finish. The Lyricon has done that a few times," Kenny said.

"I can't think of any of our CDs we've played like that."

Kenny nodded. "When we did the Riders shows, we changed the order a bit." He checked the list again. "I wonder if we'll need more than twenty songs. What do you think?" Kenny asked Paul Joseph, who had wandered over to join them.

Paul looked at the list. "No more than twenty-five. How long is Emmy going to sing?"

"She agreed to do an hour-long show," Kenny answered. "She told me she wouldn't sing with us at all."

"Was she serious?" Dave asked.

Kenny shrugged. "Who knows?"

Jeff hollered at the guys, "Hey! Are you going to waste all day? I told Frances I would be home in time to grill some steaks."

Dave took his position behind the drums. Paul picked up a guitar. Adam finished programming his keyboards, and Kenny walked up to his microphone in the center of the stage.

"Are you guys ready?" he asked the tech guys.

Will Consoli hit the talk-back mic and said they were ready. Kenny glanced at Dan Belanger, who stood behind his monitor mixer and gave a thumbs up signal.

"Count us off, Dave," Kenny said.

They started with the band's first single. A tune called "Too Bad" and the lights began to flash.

"I love digital lighting," Randy Lemmert, the band's original and only lighting guru, said to Will Consoli. "I just plug in a scene and everything works. All I have to do is keep an eye on the computer."

"One of these days you will be replaced by a child with an iPhone," Will joked.

"You've already been replaced," Randy teased back. "You just don't know it. Kenny uses his laptop to mix the whole show from the stage. You only think you're doing it."

The band played for two hours, took a short break, eliminated several songs from consideration and then played for two more hours.

"Do we need to finalize the set list before we leave?" Kenny asked.

Jeff shook his head. "You and Dave can decide. I trust your judgment. Everything will be on the laptops, right?"

Dave answered, "It's great. We don't have to write out a bunch of set lists like the old days. We create a document and network it to all our computers. It saves paper."

Kenny laughed. "Yeah, but Dad has a ton of old set lists at home. He says he's saving them for when he needs the money. He claims he can get over a hundred bucks for each one on eBay."

"Shoot! If I'd known that, I would have saved them, too,"

294

Jeff said as he put his 1964 Fender Jazz bass guitar in its case."

The road crew would pack up the gear and move it to the stadium in the morning.

"You wouldn't need the money if you didn't keep buying every old house in SoHam that needs remodeling," Jeremy teased.

"I need a hobby." Jeff shrugged. "We only buy one or two a year, and we fix them and flip them. Sometimes we make some money. Sometimes we break even."

"Sooner or later you guys will own or have owned every house in Timberline Heights," Jeremy said.

"We're working on it," Jeff said as he slapped his old friend on the back.

"Could I ask you guys something?" Paul said.

"Sure. What's on your mind?" Kenny asked.

"I've been approached by the guys from the old band. They have a chance to do a short tour on the weekends if they can get me to join them. Would you guys mind if I did that?"

Kenny looked at the other guys.

Jeff nodded. "I thought a couple of the guys moved down south or somewhere."

"Calbert and Elijah moved to Tennessee back in 2002, but they are willing to take the time to get together."

"It's all right with me," Dave said.

Paul looked at Adam and Jeremy.

Adam replied, "I don't mind. Not that you need my permission. I'm the new guy in the band."

"You still get a vote," Kenny said. "Has your father mentioned this?"

"Not to me."

"I see Sammy Demont once in a while," Jeremy mentioned. "I think he might need the money. He said his business is struggling to make ends meet."

"What does he do?" Jeff asked.

"He owns a carpet store somewhere on the east side," Jeremy answered.

"Go ahead, P.J."

"Thanks, guys. I'm sure it won't interfere with our studio

time when we decide to start recording again," Paul assured them.

"Emmy will be thrilled. She was one of The Notable Exception's biggest fans back in the day," Kenny said.

With Emmy's old backing band away on tour, she recruited some members of the worship team to back her up for her one-off show. She and the new band gathered on the platform at the church to rehearse.

"Before we get started, I want to thank you guys for helping out. Let me pray and we can get started." Emmy prayed and then passed out a set list. "This is not set in stone. Some of the songs are ones we do in church, but there are others from my CDs you might not know. I don't mind if you need chord charts tomorrow. The songs aren't too complicated. No strange key changes or anything."

Cameron Frees adjusted his Buddy Holly-style glasses and looked over the list. "I know most of these songs, Emmy. I might need some help programming my keyboards."

"Adam said he could help with that. He will be there early. He said he might even play on a few songs if I needed him."

Robby and Regina Collins looked over the list.

"Are you going to need me to sing harmonies on any of these, Emmy?" Robby asked.

"Not really, Robby. I need you more as my drummer. Regina is all I need for harmonies." Emmy turned to the two newest members of the worship team. "I know you guys are new, but Kenny assures me you are more than capable of playing these songs." She handed a set list to Paul Mahnari.

"Thanks for the vote of confidence," Paul said.

"No problem," Emmy smiled as she looked up at Paul. She tried not to stare at the long, red scar that ran from his ear to the front of his jaw.

He caught her glance. "I'll try not to frighten anyone. I usually have a beard, but my doctor had me shave it because he going to do more surgery."

Paul had been the victim of a stabbing incident the previous year.

296

"I'm sorry if I stared. You won't frighten anyone. Kevin Michael told me you let him touch the scar."

"I'm used to the stares," Paul said.

Emmy turned to the other guitar player Kenny recommended and handed him a set list. "Kenny said you are one of the most talented guitar players he's ever heard."

Gideon T. Logan had moved to SoHam from Quezon City in the Philippines only six months previously. He stared at the floor. His long black hair flowed nearly to his waist.

"Don't be shy with me. Kenny wouldn't have said that if he didn't mean it. I don't mean to belittle anyone else's talent, but I've heard you play and Kenny was right."

"Thank you, Emmy. I appreciate the opportunity, and I will not disappoint you."

"You're welcome." Emmy didn't have to look up too high to look Gideon in the eyes. He stood only five inches taller than her and probably didn't weigh more than 130 pounds.

"Do I get a set list?" Jackson Brewster set his bass guitar in a stand and walked up to Emmy.

"Sorry, Jackson. I didn't think it mattered because you play the same notes for every song," she teased.

"You are confusing me with my uncle," he said. "Uncle Hank played with the worship band for fifty years or so, and he only knew how to play in one key."

"I'll tell him you said so if I see him again." Emmy grinned. She waved to the tech guys. "We're about ready if you are."

"Are we going to have a light show like a real band?" Robby asked.

"No, there will just be a spotlight on you, so you better not screw up."

Emmy and the band ran through the familiar songs first.

"That was easy enough," Cameron said. "Are you sure you don't want to change the arrangement of 'Glorious Day?'"

"Have you guys been doing it differently?" Emmy asked.

"Riordan switched the last chorus around, and we don't do that instrumental before the bridge anymore."

Emmy bit her lip for a split-second. "If it's too confusing, we could do it Riordan's way."

"We can handle the change, Emmy," Robby said.

"Should we take a break before we tackle my stuff?" Emmy asked.

"I could use a break," Regina said.

They headed to the music suite behind the platform. Emmy saw Gideon standing by himself and walked over. "Do you want some coffee or anything? We have bottled water."

"I'm good. I don't drink anything with caffeine," he answered.

"I've seen you play, but we've never really talked before today. How do you like living in SoHam? I'm sure it's quite different than where you're from."

"The most difficult part is the cost of everything. My rent is close to a thousand dollars a month."

"Where are you living? Where do you work?" Emmy asked. *I can't believe how straight your hair is. When I wore mine that long it was so curly. It's still curly, but a lot easier to manage.* She ran a hand through her hair.

"I work in the IT department for Coventry Shield Healthcare, and I'm living in an apartment on Janet Street. That's close to the river."

Emmy stared at him without speaking.

"Are you okay? You look like you've seen a ghost."

"What number?"

"Excuse me."

"What's your address?" Emmy asked.

"It's 312 Janet. I live upstairs in this place that used to be a single family home."

"This is so unreal," Emmy said.

"Why?"

"I moved out of my parents' house when I graduated from Roosevelt and moved into that very apartment. And I used to work for Coventry. That was my first full-time job."

"Are you kidding?"

"No, who is your landlord? Do they live downstairs?" Emmy asked.

"I make out the check to Offerman Management Company. There's a young couple with a baby living downstairs. I don't know their name yet. Why do you ask?"

"My landlords were rather mean to me even though the wife was distantly related to my mother. They made me pay cash and complained if I had any guys over." Emmy put a face to her hand. "I didn't have a lot of guys over." *I'm glad I didn't say that Kenny spent the night a few times.*

"Hey, Emmy, are we going to finish sometime today?" Robby asked.

"Be right there," she answered and then looked at Gideon. "Could we talk more after practice?"

"I don't have any plans," Gideon said.

Two hours later Emmy ended the rehearsal session.

"Thank you all for doing this. Anyone have questions?"

"What about our gear?" Robby asked.

"Kenny's crew will make sure it gets to the stadium. Dave said you could use his practice kit if you want. That way we don't have to break this one down."

Robby asked a few questions about Dave's practice kit and Emmy answered as best she could.

"Sounds like a better kit than this," Robby said.

After a few more questions, Emmy said, "I'll see you all at the stadium. You can park behind the south stands and enter there. There will be a list with your names and anyone you are bringing."

"See you tomorrow, Emmy. I'll let Reed know we're finished," Robby said.

"Do you still have time?" Emmy asked Gideon.

"Yes, I bet you want to know how the apartment looks now."

"I am curious," Emmy admitted. "We could stop somewhere and get something to drink if you want. I'll buy."

"Sounds okay to me," Gideon said. "I'll follow you."

Emmy laughed.

"What's so funny?"

"You might have trouble following me. I have been accused of driving like a maniac at times," Emmy said.

Gideon followed her to a coffee shop not far from the church.

She got out of her Civic Si and waited for him. "They have bottled water and herbal tea if you're interested."

They went inside and Emmy ordered coffee and a blueberry muffin. Gideon chose tea and a chicken salad sandwich. They found a table in the back.

Gideon checked out the paintings on the wall. "Interesting art."

"Those are originals by Suzanne Mydliak. She's kinda famous, and she's from SoHam," Emmy explained.

"How long ago did you live in the apartment? How long did you live there?" Gideon asked.

"I moved there in April of 1998, and I stayed for about a year. The landlord was going to raise my rent. I couldn't really pay the higher rent and couldn't take his wife's meddling any longer, so I moved out," she answered. "You said you live upstairs. When I lived there, there were two apartments upstairs. Has that changed?"

"I have the whole upstairs."

"They must have remodeled the place at some time. Could you describe the layout now?"

"I could draw you a rough diagram," he said.

"Okay."

He used the back of a paper place mat.

"Wow! They've really changed it. Where you have a TV room was my kitchen. I was never in the other apartment, but it was smaller than mine. I would guess they opened up the living room and kitchen to make it one big area. You've got two bedrooms and two bathrooms. That's better than before."

"I am using the bedroom in the front as an office, but I have a couch in there that folds out. I like the bedroom in the back better. The bathroom is right there."

"I assume they removed the door that separated the two apartments."

"There's no sign of a door ever having been there now."

"Oh! I had an old fridge that froze everything as solid as a brick. If I wanted a bowl of ice cream, I would have to let it sit out

300

for fifteen minutes or longer."

"All the appliances are fairly new. I have an entrance in the front and back. I usually park in the garage in back and come in that way."

"I always had to park in the street out front," Emmy said. "Oh, there was this old wallpaper in the living room."

"No wallpaper anywhere now, Emmy."

"It's close to work. How is the neighborhood now?"

"Most of the people I see are young couples. Some have kids, but not all. It's pretty quiet. Sometimes I can hear the baby crying downstairs but only if I'm not watching TV or listening to music."

"My landlord's wife would complain every time I played a CD. It got to the point that I always wore headphones. I didn't watch TV much, but I had a DVD player."

"I can understand why you left. It must have been a rather small apartment before the remodeling."

"Oh, I left because the building was damaged in a storm. The landlord cheated his insurance company, and was going to raise the rent, so I moved out. I found a bigger place in Crest Ridge."

"I plan to stay there until I can afford to buy a house. I could even get married and stay there," Gideon said.

They talked a while longer and then Emmy stood up. "Kenny isn't going to believe this. I'll see you tomorrow, Gideon."

Emmy pulled into the garage and saw Kenny's Civic. *Good! He's home. He won't believe what I have to share.* She got out and raced inside. She hollered his name as she entered the kitchen.

"In the family room, Em," he answered.

They raced toward each other and collided by the stairs.

"I have to tell you something," Kenny said.

Emmy said simultaneously, "You aren't going to believe this."

They looked at each other and laughed.

"You can go first because I'm sure my news is better," she said.

"Okay, but this is pretty exciting. Paul and The Notable Exceptions are getting together to do a weekend tour. Isn't that great? You always liked that band."

"That's great, and we have to go see them, but you aren't going to believe this." Her eyes sparkled as she looked up at Kenny.

He put his hands on her shoulders. "Settle down. Take a deep breath and tell me."

"Do you know where Gideon lives?"

He shook his head. "Where?"

Emmy told him.

"Are you pulling my leg?"

Emmy shook her head. "We went out after practice, and he told me all about the apartment."

"Tell me he has a different landlord."

"Some company owns it now. The upstairs is one big apartment, and he works at Coventry."

"Now I know you're joking."

"I'm not. Would you mind if I talked him into letting me see the apartment one of these days?" she asked.

"I wouldn't mind. You could show the kids."

"I could. Heather and Isa might be interested. Kevin Michael wouldn't give a hoot."

The doors to the stadium opened at noon, and at one o'clock the opening act took the stage. Emmy was scheduled to take the stage at seven.

"We're all ready," Cameron Frees said a few minutes before seven.

"Let's pray before we go on," Emmy said. She prayed for the band and the people in the audience. "Are we ready? Are you guys nervous?"

"I wasn't until you asked," Paul Mahnari said. "I've never played in front of so many people."

Emmy giggled and then said, "Just pretend they're all in their underwear."

"Does that help? Is that what you do?" Paul asked.

302

"No, but wouldn't it be funny if they were."

The guys took their positions, and this time Emmy walked out with them. Since the sun was still up, she could see the audience. She waved to a few people she recognized as the guys got ready to play. She heard someone yell. *I know that voice.* She searched the crowd and spotted Barry Newton. He jumped up and down and waved. *Holy cow! Is that Fender with you? He's almost as tall as you, Barry.* She grabbed her microphone and waited a second to give Tobias Wouters, her front-of-house mixer, a chance to turn it on. "I want to thank you all for coming. I especially want to thank Barry and Fender Newton for their support over the years." She blew a kiss at Barry and turned to look at Robby.

He nodded and counted off the first song.

Fifty-nine minutes later, Emmy thanked the crowd again, placed her microphone in the stand, waved goodbye and headed backstage.

Gideon caught up to her. "I've seen Fridays At Five live before but never you. I have to say you are just as good."

"Thanks, Gideon." She put an arm around his slim waist. "You killed on that solo in 'These Things Take Time.' I hope the tech guys recorded it. They usually record every show."

"I'm glad you liked it. I thought I had blown it, but I found my way back."

"I might have to go back on the road just so you can be my guitar player," she said and then grinned.

"I might like that." He smiled back at her and noticed a sparkle in her blue eyes.

Fridays At Five took the stage at eight thirty. They finished their last encore and left the stage just before ten thirty.

Emmy waited for Kenny backstage with the kids. He saw them and walked over.

"The kids want to stay for the fireworks," Emmy said. "Should we let them? We have church in the morning."

Kenny looked at the kids. Kevin Michael bounced on his toes. *I know you want to stay.* He looked at the girls and saw the same excitement in their eyes. "Okay, we can stay. We might miss Sunday School, but it won't hurt to miss once."

303

"We can try to get up in time, Daddy," Isabella said.

Emmy spotted Gideon and waved at him.

He walked over. "Do you need to talk to me, Emmy?"

"Are you staying for the fireworks? We are."

"I thought I would," he answered.

"You could sit with us if you want."

He sat with them.

"How come your hair is so long?" Kevin Michael asked.

"My mother likes it, so I keep it long for her. She still lives in Quezon City," he answered. "She took care of my grandmother until she passed away."

"Don't pester Gideon," Emmy said to the kids. "I'm sorry if they're being nosy."

"It's all right. I don't mind."

"Has your grandmother been gone long?" Emmy asked.

"It's been almost two years years now. She passed away just before Christmas in 2013."

"I'm sorry for your loss. I lost my father in 2008, but he was seventy."

"My father disappeared when I was three, but my mother took care of me and my sister. She lives in Los Angeles now."

Emmy looked at his long hair. "I used to have long hair, but mine was curly. It's so much easier to manage now."

"I'll probably get mine cut shorter soon, but I'll always have longer hair than most men," Gideon said.

"It feels really nice," Emmy said. *Shoot! I shouldn't touch his hair.*

They stayed until the end.

"I'll talk to you at church, Gideon. Thanks again for helping me out tonight," Emmy said.

"You're welcome. I'm glad I could help." Gideon smiled at her. Then he turned and walked away.

Chapter Thirty-Four

"Kenny, are you awake?" Emmy asked at about nine o'clock as she rested her head on his chest.

"I am now," he answered and then grinned. "Are you...?"

"Not again," she said and then smacked his hip. "Would you mind if I go to SoHam First today? I'm not singing, and I kinda want to surprise Paul and Lynette."

"Is this his first Sunday preaching? I thought they were there last Sunday."

"They decided to make a quick trip to Indiana to see her family. If I go, will you get the kids to church?"

"What time is it?" He checked the clock. "It's okay with me. Should I stop and get something for lunch, or will you come home?"

"I could stop at Darby's. It's kinda on the way if I go out of my way."

"Makes sense to me," he said and then kissed her. "Do we...?"

"No! I need to get ready."

Emmy made it to South Hampshire First Nazarene a few minutes before the scheduled service time of ten forty-five. She smiled at an elderly couple who handed her a bulletin and took a seat in the second-to-last row. She looked around and spotted a few familiar faces. *So you must have decided to switch churches, huh? Or are you just visiting like me?* She sang the hymns and noticed that half of the people didn't sing along. *I'm not sure I blame you. Some of these old hymns are so lame. They sound like funeral dirges when you sing them so slow.*

She put a twenty in the offering plate, and listened attentively as Paul Jefferson preached his first sermon in his new church. *Not bad, Paul. You got a few amens for that point.* She made notes on the bulletin and sang along to a response song at the end of the service. She waited in the background as Paul and Lynette greeted people. Finally, most of the crowd left and Lynette spotted her.

"Emmy! What are you doing here? Why didn't you tell us

you were coming? Are you alone?' Lynette glanced around.

"It's just me." Emmy put her hands behind her back and bounced on her toes. "We had a late night at the stadium, and I decided to surprise you. Did I?"

"You did. Do you have to rush off, or can you stay for lunch?" Lynette asked. She spotted Ruth and Esther talking to a couple of teenage boys.

"I can stay a little while, but I promised to bring lunch home."

Paul walked over and shook Emmy's hand.

"Don't I get a hug?" she asked as she looked up at him.

He hugged her.

"I enjoyed your message."

Paul chuckled. "It's the same one I used for my first service in Iowa City. Could you tell?"

"You must have added some new points," Emmy teased.

They talked for several minutes and then Lynette brought up the music.

"I hate to say anything negative, but," Emmy tilted her head back and forth.

"It sucked," Lynette whispered. "I couldn't hear anyone in the congregation singing, and they played that last hymn so slow. I could have written *War and Peace* in the time it took them to finish."

Emmy bit her lip. "It could use some new life."

"My thoughts exactly," Lynette said. "What are you doing next Sunday? Are you on the schedule to sing?"

"No, why?" Emmy asked and then realized she had been trapped.

"We could sure use you," Lynette said.

"Do you mean to sing a special or something?"

"Something like that," Paul said. "Sandy Petty, the lady who led the worship service this morning, will be on vacation for a couple of weeks. We need someone to lead worship, and you are certainly qualified."

Emmy shook her head. "I'm not sure they would appreciate me coming here and taking over."

"We don't have as many young people here as you do, but we have some, and they enjoy your music. I heard someone playing one of your CDs Wednesday night," Paul said.

"If I agree to sing next week, when would I get to practice?"

"They have been practicing on Wednesday after the service."

"Please, Emmy?" Lynette asked.

Emmy bit her lip but then nodded. "Okay, but I'm not switching churches permanently."

"We aren't asking for that." Lynette hugged Emmy again.

Emmy stopped at Darby's on her way home and picked up lunch for the family.

"It's about time, Mom," Heather said with her hands on her hips. "We are starving. I was so hungry I ate a banana."

Emmy set the food on the island. "Where is your father?"

"In here, Em," Kenny said from the pantry.

"What are you doing in there?"

"I didn't know when you were getting home, so I was about to make a can of soup."

"We can eat now, but I have to tell you something."

The kids took their seats around the breakfast nook. Emmy said a prayer and passed out the food.

"Why didn't you go to church today, Mommy?" Isabella asked as she dipped a fry into her ketchup.

"I did go to church, but I went to a different one so I could see some old friends," Emmy explained. She described the service to Kenny and told him about Wednesday night practice.

"What are you going to do?"

"Well, I promised to be there next Sunday, so I'm going to rehearsal Thursday and talk to Riordan and Sadie. I don't want them to think I've deserted the team."

"Like I did?"

"You didn't desert the team. They were used to you not being there."

"Does anyone want my pickle?" Heather asked. "I don't like them anymore."

307

Kevin Michael grabbed it out of her hand and took a big bite. "I like pickles."

Emmy looked around the table and sighed.

"What is it, Em?"

"We have to start eating healthier. We eat too much fast food. Especially on Sundays."

"But will Darby's go out of business if we don't eat there once a day?" Kenny teased.

Emmy stuck out her tongue.

Wednesday morning Emmy heard the kids sneaking into her bedroom but pretended to be asleep as they climbed onto the bed.

"Ready?" Heather asked.

Isabella and Kevin Michael nodded.

"Happy birthday to you...."

The kids sang the song as Emmy stretched her arms over her head. "Is today really my birthday?" Emmy asked.

"Mom! You know it is," Heather said.

"Daddy's making blueberry pancakes for you," Isabella mentioned.

"How old are you, Mommy?" Kevin Michael asked.

Emmy held out her arms and the kids snuggled with her. "Do you want to know how old I really am, or how old I feel?"

"How old are you really?" Isabella asked. "I know you're not as old as Daddy."

"I am thirty-five today, but I still feel much younger."

Kenny walked in carrying a tray of pancakes, coffee and a single red rose in a vase. "Happy birthday, Em. I hope you're hungry."

"I could eat a whole stack of blueberry pancakes," she said.

Later that evening Emmy rehearsed with the musician's from SoHam First. The musician's struggled at times, but Emmy patiently communicated with them and even showed Leona Salvina the piano player how to add some fills between chords. She showed the teenage drummer how to play in ¾ time and made sure the bass player stayed in the right key.

"How do you know all this?" the drummer Stanley Teeling asked.

She smiled. "I've picked up a few tricks over the years."

Patrick Rackouski, the bass player, who looked even younger, shook his head at the drummer. "You do know she's in a famous band, right?"

Stanley looked at Emmy without any hint of recognition, but he said, "Of course, I know. I'm no dummy."

By the time Emmy left she felt confident the band would do a good job on Sunday morning.

"How did it go?" Kenny asked later that night.

"They're young and inexperienced, but they'll be all right. We are doing easy stuff for Sunday."

On Thursday Emmy walked into the music suite in the new building and saw Riordan and Sadie in their office looking at sheet music.

"Have you got a minute?" Emmy asked.

"Of course. Come on in," Sadie said.

Riordan put down the music. "I didn't know you were scheduled this week, Emmy."

"I'm not."

"What can we do for you?" Sadie asked.

"Paul and Lynette Jefferson are old friends of mine. They're the new pastors at SoHam First, and they asked me if I would sing there this Sunday. I want to make sure it's all right with you."

"Of course," Sadie said. "You can help them out as long as they need you."

Riordan nodded. "We can get by without you, Emmy. We have so many talented singers here. We can't possibly fit them all on the schedule. Just this week we auditioned three more singers, who would be considered the top talent in most churches, but we have to find a way to fit them into the teams. You would be helping us out tremendously if you helped your friends at the smaller church. I'm assuming they don't have as many people to sing over there."

"It's a much smaller church," Emmy said. "Thank you for letting me help them." *I certainly don't want to keep someone you want to be on the team from having a spot.*

"Take as much time as you need, or as the church needs. We will survive," Riordan said.

Sadie gave Emmy a hug. "We are singing one of your songs next week. We had several people request it, and it fits the sermon topic."

Emmy forced a smile.

"I wish I had half your talent for writing," Sadie said. "No, a tenth of your talent. I can't write a song no matter how hard I try."

"I have help a lot of times," Emmy said.

"Right! You have Kenny to do most of the work," Riordan added.

Emmy looked up at him. *I actually meant I listen to the Holy Spirit and sometimes the lyrics just pop into my head.*

More people began entering the music suite and some of them waved, or at least smiled, at Emmy.

"I better go. I don't want to interrupt your rehearsal time." Emmy left without talking to anyone because she was trying very hard not to cry. *At least Paul and Lynette want me to sing.* She wiped a tear away.

Emmy's confidence in the young musicians remained unshaken even after the drummer played in the wrong time signature and the bass player's timing was off as he played his out-of-tune guitar. Still, she was able to lead worship and injected some life into the crowd of eighty-three people.

Lynette approached Emmy after the service. "You survived the train-wreck without too much damage, I hope."

"Did we sound awful?" Emmy asked.

Lynette smiled. "You sounded amazing." Lynette tilted her head back and forth. "The band on the other hand could use some work. Are you willing?"

"I can't switch churches permanently."

"No, but could you come back next week?"

310

Emmy sighed. "You're telling me to take it a week at a time, huh?"

Lynette grinned and hugged Emmy. "You've always been such a smart girl."

Fridays At Five gathered in the studio Monday morning to go over some of the new songs. Adam played two new songs for the guys.

Kenny smiled after Adam finished. "Those are better than anything I've come up with. All I've got are two unfinished scraps. I have a weak chorus and a verse and a half. I'm going on vacation and not even taking a guitar. I don't want to hear any music until we get back."

Paul and Dave played a couple of songs, but didn't have finished lyrics.

"Some of my lyrics might fit," Kenny said.

Jeff laughed. "If we put them all together we might have one decent song."

Max Kesson, the owner and founder of the Steward Music Group, made a rare appearance in the studio. He took a seat on the couch and looked at the guys. "Anything?"

Kenny shook his head. "I think we should cancel the studio time for now. We can get back together in a month or so and go from there. I'm sorry. I know you want new material."

Mr. Kesson slapped his thigh and stood up. "I'd rather wait for as long as it takes to get a quality project done than rush out some piece of crap that everyone will hate. I don't mean the public. They'll buy anything we release, but you guys have to live with what you record. I know you won't be satisfied with less than your best." He checked the time. "I'll see you guys later. I have an important appointment on the first tee."

Kenny waited until Mr. Kesson was out of the room. "Do we agree with Mr. Kesson?"

"I don't want our name on something we don't like," Jeff said.

"I suggest we all take some vacation time," Dave said. "Macy wants us to spend some time in New England this summer.

She wants to go to Maine."

"Did you guys buy another hunk of land?" Jeff asked. "Is Maine even part of the country anymore? I thought Clinton sold it to Canada to pay his legal fees."

"She wants to buy something," Dave admitted.

"Do you even know how many properties you own?" Kenny asked.

Dave sighed. "I know because I have to pay the bills to maintain them."

Paul looked at the calendar on his phone and suggested, "We could meet again on September 21. That's a Monday."

They agreed to meet on that day and left the studio.

Emmy rehearsed with the young musicians at SoHam First again on Wednesday. She chose three well-known contemporary songs for Sunday and two upbeat hymns. After rehearsing for an hour she felt satisfied.

"I'd like to go over the songs Sunday morning. Can everyone be here by nine?" she asked.

Everyone said they would be at the church for rehearsal.

"Emmy, you make it fun to play music. We really like that," Leona said for the entire group.

Emmy smiled as she saw Lynette heading her way after church on Sunday. "Did we sound better?"

Lynette put a finger to her mouth. "Well," she paused. "The band sounded a lot better, but I think our singer might need to rehearse longer this week."

Emmy made a face at Lynette. "Oh, hush."

"I heard several positive comments after church."

"About the music?" Emmy asked.

Lynette shook her head. *You are still so easy to tease.* "No, they said the ushers did a great job taking the offering." Lynette kept a straight face.

"Oh," Emmy said sadly as she stared at the floor.

Lynette lifted Emmy's chin. "Don't you know when I'm teasing you? They liked the music."

312

"They did!?" Emmy exclaimed.

"You are such a goof, Em." *You never hide how you feel like some people.*

Emmy smiled but then bit her lip. "Oh, shoot!"

"What is it?"

"We're leaving for Montana tomorrow. We'll be gone for two weeks. Kenny really needs to get away. Will you still want me after we get back?"

"Let me think about it. I'll get back to you," Lynette said tapping her chin with a finger.

"You're kidding, right?" Emmy asked.

Lynette shook her head and kept a straight face. "No, I'm totally serious."

Emmy started to look sad, but then understood. "You're such a stinker, but I love you anyway."

"Have a nice vacation, and we'll see you when you get back. You could always bring Kenny and the kids if you want."

"I'll think about that," Emmy said.

Emmy drove home, walked into the kitchen, noticed a message on the landline and returned the call. "Frances, I'm sorry I missed your call, I just got home from church. How are you?"

"I'm fine. A little worn out from painting the bedrooms, but all right otherwise. Has Kenny mentioned anything about the band lately?"

"Nothing out of the ordinary. Why?"

"I didn't want you to hear about this until I knew for sure, but Macy and Dave are separated," Frances said.

"Separated like in not together?"

"Yes, Amanda Lenhart told me yesterday."

"Shoot! That sucks," Emmy said. "Kenny hasn't mentioned anything. Did Amanda say how Jennifer's doing?"

"Her leukemia is still in remission," Frances answered. "According to Amanda Dave moved out of the house and is living with a friend for the time being."

"I will pray for them. Thanks for calling." Emmy stared at the phone for a moment. *Frances, you sounded too happy about this. Why are you like that?*

Chapter Thirty-Five

"Did you remember to thank Mr. Robertson for letting us use his plane to get to Montana?" Kenny asked as he took a seat in the Gulfstream III.

"Yes, I thanked him personally," Emmy answered.

"Did you double check about the rental car?"

Emmy used the move made famous by Garry Rodgers and said, "Yes, I double checked. We have a Jeep Grand Cherokee for two weeks. Anything else?"

"Did you stop the mail?"

"Tony will get the mail."

"Did you tell Darian we would be gone?"

"Yes."

"Does he know the code for the gate?"

Emmy frowned at Kenny and folded her arms over her chest. "Will you relax already? I took care of things. We are going on vacation so you can forget about stuff and recharge your batteries. You are going to enjoy this vacation if I have to kill you."

Kenny didn't react.

"I meant that as a joke, but now I'm having second thoughts."

"Did you turn off the oven?" Kenny asked.

Emmy got up. "I'm moving to the back of the plane."

"I was kidding, Em. That's what Dad always asked Mom whenever we went away. Don't you remember?"

"No, and I didn't always go everywhere with your family."

"Yes you did. I can't remember a single vacation where you weren't along," Kenny said and then pulled her back into the seat.

"Then you guys either didn't take more than two family vacations, or else you're losing your memory."

"My what?" Kenny asked.

Emmy rolled her eyes. "I'm throwing you out the door as soon as we get over the mountains."

They landed in Missoula, Montana, with Kenny still in the plane.

"I will check on the rental car if you take care of the luggage," Emmy said. "Make sure the kids don't wander off into the wilderness."

Kenny looked around. "What wilderness?"

Soon they were heading north on a narrow road to the small town of Abbot Village.

"Slow down, Kenny, I think this is the town," Emmy said.

"I don't see a town," Kevin Michael said as he stared out the window. "I don't see a police station or any firetrucks."

Heather looked up from the movie she was watching on her tablet. "Are we there yet, and where are we? Are we still in the United States? I can't get a signal on my cell phone." She didn't bother removing her earbuds to hear an answer.

"Is that a wolf?" Isabella asked.

Emmy saw the large animal. "It's just a big dog, Isa. I doubt if there are any wolves around here."

"Where do we turn?" Kenny asked.

Emmy checked her printed directions. "Look for Winnett Mountain Road."

"I think we're lost," Kevin Michael said.

"We are not lost," Emmy said. "Daddy just doesn't know where we are."

"I know we're in Montana," Kenny joked.

Emmy rolled her eyes and glanced out the passenger window. "Stop!"

Kenny slammed on the breaks. "What?"

"That's Winnett Mountain Road according to the sign."

Kenny and the kids looked out the window.

"Are you sure that's a road?" Kenny asked.

"It looks one of the trails in the woods back home," Heather said.

"Will we fit?" Kenny asked. "I don't want to buy this thing because we damage it."

"Probably, but I hope we don't meet someone coming down the mountain," Emmy said.

Kenny made the turn and looked up. "I'm glad we've got a Jeep."

315

"Look out!" Emmy yelled as a multi-colored, rusted, fifty-year-old pickup truck careened toward them. A head-on collision was only averted because the truck used the ditch to get around the new Jeep without slowing down.

"That was cool!" Kevin Michael shouted.

"Are we there yet," Heather said.

Isabella screamed. "I just saw a bear!"

"There are no bears," Kenny said.

"I'm hungry," Kevin Michael said. "How much farther?"

Emmy checked. "Five miles according to the directions."

"I still don't have a signal," Heather said.

Isabella stared out the window. "I'm pretty sure it was a bear."

"We should be there in a few minutes," Kenny said.

Two hours later he stopped on the narrow dirt road in front of a genuine log cabin.

"Is that it, Em?"

"Well, there is a red pickup truck on blocks," she answered. "It has a green tin roof. Must be it."

"Are we there? I have to pee," Heather said. She looked out the window and screamed. "I am not staying here. It looks like it's ready to fall down."

"Yeah, cool!" Kevin said as he jumped out and ran up to the front porch.

"I think that bear is following us," Isabella said.

"Mom! I really have to go," Heather said.

Kenny pulled into the dirt driveway, drove over a couple of large rocks that rocked the Jeep back and forth and stopped in front of the cabin.

"The key is supposed to be under a flower pot on the porch," Emmy said.

They got out and walked up the steps.

"This is so cool!" Kevin Michael peeked in the dusty window. "There's a fireplace and a stack of wood, and I see a moose head on the wall inside."

"I am not sleeping in a house with a moose head," Isabella insisted.

"Here's the key," Emmy said and handed it to Kenny.

The door creaked loudly when he opened it. Kevin Michael rushed past everyone.

"Are there any bears?" Isabella asked.

"No, but there's a stuffed animal. I think it's a beaver, and there's a dead deer head over here."

"Is there a bathroom?" Heather hopped from one foot to the other. "Is there electricity?"

Emmy found a light switch and flipped it up. "Ah! There is electricity. There might be running water, Heather. Check that room over there," Emmy said as she pointed to a door.

Kevin Michael rushed over to the door and threw it open. "Nope! It's a bedroom, I think. It smells funny."

Kenny wandered into the kitchen. "The bathroom's in here, Heather."

Heather and Isabella dashed into the kitchen. Heather won the race to the toilet. "Will you shut the door?"

Isabella closed the door, but it opened on its own.

"Close the door!" Heather yelled.

"I did, but it won't stay closed," Isabella said.

Emmy walked over and closed the door. It opened as if by magic.

"Cool! There's a ghost!"

"I'm sure it's not a ghost," Kenny said. "The door just needs some adjustment."

Emmy picked up a note from the dusty, wooden table in the middle of the kitchen. "According to this, the door won't stay closed. The owner says he will try to fix it next week or the week after."

"What else does it say?" Kenny asked.

"Close the door!" Heather hollered again.

Isabella held the door closed.

"We need to be careful when we light the stove and make sure the damper is open. What's a damper?" Emmy asked.

"It's..."

"I know what a damper is, you goof. We have a fireplace at home."

317

"Is this a real wood-burning stove?" Kenny asked.

"It looks like it."

"Have you ever cooked on anything like this?" Kenny asked.

"No, but I bet my great-great grandmother did. I'm sure we can figure it out. There's the pantry." Emmy walked over to an area closed off from the kitchen by a sheet. "We have enough canned food to last for at least a year. There's bottled water, too."

Kenny opened the fridge. "It feels kinda cold, but it's empty."

"Mom! The toilet won't flush!" Heather hollered. "And this toilet paper sucks."

"We don't use that word, Heather."

Kenny came to the rescue by turning on the water to the cabin.

"Well, we can cook, sort of. We can use the toilet, and maybe take a shower. Is there a hot water heater anywhere?" Emmy asked.

"It's out here, but it's kinda small. We will have to take quick showers"

"I don't want to take a shower," Kevin Michael said. "I'm going to wash up in the creek like in that movie."

Emmy looked at Kenny. "Did you guys watch *Jeremiah Johnson* again?"

Kenny shrugged. "We like that movie."

"He's only seven. He will try to catch a bear or something."

Kenny put his hands on Emmy's shoulders and kissed her forehead. "I'm pretty sure there aren't any bears around."

"I see that bear again!" Isabella screamed.

Everyone pitched in to unload the Jeep. Heather and Isabella put their suitcases on the single beds in the second bedroom. Kevin Michael walked into the room.

"Get out! This is our room," Heather said. "Go away."

"Mom! Where am I supposed to sleep?"

Kenny pointed to a cot under the moose head. "I guess you can either sleep on that or else drag it into our bedroom."

Kevin Michael looked up at the mounted moose head. "I'll

318

sleep out here. Moose will protect me." He held up his stuffed animal.

"I am starving. When do we get to eat? I want some nuggets or a pizza," Heather said.

"We can have soup if I can figure out how to work the stove," Emmy said.

They ate peanut butter sandwiches and snacked on walnuts. Everyone went to bed early that night.

Emmy cuddled against Kenny. "Does it still smell like smoke in here?"

"It's not that bad now, Em. I opened all the windows and there's a breeze."

"Are you going to tell the kids you have your satellite phone?"

"Not unless I have to. I only brought it for emergencies."

"According to the note there is a landline at the next cabin up the road. We aren't totally isolated," Emmy said. "My feet are cold. I'm going to wear socks to bed."

"It will be fun to see how the kids adapt to living like our ancestors," Kenny snuggled closer to Emmy. "Your feet are freezing."

"Ya think! I can see my breath. I'm afraid the toilet will freeze."

The next morning Emmy figured out how to cook on the stove without filling the cabin with smoke. She made biscuits and heated up a can of Bush's Best baked beans.

"Breakfast is ready. Come and get it."

Everyone walked into the kitchen and sat at the now clean table.

"I'm freezing. I thought it was still summer," Heather said as she wrapped a blanket around her shoulders.

Isabella wore her jacket.

"Beans!?" Heather pointed. "Yuck! I want some pancakes and sausage."

"We can make pancakes tomorrow, but you better get used to beans. The pantry is full of them," Emmy said.

319

"I like beans," Kevin said. "They make you fart."

Heather rolled her eyes. "I can't get a signal on my phone and what's wrong with the Internet? Does anyone know the password for the WiFi?"

"There's no Internet out here, Heather," Kenny said.

"Very funny, Daddy," Heather said. "What's the password?"

"He's not kidding," Isabella said. "There's not even a telephone or a TV. That old radio in our bedroom turns on, but I can't get any stations. It's just static."

Heather held out her hands with the palms up. "How will I talk to my friends? I have to be able to text my friends. Mom! Can you fix it?"

"This will be fun," Kenny said. "No distractions for two weeks."

"Mom!" Heather and Isabella shouted.

"Who wants to go for a hike?" Kenny asked an hour later. "I found a trail guidebook and there's a trail that goes up the mountain right down the street."

"What street?" Heather asked. "If there's a street, there must be civilization close by."

"I meant the dirt road in front of the cabin."

Heather groaned.

"I'll go for a hike, but I need to take my gun. We might need to shoot a bear or a mountain lion." Kevin Michael grabbed his plastic water gun. "I'm ready."

"I am not going for a hike until I can wash my hair," Heather said. "I tried to take a shower and the hot water only lasted for ten minutes. How on earth will I survive?"

"Poor baby," Kenny said. "We could cut it off."

"Very funny, Daddy." Heather tried to run a hand through her thick curly hair. "It's all tangled, Mom."

"My hair was tangled for years when I was a kid. Get used to it."

Everyone followed Kenny up the mountain. They reached a lookout after a half mile.

"Now isn't that view worth it?" Kenny pointed.

"I don't see anything but a green valley," Heather said.

"Exactly," Kenny said as he hugged Emmy.

The owner stopped by three days later, dropped off more firewood and fixed the bathroom door. Now the twins didn't have to use a piece of firewood to hold the door closed.

"Let's take a ride into town," Kenny suggested. "Maybe we can find an Internet or a cell phone signal somewhere."

The trip back into Abbot Village only took thirty minutes since they were going down the mountain and didn't get lost. Kenny turned right at the end of Winnett Mountain Road, and they located what served as downtown Abbot Village.

"I still don't have a signal," Heather complained. She gave up trying to use her cell phone.

"Is that a grocery store?" Isabella pointed. "The sign says general store. Is that the same thing?"

"They probably have some groceries," Emmy said.

They stopped, went inside and the kids loaded a basket with junk food.

Emmy saw it. "No way! We are eating healthy food on this vacation."

"Mom! We've been eating beans every day. I don't think that's healthy."

Kevin Michael farted right on cue.

Heather and Isabella waved their hands in front of their faces.

"You are so gross," Heather shouted.

"I found some maple syrup and bananas," Kenny said.

Isabella pleaded. "I need ice cream."

Emmy found a small freezer with ice cream novelties. "You can each have one."

Kenny walked up behind Emmy and put his hands on her shoulders. "Do you remember the gas station that used to be around the corner from Darby's?"

She glanced over her shoulder at him. "Yes, why?"

"Do you remember going there with a couple of dollars to

buy ice cream bars?”

“I kinda remember.”

“That was a special treat for us back then.”

“What are you trying to say?”

Kenny opened the freezer top and picked up two ice cream bars. “My treat, m'lady.”

Emmy rolled her eyes. “You are such a dork, but I love you, m'lord.”

Heather and Isabella looked at each other and shrugged. Heather made a circle around her ear with a finger.

“I found some cookies. Can we buy them?” Kevin Michael asked.

“Fine! Junk food for everyone,” Emmy said. *Why do I always cave?*

“Do we have to go for another hike?” Heather asked on the morning of their last day of vacation. “All we've done for the last year is go for hikes and drive into that stupid town that doesn't even have cell phone service. I can't wait to get home. It's going to take me hours to catch up on everything. My friends probably think I'm dead.”

“We haven't been here for a year, Heather. Two weeks. This will be your last chance for a hike,” Emmy said.

“We can go hiking through the woods at home, and still have cell phone service,” Heather countered.

“I certainly never had a cell phone when I was nine,” Kenny said. “You should be grateful you have one.”

“Daddy, that's because phones weren't invented when you were a kid,” Heather said while rolling her eyes. “These aren't smartphones. All we can do is text and talk.”

Emmy took a deep breath. “The air smells so clean.”

“Is that a pile of bear poop?” Isabella pointed.

“It's probably not from a bear, Isa. Maybe a deer,” Kenny said.

“It smells like fresh bear poop,” Kevin Michael said as he stood over the pile of whatever it was. “I have to pee.” He turned away from his sisters and relieved himself. “I haven't used the

322

bathroom to pee for a week."

"Mom! Can we leave him here?" Heather asked. "I'm serious. Totally serious."

"We can not leave your brother in the woods," Emmy said slowly. "We have to take him back to Missoula at least."

"Should we wash the Jeep before we return it?" Kenny asked on the way back to Missoula.

Emmy stared at him. "I don't think they expect it to be in showroom condition."

"I'm going to build a new fort in the woods and live out there," Kevin Michael said.

Heather screamed and startled everyone.

Kenny slammed on the brakes. "What is it?"

"I have a signal on my cell phone! We're back in civilization at last."

Emmy sighed.

"There's that wolf again," Isabella said as she pointed.

"Can we order a pizza at the airport?" Kevin asked.

"I am never eating beans again for as long as I live," Heather said. "Oh, crap!"

"We don't use that word," Emmy said. "What's wrong now?"

"I lost the signal."

"You should have a signal when we get to the airport."

"Can we come back to Montana again sometime?" Kevin asked.

"I suppose so," Kenny answered.

"Good! I didn't take a shower all week."

"Mom!" Heather and Isabella hollered.

"He's kidding. I saw him take a shower a few days ago," Emmy said. "What is that smell?"

"Should we rent the same cabin for next year?" Kenny asked.

"No!" Heather yelled.

"I just farted," Kevin Michael said.

Isabella shook her head. "I can still see that bear when I

323

close my eyes."

"There are no bears within a hundred miles," Kenny said.

"Sorry, Mom, but I ate more beans."

"How much farther to the airport?" Heather asked. "I have to call my friends and let them know I didn't get eaten by a bear."

"There are no..." Kenny slammed on the brakes and the Jeep swerved to the left and slid to a stop.

Everyone watched as a female black bear walked across the road with her cub.

"Was that the bear you saw, Isa?" Emmy asked.

Isabella shook her head. "No, the one I saw was bigger."

"This is so cool!" Kevin Michael aimed his plastic water gun at the bear and shot it.

"Mom! Kevin Michael just squirted me with water," Heather yelled.

"Has this been a great vacation, or what?" Kenny smiled.

They arrived home without being eaten by bears, or attacked by wolves, or even suffering from malnutrition because of a total lack of chicken nuggets and pizza.

"Who is going to help me unload the van?" Kenny asked as Tony pulled up by the garage to let them off.

"Sorry, Daddy, but I have to call my friends," Heather said.

"I have to take a shower," Isabella added.

Kevin Michael sprinted for the woods firing his water gun. "I have to pee."

Kenny looked at Emmy.

"I have to check the oven. I think I might have left it on," she smirked.

Tony looked at Kenny and laughed. "Well, I guess I can help."

An hour later Kenny called for a family meeting in the family room.

"No cell phones! No tablets! I don't want to see any electronics," Kenny insisted. "We are going to talk about making some changes around here. Are you coming, Em?"

"Be there as soon as I finish checking my email," she

answered from the kitchen. "Crap!"

"We don't use that word," Heather said and then giggled.

"Emmy!"

"Be right there." She walked into the family room. "Diane sent an email saying that Mom decided to move to Las Vegas and become a professional gambler."

"For real?" Kenny asked.

"No! Actually Mom wants to get a job as a chorus girl." Emmy plopped down on the couch. "Go ahead."

Fine!" Kenny coughed to get everyone's attention. "Like I said, we are going to make some changes." He held up one finger. "First of all. There will be no more watching TV in your bedrooms."

The kids stared at him.

"Secondly," he held up another finger. "No more cell phones or whatever those game things are at the table while we eat. And we are going to start eating healthy food."

"Are we going to plant a garden?" Kevin Michael asked.

"It's too late for this year, but that's a great idea for next year." Kenny checked his list. "Your rooms have to be cleaned once a week."

Heather looked at Isabella and they both laughed.

"I'm serious," Kenny said. "We are going to start living more simply. It's time you learned that life is not all cream and sugar. We need to make some sacrifices, and I will go first. I am going to give up..."

"Kissing Mommy?" Kevin Michael said and then laughed.

Emmy stood up and put her hands on her hips. She winked at the kids and then yelled at Kenny. "I am all for living a simpler life, but I will not give up kissing."

Kenny let his shoulders sag.

Emmy walked over to his recliner, sat on his lap and pulled on his ears. "I know you mean well and all, but you're a dork and I love you. Please don't change."

"Could we at least agree on no TV in the bedrooms?" Kenny asked as he grinned.

Chapter Thirty-Six

Emmy kissed Kenny's cheek the next morning as he drank his coffee at the kitchen island. "I'm leaving now. You promise to get the kids to church?"

"We will make it to church, Em," Kenny said.

"You need a shave, and don't let Kevin Michael eat any beans for breakfast. Make him pee in the house. I'll be home as soon as I can."

Kenny rubbed his jaw. *I just shaved yesterday.*

Emmy made it to SoHam First Nazarene twenty minutes early. She parked her Civic Si and walked into the foyer. She saw Paul Jefferson in the church office folding the bulletins.

He looked over at her. "Want to help?"

"Sure, I'm early, huh?"

"The worship team should be here soon. Did you get my email?"

Emmy looked to see how Paul was folding the bulletins. "I did, and I know all those songs."

"I hope so because you wrote two of them."

"Did your worship leader say anything about using them?" Emmy asked.

"She did wonder why we are singing two contemporary songs," Paul admitted.

"I don't want to cause any hard feelings."

"And I don't want the music to drive people away. There! That's the last of them."

Sandy Petty stopped playing a hymn at the piano when she saw Paul and Emmy approaching.

"Hello, Emmy. It's nice to meet you. We don't normally do contemporary songs, but Pastor Jefferson requested them."

Emmy bit her lip and looked up at Paul.

"Thank you for being flexible," Paul said and then walked away. *I knew I'd get some blow back, but not from someone in their thirties.*

Emmy joined one of the Sunday School classes but felt too shy to participate. Gary Chisholm, the teacher, called on Emmy to answer a question.

"Uh, I think Paul meant we need to focus on our relationship with Jesus and not worry about how people see us," Emmy answered.

"Good answer," Gary said.

Emmy heard someone on the other side of the room cough. She thought it might be Sandy Petty.

The worship team showed a definite improvement today when they played Emmy's songs, but they still had trouble with the hymns. Emmy said goodbye to Paul and Lynette and left quickly.

"How did it go today?" Kenny asked as Emmy walked into the kitchen and plopped down onto a barstool at the island. "That good, huh?"

"I met the worship leader today." Emmy used air quotes.

"Did you get along with her?"

"I felt like she was mad because I was there. She flat out told me she doesn't like to do contemporary songs."

"Your songs, or all contemporary songs?" Kenny handed Emmy a can of Dr Pepper.

Emmy shrugged. "The worship team sounded pretty good on my songs, but they struggled with the hymns."

"Why? I thought hymns were easy to play."

"They are for the most part, but Sandy..." Emmy didn't finish her thought.

"Sandy what?" Kenny asked.

"She plays too much. She adds all this extra stuff and doesn't leave any space for the band."

"Maybe that's how she's always played," Kenny said. "Is she an older lady?"

Emmy took a sip of her pop and then shook her head. "No, she's my age."

"I don't know what to tell you, Em. She's the worship leader."

"They need a guitar player. Sandy and Leona play the piano and they don't always mesh." Emmy sighed. "I suppose I shouldn't worry about it. It's not like I'm going to change churches."

"Do Paul and Lynette know that?"

"I told them I wasn't going to switch."

Heather and Isabella dashed into the kitchen.

"Have you been running? Slow down and catch your breath," Emmy said as she straightened up and turned to face them.

"Mom, will you tell Kevin Michael to stop peeing in the woods? He is so gross," Heather said.

Kevin Michael walked in with a smile on his face.

"Kevin, will you stop peeing in the woods in front of your sisters, please?"

"I didn't pee in front of them," he said. "I had my back turned."

"Doesn't matter," Kenny said. "Don't pee in the woods if other people are around. Especially if girls are there."

"Can I pee in the woods if it's just boys? Or if no one is around?"

Kenny looked at Emmy. "Your call."

"Why me?" Emmy asked.

"Because you're the mom."

Emmy rolled her eyes. "You can pee in the woods if no one is around."

Kevin Michael made a face at his sisters and ran back outside.

"We didn't go to church today," Isabella said.

"Thanks, Isa," Kenny said.

"Why not?" Emmy stared at Kenny.

"We stayed home, but I read the Bible to them."

"That's good, but they need to be in church."

Everyone looked as Father James walked into the room with Kevin Michael.

"What's this I hear about missing mass?" Father James looked at the kids. "And I heard a rumor that someone is thinking about switching parishes. Would that someone care to explain?" He stared at Emmy.

"I am not switching parishes. I'm just helping out my friends, and besides no one cares which parish I attend."

"I've been peeing in the woods."

328

Father James sat next to Emmy after hugging the kids. "TMI, Kevin Michael."

"Too much information," Kenny explained to his son.

"So how did things go at church today, my child?"

"Fine! Why are you here already? Did you skip mass?" Emmy asked.

"Short sermon," Father James answered. "Do you still feel unwanted by the new worship leaders?"

"Riordan practically told me to help out at the other church for as long as I wanted. He claimed he has more singers than he knows what to do with."

"Did he make it sound like singers were easily replaced?"

Emmy stood up and stared up at her half-brother. "What are you getting at?"

"I'm not saying all singers are easily replaced. Don't get your claws out." He put his hands on her shoulders. "Did you guys eat yet?"

"No, I just got home. What do you have a taste for?"

"Pizza!" Heather hollered.

"I would like spaghetti, please," Isabella said.

Kenny put in his request and Emmy rolled her eyes and looked at Father James for his answer.

He put his hands together as if praying. "I am but a humble servant of our Lord. I will accept any nourishment you offer."

"What a bunch of bull..."

"We don't use that word," Heather and Isabella said together, started giggling and then took off running.

Emmy joined the other musicians on the platform on Wednesday night for the weekly rehearsal. She smiled at Stanley Teeling and Patrick Rackouski but kept to herself on the side of the stage.

Stanley walked over and asked, "We're glad you're here. We get to play some modern music. I'm not a big fan of those old hymns."

"There are a lot of really good old hymns, but most of them weren't written to make it easy on a rhythm section," Emmy said.

329

"Yeah, right," Stanley looked at Emmy for a moment and then walked away.

Sandy Petty joined the group. "Is this all we have for tonight?"

"I'm here, too," Emmy said.

"Okay, well, let's get started. I need to get home and get ready for tomorrow morning. I picked out two hymns. We've done them before, and Pastor Jefferson asked if we could do a couple of contemporary songs." Sandy looked at Emmy and forced a smile. "Do you have any suggestions?"

"Do you know what Paul's message will be about?" Emmy walked over to the piano.

Sandy shook her head. "It doesn't matter. Most of those new songs are pretty similar."

Emmy looked at Sandy. *I think you're wrong, but I'm not going to get into a discussion with you.* "We could try a couple of Chris Tomlin songs. Most people are familiar with them."

Emmy suggested two songs and Sandy printed them out. Emmy went over the arrangement and they rehearsed the songs.

Sandy stood up from the piano and stopped them in mid-song. "Stanley, I can't hear my piano. Do you have to play so loud? Can't you back off just a little?"

"Sorry, Mrs. Petty. I got a little carried away. I'll do better this time."

Emmy asked Sandy, "Do you want to sing harmony?"

Sandy smiled. "No, I'll let you do these songs. I'll sing the hymns, and you can sing a part."

"Okay," Emmy said softly.

"You have a lovely voice. I'm glad you sang a couple of newer songs."

"Thank you," Emmy said.

"It's about time someone brought the music into this century."

Emmy was talking to some women after the service on Sunday morning when she overheard two older ladies talking about the music behind her back. Literally.

One of the ladies said, "That girl from Crest Ridge has a beautiful voice, but if I wanted to hear songs like that, I would go to that church. I'm concerned that our new minister is trying to change too much too soon."

"I agree," the other lady said. "I've been going to this church for thirty years, and we've never had to sing that kind of songs before. I prefer to sing hymns, and I don't think I'm alone in that. Plus, this is no place to be dancing around. Did you see how she moved around and looked at everyone?"

"I did notice. She seemed to be trying to make sure we were all singing. She probably doesn't realize a lot of our people have never heard those songs."

Emmy cringed. *Who hasn't heard 'How Great Is Our God' and 'Holy Is the Lord'? Come on! And I was not dancing all over the place. You may not realize it, but most of your people don't even sing the hymns either. I was trying to inject some enthusiasm into the service.*

The ladies continued to talk about the music after Emmy walked away.

"I will have to talk to the new pastor about the music if this continues. I'm sure the church board didn't know about his preference for that kind of music."

"I'm good friends with two of the people on the board. I will talk to them."

Emmy left the building and sat in her car for a time. She closed her eyes and let the tears flow. "Lord, what do you want me to do? Where am I supposed to be?" She waved her hands around. "I feel as though I don't fit in here, and I don't feel needed anymore at my church. Am I not supposed to sing for you? I don't understand why this is happening."

"Yes, I can meet you for lunch," Lynette answered on Monday morning. "Where would you like to meet?"

"I saw a Mexican food place not far from your church. Would that be all right?"

"Yes, we had dinner there last week. It's really good. It's authentic food like my grandmother used to make."

Emmy drove to the east side of SoHam and waited in the parking lot for Lynette. Lynette pulled up a few minutes later, and they walked into Los Toltecos Restaurante together. The hostess seated them at a booth by the front windows. They chatted about family until the waitress took their order.

"Okay, now spill it," Lynette insisted. "Why are we really here?"

"I overheard some people talking about the music. They don't like the way I sing and move around. They don't like the new songs, and are worried about the church never singing those awful hymns again."

"Oh, is that all? I thought it might be something serious," Lynette teased.

"It is serious! Apparently, people don't want me at your church. Riordan doesn't need me either. He says singers are as common as flies on a... as common as books in a library."

"Okay, I have to be completely honest, Em. I heard the same thing. Paul has received a bunch of emails, and they aren't all from the senior citizens. There were a few from some of the younger people. It seems they like the old-fashioned, conservative music, but they wish we had better musicians."

"That's another thing. The ladies I heard claimed I was performing. Like I was trying to put the spotlight on me," Emmy said and then took a sip of her horchata. "I was only trying to inject some enthusiasm into a lifeless crowd. I think you guys have your hands full with that church."

"We realize it will be a challenge, but this is where God wants us. Where does God want you, Em?" Lynette asked softly. "It might not be at SoHam First."

Emmy bit her lip and then replied, "I don't know. Can you help me? You always had some wise advice for me when I was a kid."

Lynette chuckled. "All I ever did was listen, and that's what you need to do. You need to pray and listen to the Holy Spirit. He will let you know where you belong."

"I still feel like Crest Ridge is my home church, but what if I can't sing there?"

"There are many other ways to be a part of the Kingdom. In a church that large I am sure there are hundreds of opportunities. Maybe you could sing for the younger kids. I assume the teens still have a band, right?"

"They do and they even get to sing on Sunday mornings."

A server arrived with their food.

"I will pray for us," Lynette said. "Lord, thank you for your blessings. Thank you for this food, and thank you for the answers you are going to give Emmy. Amen."

"You sound pretty optimistic."

"Em! Has God ever failed you?"

Emmy bit her lip and shook her head.

"Good. Let's eat."

Emmy prayed for a solid hour after returning home. Then she called Liz Hammond.

"About time you called me. I miss you. What's up?" Liz asked.

"You know I've been helping out at SoHam First, right?"

"Yes."

"Well, they don't want me to come back. I just don't fit in with their style of worship," Emmy said with some bitterness.

"I thought you were only filing in over there. This is your real home. You belong here, Em. We need you."

"Ha! Riordan doesn't need me. He says he has lots of singers."

"Emmy, everyone can sing. It's just a matter of making a noise. But you have a special gift. You have a beautiful voice, and the sweetest spirit. You know how to help people worship. We are missing that right now."

"What do you mean? Riordan and Sadie know how to worship."

"Yes, they are very talented, but I've noticed the church doesn't have the same spark if you want to call it that without you there. The band and singers can do a perfect job, but if the spirit isn't there, it doesn't work. We need you. Please come back, Em!" Liz waited for an answer. "Em, are you crying?"

Emmy nodded.

333

"I can't see you nodding over the phone, Em."

Emmy blew her nose. "I was crying, but I'm all right now."

"Will you come to practice on Thursday? I will be there for you."

"Yes, I will be there, Liz. I promise."

Emmy called Liz on Thursday from the parking lot to let her know she was there.

"I'll meet you in the new sanctuary, Em. I'm in Tyler's office now."

"Thanks, Liz. I appreciate it." Emmy got out of her car and started walked toward the church.

"Are you nervous about seeing Sadie and Riordan?" Liz left Tyler's office and headed down the hall to the new sanctuary.

"I guess so," Emmy admitted. She entered the new building, saw Liz and ended the call.

Liz rushed over to Emmy. "I've missed you. How are you? How was your vacation?"

"The vacation was all right. The girls were bored, but Kevin Michael had a blast."

"I think Sadie is inside." Liz grabbed Emmy's hand and pulled her into the sanctuary. "They're on the platform. Come on."

Emmy hesitated, but then followed Liz. Riordan and Sadie turned around when Liz called out Sadie's name. "Look who I found wandering around lost."

"I was not lost or wandering around," Emmy whispered.

Sadie turned around, saw Emmy with Liz and ran down the steps. Sadie almost knocked Emmy over as she wrapped her arms around her. "It's so good to see you. We've missed you."

"Really?" Emmy asked.

Sadie released Emmy, grabbed her hand and pulled her up the steps and over to Riordan.

Riordan glanced at a chord sheet and then set it on his music stand and smiled. "Hi, Emmy. I owe you an apology." He held out his hand. "We both need to apologize."

Emmy shook his hand, but didn't speak.

"We thought we were doing you a favor by telling you to

help out your friends, but we were wrong." Sadie looked at Riordan. "We thought we could get by without you, but we kinda fell flat on our faces."

Emmy bit her lip.

"We need you on the team, and we would like it if you could sing more often than once a month. If you're willing, of course."

Emmy nodded and a smile appeared.

"If I'm completely honest, I was a little intimidated by you," Sadie confessed. "I was a little jealous, too. Everyone here loved you, and I felt kinda threatened."

"Why?" Emmy asked.

Riordan chuckled. "Because you're kinda famous, but now that we know you a little better, we realize you are just as normal as anyone."

Liz put an arm around Emmy's waist. "You don't know her at all if you think she's normal."

Emmy made a face at Liz and poked her in the side. "Oh, hush."

"Emmy, would you be available to sing this week?" Sadie asked.

Emmy nodded. "What songs are you singing?"

Sadie mentioned the songs. "I'm sure you know them by heart. We were thinking this one would be perfect as a duet, but Riordan can't sing it very well," Sadie said as she grinned at her husband.

Emmy laughed. "I know all about that. I have a husband who thinks he can sing, too."

As Sadie and Emmy finished their duet on Sunday morning they looked at each other and then hugged.

"I'm so glad you're still a part of the team, Emmy."

"I'm so happy to be back," Emmy sighed, took a deep breath and let it out. *You will never know how happy I am to be back.*

Chapter Thirty-Seven

Emmy sat at the back of Ms. Alexandra Dalton's classroom and watched as Heather and Isabella interacted with their friends. *How is it possible they're in fourth grade already? How can my baby boy be in second grade?* She shook her head and sat quietly. *Since I have the time I should volunteer more often. I enjoy helping out. I could even see myself as a teacher one of these day.* She laughed as Heather read aloud. *I should talk to Randy Braun. He could tell he how many hours I would need to get a teaching degree.*

"How did you like your first day of school?" Kenny asked as Emmy and the kids arrived home around noon.

"I had fun," Kevin Michael said.

"Who is your teacher?" Kenny asked.

"Miss Redmon," Kevin replied. "She's real tall and she has red hair, but she seems nice. She had to yell at one of the kids because he tried to hit Ben."

Kenny watched as Heather and Isabella walked into the kitchen and sat at the island. "You look tired. Did you have a rough day at school?"

"Ms. Dalton gave us homework," Isabella answered. "Dotty said she would be a mean teacher because she was in her class two years ago. Can we go to another school?"

Emmy shook her head. "You are not going to another class, and Ms. Dalton isn't mean. You are getting older, so she will not treat you like babies."

"Are you going to be a teacher's aide all the time?" Heather asked.

Emmy opened the fridge and brought out the taco salad she had made earlier. "I'm not going to be there every day, but I will be volunteering more than last year. Didn't you like having me in your room?"

"It was all right, but some of the kids kept asking if you were going to teach music. Are you?" Heather asked.

"No, but I could help out."

"I saw Ben's mom," Kevin Michael said as he poured

336

himself a glass of chocolate milk. "Carson said she is his math teacher."

"Carson's in eighth grade this year, right?" Kenny asked.

"Yes, and Caden's in fourth grade like the girls." Emmy added some Western dressing to the taco salad and stirred it up. "It's ready. You can fill your own bowls."

"Since the church is not going to add a high school, where will Carson go next year?"

"Diane wants him to go to Roosevelt, but I think Brady wants him to attend Barclay Academy," Emmy answered.

"He could always go to St. Raymond's," Kenny suggested.

"At least we have several years before the girls are ready for high school."

Kenny scooped out some taco salad for himself and sat down with the kids. "It will be here before we know it, Em."

Emmy leaned against the island. "Have you seen Randy Braun at church lately?"

Kenny pulled on his ear. "I saw him a couple of weeks ago, but didn't talk to him. Why?"

"Nothing special. Just want to talk to him about something."

"We're not doing anything right now," Emmy told Mary Galves on Saturday morning. "Come on over. We haven't closed the pool up yet, so if you want to swim, you can."

"We won't have time for that," Mary said.

"Well, come on over whenever you want. You know the code, right?"

Mary still knew the six-digit code to let herself in the garage service door. She and Jonah arrived forty-five minutes later and they walked into the kitchen just as Emmy walked out of the laundry room with a basket of folded clothes.

"Hi, guys. Let me run this upstairs. Be right back."

Emmy ran upstairs and hollered, "Girls, Mary and Jonah are here."

The girls raced down the stairs and into the kitchen.

"Are you here to go swimming?" Heather asked.

337

Mary shook her head. "We stopped by to talk to your mother."

"Do you think Ms. Dalton is mean?" Isabella asked.

Emmy walked around the corner just then. "She is not mean."

Mary smiled at the girls. "She has a reputation for being strict, but I wouldn't call her mean."

"Can I get you something to drink? You guys hungry?" Emmy asked over her shoulder as she carried another plastic laundry basket into the laundry.

"We're good," Jonah said as he put an arm around Mary's shoulders and smiled at the girls.

Emmy returned. "Sorry, I didn't hear your answer."

"We're good, Emmy," Mary said. "We have some good news."

Emmy looked at Mary first and then Jonah.

"Are you?"

"We are expecting in May..."

Mary didn't get to finish because Emmy nearly knocked her over as she hugged her. "Oh, Mary, I'm so happy for you guys. May, huh? I suppose it's too early to know the sex."

"It is," Mary said after Emmy let go.

"Are you really going to have a baby?" Isabella stared at Mary's belly. "Are you having twins?"

"We aren't having twins. We do know that much," Jonah chuckled.

Isabella and Heather hugged Mary. Mary ran a hand through the girls thick, curly hair. "You are growing up so fast. I remember when I started taking care of you. You were both so little."

Heather left go of Mary and ran out of the kitchen and back upstairs.

Isabella held on and looked up at Mary. "I want to be the baby's nanny when its born. Can I, please?"

Emmy shook her head. "You might be a little young to be a nanny, Isa, but maybe when you get a little older you can babysit for Mary and Jonah. How would that be?"

338

"Okay, but I could probably be a nanny, too." Isabella hugged Mary for a few seconds before racing away to join Heather.

"Have a seat and tell me all about it," Emmy said as she pointed to the island. "I don't mean... you know."

"We went to see Dr. Walsh, and he thinks my due date is May fifth."

They talked for fifteen minutes before Jonah said they needed to leave.

"I'm so happy for you guys. Is it all right if I tell people at church tomorrow?" Emmy asked.

"You can tell anyone you want, Em. We're going to post the news on Facebook later today," Mary said.

Emmy laughed. "You mean I'm not the last to hear about this?"

Mary shook her head and laughed. "Other than immediate family, you are the first to know."

"Oh, thank you so much," Emmy said as she squeezed Mary again.

A week later Blaine Dickinson approached Emmy in the hallway after Sunday School. Blaine waved to get Emmy's attention.

"Hi, Blaine. How are you guys doing?"

"We're doing great. Do you have a minute to talk?" Blaine asked.

"Sure. What's up?"

"Wade and I are in charge of the Christmas program, and I would like to ask for a favor. I need some help."

"What can I help with?" Emmy smiled. *How do you keep your hair from getting split ends? And how do you keep it so lustrous?*

"I don't know if you've heard, but we're doing a new musical. Wade and I have most of the songs already, but we thought we would ask if you have the time to maybe write a song for the program. I know it's a lot to ask, and I totally understand if you say no."

"I did write some Christmas songs before."

"Yes, and we wondered if we could use a couple of them."

"Of course, you can," Emmy said and waited for a response from Blaine. "I could try to come up with a couple new ones. I have some half-finished lyrics that I didn't use for the Christmas CD."

"I'll talk to you later, Emmy. I'll call you and we can talk about our idea for the songs. Wade wants to have a meeting next Sunday for anyone who's interested in helping with the program."

"Really? It's pretty early to start. It's only September," Emmy said.

"You're right, but we want to get a head start. I suppose we're a bit nervous. We've never had the resources to do a big production before," Blaine answered.

During the week Emmy worked on the leftover lyrics from her Christmas project. By Sunday she had two completed songs.

"I'll be home as soon as I can," she told Kenny after the second service. "Blaine didn't say how long the meeting might last. Go ahead and eat lunch."

Kenny kissed Emmy and headed home with the kids. Emmy joined the other volunteers in Noah's Ark.

"Blaine and I want to thank you for letting us take up more of your time," Pastor Wade said to open the meeting. "Please, let me pray, and we'll get started."

He prayed and then Blaine passed out a synopsis of the program. He allowed everyone a couple of minutes to glance through the notes.

"We realize this might be different from what the church has done in the past, but we did something similar a few years ago in Africa. We didn't have the same resources, so we improvised."

Wade explained how he envisioned the program and then Blaine described how they imagined the set to look.

"Pastor Tyler has agreed to let us build the set and leave it up until after Christmas. We can do it without spending a lot of money, and since we're writing the script ourselves, we won't have the expense of purchasing a program."

Emmy talked to Blaine later. "I would love to help with the script."

"We do have most of it finished, but we thought you could help polish it. Especially the dialogue," Blaine said.

"I can start this week if you want," Emmy volunteered.

"That's perfect, and we love the new songs. Don't change a thing about them," Blaine said and then hugged Emmy.

The five members of Fridays At Five along with the band's managers Andy Walker and Charles La Rosse met at their office in the Steward Music Group building on the third Monday of September.

Kenny shook hands with all the guys and said, "Long time, no see. How is everyone?" He shook hands with Adam Vicini and said, "I see you at church, but it's still good to see you here."

"Before we start I have some news," Dave said. "I'm sure the wives have shared this already, but in case they haven't, Macy and I have separated. I'm living with a friend in Newcastle."

Kenny looked at the other guys. "Emmy hasn't said anything. Did you guys know?"

The guys nodded.

"I guess I'm the last to know," Kenny said. "I'm sorry to hear this."

"For now it's just a trial separation," Dave said. "It won't affect the band."

The guys took several minutes to digest this news.

"All right! Enough of this chit-chat. I've got a doctor's appointment in an hour," Andy said. "Do you guys have new material or not?" He looked around the room and the guys nodded. "Good! I've never interfered with the music, and I don't intend to start now because that's not my job. You guys could do a tour every couple of years for the next twenty years and still make a decent living, but I know you don't want to become a nostalgia act and keep playing the same old hits night after night. Am I right?"

Jeff answered for the group. "We have a hard enough time adding new material to the set now. That's why I think we need to make sure this project is better than anything we've ever done."

341

"Good!" Andy checked his Rolex. "We're out of here. Keep me in the loop."

He and Charles left, and the guys spent an hour going over the newest new material.

"Is that the best you can do for lyrics?" Jeff shouted at Dave. "This sounds like it was written for twelve-year-old kids. Did you write the lyrics, or did Danny and Deborah?"

Dave stood up and shouted back. "Leave my kids out of this. At least I bothered to write some lyrics. All you came up with is some old blues music that sounds older than you."

"Knock it off!" Paul Joseph got in between the two guys before the shouting could escalate.

Dave and Jeff walked to opposite sides of the room.

Kenny waited until everyone chilled a bit before he voiced his opinion. "I'm not happy with the material I brought in, and apparently none of us are in the right frame of mind to head to the studio and start working. It would be a waste of time and money. I think we should wait until after the new year before we try again. What do you guys think?"

"Sounds like a good idea," Jeff said. "I'm sorry for getting on your case, Dave. Your stuff wasn't that bad, and a lot better than my weak effort. I hope you and Macy can sort stuff out."

"No problem," Dave said. "You know we could do something different. I know the Riders material didn't sell as much as our other projects, but we aren't going to sell ten million copies of anything we do now. The business has changed."

Paul nodded. "I've always been into the blues more than you guys. I'm not saying we do a total twelve-bar blues album, but we could incorporate more of that influence into our songs."

"I think you're on to something. I used to listen to blues a lot more when I was younger," Jeff said. "I could even sing lead because my voice definitely has changed over the years."

"You still sound better than Tom Waits," Dave teased.

The guys agreed to take the rest of the year to explore this new direction and meet in the middle of January.

Chapter Thirty-Eight

"Hey, Emmy, I got an email from Jeremiah," Kenny said as Emmy walked into the family room after she dropped the kids at school.

"How are they doing?" she asked as she sat in her recliner and stared at the TV. "What are you watching?"

Kenny looked up from his laptop and glanced at the eighty-inch TV on the wall. "Don't know. I just turned it on out of habit."

"Maybe we should not watch as much TV. Remember how Tyler said he doesn't watch it at all now?"

"I remember. Are you suggesting we get rid of it? Football season has started."

Emmy reached for the remote on the table between the two leather recliners. "We need to keep it for the kids."

"Yeah, right," Kenny chuckled.

"Fine. I still like to watch football," Emmy admitted and then turned off the TV. "So what's going on with Jeremiah and Mia?"

"Oh, they're doing fine. BearFace is lining up some local gigs, and Jeremiah wants to know if I'd be interested in sitting in with the band."

"Are you?"

Kenny closed his laptop and scratched his ear. "Would you let me go down there if I said I was?"

"You're a big boy now. You can make decisions for yourself."

"He's talking about the first Friday and Saturday of October. Do we have anything planned?" Kenny asked.

"I don't think it's anyone's birthday or anniversary. How long would you be gone?" she asked.

"Since I know their music, I could fly down early Friday and come back on Sunday."

"Are you gonna ask Mr. Robertson if you can use his plane?"

Kenny shook his head. "I thought I could fly commercial."

Emmy laughed and said, "Don't be a dork. They aren't

343

going anywhere anytime soon. They just got back from Italy and Greece. If no one uses the jet, Mr. Robertson might decide to sell it."

"I should pay for the trip," Kenny said.

"Of course, but good luck trying to get him to accept any money. He writes it all off on his taxes somehow."

"I'll email Jeremiah and let him know I'll be there."

"And I'll call Mr. Robertson and arrange for the use of his jet," Emmy said.

"Would it be okay with you if I don't shave until I get back from Alabama?"

Emmy ran a hand over his cheek. "It's all right with me, but a week isn't long enough for you to grow a full beard like Jeremiah and the guys."

"I know, but I can start one."

"Oh, one other thing," Emmy said and then grinned.

"What's that?"

"You can't kiss me until you shave again."

"Emmy!" Kenny whined.

Kenny arrived in Birmingham eight days later. Jeremiah met him at the airport.

"Nice flight?" Jeremiah asked as he loaded Kenny's luggage in the back of his 2009 silver Ford Taurus.

"Emmy's spoiled me. I was going to fly commercial, but as you an see, I didn't. I brought two guitars. I figured that would be enough."

"We might have an extra one around somewhere."

Jeremiah drove to the house he and Mia rented in Hoover, Alabama.

"This is it," Jeremiah said. "Mia fixed up the spare bedroom for you. It's not much."

"I'm sure it will be fine," Kenny said. He smiled at Mia, waiting on the front porch. "Hi, Mia. Thanks for letting me stay."

Jeremiah helped Kenny get situated in the guest bedroom and then asked, "Are you hungry?"

"I will be soon."

344

Mia offered to make lunch.

"Let me show you the garage," Jeremiah said. "We don't need it for the car, so we converted it into a rehearsal space for the band. The guys are coming over around one. We thought we could rehearse a little if you don't mind."

"Sounds like a plan," Kenny said as he and Jeremiah walked out the kitchen screen door, onto a small wooden deck and then over to the detached two-car garage.

"There's no house behind us, so we don't bother anyone," Jeremiah said as he opened the service door and stepped inside.

Kenny followed and checked out the setup. "Not bad. You've got some soundproofing and enough room."

"It's not exactly the carriage house where you guys started, but we're just a simple garage band," Jeremiah said and then laughed.

Cecil Hardin and Warren Dewar arrived just after lunch in a small U-Haul truck.

"How far away is the gig?" Kenny asked.

"Thirty minutes away. Place called Shooter's Rib Joint. Kind of a dive, but the food is great, and they have live music every weekend. We've got this weekend and the weekend three weeks from now," Jeremiah explained.

"We might be able to pick up one or two more gigs a month, but that's it," Cecil said.

"Yeah, Jeremiah's church is his first priority, and Cecil and I are working construction jobs to pay the rent," Warren added. "BearFace is just a way to keep our hands in the music."

"You guys can build a fanbase locally, and then see what happens. You do have the two CDs to sell," Kenny reminded them.

They rehearsed for a couple of hours and then Kenny helped the guys load their gear into the rented truck.

"Does the rib place have a P.A. system?" Kenny asked.

"Yeah, it's not state-of-the-art, but it's all right. They have some lights. Not many, but they have a couple of guys who are pretty savvy when it comes to mixing."

"I kinda hate to ask, but does anyone know I'm here?" Kenny asked.

Jeremiah closed the truck's rear door and jumped down. "I called the guy who books the band and told him we might have an extra guitar player for this weekend, but I didn't tell him who."

"I've been growing this beard in hopes no one would recognize me. I figured I would wear sunglasses and a baseball cap."

"You should blend in," Cecil said.

"I did bring a couple of flannel shirts to wear on stage," Kenny added.

Jeremiah grilled some steaks for dinner and then Cecil and Warren took the truck over to Shooter's. Kenny rode with Jeremiah and Mia, and the four guys unloaded the truck. Mia helped by setting up a table for the band's merchandise.

"I bet it's been a long time since you've done this," Warren said as they unloaded the amps and drums.

"We used to do everything back in the early days. I'm not saying I'd like to get rid of our crew, but this isn't bad."

All the gear was packed in road cases with wheels to make things easier. They rolled the equipment up a concrete ramp, through the double doors and directly onto the stage.

"It's not a huge stage," Jeremiah said.

"I've played on smaller ones," Kenny replied. "Looks like it's ten feet deep and fifteen feet wide. Plenty of room."

"Check this out," Jeremiah said. He and Kenny walked up to the camouflage canvas which served as a stage curtain. "It might surprise you." Jeremiah parted the curtain to let Kenny look.

"Wow! No wonder you guys are using hundred-watt Marshalls. That's a huge room."

"We made good use of the money you loaned us for gear."

"That wasn't a loan, Jeremiah," Kenny said.

The guys got everything set up, did a thorough soundcheck and had an hour before they would hit the stage.

The guy responsible for mixing both the monitors and front-of-house stared at Kenny after the soundcheck. "You're pretty good with that guitar. We don't get many pros in here."

"I've been playing for a few years," Kenny said. *Are you going to blow my cover?* He waited for the man to say his name.

"I remember seeing this band several years ago. I think their name was... something to do with a day of the week. They were pretty good, but I can't remember exactly what their guitar player looked like. Maybe it will come back to me in a few days."

Kenny nodded.

"Jeremiah, you okay?" Cecil asked as the guys walked onto the stage. "You seem nervous."

Jeremiah glanced over his shoulder at Kenny. "I'm afraid to make a mistake in front of him."

Kenny had his back to the guys as he adjusted some setting on the Marshall JVM410 half-stack, all-tube amplifier.

Cecil strapped on his bass guitar and grinned. "Hey! He straps on his guitar just like us mere mortals."

Jeremiah laughed. A minute later Warren banged his sticks together and BearFace launched into "Prodigal Sons" from their first CD.

Two and a half hours later Jeremiah looked at Cecil and Kenny. "We haven't done 'Sweet Home Alabama' yet. Should we close with that?"

"We might not make it out alive if we don't sing it. I think it's like the official state song down here," Cecil said.

They played the song for ten minutes and Kenny ended the show with the intro to 'Freebird' which they performed earlier.

"I think we played every song we know," Warren said as they powered down the gear.

"Are we going to leave everything set up?" Kenny asked.

"We can leave the amps and everything, but I'm taking my guitar home," Jeremiah said. "I never leave this baby anywhere." He lovingly placed his Gibson Les Paul Standard with the cherry sunburst finish in its case. "The pedal board can stay."

Kenny took his guitars with him.

The band spent Saturday afternoon adding some new tunes to their set list. Most of the songs were covers, but Jeremiah had written a couple of new songs.

"What did you think?" Jeremiah asked Kenny after the guys ran through the new original tunes.

"Those will be a good start for the next CD."

Although BearFace repeated most of the songs they played the night before, the Saturday night crowd showed their appreciation with boisterous enthusiasm. The guys closed with the two Lynyrd Skynyrd classics.

"We survived," Warren said as he toweled off outside after the last song.

"I should have brought more CDs," Mia said. "We sold every one we had. Most of the t-shirts are gone, too. I don't think we need to order anymore smalls or mediums. Guys bought the t-shirts and they need the big sizes."

The man who had mixed both shows approached with three football-lineman-sized men. "My cousins have volunteered to do the heavy lifting."

"We appreciate the help." Jeremiah shook hands with the men.

"Y'all sounded good," one said. The others didn't talk at all as they stared at Kenny.

Kenny walked up and offered a hand. "Thanks for your help, and the energy from the crowd was amazing."

The guys nodded.

The 'mixer man' walked up to Kenny. "They know who you are, but they kept it to themselves. Thought you wanted it that way."

"I appreciate it. I never caught your name. You did a great job mixing both nights."

"Thanks, I 'preciate it. The name's Leon A. Pyle." He shook hands with Kenny.

Kenny smiled. *I bet I know what the A stands for. Your parents must have been big Lynyrd Skynyrd fans.*

Kenny slipped into the back of the sanctuary the next morning. He joined in the singing and listened to Jeremiah preach. Mia made him stay for lunch, and then Jeremiah gave him a ride to the airport.

"Thanks for coming down," Jeremiah said.

Kenny shook hands. "Thanks for letting me sit in. Tell Mia

348

thanks for the hospitality."

"Do you think Emmy will let you come back in three weeks?"

"I hope so because I had a blast. It felt great to just stand in the back and play my guitar. I could get used to that."

"Is that his plane?" Kevin Michael pointed to a corporate jet as it taxied to a terminal.

"No, but I think his plane just landed." Emmy pointed to another plane. "See the blue along the bottom?"

"Kinda," Kevin Michael answered.

"Mr. Robertson's plane is painted like that."

Five minutes later Kenny loaded his luggage and guitars in the back of Emmy's gray BMW X3.

"Did you have fun playing guitar for Pastor Jeremiah?" Heather asked.

"I did. He told me to say hi to everyone."

The kids soon lost interest in Daddy's weekend and concentrated on their electronics during the ride home. Kenny carried his guitars downstairs as Emmy watched. He retrieved his suitcase from Emmy's car and carried it upstairs to the bedroom.

"I see your guitars are more important than your clothes," Emmy said as she stretched out on their bed and watched as Kenny unpacked.

"Clothes can be replaced a lot easier than those guitars." He unpacked quickly and joined Emmy on the bed. "Did you miss me?"

She grinned. "Oh, were you gone?"

"I bet you missed me," he said and then kissed her briefly.

"How did it go? How's Mia doing?" Emmy asked.

Kenny told Emmy about the house and the church before he brought up the gigs.

"Did anyone in the crowd recognize you?"

"I don't think so, and if they did, they didn't make a big deal about it. I really liked that part. I didn't even sing harmony. I just played my guitar. It was great."

"People might have recognized your voice. Good thing you

pretended to be a mute," she teased.

"Jeremiah wants me to come back in three weeks," Kenny said as he turned on his side.

Emmy turned on her side and ran a hand through his beard. "Did you already give him your answer?"

"I told him I would let him know this week. I wanted to ask you first."

You are a smart husband. She rubbed a foot against his leg. "It's all right with me if you do, but please don't plan to fly down there every time they line up a gig, okay?"

"I won't. I don't think the guys see the band as anything more than a weekend hobby."

Kenny returned to Alabama and joined the band for the next gigs. By now his beard allowed him to remain incognito throughout the entire weekend. Leon A. Pyle helped Kenny remain anonymous by giving him the nickname of Bubba Bear. Jeremiah introduced Kenny to the crowd using that name.

"Thanks again," Jeremiah said as he dropped Kenny at the airport on Sunday afternoon. "Are you sure you don't want your share of the money?"

"I appreciate the offer, but you guys keep it. I thoroughly enjoyed myself," Kenny said as he shook hands. "Let me know if you need me again."

"Will do."

Kenny relaxed on the ride home. He closed his eyes and rehashed the gigs. *This is what I love about music. Just playing in front of people and not having to travel all over the place. I wonder what Emmy would say if I decided to leave Fridays At Five. It's not like we need to keep making a ton of money every year. I'm sure we would get by on our investments. We have trusts for the kids to go to college.* He stroked his beard. *I'm sure she's going to insist I shave as soon as I get home. I kinda like the beard though.*

Chapter Thirty-Nine

"Kristen, do you see Randy Braun anywhere?" Emmy asked. "I emailed him during the week, and he agreed to meet me today after church."

"I don't see Randy, but I see Vanessa with the baby over there talking to some people." Kristen pointed to the opposite side of the large sanctuary.

"Thanks," Emmy said as she grabbed her purse and Bible. "She'll know where he is."

"Are you looking for me?" Randy asked as he suddenly appeared in front of Emmy.

"Yes, where did you come from?" Emmy looked up at him. *Oh, my God! You're losing some hair.*

Randy laughed. "I assume you mean right now and not where I lived as a child."

Emmy grinned. "You are still a goof even if you're a full professor at North Park College now. They must have relaxed their qualifications quite a lot."

"I saw you earlier and made my way over here. I was standing behind those guys," Randy explained. "How have you been, Emmy. We haven't really talked for a long time. Are your girls ready for college?"

Emmy swatted Randy's arm. "It hasn't been that long. Are you glad you finally have a daughter now after having three boys? How old is she?"

"Maisie is almost five months, and I totally adore her. She smiles at me and makes noises. I love to make her laugh."

"I bet the boys tease her a lot."

"Stephen does, but Hale and Thomas ignore her. Stephen is in third grade this year," Randy added.

"Heather and Isabella are in fourth. They grow up so fast."

"They certainly do, Emmy."

"The church is getting so big that it's impossible to talk to everyone. Sometimes I don't even have a chance to talk to old friends. I'm not using that as an excuse." Emmy stared at Randy. *You've gained some weight, but you're still pretty skinny.*

"We were gone for most of the summer," Randy said. "We were here in August when you sang with Sadie. I could tell you got a bit emotional."

"Yeah, it's a long story," Emmy said and then bit her lip.

"I heard from Christopher and Maddy last week. They are adapting to the Pittsburgh area."

"What? I didn't know they moved. When did that happen?" Emmy asked.

"Almost a year ago, Em. They are still with Liberty Manufacturing, but they work in the corporate headquarters. Christopher wants to be the CEO one of these years. Did you hear they had a daughter?" Randy asked.

"No! I didn't know. I am so out of the loop."

"Her name is Bayleigh Anne." Randy spelled it for Emmy.

"That's a beautiful name."

"And Elena is officially a teenager. She is a beautiful young lady." Randy touched the top of Emmy's head. "She taller than you."

"Everyone's tall than me. How is Elena dealing with her Crohn's disease?" Emmy asked. "I still remember to pray for her once in a while."

"You'd never know she has it."

"Do you remember I used to have a crush on your brother?"

Randy laughed. "I remember. Are you telling me you are over him? He will be so disappointed to hear that."

Emmy made a face at Randy. "Yes, I'm totally over my crush. Are you still abstaining from alcohol?"

"Yes."

"Good for you, Randy."

"I haven't had a beer in so long. I can't remember how many years," he answered. "I don't have your willpower. If I have one beer, I wouldn't stop until I was intoxicated," he said. "In your email you mentioned something about going back to school."

"I've been toying with the idea of getting a degree in education so I could teach here at the school."

"We are always in need of teachers. I'm on the school

board. Not sure if you knew that."

Emmy shook her head. "I didn't know."

"I could look into it if you want. Off the top of my head, I would think you might need twenty hours. Give or take. It would depend on what classes you've already taken. You did finish your degree, right?"

"Yes, it took me forever, but I graduated back in 2004."

"I should have remembered that," Randy said.

"I would appreciate it, Randy." Emmy grinned and then said, "Wouldn't it be weird if I took one of your classes?"

"Yes, it would because you aren't a math major, but I would love to have you for a student. I'd make sure you had tons of homework."

"I used to detest homework, and now I have to help the kids with theirs. I actually enjoy it."

"That's good because if you decide to teach, you will have to deal with a lot of homework," Randy said.

"I'll try to keep in better touch, Randy. Say hi to Vanessa for me. I've got to pick up Kenny at the airport later. He was sitting in with BearFace again."

"Is that Jeremiah's band?"

"Yeah. See ya." Emmy waved goodbye as she scooted around some people.

"Who wants to go to the airport with me to get Daddy?" Emmy asked just before four that afternoon."

"I want to stay here and play," Kevin Michael said as he lined up some cars on the stairs."

"Heather! Isabella! We need to pick up your father," Emmy hollered from the foot of the stairs. She looked at Kevin Michael. "I didn't mean you had a choice. We're all going to the airport."

"Can I leave my cars here?" he asked.

"Yes, but you will have to put them away later."

Heather and Isabella galloped down the stairs. "Can I ride in the front seat?" Heather asked.

"Who sat in front the last time?" Emmy asked.

"I can't remember," Heather said as she shrugged.

"You can sit in the front," Isabella said.

"I shouldn't let either of you sit in the front because it's probably against the law."

"Will the police arrest you and send you to jail?" Kevin Michael asked.

"I hope not."

Emmy helped Kevin get buckled in and headed to the airport.

"Who wants to play a joke on your father?" Emmy looked in the rear-view mirror of the Odyssey.

"I do!" Heather hollered.

"What do we have to do?" Isabella asked.

"I think we should pretend not to recognize him if he still has a beard. What do you say?"

The kids giggled. They arrived at the airport early. Kenny landed fifteen minutes later, and the pilots taxied into Mr. Robertson's hanger. Kenny emerged and waved. He walked over to where Emmy and the kids were waiting.

"Did you miss me?" Kenny held out his arms waiting for a hug, but no one ran over to him. "Don't I get a hug?"

Heather and Isabella looked at him and shrugged without saying a word. Kevin Michael giggled.

"What's going on?"

"Mommy said we were supposed to pretend we didn't know you if you still had that beard," Heather said as she pointed to his beard.

"Ah, she said that, huh?" Kenny ran a hand through his beard as he walked up to Emmy. "Don't you like how it feels when I kiss you?" He kissed Emmy and made sure she felt his beard on her face.

"Stop it! That scratches," Emmy said as she pushed him away. "No more kisses until you get rid of that."

They loaded Kenny's gear, got in the Odyssey and headed home.

"Did you have fun playing your guitar?" Kevin Michael asked.

"I did have fun. Did you miss me?"

354

Both girls answered, "Oh, were you gone, Daddy?"

Kenny laughed and then tried to tickle Emmy's knee.

"Stop it. I'm driving."

They got home, and the kids resumed playing. Emmy started working on dinner as Kenny unpacked. He came back downstairs and put his arms around Emmy from behind. He rubbed his beard against her neck.

"Are you trying to give me a rash? I'm allergic to beards."

"Do you really hate it?" Kenny checked the pot of pasta. "I could trim it."

"You could shave it off completely," she suggested as she waved a wooden spatula at him.

"Do we need an arbitrator?"

"No, you need a barber." She turned back to the pasta and stirred it.

"Oh, come on, Em. I've never had a beard before. I like it. No one can recognize me," he pleaded.

"Who are you, and why do you have your hands on me?"

He moved his hands lower on her hips. "Please?"

She turned around to face him. He moved her hands to his neck and pulled her close.

"Ow! That's hot," he moved back a step.

She waved the spatula at him again. "Boiling water usually is."

"Should I call Father James to settle this?"

Emmy shook her head. "I don't have to kiss him. He can grow a beard to his butt if he wants."

Kenny tilted his head.

"You know what I mean," Emmy said. She took a deep breath. "Fine! You can keep that for a week."

"Deal!" Kenny shook her hand.

"But I'm not shaving my legs or my armpits until that beard disappears," she said and then stuck out her tongue.

Chapter Forty

"Are you sitting down?" Rory Porter asked after he and Emmy had been talking for a few minutes.

"No, I'm leaning against the counter. Why? Should I be sitting down? Do you have some terrible news to share?" Emmy asked.

"I hope you don't think it's terrible news," Rory said.

Emmy moved into the breakfast nook and sat down. She looked out the window and laughed because as fast as Kenny could rake some leaves into a pile, Kevin Michael, Ben, Taylor and Scout, the Bertucci's black lab, were jumping into the pile and scattering the leaves. Emmy watched as Scout chased the boys.

"Why are you laughing?" Rory asked as he opened a cold can of Dr Pepper.

"I'm watching Scout chase the boys around the yard and destroying all of Kenny's hard work raking leaves."

"That's something you used to do when you were a kid."

"No I didn't, did I?" Emmy asked.

"I remember one fall when Owen and I had to rake the backyard, and you came along and started playing in the piles of leaves," he reminded her.

"I probably did that at Kenny's house, too," she confessed. "Okay, so I'm sitting down. What do you need to tell me?"

"Rochelle and I are getting married next year," Rory said quickly.

"Get out! Are you yanking my chain?" Emmy jumped up from her chair and almost knocked it over. "You're lying to me."

"Nope, I'm not. I asked her yesterday, and she said yes. Can you believe it? I'm going to get married again." He waited for a response for several seconds. "Em, you still there?"

"I'm here. I don't know whether I should be happy for you or mad because I thought you... Never mind." She blew her nose and wiped it on a napkin from the table. "I'm happy for you, Rory. Do you have a date set?"

"We know it will be next summer. Are you planning on touring then, or will you be available?"

"Available for what?" she asked.

"To sing at my wedding. What did you think I meant?"

"I don't know. Of course, I'll sing for you. Tell me all the details."

"What details?"

Emmy sighed as she shrugged. "You're a goof. Where did you propose? What did you say? Did you get down on a knee? Those details."

"I proposed at a fancy restaurant in Tampa."

"By fancy restaurant, do you mean a fast food joint?"

"I'm going to hang up now," he threatened.

"Okay, fine. Tell me more."

"I took her out to a nice Italian place called Nicola Batali's in Tampa. Cost me an arm and a leg."

Emmy began to laugh hysterically.

"What is so funny?"

"I was thinking it cost you another body part."

"Ha! Ha! Aren't you a laugh riot."

"Tell me more. Did you practice how you were going to ask her?"

"I worked on a little speech, but she didn't let me finish. She knew where I was heading and said yes. We were both sitting down, so I didn't get on my knee."

"Did I ever tell you how Kenny proposed?"

"Several times. You tackled him and about raped him right in front of Kristen," Rory teased.

"I did not!" she exclaimed. "I might have kissed him a few times, but that's it."

"I know about Tony's proposal, too, Em," he said.

"I don't want to talk about that," she said and didn't. "Did you tell your mother?"

"I called her last night. Rochelle called her parents."

"Where do they live?"

"Orlando. The wedding will be in Orlando somewhere because that's where Rochelle grew up. She's got a huge family. She's introduced me to all three of her brothers and both sisters. We were at a family reunion and there was over a hundred people

357

there. Tons of aunts and uncles and cousins. All four of her grandparents are still alive. Do you think you can get away for a few days?"

"Are we all invited to the wedding?"

"Of course. You should bring the kids and stay at one of the resorts. They're old enough to appreciate it now. The girls are five, right?" he teased.

"I can't believe they're gonna be ten in January," Emmy said.

"I remember some of the things you did when you were ten," he said and then chuckled.

"Don't you ever dare tell them about what I did. I will murder you... Crap! Sorry, Rory."

"It's all right, Em."

"Shoot! She has a big family and all you have is your mother."

"Amy's kids are family, but I haven't seen or talked to them since... you know. Jane and Melissa are like fourteen and fifteen now. As far as I know, they live with their father in Pennsylvania somewhere," he said. "I kinda think of you as my family."

"Really?"

"Yeah, you're like a wild cousin or something," he teased.

"Yeah, well, you're like a mean cousin who tried to get me to do naughty things with you," she retaliated.

Rory finished his Dr Pepper and tossed it in the recycling bin. " Rochelle wants to have a dozen bridesmaids and this huge reception. I don't even know that many guys. I might have to use you to be my best man."

"What's that word I'm thinking of using right now. I can't seem to remember, but I think it starts with..."

"I get the picture, Em."

"She's never been married before, right?"

"Nope! First time."

"And she's two years older than you. That means... When is her birthday?"

"April tenth."

"So if you get married in the summer, she will be forty."

358

"And your point is?" Rory asked.

"That's pretty old to be starting a family for a woman," Emmy answered.

"We realize that, but it is possible. Your mother was almost that old when she had you," he reminded Emmy.

"It can be done, and she is a nurse, so she must know the risks."

"Are you trying to ask if she's pregnant without coming right out and asking. That's not like you."

"I was trying to be tactful."

Rory laughed.

"I can be tactful, you creep."

"You're about as tactful as that North Korean dictator with a nuke pointed at us."

"Is she?" Emmy asked and then bit her lip.

"No, but we aren't doing anything to prevent it."

"Normally, I would get on your case for that, but since you're an old guy, I guess it doesn't matter," Emmy whispered.

"Thank you, I think."

"Is it all right if I tell Kenny?"

Rory chuckled.

"Not about you guys trying to have a baby! I meant the engagement part."

"You can tell the whole world, Em."

"Hey! I just thought of two guys you could use," she said.

"Who?"

"Kenny and Father James."

"Great! I only need ten more," he said and then laughed. "Maybe Kevin Michael, too."

"If you guys do start a family, you'll need a bigger place to live," she said.

"I am aware of that, Em, and I'm saving up for a down payment."

Emmy bit her lip and then said, "I could help."

"You could buy the whole state without batting an eye, but I seem to remember this stubborn kid who refused to let anyone help her pay for college."

"Did I tell you that?"

"I think it was Kenny, but that's beside the point. I really appreciate the offer, Em, but I can be stubborn, too."

"I understand you want to do it on your own, but I had to ask."

"You are the most generous person I've ever known, sweetie. Even when we were kids, you would share your last dime when we would stop at Darby's."

"We have been so blessed, Rory."

He could hear her voice breaking. "Don't cry, Em. You have earned it."

"We might have earned the money, but God has blessed me with so many other things. My family and great friends."

"Like me?" he joked.

"Yes, like you, you creep!"

"I better go. Rochelle is coming over. We've got a lot of stuff to do," he said.

Emmy laughed.

"I didn't mean that, Em."

"I'll talk to you later. Keep me informed as soon as you guys decide on a date and stuff."

"Will do. Say hi to the kids for me."

Emmy hung up but held the phone in her hand as she glanced at the mudroom door and heard voices. Kenny, Kevin Michael, Ben and Taylor entered the kitchen.

"Was someone on the phone, Emmy?" Kenny asked.

"Rory called."

"How's he doing?"

"He's getting married," she answered.

Kenny stared at her for a moment. "That's a good thing, right?"

She smiled. "Yes, it's a very good thing."

After Emmy dropped off the kids at school on Monday morning, she came home and hollered for Kenny.

"I'm up here," he answered.

She walked up the stairs and peeked into their bedroom.

"Why aren't you up and dressed? Are you gonna be lazy today?"

"I was waiting for you," he replied.

"Oooh! What did you have in mind?" She walked toward the bed.

"Not that. I waited because I've decided to get rid of this." He stroked his beard.

"Oh, thank God!"

"I wanted to wait until you got back so you could watch me shave." He got out of bed and pulled her into his bathroom.

"Why would I want to watch you shave?"

"Don't you want to watch? I like to watch you shave your legs."

She rolled her eyes. "You are such a guy."

She sat on the vanity top and watched as he shaved. "Rory mentioned we might plan a vacation around his wedding. Would you be totally opposed to that?"

"His wedding's in the summer, right?"

"Probably in June, but they didn't know the date."

"Unless something changes drastically, and we get the new CD recorded a lot quicker than I expect, we will probably be spending most of next year in the studio. I don't see us doing a summer tour at this point."

She stared at him.

"What?"

"A simple yes or no would have sufficed."

"Then no, I would not be opposed."

"Speaking of recording, did I mention the Bender Brothers Band is finally finished with their summer tour." She used air quotes for summer. "Micah wants to use your studio to record some original songs. Other than Adam, do you have anyone booked to use it?"

"Just you and me when we come up with a new song."

"I'll see when Micah and the guys want to start." She jumped down from the vanity and kissed his now clean-shaven cheek. "I still love you even if you're a dork."

"Gee, thanks."

Ross Knapp walked up to Riordan in the music suite on Thursday evening and held up his left hand. "I'm finished."

"Finished with what?" Riordan asked.

"Remember how I told you about the arthritis in my hand?"

Riordan nodded. "We prayed for your hands."

"It didn't work. The pain is worse than ever. I can't play anymore. It hurts too much to make the chords. I just wanted to let you know. It's a good thing there are other guitar players available."

"The Bender brothers are back in town. I can add them to the schedule if they're willing." Riordan looked at Ross's hand and thought about something.

"What?" Ross asked.

"Have you thought about trying the bass. I know you can play bass, but I was thinking it might be easier on your fingers."

"I could try it. I would really like to still be part of the team in some capacity."

"Let's try it and see how you feel," Riordan suggested.

Ross switched over to the bass guitar for the rehearsal. Riordan asked him how it felt after they finished.

"Not bad. It still hurts, but the pain is more manageable. I don't want to take anyone's spot away, but I think I could handle playing bass a lot easier."

"Good! I'll work with the schedule. I'll try to schedule you and Heidi together."

Diane glanced out the window behind the couch in her living room and saw Brady's black 2013 Mercedes E-Class pull up the driveway. "You're back a bit early."

"Who?" Emmy asked.

"Brady just got back," Diane answered. "I didn't expect him until after five."

"Should I leave?" Emmy asked and then giggled. "I could sneak out the back so he wouldn't know I've been here and that we were talking about him."

"You can stay. I didn't mean to complain so much, but I still feel Bennett should have to assume more responsibilities with the company. He is a full partner after all."

"I won't stay long, but I agree with you. The company is making enough money to support Bennett. He should leave the Barclay Academy. He wouldn't have to work as many hours if he took a position with Carson & Caden," Emmy said and then chuckled. "I still think that's a funny name for a technology company. Is he going to start one called Conor and Lily and use it to create satellites for outer space?"

"I think it's wonderful that he named the company for the boys. It shows he thinks of them as his own kids. You know what I mean, right?"

"I think it's cool but funny."

"I'm home! Is anyone here?" Brady hollered from the kitchen.

"He came in through the garage," Emmy said as she got up and ran toward the kitchen. "I'm going to surprise him."

Diane followed as Emmy raced into the kitchen. Emmy ran up to Brady, threw her arms around him and hugged him close.

"I'm glad to see you, too, Emmy." He looked at Diane and mouthed the words, "What's up with Emmy?"

Diane shrugged. "Your guess is as good as mine."

"How was your week? Are you hungry? I can make an early dinner," Emmy said as she released Brady.

"It was all right."

"I am so glad you're home. I missed you so much."

"Emmy!" Diane yelled. "What are you doing?"

Emmy turned to face Diane. "He's been gone so much lately I wanted to see if he still remembered who he was married to."

Brady laughed.

Diane frowned. "I think he still remembers, Emily Olivia."

It is good to be home," Brady said as he walked over and kissed Diane. "Yes, you are definitely my wife."

Emmy giggled and then waved a hand. "I'm outta here! Call me later, Diane. If you're not too busy."

"Goodbye, Emmy!"

"Will you make sure you eat lunch?" Emmy asked kissing the top of Kenny's head while he sat in his recliner. "I gotta run. Practice is supposed top start at ten. There's stuff for sandwiches and soup or make yourself a pizza. I'll be home as soon as I can. I need to stop and see my mother for a few minutes."

"Have fun at practice," Kenny said.

"We will," Isabella answered. "We already know all our lines. We've been rehearsing all week."

Emmy made it to the church a few minutes early. She parked her BMW next to Tony and Sloane's Toyota Sienna.

"Watch out for cars!" Emmy hollered. She headed into the building and saw Tony talking to Reed Shafer and Bill Griffith.

"What are you doing here? Where's Sloane?" Emmy asked.

"She's home. I told Reed I would help," Tony answered.

"Since when do you know anything about building stuff?" Emmy teased.

"Hey, brat! Have you seen that new building next door? I built it."

"You don't know which end of a hammer to use."

"I've learned a lot since I retired from football. I even know how to read blueprints," he said.

"You better keep a close eye on him," she said to Reed and Bill. "He could screw up building a two-piece set of Legos."

"Do we have a closet we could lock her in?" Tony asked. He tried to grab her arm but she scampered away. "Try not to mess up the music too much, brat."

Emmy headed to Noah's Ark and stood inside the door listening to Blaine praying.

"I'm glad you made it." Blaine waved at Emmy. "I do okay with the motions for the songs, but my voice isn't as good as yours. Could you and Wade work with the children on the songs while Allie and I work with the kids who have speaking parts?"

"Sure, no problem," Emmy said. "When is the program?"

"The second Sunday in December. The thirteenth," Blaine said.

"Well, we have a month. That should be plenty of time."

Chapter Forty-One

"Why do you have such a funny face?" Blaine asked Emmy as they took a little break from rehearsing the songs for the Christmas program.

"It's the only face I have," Emmy answered as she sat on the edge of one of the tables in Noah's Ark.

Blaine laughed. "No, I didn't mean you have a funny-looking face, but you have a weird expression right now."

"Oh, I guess I feel kinda silly doing the motions. I'm not used to it. I've never been a part of the kids' program," Emmy explained.

Blaine smiled as she went through some of the motions. "These kids are too young to do much more than move their hands while they watch us."

"Do we really have to be in the front where everyone can see us?" Emmy asked. "Couldn't we stand at the back?"

Blaine shook her head. "The kids wouldn't be able to see you. It will be all right. There will be at least four of us leading them, and the parents will be watching their children. They won't even notice us."

Emmy stood up. "Okay, what's next?"

Forty-five minutes later they finished.

"Our next practice will be the same time next Saturday. I'm proud of the progress everyone has made," Blaine announced.

"I'll see you tomorrow," Emmy said gathering the kids.

"Mommy, we are the only ones who know all of our lines," Heather said.

Isabella nodded. "Some of the kids have trouble memorizing simple lines."

"I'm sure they will do better. I want to see if I can find Tony. He might need me to take Ben and Taylor home."

Heather pointed down the hall. "There's Aunt Sloane talking to someone."

Emmy saw Sloane and waved. She whispered to the twins, "That's Mrs. Frees. Eloise and Nadine's mom.

"We know who she is. Lindsey is married to Cameron and

he plays keyboards for the worship team. You always say he looks like Buddy Holly whoever he is," Heather said.

"Eloise is in our Sunday School class, but she doesn't come to our school. How come?" Isabella asked.

"I'm not sure, but it might be because her parents both teach at McGee Junior High," Emmy said as she walked toward Sloane and Lindsey. "Do you remember when Cam and Lindsey lived in the guesthouse?"

The girls shook their heads.

"No, I guess you were too little. You might have not even been a year old at the time." Emmy smiled at Sloane and Lindsey.

"Hi, Emmy. I didn't know if you would have room for the boys, so I left Coby with Mama," Sloane said.

"I would have had room, but that's all right. I might stop by to see Father James if he's not busy. Oh, Lindsey, Eloise is doing great. She has a beautiful voice and she knows all the motions."

"She has been singing the songs at home every day. Cam has been helping her while I work with Nadine. She's only four, but she knows the alphabet and can count all day long if I let her."

"It must be quite an advantage to have parents who are teachers." *I wonder if Nadine will be tall like her sister. Eloise is probably the tallest kid in her class.*

"We try to make learning interesting."

"Mom! Can we stop at Darby's for lunch?" Kevin Michael asked. "I really, really, need a chili dog."

"We'll see," Emmy answered.

Tony walked up behind Emmy. "Can I have a chili dog and fries?"

She spun around and poked him in the belly. "I thought you were cutting out fast food. You look like you lost a couple more pounds. Have you?"

He patted his flat stomach. "Maybe. I haven't been on a scale lately, and I still each hot dogs. Just not as many or as often as before. Sloane is hinting at becoming vegetarians, but Mama won't buy into it."

Emmy reached out and touched his shirt. "Did you get all the paint on yourself, or did you manage to get some on the sets?"

Tony glanced down at his Bears t-shirt. "I didn't do much painting. The teens are doing that. I spent my time helping Bill cut lumber and actually putting the sections together."

"I hope you didn't mess things up."

"I know what I'm doing. The set is designed to be built in sections to make them easier the move around," Tony said.

"Was that your idea, Uncle Tony?" Kevin Michael asked.

Emmy laughed and shook her head. "Uncle Tony hasn't had a good idea for years."

Tony picked up Kevin Michael and sat him on his shoulder. "Don't listen to her, buddy. She's jealous because all she knows how to do is sing songs."

"FYI. I can write songs and I've even written some books. You'd know that if you knew how to read." Emmy made a face at Tony. "Oh, wait. You used to know how to read, but you got hit in the head so many times playing football that you can't remember."

"You better not let the press hear you say that, Em."

Emmy put a hand to her mouth. "Sorry. I guess that's a rather sensitive topic now. Did you have many concussions?"

"I only remember one, but it was pretty mild. God kept His hand on me."

"Good! I'd hate for you to end up like some of those other players who..." She looked at her son. "You know."

"Hopefully, John and I retired in time. Other than his knees, John's in good shape." Tony set Kevin Michael down.

"Mom! We're hungry," Heather whined. "Can we go eat now?"

"Okay, we can go now." Emmy waved goodbye and they headed out to the Odyssey. *I wish you girls were singing every song. That would make things so much easier.*

367

"Emmy! Emmy!" Kenny hollered Tuesday morning. "There's someone on the landline from Sunrise Garden."

"Can you take a message?" Emmy hollered back. "I'm in the middle of doing laundry."

"I think you better talk to them, Em. It's serious." He walked into the laundry room and handed her the phone.

Emmy bit her lip as she stared at Kenny.

"Em, you need to talk to them," Kenny whispered as he rubbed her back.

She looked at the phone as if it were about to bite her but then answered.

"I'm sorry, but I didn't get an answer at Mrs. Robertson's home," the voice said. "We called 9-1-1 for your mother. She was complaining of chest pain, and we don't take any chances..."

Emmy handed the phone back to Kenny. "I'm going to get Diane. We're going to St. Bart's."

"Drive carefully, Em," Kenny said and then talked to Sunrise Garden for a couple of minutes.

Emmy threw her Civic Si into reverse, backed out of the garage, slammed the transmission into first and floored it. She raced over to Brady and Diane's house and arrived just as Diane was getting out of her minivan.

Emmy rolled down her window and shouted, "Diane! We have to go to St. Bart's! Like right now!"

Diane ran over to Emmy's car. "Unlock the door!"

Emmy did and Diane got in. "What happened?"

"Buckle up and I'll tell you on the way."

Diane buckled up. "Try not to kill us, okay?"

Emmy explained what she knew, and they arrived at St. Bart's in one piece without getting a ticket. Emmy threw her keys at the parking valet, and she and Diane raced into the ER section.

"May I help you?"

Diane explained why they were there, and a man in a white lab coat led them back to where their mother was being examined.

"Hi, we're her daughters," Diane said.

The ER doctor introduced himself. "We will have to do more tests, but it appears your mother might have suffered a... to use non-medical terms... a mild heart attack. She is stable, but appears to be very confused."

"She lives in the memory care facility at Sunrise Garden," Diane explained.

"She will be admitted to CITU. You can stay with her." The doctor glanced at Patricia. "She doesn't seem as agitated now."

Diane and Emmy sat with their mother for an hour before she was moved upstairs.

"I need to call Brady," Diane said. "Have you let Kenny know what happened?"

"No, I left without my phone or my purse. Can I use yours?"

Diane nodded. "Hi, Brady. Emmy and I are at St. Bart's with Mom."

Brady listened without asking any questions.

"I just got home from dropping off the kids at school when Emmy raced up to the house. Bill and Mona have Lily and Conor, but I need to call them."

"I'll call them, Diane. I just arrived in Atlanta. Should I turn around and come home?"

Diane shrugged. "I wish you were home, but it looks like Mom is going to be all right. It's your call."

Brady sighed and made a quick decision. "I'm coming home. I'll be back in the air as soon as we can get out of here."

"Thanks, Brady, I appreciate it."

"Family is more important than business, sweetheart," Brady said.

Diane called her father-in-law and explained everything.

"You can stay with your mother as long as you need. Mona and I will take care of the kids."

Diane handed her phone to Emmy, and she called home.

"Hey, Diane. How is your mother?"

"It's me. I forgot my phone and purse," Emmy explained. "Could you come down to St. Bart's and bring them. I'm going to be here for the rest of the day."

Emmy explained what was going on and where they were.

"Anything else you need?" Kenny asked.

"Not sure. I don't plan to spend the night unless she gets worse. Right now she's resting comfortably."

"I'll be there soon, Em. Is there anyone I should call?"

"Pastor Tyler and Father James. They need to know."

"I'll call them both."

Father James answered his cell phone as he walked down the hall of the ninth floor of St. Bart's. "What's up, little sister?"

Hi, Father James," Kenny said and explained the reason for the call.

"I will head there now," Father James turned around and headed to the elevators. He knew exactly where to go and spotted Emmy talking in the hallway to a nurse.

"How did you get here so fast?"

"I was in the building just wandering around when Kenny called. How is she?"

Emmy poked him in the arm. "Aren't you ever serious?"

"I really was wandering around. One of my parishioners was supposed to be in room 90115, but it was empty. I was looking for him when my phone rang, and I thought it was you calling."

"Oh, sorry," Emmy said and then bit her lip.

Father James hugged her. "Tell me what you know."

Emmy did.

"Okay, any heart attack is serious, but this one doesn't appear to be life threatening."

"Do you want to see her?" Emmy asked.

"No, I'm concerned about you and Diane. The last time your mother saw me she thought I was your father. I don't want to give her another heart attack."

"Good thinking," Emmy said.

"If it's all right with you, I'll stay in the waiting room down the hall. I can say a few prayers."

Pastor Tyler arrived an hour later, saw Father James pacing up and down the hallway, walked up to him and tapped him on the shoulder. "How is everyone doing?"

"Hello, Pastor Tyler. They just did some kind of test on

370

Mrs. Colasanti. It appears she might have suffered a second attack earlier. Diane and Emmy are with her. I haven't been inside for obvious reasons, but I'm sure Emmy would like to see you."

Emmy spotted Tyler and came out into the hallway.

"How are you doing, Emmy?"

"Okay, but it's good to see you."

"Father James mentioned..."

"The cardiologist examined her. He spouted off some medical stuff that I didn't understand, but said Mom will be here for a few days." Emmy looked up at him and bit her lip. "I know she isn't the same anymore, but I'm not ready to say goodbye."

"I understand. Would you mind if I pray right here for you and your mother?"

Emmy shook her head. Father James stood behind her with both hands on her shoulders as Tyler prayed.

"Thank you, Pastor Tyler," Emmy said. "I know you're not a hugger, but would you mind if I gave you one?"

"Go ahead," he said with a nervous chuckle.

Three days later Diane and Emmy waited just inside the entrance to the Astoria Estates Care Center for the ambulance bringing their mother.

"Are they sure they can handle her here?" Emmy asked Diane as she paced back and forth.

"Will you chill out! They have an entire wing for patients like Mom," Diane said. "She will be better off here than at Sunrise Garden."

Five minutes later the ambulance arrived.

"Mom, can you hear me?" Diane asked later as she stood beside her mother's bed.

Patricia opened her eyes and tried to sit up, but Diane gently urged her back down.

"Am I in the hospital?"

"No, Mom, you're at Astoria Estates," Diane tenderly ran a hand through her mother's hair. "You're doing better, so you're not at St. Bart's."

"Is your father still here?" Patricia asked. "I remember

when he came to this place."

"No, Mom. He's not here, but Emmy's here." Diane motioned for Emmy to move closer and when Emmy didn't move, Diane frowned and said through clenched teeth, "Get your butt over here!"

Emmy moved closer and stood on the opposite side of the bed. "Hi, Mom, you look better. Do you feel better?"

Diane shook her head. "How do you think she feels?"

"Sorry," Emmy whispered.

"I had a dream that I saw your father, but he looked younger," Patricia said.

Emmy and Diane looked at each other.

Emmy said, "You might have seen..."

"It was just a dream, Mom. It's all right if you dream about Dad," Diane assured her.

Emmy left an hour later, but Diane stayed until after dinner.

"Mom, you should try to eat something. You like mashed potatoes."

"I'm not hungry. I need to get some sleep. I want to watch my shows later," Patricia said.

Diane set the fork down and moved the tray of food out of the way. "Your shows won't be on until tomorrow. I'll be back in the morning to see how you're doing. We can watch your shows together."

"Thank you, sweetie." Patricia reached up to stroke the side of Diane's face. "You've always been so thoughtful and caring. Tell your sister to come and see me sometime."

"I will, Mom." Diane kissed her mother's forehead and left. *Oh, Mom. Everything must be so scrambled up in your head. I was never thoughtful or caring about you when Em and I were growing up. I guess I'm trying to make up for that now.*

"Kenny, will you carve the turkey, please? It's done," Emmy asked as she checked the oven.

"No way! I cooked that bird, and I'm going to carve it," Andy Walker said in a loud voice. "Stand back and give me room. You can take care of the other food, cuz."

A few minutes later the adults gathered around the table in the dining room. Emmy looked at the food on the table and even more dishes on the buffet. "I'll pray and then we can eat."

"Mom! I need more milk," Kevin Michael shouted from the breakfast nook where Emmy's and Diane's children sat. Only one-year-old Conor ate with the adults in the dining room.

"I'll take care of him," Kenny said. "You guys can get started."

Emmy prayed and everyone took a seat.

"If the turkey's too dry, we can blame Andy," Emmy said.

"My turkey is never dry," Andy replied. "I hope these mashed potatoes aren't lumpy, or did you use instant?"

Emmy shook her head. "I made them the old-fashioned way just like Mom used to. If there are lumps, that's too bad. Her potatoes were never perfect."

For the next hour people passed platters and bowls around the table as everyone gorged on the Thanksgiving meal.

Dad Colwell scooted his chair back and patted his stomach. "I will pop if I eat another bite. Everything was delicious, Emmy."

"Thank you, but I had help. Diane, Mona and Mom Colwell all brought food over," Emmy said.

Father James smiled at Andy. "I thought the turkey was a little dry, but that's just me."

"I should have cooked it at home. I'm not used to Emmy's old oven," Andy slapped Father James on the back. "I have a brand new state-of-the-art professional oven at home."

"Are you suggesting I need to replace mine?" Emmy asked.

"Well, it is several years old."

"We've been living in this house for ten years now," Emmy said as she looked around the large dining room. She paused for a moment before she continued. "Sometimes I still can't believe we're living here. I never could have dreamed I'd ever live in a house like this."

Kenny smiled from the opposite end of the table. "We've been very fortunate, Em."

"I'd say God has blessed you rather abundantly," Dad Colwell said. "I'm going to check on Kevin Michael."

"Make sure he has tasted the cranberries," Emmy said. "He has to try one bite."

Dad Colwell got up and walked into the breakfast nook.

"I'm done, Gra. Can I go play?" Kevin Michael asked. "Everyone else is playing."

Grandpa Colwell looked at Kevin's plate. "Your mother wanted you to try the cranberries. Did you?"

"No, they smell funny." Kevin held up the plate for Gra to check.

Grandpa sniffed the cranberries. "They smell all right to me. I ate two helpings. Could you taste one little bite for me?" He set the plate down.

Kevin Michael stared at the cranberries. "They're too runny."

"Please? Just a tiny bite for me."

Kevin Michael listened to the other kids playing outside on the deck and surrendered. He placed a single cranberry on his spoon and put it into his mouth. The cranberry immediately flew across the table and splattered against a chair. "That was yucky."

"He tried a bite," Dad Colwell hollered. "Can he go play?"

"Yes, he can go," Kenny said as he brought some empty plates into the kitchen.

"I'm never eating another cranberry as long as I live," Kevin Michael said as he raced into the mudroom for his coat.

Kenny and his father rejoined everyone in the dining room.

"Emmy, do you like cranberries?" Andy asked. "I didn't see you eating any."

She shook her head. "I can't stand the stuff, but it's a holiday tradition. Mom used you make them every year, and I fought like hell to try to avoid eating any."

Emmy bit her lip as everyone laughed at her.

"Em, did you make all this stuff that Mom used to make for any particular reason?" Diane asked. "I know you don't normally make cranberries or whatever kind of Jello that is."

"I found some of her old recipes, and I thought I would try them. I was hoping she might be able to be here," Emmy said and then let the tears flow.

Chapter Forty-Three

"Are we doing anything special tonight?" Kenny stood in the doorway of Emmy's bathroom and watched her drying off after her shower."

She wrapped the towel around her and ran her hands through her wet hair. "I thought we were going over to John and Kristen's after dinner."

"Maybe one of these days we could have another party at our house," Kenny suggested. "We could invite all the neighbors and their kids."

"You know Kristen has been looking forward to this night." She walked past him and over to the bed. She dressed as they talked. "We don't have to stay real late."

"We'll see. We don't have to get up early, and my parents have the kids," he reminded her.

She grinned and her blue eyes sparkled, "That might be a good reason to come home early."

"Should we even bother to go over there?"

"I told Kristen we would be there. She invited the Plants and one of those other new couples. I can't remember their name, but we've met them."

"Should I shower now or wait until later?"

"You can take more than one shower a day," she said as she touched his face. "And you better shave today."

He rubbed his jaw. "I thought you liked the scruffy look."

"That was twenty years ago. I'm going to fix some breakfast. You got any requests?"

He grinned.

"I didn't mean that. Pancakes or a fry-up. Your choice."

"If you wait, I'll help with a fry-up. We haven't done that in forever."

"I'll get it started."

Later as they sat in the breakfast nook, Emmy watched the rain falling.

"Are we supposed to get much rain? If it was a little colder, this could turn into snow."

"I heard we might get an inch of rain. If it did turn into snow, it would just be flurries." Kenny poured more ketchup on his plate. "We aren't going to snowed in."

Ya think! Emmy rolled her eyes. "We probably won't get enough snow this winter to use the snowmobile either. We might as well sell it. We hardly ever use it."

"We will. Use it, I mean. Kevin Michael asked about going for a ride last week. He meant sometime this winter. Could you pass the salt, please."

Emmy handed him the sea salt without taking her eyes off of the view outside. Do you remember the first time I ever heard you playing the drums in the carriage house?"

"What brought that up?" Kenny sprinkled some salt on his plate and then set the shaker down.

"I've been thinking about the old days."

"Do you remember it?"

"I think so. If it wasn't the first time, it was close. I was walking home from school and turned into the alley. I heard this horrible racket coming from above me," she said and then giggled.

"Hey! I wasn't that bad on the drums."

"You weren't terrible, I guess," she admitted.

"I always liked playing the guitar better, but I wanted to learn how to play the drums, too. I could play the bass already."

"I remember the first time you asked me to sing for you. I even remember the song."

"It was "Wheel In The Sky' by Journey, right? I was learning all those early eighties songs back then."

Emmy shook her head. "No it wasn't! It was a Fleetwood Mac song. I think it was 'Storms' or maybe 'Sisters Of The Moon.'"

"I think it was the Journey song," Kenny tilted his head. "I don't remember doing any Fleetwood Mac covers. I remember it was a Steve Perry song."

"Why would I sing a song by Journey? Steve Perry was their lead singer. He's a guy. Stevie Nicks sang those songs for Fleetwood Mac. You're getting your Stevies mixed up."

"Are you sure?"

"Well, I wouldn't swear it to the Supreme Court, but I'm

376

ninety-nine percent sure it was a Fleetwood Mac song."

"Doesn't matter. Was that the same song you sang at the Youth Center with us?"

"That was your first gig. Did I sing that night, or was it the second one. I can't remember where you played your second gig."

"We'd have to ask Dad. He would know for sure, but I'm thinking it was at Larry's Uptown Grill."

"I remember the time you told me how you wanted to make a career in music. You had just started high school. I remember how excited you were when you learned how to play a whole song," Emmy said and then grinned.

"I knew how to play whole songs before I got to high school, Em," Kenny insisted.

"You were a huge U2 fan back then. When *The Joshua Tree* came out, you played it for me about a hundred times."

"I still think that was a great album."

"I remember how much you whined when they released *Pop*. You hated that one."

"I didn't like the direction they took," He stabbed a piece of sausage and waved it at her. "Do you remember the *Monster* CD by R.E.M.?"

"Is that the one with the Kenneth song?"

He nodded. "'What's The Frequency, Kenneth' is the actual title."

"Whatever! You played that one so much I ended up hating it." She tried to steal his sausage, but he pulled it away from her.

"Does that mean you hate our early songs because we've played them a million times?"

She bit her lip. "There are some early tunes I wouldn't complain about if I never heard them again."

"Like what?"

"Like 'Broken Hearts' off the first CD."

He raised his eyebrows, "I thought you liked it. You never said anything before."

"I might have liked it at first, but if I listen to it now, it sounds too sappy. The lyrics are sweeter than syrup and too simple. I like edgier lyrics now."

377

"I wrote it for you," he claimed.

Emmy shook her head. "No, you didn't!"

"Are you sure?"

"Positive! But you did write 'Sweet Girl' for me. That one's about me."

Kenny laughed. "That has to be the sappiest song I ever wrote."

Emmy frowned and tried to smack his hand, but he jerked it out of reach. "It's not sappy. It's about me. Are you saying I'm sappy?"

"No, of course not."

"Yes, you are, and you can forget about coming home early from the party."

"I'm just teasing. We still sing that song every night."

"Yeah, so what. You have to sing it because the crowd demands it."

He waved a finger at her. "No, no, no! We don't sing every song the crowd demands. We haven't done 'Freebird' in years."

"I hate it when people request that one. I've heard people call out 'Freebird' at some of my shows. Do they really think I'm going to turn into Lynyrd Skynyrd?"

"I've seen you go barefoot on a stage before."

She frowned at him. "One time," and then she stuck out her tongue.

"Those were the good old days," Kenny sighed.

Emmy rolled her eyes. "Give me a break. You make it sound like it was fifty years ago. You guys haven't been together for twenty years yet. Look at The Rolling Stones! They got together back in the sixties. That's the good old days."

"We got together in the fall of 1994, so it will be twenty years pretty soon. That's a long time for a band to stay together."

Emmy grinned, "Especially one without any talent."

"Ha! Ha! You are so funny, Em."

They stared at each other for a moment without speaking.

Emmy whispered, "Are you still thinking about leaving Fridays At Five to go solo?"

"Maybe."

"I wish you wouldn't. It's been a lifelong dream of yours to be in a band. You guys are such a perfect fit. I'd hate for it to end."

"Nothing lasts forever, Em," he said and immediately regretted it.

"Are you planning to leave me, too?"

"I didn't mean that, and you know it. Lots of bands take a break to do side projects..."

"And most of them never get back together, or if they do, their fans have moved on. Do you want that to happen?"

"No."

"Then don't leave. I know this last project has been difficult, but it will work out."

"I've got all these songs recorded, or partially recorded, that are good songs but just not Fridays At Five songs. You know what I mean?"

"Yeah, I know. You want some coffee or something?" Emmy got up and walked into the kitchen.

"I could use a cup," he answered.

Emmy started the coffee and then leaned against the island. "Just because you have these songs for a solo album, which is what it sounds like you plan to use them for, doesn't mean you have to break up the band."

"The band wouldn't break up if I left. The guys would find another singer." He brought their empty plates back into the kitchen and set them in the sink. "Remember that tribute band we saw last year?"

"I remember seeing them. Can't remember their name."

"Johnny March Combo. They had this singer you claimed sounded more like me that I do. Remember?" He grabbed two coffee cups from the wooden mug tree on the counter.

"I remember."

"Journey did the same thing. They found a singer in a tribute band."

Emmy shook her head. "If you think Steward Music is going to let Fridays At Five go on without you, you're bonkers."

"I think you're exaggerating my importance to the band."

"And I don't think you're realizing how important you are.

Would U2 carry on if Bono decided to leave?"

"That's different."

She pointed to the Mr. Coffee machine. "The coffee is ready. Would you pour me a cup, please?"

Kenny poured the coffee, and they moved back to the breakfast nook.

"It's raining harder," Kenny said.

"Quit trying to change the subject."

They stared out the window for a time without talking.

"I'm not going to leave the band until we finish this project," Kenny promised.

"But you might after that, huh?"

"I'm not saying I will, but I might take another look at those songs. They would be a strong foundation for a side project."

"Are you thinking about that because of Adam's solo CD?"

"Maybe."

"Adam doing a side project is not the same as you doing one. People hear your voice and immediately know it's Fridays At Five." She waved a finger. "Not so with Adam."

Kenny finished the last of his coffee. "Want another cup?"

"Warm me up, please."

Kenny refilled his cup and added some to Emmy's half-filled cup. He stared out the window. "We could go for a walk after the rain stops. It's not that cold."

"Maybe later. I don't want you to feel you have to stay in the band because of financial reasons. You aren't, are you?"

"Not at all." Kenny sat down.

"We would be all right if you never made another dime from the band," Emmy said. "We have trusts for the kids, and our investments are solid. We could cut back on expenses."

"I could get a job teaching music."

"I could get my education degree and teach school."

Kenny laughed. "Who are we kidding, Em. My dream has always been to be a rock star."

"I know," Emmy's eyes sparkled. "And if you keep working at it, one of these days it might come true, m'lord."

Check out these other titles by the author. Visit the website:
kennethleemcgee.com

The Emmy's Story Series

1. We We're 'posed to Get Married
2. One Of The Guys
3. A New Friend
4. Did You Like the Ravioli Tonight?
5. Completely and Forever: A Wedding
6. It's Time To Go!
7. How Difficult Can It Be?
8. Forever... Isabella... Forever
9. The Forgettable Year
10. Turning Thirty
11. Hello, I'm James
12. Remember The Struggle
13. But God! I Write Songs

The Annie Mercer O'Dell Series

1. Roosevelt High
2. North Park College
3. Smoky Mountain Summer

Stand Alone Books

1. Growing Up In Kinmundy Junction
2. Grandpa, Lions and Kitty Cats: A Collection Of Short Stories For Children Of All Ages

www.ingramcontent.com/pod-product-compliance
Lightning Source LLC
Chambersburg PA
CBHW052006240626
47153CB00012B/109